NICK BRIAN

Praise for *A Spy's Life*:

'Right to the very penultimate page, these are the doubts and fears that keep up the suspense in a thrilling, action-packed story of deceit and double-dealing – the very essence of a spy's life. All of which is, necessarily, very confusing. But this is exactly where the book shows itself to be in such a high class. A second-rate writer would have turned a dog's dinner where the reader gets to the end only to have to turn back to re-examine past passages ... Those who pick up *A Spy's Life* are spared such shoddy treatment. This is a well constructed novel and Henry Porter is emerging as a thriller writer of tremendous verve who takes his readers on a white-knuckle ride but never leaves them for dead'
Graham Stewart, *Spectator*

'None of this complexity prevents *A Spy's Life* from being compulsively readable ... He has, moreover, begun to create himself a comtemporary landscape that's authentic and authentically thrilling. *A Spy's Life* is going to be an essential part of this summer's airport and beachscape'
Michael Williams, *Observer*

'Plot, fiercely paced and elaborately developed, is what this novel really gives you. Its intricacies, the pleasures of which have been forgotten by so much "literary" fiction, are what readers want from this genre. Here they will get them'
John Mullan, *Guardian*

'Magnificent ... Mr Porter's particular gift is his ability to make technology interesting ... [he has] learned the oldest lesson: that characterisation and narrative are all' *Economist*

P9-CQH-791

'As with his first thriller, *Remembrance Day*, Porter demon-strates great technical ingenuity ... Yet this is embedded in a complex web of emotional realtionships – between lovers and comrades, father and son, son and stepfather, mother and daughter, torturer and victim – that seems entirely authentic ... Porter has proved that he is a torchbearer in a great tradition' Christopher Silvester, *Sunday Express*

'The big problem for writers of spy fiction after the Cold War is to find credible enemies, and to explain why we should be scared of them. There are even those who suggest that the entire spy-fiction genre is dead or dying. Henry Porter proves it is alive and well – this is top quality stuff. If you enjoyed Henry Porter's first novel, *Remembrance Day*, you will not be disappointed' Gavin Esler, *Daily Mail*

'Porter's novel demonstrates that the spy thriller is far from exhausted, and that the genre is capable of regenerating itself by responding to new developments in technology' Andrew Biswell, *Daily Telegraph*

'Harland is an immensely sympathetic character, flawed enough to be convincingly human, stubborn and foolhardy enough to explain his feats of moral and physical heroism. His love story is subtle and poignant. At times he quietly reminded me of Sean Lemass, in John Le Carre's *The Spy who Came in from the Cold*. I cannot think of a higher compliment' Marcel Berlins, *Sunday Times*

'The drama of ambiguous loyalties, though the biggest cliché in spy fiction, is well played out, and Porter marshals potentially cumbersome material with admirable clarity. But it is the characterisation, as much as the plotting, that catches the eye ... A bedroom scene, or rather a fusion of two bedroom scenes, one in Italy, the other in London years later, is beautifully done. Amid the violence and the double-

crossing, Porter has struck a vein of real tenderness. His no-nonsense hero, battle-scarred but with a residual decency, rings heart-warmingly true'
David Robson, *Sunday Telegraph*

Henry Porter was born in 1953. He is married to Liz Elliot and has two children. He lives in London. *A Spy's Life* is his second novel.

By Henry Porter

Remembrance Day
A Spy's Life

A SPY'S LIFE

HENRY PORTER

ORION

For Liz
with Love

An Orion paperback

First published in Great Britain in 2001
by Orion
This paperback edition published in 2002
Second impression 2002
by Orion Books Ltd,
Orion House, 5 Upper St Martin's Lane,
London WC2H 9EA

. Copyright © 2001 Henry Porter

The right of Henry Porter to be identified as the author
of this work has been asserted by him in accordance with
the Copyright, Designs and Patents Act 1988.

All rights reserved. No part of this publication may be
reproduced, stored in a retrieval system, or transmitted,
in any form or by any means, electronic, mechanical,
photocopying, recording or otherwise, without the prior
permission of the copyright owner.

All the characters in this book are fictitious, and any resemblance
to actual persons, living or dead, is purely coincidental.

A CIP catalogue record for this book is available
from the British Library.

ISBN 0 75284 806 2

Typeset by Deltatype Ltd, Birkenhead, Wirral

Printed and bound in Great Britain by
Clays Ltd, St Ives plc

ACKNOWLEDGEMENTS

I owe a debt of gratitude to many people who helped me during the preparation of this novel. I would particularly like to thank my editor, Jane Wood, and my agent, Georgina Capel, both of whom provided encouragement and contributed much to *A Spy's Life*, and also Pamela Merritt, who read the manuscript and made many suggestions.

There were countless individuals in the USA, the Czech Republic and the Former Republic of Yugoslavia who took time to explain how things were and are. Some would prefer not to be named here, however, I want to mention Mila Řádová and Hasan Nuhanovic for giving me special understanding of the Czech Republic and Yugoslavia. In Prague, I received matchless assistance from one individual who was closely involved in the events which form part of my story. He knows who he is. I hope he knows how grateful I am for his hospitality and insight.

At the United Nations Headquarters in New York I encountered patience and generosity among officials who described the complexities and procedures of their organisation. Others gave me invaluable access to the building.

In matters of aviation I am indebted to three pilots – Philip Waterer, Mark Seymour and Phil Bachelor – the US National Transportation Safety Board and Sharl Stamford

Kraus Ph.D., the author of *Aircraft Safety: Accident Investigations, Analyses, and Applications* (McGraw–Hill), a fascinating and rather terrifying book.

As far as my medical researches go, I would like to acknowledge debts to the journalists on BBC Radio Four's *Science Now* programme, who made available their material on Locked-in Syndrome, and to Dr Caroline Miller who helped me understand a small but crucial detail concerning inheritance.

As always, friends have been very helpful. My thanks go to Lucy Heller, Shameen Bhatia, Xan Smiley, Lucy Nichols, David Campbell and Janine di Giovanni, all of whom gave me support and ideas.

HP
London, 2001

1

THE EAST RIVER

A lip of ice protruded from the bank just in front of his face. It was no more than three feet away and he could see it with absolute clarity in the light that was coming from behind him. He contemplated the ice through the mist of his breath, noticing the lines that ran around its edge like tree rings. He understood they were formed when the tide lapped its underside, adding a little to the surface, then receded, leaving it hanging over the mud. He was groggy, but his powers of reason were working. That was good.

Harland moved his head a little and listened. There was a ringing inside his ears but he could hear the slap of the water and the agitated clicking of dead reeds somewhere off to his left. Beyond these there was a commotion – sirens and the noise of a helicopter.

The light didn't allow him to see how he was trapped, but he felt something heavy pinning him down from behind and he knew that his legs were bent backwards because the muscles in his groin and on the tops of his thighs were burning with pain. The rest of him was numb. He reckoned he must have been there for some time.

He pulled at his arms which had been plunged vertically into the mud. The movement caused his face to fall forward nearer the mud and his nostrils to fill with the smell of the sea. The tide! He could see that the water had risen a little in the time since he had become conscious. The tide would come in and cover his face. He had to get free – shift the weight that was holding him down. But he felt weak and dazed and there was nothing for him to push against to hold his face away from the mud. He groped behind him and felt the seat. Jesus, he was still strapped into his seat! He ran his right hand up and down searching for the seat belt and found it stretched tight across the top of his chest. That explained the pain in the area of his heart. Eventually he located the buckle, flipped its tongue with his thumb and sagged forward into the mud.

It was going to be okay. He'd be able to shift the seat, or wriggle from underneath it. A little more purchase was all that was needed. But that wasn't going to be easy. Exerting the slightest pressure made him sink closer to the water. He knew that the mud had absorbed the force of his impact and had saved his life, but now he cursed it.

He began to prod and grope beneath the mud. After several minutes he touched something solid, an old plank of wood. It was slippery, but it did not move when he gripped it with both hands and then pushed upwards with all his strength, bringing his legs awkwardly into play. Nothing happened. He slumped down again and inhaled the odour of decay. He had to concentrate on controlling his breath which was coming in shallow puffs.

As he waited, the breeze peppered his face with grains of ice and he realised for the first time how cold it was. He breathed deeply, right into his stomach, and tightened his grip beneath the mud. He was going to do it. He was going to lift the damned seat because he hadn't survived the crash to be drowned in six inches of the East River.

He pushed again and this time felt the right side of the seat lift slightly. He threw his bottom up and with a desperate writhing motion managed to free first one leg, then the other, and roll over into the sea water. The cold made him gasp. He lunged upwards, knocking the lip of ice, which broke off with a chink, dug his fingers into the bank and pulled himself to a kneeling position. The mud sucked at his shins. He saw the seat now and a tangle of metal and torn plastic attached to the back of it. He looked up and across to Manhattan, ranged along the skyline like a miniature tiara. He realised that he was seeing it through a gauze of tiny ice particles floating on the breeze. But there was something else – the insides of his eyelids seemed to be imprinted with a golden light that flared every time he blinked. And there was a new sensation in his head, halfway between pain and sound.

Shielding his face from the wind, Harland turned and peered towards La Guardia. It was difficult to make out exactly what was happening against the background of the airport's lights. There appeared to be two fires that were being fed by plumes of foam from the emergency vehicles. The nearest was a few hundred yards away. The lights shot across a long horizontal shadow, which Harland took to be some form of dyke, to play across the mudflats and skim the sea. He wondered how the wreckage of the UN plane had ended up so far from him. Maybe it had kept travelling after breaking up; or perhaps there'd been a collision which would explain why he could see two fires. But that didn't match his memory of the moments as they approached the runway. He had felt no impact, just the shocking lurch to the right that came as he turned from trying to see the lights of Riker's Island to Alan Griswald's face. That was all he knew before a terrible force took hold of him and obliterated everything in his mind.

He climbed on to the bank, shook the worst of the mud from his legs and rubbed his calves and thighs to get the circulation back. The bank which he had taken for part of the shoreline turned out to be a tiny island of a few square feet. Despite the frost, the ground crumbled easily and when he moved, clods of soil and dead vegetation slipped into the water. He peered down into the darkness to see how far he would have to wade to get to the shore, his mind fumbling to make sense of his situation. He had to think about the depth of the water and the possibility of sinking into the mud and getting stuck. And he had to remember the tide because he wasn't in any state to swim, not even a short distance in the currents which he knew hurtled through the East River. There was also the ferocious cold. It was already way below freezing and the wind-chill was getting to him, sapping energy from his legs. He might die of exposure before they found him.

Where was the helicopter he'd heard? Why the hell weren't they looking? They must've worked out that the plane had broken up and there would be casualties out here in the tide. But the runway was raised quite a height above the mudflats and he knew that would mean they wouldn't spot anything by chance. They would have to be looking – they would have to know people were out here.

He looked out over the water to see if any rescue boats had been launched. No lights, no sound – nothing. He searched the dark around him and then as his eyes moved across the sea towards the Bronx he caught sight of something about forty feet away. It was a piece of wreckage – another aircraft seat, he was sure. A little closer to him was an oblong object bobbing in the water – perhaps a door. A cry rose up in him and he bellowed, 'Over here, help! Over here.'

He told himself not to be so damned stupid. No one could hear him above the wind. He cautioned himself to keep a tighter control of his fear. He must conserve his energy.

But then it struck him that someone might be out there and that they could be trapped. He looked again and thought he saw a foot projecting from the end of the seat. Without thinking more about it, he lowered himself into the water and gingerly tested the depth. The mud shelved away to the right but ahead of him it appeared to be level and, although

4

his feet sank into the mud with each step, it was just possible to wade.

He moved slowly out into the open where the breeze was skimming foam from the tops of the waves. The headlights of a truck had manoeuvred in the distance and sent a beam across the water to pick out part of the seat. He was about halfway there and he could see that the seat was tipped backwards and was propped against a stack of tufted soil. Around him was a lot of other wreckage, knocking about in the waves. He grabbed a long plastic panel and felt the rest of the way. When he reached the seat he called out once then took a step sideways to see better and prodded it with the panel. The seat fell sideways and a body slumped into a patch of light.

He knew he was looking at Alan Griswald, although most of his face had gone and part of the neck and shoulder had been torn away. He must have been killed instantly. Poor bastard: one moment draining a tumbler of scotch, the next he was out here, mangled and ruptured and dead.

Harland felt dreadfully cold. A shudder welled up in his back and ran through his entire body. He had been stupid to get so wet because it reduced his options. Before he might have waited but now he was so cold he had no choice but to wade back past the little island and strike out towards the lights of the emergency vehicles and to what he hoped was the shore. At the same time he realised that his strength was going and – more alarming – he could feel the increased drag of the tide plucking at his legs.

He turned to go, then stopped and listened intently to a new noise. He cupped his hand to his ear. It was a muffled sound – muffled but insistent – and it was coming from Griswald's body. Suddenly he understood: it was a cellphone. Griswald had kept his phone switched on and now it was ringing. He waded through the water, ran his hands over the body and felt the phone inside his breast pocket. He thrust his hand inside Griswald's jacket, steeling himself against the blood and pulp of his chest, and pulled out the phone and something else – a wallet. He was about to throw it away when something told him it would be needed for identification. He slipped it into his hip pocket.

The phone was still ringing. He stabbed at the keypad and brought it to his cheek.

'Hello.'

'Al?' came a woman's voice. She was a long way off and the wind was making it difficult to hear, but he thought he recognised the voice.

'Look,' stumbled Harland.

'Who is this?' demanded the woman.

Harland grimaced to himself. 'Look, Alan can't take your call.'

'Who is this speaking? Where's Alan?' The panic in her voice was rising. 'Why have you got my husband's phone?'

Harland saw nothing for it but to hang up. Sally Griswald would learn soon enough. He held the phone in front of him and dialled his own direct line at the UN building.

'Marika?'

'This is she.' The voice was brisk – troubled.

'Marika, I need you to listen very carefully.'

'Oh, my God! Mr Harland? You don't know what's happened. It's terrible. The plane's crashed at La Guardia. The flight from Washington. All those people. We just got the news a few minutes ago.'

'I was on the flight.'

'What are you saying? I can't hear you.'

'I was on the flight. I'm okay. But I need you to tell them where I am.'

'I don't understand. It's not on your schedule—'

'Listen, for God's sake, Marika.' He was shouting and he knew he was terrifying the life out of her. 'I was on the flight.

6

And now I'm stranded in the East River. You've got to tell them where to find me.'

'Oh, my God . . .'

'Tell them I'm in a direct line between the northeast runway and Riker's Island. The tide's coming in fast and I need them to get here quickly. Marika, now don't hang up! Keep the line open . . . Marika?'

Another voice came on the line. 'Bobby, it's Nils Langstrom.'

'Thank God,' said Harland. Langstrom had a cool head. 'I was on the flight that crashed. I'm stranded in the East River. I guess I'm about one hundred and fifty, maybe two hundred yards from the runway on a line with Riker's Island. I'm in the water and I'm going to try and get myself back on dry land. They'll see some wreckage from the plane. I'll wait there. But tell them they've got to move quickly. There may be other people out here.'

'Got it. I'll make sure they understand where you are.'

'I've got to hang up now and get to the island.'

'Don't take any risks . . .'

Harland pressed the 'off' key and clamped the phone between his teeth. He ignored the taste of blood on the phone and looked up to get his bearings. It wasn't easy. Wading out to where Griswald lay had been fine because the light from behind him had shown him the way. Going back was a different matter. Beneath the distant beam from the truck everything was pitch black. He picked up the plastic panel, which he had kept wedged between his legs, and set off, jabbing at the water ahead of him. All around him was the excited rippling of a tide in full flood.

Part of him remained aloof from the situation, a dispassionate observer, registering the difficulty he had pulling his legs out of the mud, noticing the shortness of his breath, the lifelessness in his arms, the fatigue clouding the front of his brain and tempting his eyes to close. The cold was beyond

7

anything he'd experienced. It was robbing him of his will, making his thoughts sloppy and his movements clumsy.

This part of Harland, the remote, calculating part, recognised that he had only a very short time.

It was beginning to snow. Big snowflakes were streaming across his vision making a little vortex along the line of the headlight beam. He put his head down and worked his shoulders to take several quick strides. The water had reached halfway up his thighs when he put his left leg down, found nothing and toppled sideways into the current. His lungs contracted with shock, expelling the air with a succession of hollow shouts, the first of which caused him to let go of the phone in his mouth. Then, as he flailed in the water like a child learning to swim, he lost his grip on the panel. He knew his only chance now was to make it back to the point where he could stand, but the current was very strong and his power to resist it had gone. His lungs wouldn't keep the air down and he was swallowing water. He tilted his head back and stretched out his arms, his brain grasping at half a memory of a training session he'd endured long ago in Poole Harbour. He was floating, allowing the current to take him and to twirl him around like a piece of flotsam. He was aware of looking up at the snow. The light seemed to be growing fainter and the snow was getting denser. His terror was being edged out by blankness and submission. One thought kept moving through him: this is it, I'm going to die; this is it, I'm going to die.

And then his foot hit something and the current spun him round so that his bottom grazed the mud. He had been washed up on another bank. He reached his hands out backwards and clawed awkwardly at the mud, trying to get his head above the water. He found some roots just below the surface. With the last reserve of energy he turned and brought himself to all fours and choked the water out. He stayed there heaving and gulping in the terrible cold for what seemed like several minutes. Then he looked up and squinted through the sea water that was still stinging his eyes. There was no sign of anyone. They weren't looking for him.

He listened. A seabird called out in the dark and again he heard the rasp and click of reeds nearby. He had to think. He had to think, dammit. But his mind was moving so slowly. He'd crawl into the reeds where the mud would be firm because of the roots and he would drag himself to his feet and stand so that they would see him. That's what he'd do. He would get up and wait there and not give in to the cold. Someone would come. He knew it. Marika and Langstrom must have made them understand where he was. He inched towards the clump of reeds where a mess of snow and sea foam had collected, grabbed on to a handful of stalks and hauled himself towards them. He rose to his feet and stood, swaying like a drunk.

A few moments later he heard the helicopter's roar, turned and saw a light coming towards him. He raised both arms and held them high until it was hovering in front of him and throwing up a whirlwind of snow and dead reeds. Next he saw several bent figures emerge from a cloud of snow and foam and rush towards him. They carried lights and a stretcher. He felt himself stagger on his feet, topple backwards and then lurch forwards into their arms.

2

THE MISSING

Sister Rafael was rather proud of her patient in Room 132. Since the British UN official had been brought in early on the previous evening, she had seen the TV film of him standing out in the East River with his arms raised like he was defying death. It was a miracle that he hadn't been killed with the others. The TV news had said twenty people from the two aircraft had died, and now their bodies were lying in a temporary morgue at the airport, most of them burned beyond recognition. It made her shudder to think of so many people's grief, especially now, before the holidays. She felt his wrist and touched his forehead with the back of her left hand. There was no sign of fever and his pulse was normal.

She peered at him in the sliver of morning light that was coming through the blinds. He was a big man and she guessed he was naturally strong. When he was brought in they'd needed three people to lift him to put on the Heibler vest so his temperature could be stabilised. His face interested her because it had none of the weak, fleshy appearance she associated with the British. The jaw was well defined, like his dark eyebrows which ran horizontally until they plunged down at the ends. His hair was a lighter brown and was cut short so you could see where it had receded on his forehead. She felt there was an openness in his features, except in the mouth, which even in medicated repose was clamped shut. Tension showed itself elsewhere – in the long furrows that ran from his cheekbone nearly down to his jaw, in the crow's-feet at the corner of his eyes and the single cleft at the centre of his brow. His eye sockets were blackened by fatigue.

She wondered what expression his eyes held when they were open and what his voice sounded like and whether he was married. There was no wedding ring on his finger and when his sister called from London to speak with Doctor Isaacson, she had not mentioned a partner or any family. Of one thing she was sure. Mr Harland was important. Twice that morning a woman had called from the Secretary-General's office to ask about his condition. She had instructions to pass on his concern and to let them know when the doctor said it would be okay to talk to him. Everyone wanted to talk to him – the TV and the accident investigators, and the Secretary-General was even threatening to come visit in the hospital. People understood that this man's escape was extraordinary. That's why the picture from the TV film was blown up in all the papers and why they were still playing it on the news bulletins. She could see him in her mind's eye, standing there, feet slightly apart, his arms raised outwards in an almost religious attitude.

She moved to the window and parted the blind to look down into the dazzling snow light. Four or five news crews were still there, waiting in the sunshine to hear about her patient. Then she returned to the bedside and gave the face a last glance before leaving the room. He would sleep for a while yet.

Late on the third morning after the crash, Harland woke as a breakfast tray was brought to him. He felt alert but also curiously light-headed. In snatches of wakefulness during the past forty-eight hours, he had struggled to make sense of the events that had brought him to a hospital bed. Drowsily he watched a report on TV and got more or less all he needed –

the casualty figures, the shocked reaction in the UN headquarters, the approximate circumstances of the crash and the mildly unnerving fact that he had been picked up by a helicopter that was carrying a TV crew who had filmed the rescue. It had taken a few seconds before he recognised the absurd, panicky figure, gesticulating like a maniac out on the shoreline. He had pressed the remote and had almost immediately fallen asleep.

Now he was hungry and set about the eggs and toasted bagel with relish, his mind returning to the crash. There was a lot he didn't understand, chiefly how he and Griswald had been thrown out of the fuselage and landed so far from the line of the wreckage path. He thought of finding Alan Griswald's body and hearing the telephone ringing in the dark and then speaking to Sally Griswald. He remembered her from years ago when the Griswalds were doing the rounds of East European embassies. He could see her now, a small, bubbling natural blonde from the Midwest who never took anything very seriously, least of all her husband's work as the CIA Station Chief. She was a breath of fresh air in the otherwise self-consciously discreet gatherings of spies and embassy staff. The Griswalds had two small boys then. They were now at college. Griswald had talked about them on the plane. They were home for the Christmas holidays and he was going to take ten days with them.

The door opened and the woman who had introduced herself the day before as Sister Rafael came in, followed by the doctor, who looked him over quickly and pronounced himself satisfied with Harland's recovery.

'Anything we should know about your medical history?' he asked. 'You have had one or two operations – appendectomy and . . . er?' He pointed below Harland's midrift to his groin.

'That was a long time ago.'

'And it's what I think it was?'

'Yes, but I've been clear for a dozen years or more now.'

12

'Diagnosed early then?'

'Yes,' he said with finality. He didn't particularly want to discuss it in front of the nurse.

'And these scars on your wrists and chest. Nothing that should concern me?'

'No.'

'What were they caused by?'

'An accident,' said Harland, with a discouraging look.

Isaacson nodded, a trace of doubt showing in his eyes. He told him how his body temperature had crashed below the eighty-eight-degree mark and that it had been touch and go for an hour after he was brought in. An incubator had been used to warm him on Tuesday evening. He had spent the first night on a supply of slightly heated, moist oxygen. Now all he needed to do was to concentrate on building his strength with rest and a high calorie intake. He warned that there were bound to be some after-effects. He would feel weak for some time and his muscles would continue to ache for a few days. There might also be problems of delayed shock. If he felt unusually depressed or listless in the coming weeks, he should seek trauma counselling. It was important that he should not try to deal with the experience by himself, but talk it out with a professional. Harland nodded obediently, although the idea was absurd to him. He had talked only once in his life – to an elderly woman in North London. He'd found it exceptionally hard to be precise about the effects of torture.

Isaacson noticed his expression. 'How would you feel about speaking with the crash investigators? I mean, about the facts of the crash – what you remember about the airplane journey? They're very anxious to speak with you.'

Harland agreed and after another cursory check, Isaacson left. Half an hour later, two men were shown in with great ceremony by the nurse. They introduced themselves as

Murray Clark from the National Transportation Safety Board and Special Agent Frank Ollins of the FBI.

Harland slipped his legs from the bed and indicated to the nurse that he would like the robe hanging near the door.

'Are you okay about this, Mr Harland?' asked Murray Clark. 'We can do it later.'

'I'm fine,' he said. 'Wish I'd shaved and washed before you came.' He nodded to the nurse who left, almost regretfully. He stood up and looked at them. Clark was short and a little overweight and looked as though he had been plucked straight out of a college laboratory. Agent Ollins was in his mid-thirties and was crisply dressed in a blue suit and white shirt. He had a steady gaze and seemed more purposeful than Clark. They both carried heavy anoraks and had mud on their shoes.

They sat down either side of the little table at the end of his bed.

'Why are you involved?' Harland asked Agent Ollins. 'This isn't a criminal investigation, surely.'

'Too soon to say what this case is about,' Ollins replied equably. 'We're hoping that you will be able to help with that. There were a lot of important people on board and we need to cover all the angles. Mr Clark here is going to find out what went wrong with your plane. We take over if we think some party or parties intentionally caused that malfunction to occur.'

'Fortunate about the cellphone,' said Clark brightly. 'You might still be out there if you hadn't found it. We hear you suffered quite badly from exposure – it's good to see you doing so well already, sir.'

He turned on a small tape recorder and asked Harland to take them through the flight, remembering anything that might be of use to them.

He told them how he had finished his work in Rockville, Maryland, and had gone to Washington National Airport, thinking that he had missed the ride offered to him by Alan Griswald. He explained that he had met Griswald the week before in Holland. They had travelled to Washington on consecutive days and had hoped to meet up in DC as well as fly together to New York. Both knew they were too busy and the arrangement was vague. However, he had bumped into Griswald at the airport which was how he came to be on the plane.

Harland said that there were some other UN people with him, people who had been at meetings at Congress. They were travelling together but there was some diplomatic nicety which meant that this was not an official delegation from the UN to Congress. Griswald seemed to know some, but not all of them. He remembered there were two or three young women in the party.

'How did you know Mr Griswald?' asked Ollins.

'We worked on the same diplomatic circuit back in the eighties.'

'Right – you were diplomats.'

'Yes,' said Harland. 'We were diplomats in Europe. Griswald was in Germany and Austria for a long time, with a spell in the Middle East. We served in some of the same places. I saw a lot of him and his wife in those days.' He paused and took some coffee. 'Do you want some of this? I'm sure I can get a fresh jug.'

They shook their heads.

'Were you both in the Middle East?'

'No, just Griswald.'

'So tell us about the flight.'

'We left pretty soon after we met and we flew up to New York without any trouble. About twenty minutes out of La Guardia, I went to the lavatory and noticed that the cabin had grown very cold. As I was about to take a pee, the lights went out. So I went back into the cabin which was pitch black. Then we were struck by some turbulence which was

15

uncomfortable but not severe. I think the pilot came on and told us to fasten our seat belts.'

'Did the captain says anything else at this time?' asked Clark, making a note.

'Maybe. I didn't pay much attention. We could see the lights of New York below us and we weren't especially worried.'

'What else do you recall?'

He said there wasn't much he could add. He remembered Griswald turning on his laptop to use the light of the screen. As he spoke, Griswald's face came back to him, lit by a blue-grey aura, smiling at the thought of one of his sons returning from college. Griswald lifted the computer and they struggled to fold away the table in the dark, and then looked down at the Bronx. Harland saw the white rooftops in his mind, the grid of little streets and the scrawl of new tyre tracks in the snow. Griswald made some remark about the weather.

'Did the lights return before landing?' asked Clark.

'No.'

'Can you remember anything else unusual, sir? What about the sound of the engines? Any significant increase in engine power while you were experiencing the turbulence? Do you recall a change of note in the engine noise as the plane came in?'

'I'm not sure – maybe just before the impact. I was looking out towards Riker's Island on the left of the plane and Alan Griswald said something which I didn't hear. I turned back to face him. Then, bang! I don't remember much else.'

'Let me get this straight,' said Clark. 'You were looking out at Riker's from the left of the plane? The first question is this: could you see Riker's Island?'

'I could see an orange glow which I assumed were the lights from the prison.'

'But surely you mean you were looking out to your right, not left.'

16

'No, I was in a rear-facing seat, across the table from Alan Griswald.'

'Ah, I see. I guess that's one of the reasons you're here. Being at the back of the plane and facing backwards meant that you avoided the whole force of the impact. Tell me, was anything about the approach unusual?'

'No.'

'You didn't think that the plane was unusually low?'

'No, I didn't. Have you any theories yet?'

'Right now, we're considering a number of possibilities. The flight data recorder and the voice recorder were recovered on Wednesday; both are being analysed at our headquarters in Washington. We'll get the results at the weekend.'

Ollins plucked a piece of fluff from his suit, looked up at the ceiling and began speaking.

'As yet we don't know why the plane crashed, Mr Harland. None of the theories about icing, wind-shear, poor visibility or a freak collision with Santa's reindeers comes anywhere near to explaining it. How could this aircraft, flown by a pilot with over ten thousand flying hours, come in without any reported problems and just nose-dive into the runway?'

Harland got up from the edge of the bed, walked a few paces and worked his bare toes up and down to get rid of the prickly sensation in his feet. They watched him.

'Nobody has told me what actually happened,' he said, looking at Clark. 'I mean, I still don't see how the other plane was involved. Surely it was nowhere near where we came in?'

Ollins exchanged a look with Clark, as if asking his permission.

'It's simple,' he said. 'Your plane comes in too low, banks right and clips the light tower with the starboard wing. An explosion occurs in the fuel tank, debris flies back, tears into the cabin at the rear and loosens the spars supporting the starboard engine. The engines have already been put into

17

maximum thrust because the pilot realises he needs altitude. All three engines are full on. The Falcon climbs momentarily, comes down, rolls through ninety degrees, banks right and hits more light towers with incredible force. The fuselage sustains more damage and the starboard engine becomes detached and is thrown forward for a considerable distance. It hits the wing of a Learjet waiting to take off. The Learjet explodes and catches fire, killing all seven passengers and the pilot. Meanwhile the Falcon is ploughing a trench at a thirty-degree angle from the runway towards the Learjet. Then your plane also catches fire.'

'Jesus,' exhaled Harland. 'How on earth did I get out?'

'Some time at an early stage in this sequence,' replied Ollins, 'the seat anchors in your section of the Falcon break free and you are propelled out of the fuselage and land in the soft terrain at the edge of the East River.' He paused and gave a bleak smile. 'The chances of anyone surviving this crash without injury must be one in fifty billion, Mr Harland. People don't get breaks like that too often. I think you'll realise that when you see the wreckage.'

'You want me to see the wreckage?'

'Not so much the wreckage, but I would like to take you over the crash scene and have you look at a reconstruction we've set up there.'

Harland sat down on the bed. Clark asked if he wanted them to leave. But Ollins was clearly disinclined to go just yet.

'There are a few more questions I want to ask you before we leave,' he said. 'It's important that I have your attention for just a few more minutes, Mr Harland. One of the things we need to do in this investigation is to construct profiles of all the passengers and crew. We need to know a little more about your life also.'

A part of Harland went on guard. 'What do you want to know?'

'First off, tell me about your work, sir. You're doing a special report for the Secretary-General's office. Is that right?'

'That makes it sound more important than it is. I'm looking into the ownership of the supplies of fresh water in Asia and Eastern Europe.'

Ollins looked puzzled. 'Please explain.'

'One of the big problems facing the developing world – in fact, the entire planet – is the shortage of fresh water. There are too many people and the major fresh-water resources, chiefly lakes and aquifers, are being drained at a very fast rate. The reduction in some of the bigger lakes, like the Aral Sea, is showing up on satellite photographs. Others, like Lake Baikal, which contains about a fifth of the world's fresh-water supply, are being polluted by industry – a big paper mill in that instance. What this means is that fresh water is becoming a very scarce and valuable commodity. The Secretary-General wants to know who owns what. He believes that it's going to become an important issue. He wants a briefing as much as anything else.'

Ollins listened to this impatiently. 'But this wasn't always your line,' he said rather too quickly.

Harland realised that Ollins had already talked to people at the UN.

'You probably know that I've done a lot of things. Banking for a short time when I was young, British Foreign Service, Red Cross for ten years. I started out as an engineer – that's what I studied at Cambridge and that's how I can find my way around this subject.'

'That's a lot of different careers to cram into one life. You're only in your late forties?

'Forty-nine.'

'The Foreign Service – that's the diplomatic service, right?'

'Yes, I just said that I knew Griswald in the diplomatic service.'

'Were you hired by the UN to do this report?'

'Not specifically. I came to advise about rapid relief programmes. Three years later, I'm still here. I'll be ready to report in six or seven weeks. Then we'll see what happens.'

'And you were visiting Rockville in connection with this report?'

'Yes, there're a couple of companies down there that have large water interests. I'm trying to assess their current holdings and the extent of their ambitions.'

'A kind of investigation, then?'

'In the loosest sense, yes. It's a case of tracking down who owns what.'

'So you could make some enemies in this line of work?'

'Not really, most of the material that interests me is in the public record – somewhere. It's just a question of finding it and, as I say, establishing the plans of some of the big multi-nationals.'

He could see that Ollins was tiring of this line of questioning. He'd give it ten minutes, then make an excuse to get rid of them both.

'So tell me a little more about the flight. Did you talk to anyone besides Mr Griswald?'

'I said hello to Chris Lahmer and André Bloch. There were a few other faces I recognised – a man from UNHCR but I forget his name.'

'Philippe Maas?'

'Yes, that's right. They were all sitting near each other. I assumed they'd been at the same meetings in Washington.'

'So you can only put names to three or four people on the plane?'

'Yes, I suppose that's right. Is that important?'

'Well, it's like this. We have one unidentified body – a man. And we're not even sure that we have the right toll yet, because we could have lost people in the water. It took a while to find you and it's conceivable that other victims were washed out into the ocean.'

20

'But surely there was a passenger list – a manifest of some sort?'

'No. There should have been. But this was a private flight that didn't cross any national borders so it was forgotten, I guess.'

'Yes, but this man must have been missed by his relatives.'

'That's what we thought. But we've had no calls. The problem is that pretty much everything was burned. A few personal possessions escaped the fire – thrown out of the plane with you and Mr Griswald – and we are working on those. We may retrieve more material and there is the possibility of identifying bodies by dental records, jewellery and other possessions. It's going to be a long operation. But you're right, it is kind of strange that we haven't gotten a call.'

All this time, Clark remained silent, occasionally checking that his tape was going round, but otherwise studying Harland benevolently.

'What does that suggest to you, Mr Harland?' continued Ollins.

'I don't know – possibly no one knew he was on the plane. Maybe he was a foreign national who would not be missed immediately by his family. But presumably if he was on the UN plane, he was connected to the UN in some way and someone – a secretary or a department head or people at one of the national missions – would notice his absence?'

'Exactly the same thoughts occurred to us. It is odd. But look at it this way. If you'd been killed it might have been some time before anyone made the connection between the crash and your disappearance. Might've been a few days before anyone went back over your schedule and made some inquiries in Maryland and then put it all together. That's why we need very accurate descriptions of the people you saw on board. Then maybe we can start to work out who he was. I want you to think about them all and make some notes for me. I also want you to go over the journey again and record anything out of the ordinary – the smallest detail may be of crucial importance to this investigation, as Mr Clark here will tell you. Think of the passengers, Mr Harland – what they were carrying, where they sat, who they talked to. Think about the behaviour of the crew, what the captain said to the passengers – everything. I know it may be painful for you at this time, but I'm telling you, we need some help here. We'll talk again tomorrow and maybe you'll feel strong enough to come out to the airport and look over the model of the plane we have out there.'

He looked to Clark who nodded and turned off his tape recorder. Both gave him cards with cellphone numbers. They took his number and address in Brooklyn.

'Call us when you want to come out to the airport,' said Ollins from the door with a brief, wintry smile. 'And hey, don't forget to bring those notes you're going to make for me.'

With a sudden inward start, Harland realised that he had lost nearly three days. He phoned his sister, Harriet, in London and discussed staying with her family for Christmas. At the back of his mind he wondered how he was going to get on another plane so soon. But he was also certain that he did not want to spend the holiday in New York. Most of the UN would be shut down, with a lot of people returning to their home countries for a full fortnight. He said he would let her know in the next day or so. Then he talked to his office and told Marika what he would need in the way of clothes from his apartment. He asked her to get a new cellphone. His had been destroyed along with his briefcase.

After lunch he slid down into the bed and watched the sun descend behind a pearl grey shroud. It reminded him of the light over the Fens in England and the enormous cold skies of his youth. Harland tended to avoid introspection, but he knew there was now a before and an after in his life, divided by the few minutes when he was taken by the current and was certain he was going to die. He looked into himself without sentiment or fear and understood that his fortune at surviving might come with a penalty, an essential loss of confidence perhaps, like he'd suffered before when he was brought to another hospital bed, beaten so badly that the nurses at first hid their eyes from the sight of his injuries. That had taken a long time to get over, but he had managed it and he would this time too.

He closed his eyes and thought of Griswald and the party of people standing a little way off in the airport. It was a pretty typical UN crowd, with their cellphones and laptops. All of them good people, bubbling with brave initiatives, yet each in varying degrees mistaking furious animation for achievement. He tried to hold the scene in his mind. There were two or three groups of people, waiting to catch the minibus out to the UN plane. A few went outside the terminal building to smoke. The others stood in twos and threes inside. Something wasn't quite right about the way he was remembering it; something was tripping him up. His mind's eye moved across the groups, trying to pick up information. The young men both with computer cases. The woman in a long, black coat. Lahmer's anorak with a fur-trimmed hood. A lot was missing.

He'd give some thought to it later. Now he would sleep. He drifted off, this time thinking not about the flatlands of his boyhood, but an empty square in a hilltop town in central Italy. The unbidden image haunted him only rarely these days.

Next day he woke early. Having nothing else to do, he went to get a pen and paper from the duty nurse down the hall. He was moving more easily now. The bruises across his back and chest were still causing stabbing pains when he breathed deeply, but his legs were less stiff and the mysterious neuralgic patches on his stomach and thighs, which had woken him in the first nights after the crash, had gone. He cadged some coffee and returned to his room.

Dawn was breaking with a mustardy smear in the west. He sat down on the bed and noticed a small black bag. Marika must have dropped by with his things the previous evening. Inside there was a note from her, some of his own clothes, three hundred dollars in advance expenses, a new phone and a set of keys to his apartment. He smiled at her efficiency. He swung his legs onto the bed, and settled back on the pillows to write an account of the flight. He found he wasn't able to add much to what he'd told Clark and Ollins until he sketched a plan of the interior of the cabin and placed some names in the little oblong grid of seats. He marked himself and Griswald facing each other in the two rearmost seats on the starboard side. He knew that André Bloch was a little forward from him and that he had sat down opposite one of the women. On the other side of the aisle to him, on the port side, was Chris Lahmer. Before they took off, he recalled that Bloch leaned across the aisle to show Lahmer something. They were laughing with the man from UNHCR – Philippe Maas – which meant he must have been facing Lahmer.

It was difficult to say what people were wearing, and even more so to recall what they had carried on board, something which was obviously of interest to Ollins. One of the passengers, maybe one of the younger men who had sat up front, had carried a suitcase on board. He remembered there was a fuss from the flight attendant about stowing it. He wrote it all down as dispassionately as he could and annotated a diagram of the seating with the names of the passengers that he could remember.

He focused again and again on the scene, trying to glean more detail. The sensation of the first impact came back to him, the terrifying lurch to the right which threw him against

24

the cabin wall. He saw Griswald's face again, contorting in a flash from the window. He held that image in his head and then let the paper slip from his lap and the pen drop to the floor.

The young man left the hotel on Tenth Avenue and 23rd Street early in the morning. His body was still on European time and he couldn't sleep. He bent his head to the wind and trudged to breakfast at the café he'd used a couple of times since arriving. It wasn't much of a place but it suited him fine because it was cheap and he had to watch his cash supply. There was also a table by the window which provided a good view of the intersection and the hotel entrance. He doubted very much that he had been spotted, but it was as well to be on the lookout.

He ordered from the waitress, a tired little brunette with too much eye make-up and an accommodating manner who seemed to be there at all hours. She was the other reason he liked the café. As she took down his order he thought how remarkably pretty she was – an exquisite pale face and beautifully shaped mouth that twitched nervously into a smile as she spoke.

When she had gone, he laid out the newspaper cutting which he had brought from England and examined the photographs of the sole survivor of the plane crash. The picture was given prime position on the front page, hardly surprising, given the starkness and drama of the image. That was what had caught his attention; what had held it was the inset of a small portrait of Robert Cope Harland which had been released by the UN following the crash. He realised at once that he had found the man he was looking for, which was why he'd packed a rucksack and had got on the plane within six hours of picking up the newspaper.

The waitress returned with the food and he laid the newspaper clipping aside. She made some comment about the picture and the crash and then asked where he was from. He told her Sweden. Was he on vacation? 'Something like that,' he said. He read the nametag on her breast – Shashanna – and remarked that he had never heard of anyone called that before. She said that she believed her father had made it up. Then she complimented him on his English and told him that he looked like he belonged in the city. That pleased him because he took pride in his ability to merge. She went away, darting a look over her shoulder.

He was calm, unusually so considering what he expected to happen in the next few days. He felt pretty pleased with himself, having obtained Harland's address so easily. He wondered if they were usually so lax. After all it had been a simple matter to go to the UN as a tourist, buy the current United Nations handbook and look up a suitably impressive name, in this case the one belonging to the Assistant Secretary-General for External Affairs, a Dr Erika Moss Klein. Posing as her assistant, he called Robert Harland's office and told them that the Assistant Secretary-General needed the address before the weekend. He said there was a package that had to be urgently delivered that evening. The woman, by now a little flustered but also charmed by his manner, gave it to him without a second thought.

Now all that remained was to decide on the approach. That was going to take a lot of thought. The actual words with which he was going to break this astonishing news had so far eluded him. He had made the speech several times in his head since seeing the newspaper photograph – it was all he thought about on the plane trip – but each version seemed hopelessly melodramatic and artificial. Thank God he had remembered to bring the identity cards with him. If all else failed they would surely persuade him that he wasn't a crank.

He went over to a pile of newspapers on the counter and selected the news section of the *New York Times*. He wanted to see if there was anything more about the crash. The day before, the paper had said Harland was still in hospital but was expected to be well enough to leave by the weekend. As he flipped through the paper, he wondered if he should leave it a couple of days before going over to Brooklyn. No, he thought, he would try that day.

There was nothing more in the paper and he put it down. Shashanna took this as a signal that he was available for a chat. She offered him more coffee and asked his name. 'Lars,' he replied, thinking how much he disliked it. But Lars Edberg was the name on his Swedish passport and he had to live with it for the time being. There was no reason to tell this girl his real name.

'What do you do, Lars?' she said, perching on the side of the chair opposite him.

'I'm in the music business.' That wasn't strictly true, but it had been. 'I'm part of an outfit that publishes original music on the Net. In a way I guess it's an anti-music business.'

'Do you have a girl in London?'

'Yes, I do,' he said. He thought of Felicity – Flick – who was ten years older than him and ran a successful flower business. She had picked him up in a bar, given him a place to live and asked no questions about his past.

'Does that mean we can't go to the movies tonight, Lars?'

'I guess it does.'

The rejection registered in her eyes. He put his hand on the table not far from hers. 'I have a lot on, Shashanna. Another time and we would go to the movies. But . . .'

She silenced him with her hand.

'That's okay,' she said and rose from the chair.

He didn't want to mess about with this girl and he had no time, but that wasn't the point. The problem was the thing that he carried inside him, the heaviness of heart – the guilt – which, far from dissipating over the years, had grown and now occupied much of his being. Flick had somehow discerned this and devised a way of living which meant that this unspoken secret did not dominate their relationship. He was sure she knew that it was there.

3

GRISWALD'S MUSIC

As the car neared La Guardia, Harland remembered that he'd left the notes and diagram that he'd made for Frank Ollins back at the hospital. It wouldn't matter. He could arrange for them to be faxed later when he returned to collect his things and to receive a final check-up.

The car dropped him off at the old marine terminal building. Harland was directed to a hangar that was plastered with temporary signs, warning that entry was restricted to the FBI and Federal Aviation Authority and Safety Board personnel. He rang the bell labelled VISITORS and looked across the black water of Bowery Bay towards the end of the runway where the UN flight had crashed. A medium-sized jetliner was landing, its wings visibly seesawing over the last hundred yards of its flight. Harland grimly watched for the puff of smoke from the wheels as it touched down. Then he turned to find Ollins scrutinising him from the doorway.

'When you've seen what's in here,' he said, gesturing behind him, 'you realise what a helluva miracle it is that they don't crash more often.'

Ollins led him into the vast cold space of the hangar in the middle of which lay the remains of the Falcon jet, crudely assembled into the configuration of an aircraft. The temporary lights erected around it gave the wreckage a stark, fossilised look. 'See what I mean?' said Ollins matter-of-factly. 'It doesn't take long to reduce several million dollars'

29

worth of sophisticated machinery to this. Just a matter of seconds.'

Harland said nothing. He was watching the accident investigators move round the plane. Each piece of wreckage was numbered with spray paint and here and there ribbons and tags were fixed to the twisted metal. Almost nothing of the plane's original white and red livery remained, except on the tailplane and one of the three engines. The cockpit was unrecognisable, as was the starboard wing, although a light was visible on its leading edge. The fuselage was crumpled like an old beer can. The dull, inky-coloured metal reminded him of the clinker produced by the boiler in his childhood home.

'What are they doing?' he asked Ollins.

'Determining the precise sequence of events at impact, looking for clues, selecting pieces of the wreckage for further analysis – that kind of thing. A lot will go away for further testing. Clark would tell you better than I can.' He stopped. A hint of disdain passed across his face. 'But Clark and his people already believe they've got this investigation tied up like a Christmas gift with a fancy bow on top.'

'And you don't?'

Ollins gave him the thin professional smile that Harland remembered often seeing in his colleagues back in Century House in London. It was an expression that came with knowledge and enforced silence.

'The Safety Board no longer believes there's a need for criminal investigation,' Ollins said. 'But I can't hide from you the fact that there are unresolved issues here.'

So brisk and confident when he appeared in his hospital room, Special Agent Ollins was now weighed down, fatigued. Harland knew that look too.

They walked around the wreckage in silence. Harland was struck by how small the plane seemed, and also by the smell, which contained several elements – burnt plastic, aviation fuel and a scorched, rusty aroma.

When he had seen enough, Ollins led him up a flight of open stairs and into an office where a ten-foot model of the plane was set out on a large board. The top of the fuselage had been cut away to reveal the inside of the cabin. It was clear that the model was being used as an aid to thought rather than any kind of scientific measurement. Around it were tags and arrows leading to the seats. His name and Griswald's were attached to the two facing seats at the rear of the model. The labels for Maas, Lahmer and Bloch were beside the plane, as were the ones for the three women on the plane – Elsa Meinertzhagen, Courtney Moore and Noala Shimon. Three other labels were named Male: A, Male: B and Male: C. There were also red markers which apparently indicated baggage that had been identified as belonging to one or other of the victims. Ollins told him that most of the bags had been incinerated, but here and there were clues that enabled identification.

'Have you got the name for males A, B and C?'

'A and B have been identified as Roger Clemence and James Gleeson. Mr Gleeson had served the UN in Iraq and was subsequently attached to various observer missions run by the Security Council. Clemence was a lawyer from New Zealand who worked in Africa – Sierra Leone, Rwanda.'

'What about C?'

'We've got no further with him. He's a complete mystery.' Ollins went over to a coffee pot, gestured to Harland who shook his head, and poured himself a cup. 'Why don't you take that chair, Mr Harland, and talk me through the people that you saw at Washington National Airport last Tuesday afternoon – the people who boarded the plane with you? Did you bring your notes?'

'I'm sorry, I stupidly left them at the hospital.'

'That really is a pity,' said Ollins curtly.

'I can get them later,' said Harland. 'I'll fax—'

Ollins put his hand up. 'Could you wait a second?' He leant back and tapped on the window of the adjacent room with a key. 'You people need to hear this.' Four men came in. Each nodded to Harland and found a perch. They had all brought notepads with them.

Harland was puzzled by the FBI's behaviour. If the Safety Board was satisfied that the accident was not the result of sabotage, why was Ollins working under the assumption that it was? Ollins nodded and Harland took them through what he could remember of the meeting at the airport and the minibus ride to the plane. He could now definitely say that Bloch and Lahmer and one of the women were in a huddle inside the terminal and that outside another woman was smoking with Philippe Maas. A third woman, with dark hair cut in a bob, was talking to two men that he didn't recognise. He could not be sure until he saw some photographs. Standing apart from all these was a man in his early thirties – good-looking, obviously fit and with a standoffish manner.

'That's C,' Ollins cut in. 'The woman with the dark hair was Courtney Moore, which means she was talking to Clemence and Gleeson. Can you remember what any of them was carrying, Mr Harland?'

'Most of them had small pieces of luggage – overnight bags and work bags. Alan Griswald and I both had larger cases – we'd been travelling for longer.' He thought about boarding the minibus. He and Griswald had had to stow their suitcases at the back while the others had held them on their laps. 'The man you call C had a large shoulder bag and placed it on top of Griswald's stuff. I think he may have been carrying something else – a smaller bag perhaps.'

'When you got to the airport,' said Ollins, rolling the cup between the palms of his hands, 'you expected to be taking the shuttle. Then you came across Mr Griswald. Who saw whom first?'

'I think I spotted Al.'

'Who was he talking to?'

Harland thought for a moment. 'He was with C. They were standing together, but not talking.'

Ollins looked around the ring of FBI agents to make sure they had understood the significance of this.

'And he didn't introduce you to him?'

'Nor to anyone else, although I'm not sure how many people he knew on the plane.'

'So where did C sit on the plane?'

Harland went to the model. 'Here at the front. One of the women, a blonde of about thirty-five, sat opposite him. She had been looking him over at the airport.'

'That's Elsa Meinertzhagen ... And his baggage would have been placed in the hold with the bigger pieces?'

'No, I think there was some trouble stowing it in the hold. He brought it into the cabin and the flight attendant dealt with it.'

'And he didn't talk to Griswald during the flight?'

'Nope, I was with Griswald the whole time, except when I went to the toilet.'

'That was what – ten, fifteen minutes short of La Guardia?'

'Yes, about that.'

'The lights were extinguished and you returned to your seat. You say you noticed the heating system was malfunctioning at that time. It was cold in the cabin, right?'

'Yes.'

Silence descended on the group as Ollins mulled this over. They all looked tired. The room held the sour atmosphere of long and unrewarded labour.

'Do you want me to try and place people on this model?' asked Harland.

'Sure,' said Ollins, 'and then we'll go out to the crash site. They're switching the landing runway and delaying all takeoffs for a half-hour. I need you to try to trace your movements out there.'

Harland went through the cabin placing labels by the seats. He wasn't sure about Male A and Male B and he couldn't remember which of the women had been sitting across the aisle from him. But Ollins appeared to have lost interest and was anxious to get out on the runway. A call was made to the air traffic control tower and in a few minutes they got clearance to drive out to the far end of the runway.

On the way, Ollins laconically indicated the positions where the main parts of the fuselage had come to rest and the Learjet had been hit. All the wreckage had been cleared away and on the spot where the tarmac had been damaged by the Learjet explosion a new surface had already been laid. They moved up the runway, beside the huge blackened scrape which marked the wreckage path of the Falcon. The distances seemed much shorter in daylight and when they got out of the Cherokee Jeep, Harland was astonished how close he had been to the side of the dyke. Now he understood why he hadn't been seen. The main beam from the fire trucks, although appearing to illuminate his surroundings, must have overshot him. He could see that he'd been about twenty feet below the level of the runway.

He walked to the edge of the dyke with Ollins and looked down. Out on the mudflats were several men wearing Day-Glo jackets, sweeping the surface with metal detectors. Two other men were in a rubber inflatable. One punted up the little rivulets while the other operated two probes. The tide was still low. Marker buoys floated on slack lines in the water and flag-sticks protruded from the mud. There was a fair amount of ice about and for a moment Harland's eyes settled on a brittle white shelf which projected over the mud.

'That's where we located the cockpit voice and flight data recorders,' said Ollins, pointing to the furthest flag. 'They were carried in the tail section which is why they were thrown out along this line.' He made a sweeping gesture with his hand. 'Over there is where we found Mr Griswald's body. And right over there is where the chopper picked you up. It's a long way between the two points. How'd you get there, Mr Harland?'

Harland was finding this harder than he'd expected. He stared down at the tufts of grass and the little streams that snaked through the mud. It all looked harmless enough now, but down there in the dark and with the tide rushing in, he had been damned certain that he was going to lose his life. He thought of Al Griswald's body propped up grotesquely in his seat and the freezing water swirling round his chest and sucking at his legs.

'Mr Harland!' shouted Ollins over the roar of a plane that had just landed on the other runway. 'What happened? How did you get there?'

'Swam,' he shouted back.

'That's a hundred yards or more. You were swimming out into the East River?'

'I was being swept out there – I was taken by the current.'

'And the phone?' asked Ollins, leaning into Harland's face and shouting over the noise of the plane that was now manoeuvring towards the terminal. 'Can you say where you were when you dropped the phone?'

Harland looked down at the place where Griswald's body had been and worked out that he had waded in a line that was parallel to the runway. With the tide being so low now, it was difficult to pinpoint the spot where he'd dropped down into the water and let go of the phone, but he hazarded a guess that it was where the mud shelved down sharply into a gully. At high tide it would be way out of his depth and he could see that what was a trickle of water would become a channel for the tide flowing from the west. Ollins produced a radio from his pocket and guided his beachcombers to the area. A voice came back to tell him that they had already searched there several times. The phone had probably been taken out on the tide. It could be anywhere.

'Why's the phone so important to you?'

'We're just researching as much as we can about all the victims.'

It occurred to Harland that they would want it to see who Griswald had been calling.

Ollins looked out towards Riker's Island and then turned to him. 'I have to ask you this: did you take anything from Alan Griswald's body?'

'No,' said Harland, mystified. 'I thought I was about to lose my life. I wasn't in the business of ripping off the dead.'

'Nothing?'

'No.'

Ollins looked at him intently. The wind made his hair stand up vertically in a crest. 'Were you ... er ... involved with Mr Griswald in any way? I mean his business at the War Crimes Tribunal. You had nothing to do with that?'

'My work is much less glamorous, if I can put it that way. I barely knew what Al was doing and I expect you've found out that he was an exceptionally discreet person.'

'Yes, that's what the agency said. You're sure that you didn't take anything? It could be important.'

'Why are you asking this?'

Ollins didn't answer. He turned towards the car and said, 'Let's get out of the cold, Mr Harland.'

They climbed in. 'Clark says the two black boxes have been retrieved,' said Harland. 'Surely they will tell you all you need to know about the plane? As I understand it, they record everything that happened during the flight. They're very sophisticated these days.'

Ollins started the engine distractedly and executed a lazy turn towards the Marine Terminal, steering the car with just a couple of fingers. 'You're right. The data recorders are very good – a near-perfect record of that flight. Mr Clark and his colleagues at the NTSB think they've got enough evidence to say what happened to your plane. But I find I want to know more than they can answer.'

He drove in silence to the hangar where he deposited Harland by the cab that would take him back to the hospital. 'We'll be in touch,' he said, moving off. 'And don't forget to fax me those notes you made. The number is on the card I gave you.'

At the hospital, Harland ate lunch and dozed for a short time before receiving a final examination. While waiting for the cab from Queen's Limousine Service to arrive he got his few possessions together. As he cleared out the drawer of the bedside table he found a black wallet. It was bulkier than his own but, like his, the leather was distorted from being immersed and then dried out. He opened it and found Griswald's credit cards.

Slowly he remembered how the wallet came to be there. At the moment of trying to answer Griswald's phone he had slipped it into his pocket and forgotten about it. The hospital staff must have dried it out with the rest of his clothes and placed it with his own wallet in the drawer. He looked again and found pictures of the Griswald children. The photos had suffered from the water, as had the receipts and the cover of a mini-disc which was in one of the wallet's compartments. Harland pulled it out and saw that it was a compilation of work by Brahms, Chopin and Mendelssohn. This surprised him since Griswald was famously hostile to any music which did not involve saxophones and trumpets. He looked at the disc then returned it with the box to the wallet, at the same time remembering the many evenings he had spent with Griswald – more from friendship than shared enthusiasm – searching out increasingly arcane jazz haunts in West Berlin.

He put the wallet with the rest of his things, reminding himself to tell Ollins about it, and went to find out what had happened to the cab. Sister Rafael made a call and a few minutes later put her head round the door to say that the car was on its way, but that there was another call waiting – a Mr Walter Vigo from England.

Vigo! What the hell did he want? He hadn't seen Vigo for at least a decade. On the day he left MI6 for good in 1990, Vigo had come to him and offered a limp hand of regret together with the assurance that their masters would take Harland back if he found he could not make a go of things outside. They both knew this was impossible.

Harland picked up the phone.

'Bobby,' said the voice. 'It's Walter here. How are you? I was phoning to say how concerned we've all been to hear about your ordeal.'

We, thought Harland. Who the hell is *we*? A great crowd of well-wishers at the new headquarters of SIS, unable to think of anything but their ex-colleague's health?

'Thank you,' he said. 'It's good of you to call. Where are you ringing from? It's nine p.m. in London and it's Saturday – you can't be at work.'

'I'm here in New York. Davina wanted to do some Christmas shopping and see a show or two. I took a few days off and came along with her. I'm pleased to say that our flight was rather less eventful than yours.'

Harland remembered that Davina Vigo was wealthy. She had the kind of background – Vigo's euphemism for money – that enabled Vigo to treat his government salary almost as loose change. They lived in a large house in Holland Park and were always nipping off for weekends in Italy or Switzerland. People wondered why he hadn't left the service when his wife inherited in the mid-eighties, but that was to misunderstand Walter Vigo and his profound commitment to the profession. He liked intelligence work and was prodigiously good at it. Harland knew he was pretty near the top of the service now.

'How long are you staying in New York?'

'Until Monday – just a short trip. I was wondering if you'd like me to visit you. I'd do a lot to get out of the play Davina has fixed for this evening. If I came late this afternoon, I could reasonably excuse myself for the whole evening.'

'They're letting me go home,' Harland said. 'I'm waiting for a car to pick me up now.'

'Really! That is good news. Then what are you doing this evening? Can't be much fun going back to an empty flat in Brooklyn.'

How uncharacteristic of Vigo to make a mistake like that, thought Harland. Vigo could only know he lived in Brooklyn if he had been making inquiries about him. Harland was not in the phone book and, though he never made any secret of it, few people knew where he lived.

'How do you know it's empty?' asked Harland, smiling to himself.

Vigo laughed. 'I admit to the assumption, unwarranted perhaps, that your personal life is in its usual state of disarray. Otherwise I imagine that someone would be collecting you and that you wouldn't be waiting for a car.'

A fast recovery, thought Harland. Maybe he wasn't losing his touch after all.

'But forgive me, if I'm wrong,' said Vigo. 'Look – it would be lovely to see you. Why don't we have an early dinner? Shall we say Noonan's Steakhouse at seven? It's at Lexington and forty-eighth Street. I'll book – it's on me.'

Harland was about to decline, but then thought that an evening by himself was precisely what he did not need. He was feeling rested and, besides, he was curious to know what Vigo wanted. He'd bet his life that there was a very specific reason for the call. Walter Vigo always had a purpose, even if at first he did not declare it.

4

PHILOSOPHER SPY

Harland was late at Noonan's, arriving at twenty past seven. As he waited to check the old blue overcoat he was using as a substitute for the one lost in the crash, he looked around the restaurant and decided it was an odd place for Vigo to choose: a phoney club atmosphere; hearty back-slapping men, and women with the expensive, caramelised look of over-decorated pâtisserie. No, Noonan's was not at all Vigo's natural habitat.

The maître d' gestured to a booth in the far corner of the restaurant and told him that Mr Vigo had been there for some time. He found Vigo tucked into the booth, with his back to the rest of the diners. The fingers of one hand rested on the stem of a vodka martini, while the other held down the pages of a Sotheby's auction catalogue.

He rose as Harland approached and proffered his hand. 'Bobby, what a pleasure to see you – and looking so well too. Slide in there and let's get you a drink.' He examined Harland in the light of the lamp over the table. 'Let me look at you. Gracious, there's not a scratch on you. You're a bloody miracle and a famous miracle at that. I suppose you know that every daily newspaper in the world published the picture of your rescue.'

'I'm beginning to appreciate that,' said Harland regretfully.

'You're going to become one of those icons of photography, an exquisitely comic fate for an ex-spy, don't you think?'

He paused to irradiate Harland with a smile. 'Now, what are you going to have to drink, Bobby – champagne?'

Harland accepted and reminded himself to guard against Vigo's we're-all-in-it-together bonhomie.

Vigo clapped his catalogue shut and held it up for Harland to see. 'Incunabula!' he proclaimed. 'Isn't that a marvellous word? It refers to all books printed before 1501 – just a few years after Caxton's press.'

'Yes, Walter, I think I knew that.'

'But do you know what it means in Latin? I learned the other day that incunabula are swaddling clothes – I suppose it's the idea of the very first stage in any given development.'

Vigo hadn't lost his pedagogical style. And physically he hadn't changed much either, although Harland knew that he must have passed his fiftieth birthday. He had the same polished skin, the same prominent, fleshy nose and slightly popping eyes. Even his hair, a unique mass of tight curls that bunched at his collar like the improbable locks of a wig, seemed as thick and vigorous as it had been when Vigo had come to lecture Harland's SIS intake at the Fort training school on Euro-communism. But he had gained weight around the shoulders and chest, and his face had thickened at the jaw, which added to his appearance of substance. A stranger might have taken him for a professional connoisseur, an art dealer or wine merchant. But there was nothing refined about Walter Vigo, nothing ponderous or precious about him. He could mix it with the best and, when circumstances required, was capable of demonic application. As he sat beaming across from Harland, he seemed more than ever to project a massive and protuberant cleverness.

Harland's champagne arrived. Vigo ceremoniously raised his own glass. 'Here's to your survival, Bobby. Good health.' He drained the martini, never letting his eyes leave Harland's. 'From what I hear, it was a remarkable feat. You were half-dead when they got to you.'

'I was lucky, the others weren't. It's as simple as that.'

'Yes, but surviving in those conditions. That took some guts – not that there was ever any question about your personal courage, Bobby. We know that. We know what you did in Germany and Czechoslovakia. And I hear you've been in some pretty tight situations since you left us.'

'As I say, I was lucky.'

'I suppose in one sense you were. I mean happening upon that phone. What an extraordinary piece of fortune that was. And you knew the man whose phone it was.'

'Yes, it was Alan Griswald's.'

Vigo was certainly on top of things. Almost none of this had been released to the press. Harland realised that the information would have been quickly picked up by the SIS contingent at the UK mission who had any number of friends in the UN.

'Ah yes, of course. Alan Griswald. Now we've come across him before, haven't we?'

Harland wasn't going to help. 'Have you, Walter? I wasn't aware of that.'

'Yes, where did we meet Mr Griswald before?'

'He was in Europe – Vienna and Berlin. Also in the Middle East.'

'Oh yes, Alan Griswald. CIA to his boots, a good soldier, a good solid Cold War warrior. I remember him. He had a wife . . . um?'

'Sally.'

'Yes, Sally. Poor woman. Of course there were many other casualties, but it means a great deal more when you know someone. Griswald retired from the Agency. What did he go on to do? Was he involved with the UN?'

'He was working for the War Crimes Tribunal. I saw him in The Hague last week. I was there for the World Water Convention. We bumped into each other outside the convention centre and then both of us walked slap-bang into

42

Guy Cushing – you remember the man in the Far East Controllerate who had the money problem? Pushed out because of his debts and the gambling thing?'

'Of course,' Vigo said unenthusiastically. 'Yes, Cushing.'

'Guy works for the UN chemical weapons agency in The Hague. We all had dinner that evening in the old town – a place near the Palace. Griswald didn't say much about what he was doing because Guy was there. He said that he had been engaged in some follow-up work for the Tribunal. I didn't know what that meant. He said he was going to Washington and we loosely arranged to hook up because I was going to be in Rockville, which is no distance from DC. That's how I came to be on the plane.'

'Yes, I heard that from someone.' He signalled for another martini. 'Any idea whether he was going to see his former employers at Langley, Virginia? That's not far from DC either.'

'No,' said Harland, now certain that this was not a friendly fixture. He thought suddenly and rather guiltily of Griswald's wallet. Griswald had gone on about some big breakthrough he had made and on the cab journey to the restaurant Harland distinctly remembered how he had patted his breast pocket and said that he had found everything he needed for a hell of a case. 'One day,' he had said, 'I'll tell you the whole goddam frigging story and you, Bob, will be especially interested.' That was the trouble with the last few days, Harland thought. He was so bloody vague; things were coming back to him, but very slowly.

'So, then you flew back on the UN plane to New York,' continued Vigo gently. 'Had you seen each other in Washington?'

'No, in the end it wasn't possible.'

'But you had arranged to fly back together on the UN plane.'

'Not really. Vigo told me the time of the departure and

43

said where they'd be. I thought I had missed it by a long time, but then I found them in the airport and took the ride.'

'Anyone else on the plane that I'd know?'

'I don't think so, but they haven't all been identified.'

'How many remain unidentified?'

'One – a man.'

'Odd, that. I mean you would think he would have been missed by now. What did the investigators say to you? They've been to see you?'

'Yes, I've seen them twice. I went out to the airport today – went over the crash scene.'

'Did they have any ideas about this individual?'

'Not that they told me.'

The maître d' appeared at their booth. Harland ordered soft-shell crab and lamb chops, Vigo lobster bisque and blinis of almas caviar – the roe of an albino beluga sturgeon. Vigo told the man to bring the wine they had discussed before Harland arrived.

'How's your sister?' he asked, suddenly snapping a bread stick. 'You knew Harriet was at Oxford with my wife, Davina. Davina always says that she was far and away the most able of her generation at LMH. What's she doing now?'

'She's married to Robin Bosey, the advertising man. You may have heard of White Bosey Cane. That's his agency.'

'Oh yes, I know exactly who you mean: always in the papers; designs his own clothes, works for the Labour Party.' A flicker of disdain swept through Vigo's eyes. 'And she's happy with *Robin*?'

'I think so. She does some financial consultancy, but brings up the children mostly. She had three, the last one four years ago.'

'Seems an awful waste of such a good mind – I mean Harriet sitting at home and being married to a man like Bosey. You're frightfully close, aren't you? I believe she was a great support when you had that terrible year. What with

Louise leaving and your getting ill, it must have been an extremely difficult period for you, Bobby. That's all all right now?' Harland nodded and smiled at Vigo's parenthetic concern for his health.

'What a year that was, eh?' mused Vigo. 'Stumps drawn on the great game. Enemies and friends wearing the same suits and driving the same cars and suddenly we had to look very hard indeed to understand the new patterns of play. It was unsettling, and yet deeply stimulating at the same time. The people who suggested that the twentieth century ended in those months are absolutely right. Look at what else happened – the technical revolution and the leap to globalisation. It took some time, I have to confess, for us to get the point that digital information was infinitely more fluid than the information that's written down on a piece of paper, placed in a file and locked up in a steel vault. Secrets developed wings of their own. Things that had been stationary became fleet of foot; those that were solid and impenetrable became porous. Secrecy was no longer an absolute condition, but something that was measured in degrees.' He stopped to taste the wine that the maître d' had brought, nodded and waited as it was poured. Harland picked up his glass, reflecting on the fact that he'd need the drink to get through the evening. 'But, of course,' continued Vigo, 'what was our weakness was everybody's weakness. There were new lines of attack, new pathways to explore and new friends to be made. You've missed a lot, Bobby. It's been challenging for the old lags who've clung on.'

Vigo had certainly clung on. Harland had heard the details from a colleague who was brushed aside in his ascent. Vigo had served for a brief period in Washington. In 1995 he had manoeuvred to take over the newly formed Controllerate responsible for the Middle East and Africa. Five years later he had become Controller, Central and Eastern Europe. Recently he had got an even grander position which required a special title which no one could remember, but which seemed to incorporate security and public affairs.

'But you've done very well for yourself, Walter. I hear you're a great power in the land. You must be going for the top job?'

'No, no. I am sure that won't come my way. Robin Teckman may be asked to stay on for three more years, which means that his successor will be chosen from the generation below me. Tim Lapthorne or Miles Morsehead are the obvious candidates. I'm content with my lot and there's much to do in the years that remain to me in the Service.'

Harland remembered Lapthorne and Morsehead, two bright stars of the early eighties' intakes. Morsehead was the obvious choice. From an early moment in his career he had managed to seem bold and reassuring at the same time.

'You're sounding like a politician, Walter,' he said.

Vigo ignored the remark. The food arrived and he set about drawing up the bisque to his lips in a fluent scooping motion. 'Of course,' he said eventually, 'you would have gone a long way up the ladder yourself, Bobby, if you hadn't bailed out. You've got what it takes – intelligence, imagination, discipline, charm. You were good at winning people's confidence, a very light touch with the most difficult of characters. Remember that Russian diplomat in Turkey you persuaded to drive over the border with a chunk of the new Soviet armour welded into his car engine? What was his name?'

'Tishkov – Avi Tishkov.'

He paused and glanced around the restaurant with an air of someone experiencing public transport for the first time.

'Why did you go?' he said emphatically. 'Why? There was no need, surely? We would've made certain you had time to recover properly. You were marked for the top, Bobby.'

Harland opened his hands in a gesture of appeal. 'When

you've had a brush with cancer, you think through your life and see it in a different light. It's a terrible cliché, but it's true. I decided to do something else. That was all. What I didn't appreciate at the time was that Louise was thinking along the same lines.'

'Yes, discipline,' mused Vigo, failing to follow the trail about Louise's departure. 'That really is your foremost quality. You never gave in to what I would guess was an essentially turbulent nature. It was that tension between impulse and control that made you a good agent. You watched yourself as carefully as anyone else. You became a philosopher, a thinker, because that way you would survive. I admired you for that thoughtfulness and the way the habit of weighing things extended into your work. Yet I have to say that I feared what would happen if you let go of the reins. That would be the end of the philosopher spy, I was always sure of that, the end of the man who talked Descartes to some poor Polish trade official and induced him to donate all his country's economic information to our data bank.'

Harland saw that the nature of the conversation had changed entirely. He had the impression of a very large ship edging towards its berth.

'What's this about, Walter?' he asked. 'Is there something you want to know?'

Vigo looked up from the nearly drained bowl, his eyes glittering with purpose. Harland was momentarily fascinated by the size and sensuality of his face. He remembered how someone in Century House had found a picture of a ceremonial mask from a Pacific island in one of the Sunday supplements and had pointed out that it looked exactly like Walter Vigo. For a short while afterwards he was called the Love Mask.

'Oh yes, Bobby. There's a lot I want to know. I want to know who was on that plane and what Griswald was taking with him to Washington. And, more particularly, I want to know whether your relationship with Griswald holds any significance. I ask myself, can it be that you really just happened upon each other in The Hague and had dinner at the Toison D'Or? Or was it that you two had some business there and in Washington? I want to know whether your presence is important on the flight, or whether it is simply Alan Griswald I should concern myself with. Yes, I would like to know the answers to these questions. Can you help?'

'Not really, Walter,' said Harland. 'By the way, I didn't mention the Toison D'Or. How did you know?'

'I assumed it. The Golden Fleece is the only place there.'

Smooth, thought Harland, but unconvincing. 'I have had no professional dealings with Griswald whatsoever for more than a dozen years,' he said. 'I liked him and that's why I was sitting with him on the plane. Indeed, that's why I was on the plane. There's nothing sinister about it.'

Vigo sat motionless with his hands splayed on the table while the plates were removed.

'I'm right in thinking that you and Griswald knew each other very well once,' he said, when the waiter had gone. 'You worked together in the eighties and you were both involved in that operation after the Wall came down – the operation to lift the Stasi files in East Berlin. God, what an excitement that was! And with good reason. Those files were matchless. They contained everything we could have wished to know about the East Germans and their intelligence service – absolutely everything.'

He paused, as if to catch hold of the fading memory, eyes to the ceiling, hands stroking the tablecloth. 'Yes ... they were handed over in a villa in Berlin – Karlshorst – but not to you, not to the CIA, but astonishingly to the KGB. Then Griswald's pals in Moscow station obtained them for an exceedingly large sum of money. I recall your excellent report, describing Alan Griswald's pivotal role in the coup, and outlining what those files would mean to West German society and to us – the understanding of the Stasi's strategy, the highly placed agents who'd been working for the East, to say nothing of their ingenious trade-craft. They *were* good, weren't they?'

'Yes, I suppose they were, but it all seems so long ago. The world's moved on, as you say yourself.'

Vigo was not easily diverted.

'But then you and Griswald overreached yourselves and went south, to Czechoslovakia, on an extremely dubious fishing expedition to seize the files of the State Security Service in Prague. That was an occasion when you may have been driven by impulse rather than reason, I fear. But we were all carried along by your enthusiasm. Bobby Harland, the magician of the East European Controllerate, was going to bring home the bacon – everything we wanted to know about the StB. Your argument was so alluringly pitched. If I remember rightly, you pointed out that we couldn't know what would happen in Eastern Europe. It might all be a flash in the pan, you said, so we'd better move quickly. We knew it was blue-chip intelligence, the real stuff, and we all desperately wanted it.

'Everyone liked the idea,' said Harland, knowing he was sounding defensive.

'Oh yes, I know your plan was cleared by the Head of Soviet Ops and the Security Branch Officer – who incidentally had no business sanctioning such a harebrained scheme. Operational security! There was no operational security and everyone knew it. You didn't know the set-up in Prague and our people there were extremely doubtful about the contacts you and Griswald had conjured from nowhere. But you insisted that cash would open the right doors and, well, I suppose we were all guilty of greed, weren't we? A matter of days and you were arrested and beaten so badly you couldn't walk. If The Bird and Macy Harp hadn't got you out I doubt whether you would be alive today.'

Harland suddenly saw the loping figure of Cuth Avocet, known to all as The Bird, and his equally improbable partner, Macy Harp. Both MI6-trained, they'd turned freelance and during the Cold War went behind the Iron Curtain to sort out problems which were underplayed as 'situations' in the argot of the great game.

'How long were you in that Austrian hospital – five, six weeks? It all still puzzles me. I felt there was more to it than met the eye. Worth further thought some day, I said to myself, because it seemed to me that they were expecting you. You weren't held in a standard prison, were you? Some bloody house on the outskirts of the city.'

He stopped to let the waiter set down the second course, then looked down at his caviar with an expression of regret, perhaps caused by the thought that he would not be able to devote his full attention to it.

Harland fought to put the image from his mind, the image of the room where he had been held for all those days and beaten senseless. But he didn't succeed. He saw The Bird stepping into the doorway and saying, 'Hello, old lad. Time to be on our way, don't you think?' And then The Bird had freed him from the leather restraints and virtually carried him out of the deserted villa. On the way they passed two guards who had been dispatched by him. And then they found Macy Harp waiting patiently in the street behind the wheel of an old but very fast BMW, and they had driven like the blazes to the Austrian border, where The Bird had squared things with the Czech border guards. There had been others involved in the operation, but he never knew their names, and when at length he visited The Bird and Macy to thank them, they had been stubbornly mysterious about how they had found him and who else had helped. It was part of their service, they said, and they had been well paid for it. However, they would prefer not to discuss the matter any more.

Vigo was watching him now.

'Was it the beating, Bobby? Was that what finally turned you against the Service? I know it must have been a terrible experience, but it's not as though you went into some quieter line of business afterwards. I mean, Kurdistan in the early nineties, followed by Tajikistan and where else? Azerbaijan, Chechnya? Not a sheltered life, by any means. To tell you the truth, it always looked to me as if you were going out of your way to find danger. I used to ask myself why that might be.' He paused to let the thought hang in the air. 'In another man I would hazard that such compulsion was an indication of guilt.'

Harland looked at him mildly. 'Not guilt, Walter, just a change of interest. The reason I went to those places was that I could speak Russian. As you can imagine, the Red Cross didn't have too many Russian speakers in those days. And, you know something? We did some good in those places, which is what I liked about the job.'

Vigo returned a knowing smile and then sighed. 'But let's just go back to the matter in hand, if you wouldn't mind – this thing you had with Griswald, this association, this alliance. He must have given you a hint of what he was doing. You see, we know he was bringing something to New York of great value. When I saw you were on the same flight I said to myself that this information might be the sort that Griswald would share with an old and reliable friend such as Bobby Harland.'

'The answer is no. I really haven't the first idea what he was up to. I guessed that it was important – in fact, he said so. But really I can't tell you any more than that.'

'But I have a steer that you did indeed know about it all.'

Harland remembered Guy Cushing in The Hague and wondered whether Vigo had prevailed upon him to bump into Griswald and find out what he could at the Toison D'Or. Harland was certainly not put off by the nauseous look

51

that came into Vigo's expression when he first mentioned Cushing. It was quite possible that Cushing had been keeping an eye on Griswald for some time. He must owe Vigo all sorts of favours after his unceremonious expulsion from the Service, which was said at the time to be a lenient punishment. Yes, he would owe Vigo, and Vigo would have pressed for repayment. That was Vigo's way.

'Walter, you asked me why I left the Service. It was partly to stop wasting my life on this sort of crap. Let me be clear about this. Griswald and I collaborated at one time and I really was genuinely fond of him, but our lives developed in different directions. The steer you have is a bad one.'

Vigo said nothing.

'The other thing you're forgetting,' Harland continued, 'is that the crash appears to have been an accident, which stands to reason. If you were to sabotage a plane, you would arrange for it to blow up at twenty-eight thousand feet, not at fifty feet as it was coming in to land.' He pulled his napkin from his lap and began to work his way out of the booth. 'Walter, I can't give you the answers to your questions because they're too damned silly.'

'There's no need to leave, Bobby,' said Vigo, holding up both hands. 'Please do stay. I'll explain as much as I can. You see, we believe that Griswald had benefited from an unusual source.'

'What kind of source?'

'I'm not at liberty to say, but I can tell you that the source is random in focus and sometimes oddly juvenile. We are anxious to learn a little more about the source and so naturally I came to you, believing that perhaps Griswald had told you about it.'

Harland felt his temper rising. 'Look, I had absolutely no connection with Griswald. He wouldn't tell me what he was doing. You must understand that. Why don't you ask this bloody source?'

Vigo considered this while adding sour cream and caviar to the mound of chopped egg on one of the blinis. When he had finished, he picked up the pancake, squeezed the sides gently and placed it in his mouth. Silence ensued. Then he spoke. 'I can't talk to this source because at present it's anonymous.'

'Look, somewhere along the line there's a physical entity who you can grab by the throat and demand he tells you what he's talking about.'

'In this case we can't. Things aren't nearly as simple as they used to be and this is a very delicate, not to say dangerous, situation.'

'Are you getting this all off the Web? Some crackpot intelligence site?'

'No, it's rather more specialised information – designed for the trade only, I suspect. I believe Griswald was in receipt of a bespoke service, if I may call it that.'

The trade only! Bespoke service! He wished Vigo would stop talking like a fucking butler. He looked at him and wondered vaguely if he had any concept of life outside the Secret Intelligence Service.

'But this source is some kind of friendly voice?' ventured Harland.

'I couldn't say.'

'Then what the hell are you talking about?'

'I can see you're sceptical about all this, but I assure you that we believe it to be important.'

'Yes, I'm sceptical, but I was also thinking that it's a long time since I've had a conversation like this when I haven't the first idea what is being said to me.'

'Oh, come on, Bobby, you do yourself a disservice. As you well know, you are rather good at all this. Don't tell me you've been converted by the happy-clappy folk at the UN, because I won't believe you.'

'For fuck's sake,' Harland snapped. 'Out there, there are

vast problems of poverty and with the environment. These problems are getting worse and they need people to think about them. When it comes down to it, the intelligence community – as it is laughably called – does damn all to help.'

Vigo sat back to examine Harland with ironic amusement, his eyes popping with superiority and malice.

'I see the philosopher spy is in the grip of a moral imperative – or is it a categorical imperative? I am never sure. However, before you get too carried away, let me just point out that a great number of people at the UN belong to the community you so despise. No less than a fifth of every national mission at the UN is devoted to the unlovely practice of your former trade. They're ferreting around, snooping, poking, prying, stealing, poncing and generally doing their level best to find out what each other is up to. They may wear national costumes and talk humanitarianism while queuing at the vegetarian counter in the UN cafeteria, but let me tell you that a good many of them are spies, and pretty second-rate spies at that.'

Harland drank some wine and decided not to reply. Time to go.

'Look, Walter, I'm not much company. I wish I could help you about Griswald, but I can't. And now I really do think that I should go to bed. I'm still feeling pretty done in.'

He got up.

Vigo looked disappointed. 'Yes, of course. I quite under-stand, Bobby. It's been a pleasure to see you. I hope you haven't minded our talk. You can probably see that it's important to me. I hope also that you'll understand if I have to call on you again.' He composed himself and smiled. 'What are you doing for Christmas? Going back to dear old England or staying here?'

'No plans yet.'

'Well, keep in touch. And Bobby, all of what we've talked about aside, I'm really very pleased to see you alive.'

Harland shrugged and thanked him for the meal. He went to collect his coat at the front desk. The girl at the coat check had some trouble finding it. As he waited he cast a look back at Vigo in the booth. His hands were just visible, leafing through the catalogue of incunabula. Then a man appeared, perhaps from a table on the opposite side of the restaurant, and went over to say something to him. Vigo did not raise his head to look at the man.

Harland walked down 48th Street towards the East River, relieved to be out of Vigo's oppressive company and also a little angry with himself for allowing Vigo to nettle him. He was sure that the stuff about Prague, dropped like an iron bar into the conversation, was there to menace him. Of course, Vigo didn't know anything about Prague, but he must have had suspicions at the time which he had resurrected now to use as a lever. Well, he could forget it! There was no way he was going to succumb to a clumsy threat like that.

Try as he might, he couldn't stop turning over the conversation in his mind. What was it Griswald knew that Vigo was so desperate to get hold of? It had occurred to Harland beforehand that the mini-disc might just carry something, if only because the choice of music was patently not Griswald's. The next day he would take it to Sally and ask her if she thought it had any special significance. He would also see if she knew what her husband was working on. The Griswalds had an unusually close relationship and he was sure that Al kept few secrets from her.

But what about Vigo? What the hell were his motives? On reflection, Harland felt he'd almost been sitting with some-one who was playing Vigo, rather than Vigo himself. The humour and effortless speed of mind had been replaced by a pantomime version of the original – an indication perhaps of his desperation. There was no doubt that the problem was consuming all Vigo's considerable resources because he was well informed about the crash. Maybe he had a line into the FBI? But it was more likely he was getting this stuff from someone in the UN, someone who was being kept informed of the progress of the investigation.

Harland turned right at Second Avenue and kept walking simply for the pleasure of the bracing night air and the glittering vistas of midtown Manhattan. His mind was clearing and with that came a burst of optimism, which had been waiting to break out since he left the hospital. He had survived, dammit, and that was all that mattered. He stopped at a Korean deli and bought himself a small container of freshly squeezed orange juice to clear his mouth of the thick, musty taste of the wine. He undid the top as he waited for the store assistant to change his twenty-dollar bill and swilled the juice in his mouth before swallowing it. Then something occurred in a deep part of his consciousness. An old nerve ending tingled which made him look round through the doorway and catch sight of a man on the other side of Second Avenue. He had stopped and was fiddling with one of the newspaper vending machines that are on every corner in midtown. Harland understood that he had been followed from the restaurant. He took his change and lingered to the side of the doorway, waiting for a cab with an illuminated sign to draw up to the lights. The man threw one or two glances his way, then withdrew a newspaper from the machine and ostentatiously started leafing through it.

Bloody amateur, thought Harland as he walked smartly from the doorway and flagged down a cab. What the hell did Vigo think he was playing at, sending his idiot footpads to follow him?

5

THE WOODEN HAT

The young man waited to catch sight of Harland outside the Flynt Building in Brooklyn Heights for much of the day. But the wind was blowing straight off the East River and several times he had been driven inside by the cold, first to find refuge in a bar and then in the cinema on Henry Street. After the movie, he decided to find out whether Harland was expected back that day. He talked to the surly Russian porter at the Flynt and discovered he'd missed him. Harland had returned from hospital and gone out again. At 10 p.m. the young man returned to his post behind some recycling bins across the street from the building. He would give it an hour and if Harland didn't show he'd go back to the hotel.

Ten minutes later a cab drew up and a man in a long overcoat got out and walked slowly to the building's entrance, patting his pockets for keys. As he reached the door, he paused and shot a glance quickly up and down the empty street. It was then that he caught sight of the man's face. Although he was thirty yards away and the light was not good in that part of the street, he was certain that the tall, slightly stooping figure was Robert Harland. But now that the moment had arrived, he found his mind tripping over itself in an effort to choose the right words. Hell, he'd had enough time to think of what he was going to say, but he couldn't find a coherent sentence in his being. And so he watched while Harland pulled the door open and passed into the lobby.

He was just pondering how long he should wait before asking the porter to call up to Harland's apartment when another cab coasted to a halt at the end of the street and two men got out. Instinctively he withdrew further into the shadows behind the bins. He saw one of the men jog a little way down the street, stop and hold up his hand to shield his eyes from the light of the street lamp. He seemed to be interested in the cab which had dropped Harland off, and was only now moving away. After a few seconds the man retreated and disappeared with his companion into Henry Street.

Harland could never enter the Flynt Building without marvelling at his good fortune in landing the apartment when the previous tenant left for Rome. He made for the elevator, raising a hand cheerily to the young Russian who served as the weekend doorman. Boris grunted something but did not look up from the mini TV balanced in his lap.

When he unlocked the door of his apartment he would sometimes go in without turning on the lights, take a drink from the fridge and look at the view for a few minutes. The room was large and airy, and all along one side was an uninterrupted view across the East River to Wall Street and the World Trade Center. But now he flicked the switch because the answerphone light was blinking. He pushed the play button and heard the machine announce in its hesitant, half-feminine voice, 'You have ... five ... new messages.' The first caller hung up without speaking. The next three were well-wishers from the UN, and then came Harriet, again insisting that he should spend Christmas in London.

As he listened to her, his eyes ran over his desk. Something was wrong. The letters he'd picked up from the mailbox that afternoon had been placed in a different order. And the bill from the electricity company, which he'd left on top of his laptop so he wouldn't forget to pay it, had been moved to the side and turned over. Also, the lid of the computer was fractionally open. He knew he had left it shut tight.

He looked round the apartment. Nothing else seemed to have been disturbed. He went back to the computer and turned it on. All the files on his water report were in order and appeared not to have been tampered with. His e-mail, however, had been downloaded from the Internet provider and read. Some sixteen messages that he had not seen before were displayed in the inbox. None was in the bold type that indicated an unopened message.

His first thought was that Vigo had arranged for the search, knowing he was safely at dinner with him. His hand rose to feel the lump of Griswald's wallet in his jacket and the hard edge of the disc's cover. That was the only thing Vigo could want unless he was convinced that Harland's laptop contained some clue to Griswald's secret. Still, it didn't seem quite right to him. A professional team from SIS would have stolen into the apartment and gone through his things without leaving a trace. They certainly would not have made the mistake of opening his e-mail and then leaving the computer open and in sleep mode.

He left the apartment and went down to the lobby where he found Boris who was leaning back in his chair, distractedly pulling a strand of gum from his mouth.

'Did I have any callers when I was out, Boris?'

'World and fucking wife try reaching you,' he said without turning round. 'Too many people looking for you come here.'

'Too many people? What do you mean – the media?'

'Many people. Not media.'

'Well, who then?'

Boris's sallow features looked up at Harland. 'Two men from UN. I show them apartment.'

'What! Which men from the UN?'

'They have ID and documentations. They take nothing. I check.'

'You mean you let some strangers into my apartment.'

'They have documentations; they have ID.' Boris stood up and thrust his hands out with the exaggerated innocence of a footballer caught fouling. 'Like the woman she come yesterday.'

'Which woman?'

'The woman who take clothes to hospital.'

'Yes, that was my secretary who you gave a spare set of keys to. But who were these men? What did they look like?'

'One tall with grey hair, like Bill Clinton. Other man, younger. They stay in five minutes. I wait outside door. Then they go.'

'This isn't bloody Russia, Boris. You don't have to do what everyone tells you just because they flash an identity card at you. Why didn't you say something when I came in just now?'

'You deen aks me.'

Harland briefly marvelled at Boris's mastery of street idiom.

'How on earth was I supposed to know that you had let a couple of complete strangers into my apartment? I think we're going to have to talk to the building manager about this, Boris.' He turned to the lift.

'You deen aks me about kid neither!'

'What kid, for heaven's sake?'

'A man like my age – maybe more young. He speak Russian and English like me. Smart kid. He say he come back later.'

'What did he look like?'

'Tall like you, Mr Harland. He wears big jacket and hat – like this.' Boris clamped his hands over his head.

'A woollen hat?'

'Yes, a wooden hat,' said Boris triumphantly.

'Did he say what he wanted?'

'He say he see you when you come back.'

'Fine, call me if he appears. But don't let him come up to the apartment. Have you got that?'

The moment Harland closed the apartment door behind him, the buzzer went. Boris was on the other end, now evidently anxious to help.

'Kid with wooden hat is in street. I see him now. He come in building . . . No . . . He stand outside door. Now go away.' The commentary trailed off.

'I'll come down.'

He got downstairs to find Boris lurking at the side of the front door. Without bothering to hide himself, Harland peered through the glass and saw the figure across the street.

'Are you sure it's the same man?'

'Yes,' said Boris definitely. 'I tell him fucking get lost?'

'No, let's see what he wants.' Harland opened the door and saw the man more clearly. He had moved into the light of the street lamp and was looking in his direction, stamping his feet in the cold. Harland moved out into the wind and called out.

'What do you want?'

The figure made a hopeless gesture with his hands and seemed to smile, although it was difficult to tell in the dark. Then he started across the empty street.

'Do you need something?' Harland shouted again.

'Is that Mr Harland?' called the man. 'Yes, I would like to talk to you for a few moments.'

Boris had moved to stand behind him, apparently expecting trouble.

'He looks okay,' said Harland. 'Why don't you go back inside, Boris? You can call the police if there's a problem.' But Boris wasn't in any hurry to leave.

The man came up to them wearing a rather odd, eager

61

smile. Harland gauged he was in his mid to late twenties. He had a thin, fairly handsome face and a sparse growth of stubble on his chin. He wore a padded ski jacket, black denims and tan-coloured boots. A dark blue woollen hat was shoved tight over his head and around his neck was wrapped a bulky olive green and black scarf.

'Mr Harland?' he said, still smiling.

'Yes. What do you want?'

'To talk to you. I have some things to say – important things.'

Harland registered an educated foreign accent and a pair of light brown eyes, which were perhaps a little troubled – or at least hesitant.

'What things?'

'It's quite difficult to explain.' He was now standing about three feet from Harland. The wind whipped the steam of his breath from his lips.

'What's this about?' said Harland impatiently. 'I'm not standing out here all bloody night.'

The man opened his jacket and rather deliberately slid his hand inside, which caused Boris to shift his position at the door. The young man held up his other hand and said to him in fluent Russian, 'There's nothing to be worried about. I am a friend.' Harland noted that the accent was again faultless.

He pulled out a wallet and withdrew a card which he shielded from the few flakes of sleet that were being borne down the street by the wind. 'I wanted to show you this.'

Harland took it and held it up to the light. It was an Italian identity card, frayed at the edges and discoloured. A picture of a young woman was rippled with the impression of an official stamp. He looked closely. There was no mistaking her. The name on the card confirmed his fears. EVA HOURESH was printed in capital letters and below the photo and in a different type face were the words 'Design Student'. The card was dated 1975.

Harland felt his stomach churn. But he did not react – he could not react, because he was certain that Vigo must have put the boy up to it. He wondered wildly whether the encounter was being observed. Was he being filmed? He glanced to the darkened windows of the apartment opposite and then to a blue van which stood under the line of gingko trees on the other side of the street.

'You don't recognise her?' said the young man, who had removed his hat and now stood looking rather crestfallen. His eyes were watering and his face was pinched with cold. 'Then I will show you these.' He took out two further cards and presented one to Harland. 'They have different names. I will tell you why in a moment.'

Harland examined the first one, a membership card for the Communist Party of Czechoslovakia, dated 1980. Eva Houresh appeared as Irina Rath. No occupation was given. Her hair was shorter and her face was a little older. If anything, she looked more attractive. The photographer had caught the expression of mockery that he remembered so well. Her eyes looked boldly at the lens and her lips seemed about to part in a smile.

The last card was party membership for 1988 and had belonged to Irina Kochalyin. The photograph was almost identical to the one taken eight years before. The card was in better condition and everything seemed in good order – the stamp, the serial number and regulations appeared authentic. Harland concluded that the outfit in SIS that had undoubtedly produced the cards had done a pretty good job. But how had they obtained the pictures of Eva? That worried him a lot.

He handed the cards back. 'I don't know why you think I should be interested in these.'

The boy looked confused. 'I thought you would recognise this woman.'

'I am sorry. I haven't the first idea who she is.'

63

'You must do! You must remember her! This is the woman that you knew as Eva Houresh! Her real name is Irina Rath and her married name was Kochalyin.'

Harland shook his head. 'I'm sorry, I think you must have got the wrong man.'

'But you are Robert Harland, are you not? I saw a photograph of you in the newspapers after the accident and I knew it was you. I knew you were the Robert Harland I wanted to find.'

Harland was watching him closely. He was obviously bright and he spoke excellent English, but he was no professional. There was too much raw emotion playing in his face. No one but a very talented actor could fake the oscillation of hope and embarrassment in his eyes. Still, Harland wasn't willing to take him on faith yet – not by any means.

'Look, I'm sorry,' he said, 'but I'm afraid you're very much mistaken if you think I know this woman. I wish I could be of some help to you. But there it is, I can't.'

He nodded to Boris who opened the door and went in. Then he turned towards the door himself.

'I don't need help,' said the boy indignantly. 'I came because I believe you are the man that this woman loved.'

'Well, I'm sorry,' Harland said with a finality that would deter most. 'You've got the wrong person.'

The boy continued, 'If you are that man, I need to tell you something very important.'

Harland kept walking because he knew he didn't want to hear any more. There were things in the boy's manner which had made him feel uneasy, and when a certain look had flared in his eyes, a very troubling doubt crept into his consciousness.

'Mr Harland, please,' he said more urgently. He came forward a few steps and caught him at the door. 'I think you are lying when you say that you didn't recognise her. I tell you this – she is my mother. If you are the person that loved her when she was a young woman . . .' He looked down and then up into Harland's face with urgency. 'If you are that person it is very possible that you are my father. In fact, I believe it is certain.'

Harland was speechless.

'I know where you met, you see. I know you went to a town called Orvieto in Italy and that you had to keep your affair secret because she was Czech and you were working for British Intelligence. I know about Cleopatra's Needle.' He suddenly seemed to lose momentum and stammered, 'I – I did not want to tell you in this way.'

Only Eva knew about Cleopatra's Needle – the place where they had arranged to meet in London but hadn't, for what reason Harland never knew because that was the last he had heard of Eva Kouresh. Still, the point remained that nobody else could know about it. It was conceivable that Eva had been traced by Vigo and had told him how she had failed to turn up – and about everything else, no doubt. But why would Vigo bother with this nearly thirty years later? What would be the point? He struggled to fit it into the conversation he had had with Vigo and tried to work out his motives. Nothing came to him.

'What do you mean by coming here with this tale?' he demanded. 'Maybe you should seek some kind of medical help because I can tell you that this idea you have is a dangerous fantasy.' He stopped. 'Is there something else you want. You want money?'

The young man shrugged and looked down at his feet again. 'I want nothing from you. Nothing at all.' He emitted a short ironic laugh. 'That's the odd thing. Now that I have told you, I don't want anything from you.' He paused as if remembering something then put his hand out with a disarming smile. 'I'm sorry I haven't introduced myself. My name is Rath – I am Tomas Rath.'

'You may find this amusing. I don't. Now, please would you leave.'

Harland knew he was playing for time. There was no reason why Tomas couldn't be Eva Houresh's son, that much he was prepared to concede. In fact, it had occurred to him the moment he saw the first identity card which showed Eva exactly as she was when he met her in Rome. The boy looked like her. His colouring was right, particularly the lightness of his eyes and the fine dark hair. And though he hated to admit it, he had much of Eva's manner. The photographs had stirred his memory and moments that he had not recalled for decades were flashing into his mind. He saw Eva, turning from some frescos in Orvieto to argue about their meaning. He could be Eva's child, certainly, but it didn't follow that he was his son. There was nothing of himself in the boy. Nothing whatsoever: not a cell, not a look, not a hair, not a gesture. This was not his son.

6

THE BOY'S STORY

'Who put you up to this?' Harland asked. 'Is this some kind of stunt? Is Walter Vigo responsible for you coming here?'

Tomas shook his head, confusion clouding his face. 'I have never heard of this Vigo. No one knows I'm here. I came from London when I saw your picture. I didn't tell anybody that I was planning to do this. It was an impulse when I saw your photograph.'

'How did you know where to find me? I'm not listed in the telephone book.'

The boy told him how he had got the address from the UN. When Harland questioned him closely about whom he had spoken to, he produced the name of the Assistant Secretary-General. It sounded unlikely that he'd be able to bluff the address out of them. On the other hand, it was perfectly possible that one of the people on his floor had taken the caller on trust.

He opened the door and gestured Tomas inside.

'You wait here,' he said. 'I'm going to get a coat. Then we're going somewhere to talk and you will tell me what the hell is behind all this.'

It would have been much easier to take Tomas up to his apartment but Harland wanted to have the conversation in a public place. There was something about him that was desperate and uneasy. Besides, there seemed every possibility that his apartment had been fitted with eavesdropping devices by the people who had broken in. As he collected his coat he made a mental note to search the place later on.

When he returned Tomas had put his hat on and was sitting quietly on the polished bench near the door under Boris's suspicious gaze. Harland thought he looked like any of the thousands of young men on New York's streets.

They walked a few blocks to a restaurant where there was a bar at the front. It was late on a cold Saturday night and the place was pretty full, but they found a good table by the window at the rear of the bar area. Harland ordered a couple of beers from the waiter and told Tomas to sit down.

'Right,' he said abruptly, 'tell me your date of birth.'

Tomas was not going to be hurried. He unwound his scarf then took his jacket off to reveal a charcoal grey and navy plaid shirt. He folded the scarf deliberately and put it on the chair next to Harland, together with his gloves and hat. He looked around, wiped the condensation from the window with a serviette and peered into the street.

'Are you quite ready?' Harland said.

'I was born on the fifteenth of November 1975,' said Tomas evenly. The colour was returning to his cheeks.

'Where?'

'In Prague.'

'What age was your mother when you were born?'

'She was was twenty-two on the twelfth of October that year.'

The dates were just about right, thought Harland.

'And where does your mother live now?'

'Outside Prague, but we moved around a lot when I was kid.'

'Your mother is married?'

'She married a Russian citizen, but they are divorced now.'

'And she lives in the Czech Republic?'

'Yes.'

'And you? Where do you live?'

'I was living in Stockholm where I worked. Now I live in London for a while. Maybe I will move soon.'

There was a good deal that was unconvincing about the boy: while he had become more confident in his attitude to Harland, there was also an edginess in his manner. His eyes kept darting to a mirror behind Harland.

'I can tell you about my mother if you want,' he said. 'Ask me some questions.'

Harland thought for something else to ask him. 'Does she have any distinguishing marks?'

'Yes, on the nape of her neck, below the hairline – a patch of dark brown skin.'

He remembered the moment when he'd made the discovery of her oval-shaped birthmark in bed. They had fled, for that was what it seemed to both of them, to Orvieto in the dead of winter. It was early in 1975, when they had known each other just five months. They needed time together, both being too young for the pressure of their professions. They had stayed there for four nights in an ancient hotel's best suite. The town was empty, standing still and cold about them as though it had been struck by the plague, without a soul, it seemed, to hear the ceaseless tolling of the bell towers. It was quite simple: for those four days they had merged into each other. He was closer to her than he had ever been to another human being in his life. But it was just a few weeks before he had had to return to London to complete his training. By then there were no secrets between them. He knew what she really was – an agent working for the StB, the Czech Security Service. Her language skills and considerable beauty had been deployed in Rome, initially against the Czech dissidents who were running a propaganda operation there, and then with a view to compromising diplomats at the American and British embassies. She told Harland that he had been singled out as an inexperienced SIS officer who would be susceptible to her charms. She told him everything, but she never gave him her real name because she was too frightened. They had got something on her. He never knew what it was. Then they had parted on Rome station one morning. Harland thought back to the scene. At the time it had felt like an amputation.

'So how did your mother meet the man that you think is me?'

'It was in a bar. You were introduced by an American diplomat my mother knew. You were his regular tennis partner, she said. You went out with a big crowd of people that same evening. You talked about the books you had been reading. It was a great evening for her – very exciting, being in Rome with Westerners and drinking and laughing. A big change from the life she had known in Czechoslovakia. Even though she was working for the State Security Service, she said it was one of the most carefree evenings of her life. She said that afterwards you strolled through the city for most of the night. It was late summer – the month of August or September – and you walked until you found a café at dawn in a market near the French embassy. You had to catch a taxi and go straight to work. See, Mr Harland, I do know about it.'

Harland ordered another beer for himself, the boy not yet having touched his, and asked the waitress if she could find him a cigarette. She delved under her apron and shook a Marlboro from a crush pack. Tomas lit it from a matchbook on the table and sat back with a smile.

'I did not imagine you as smoker,' he said.

Harland ignored the remark. 'Who gave you the idea of approaching me?'

'Nobody,' said Tomas earnestly. He leaned forward to place his elbows on the table. 'You think I make all this up. How can you believe that?'

'You tell me. I mean, you walk up to me in the street like some kind of professional stalker, announce that you are my

70

son and expect me to greet you with open arms. So what am I supposed to do now? Change my will? Put the family silver in your name – eh? You can't seriously expect me to believe all this?'

'I know about Cleopatra's Needle,' he said. 'That will prove I'm speaking the truth. No one but you and my mother knew about that.'

'You mentioned it before,' said Harland indifferently. 'So why don't you tell me about it?'

'My mother said you had a joke that she was Cleopatra because you believed that your love for her would destroy you. There was some dark humour there, she said. A few weeks after you left Rome she rang you and said that she was in London. You arranged to meet that evening at Cleopatra's Needle by the River Thames because you did not want to risk being seen with her. She understood this. It was very difficult for you – she knew that. She said she remembered it very well. It was a beautiful day in spring. She found the rendezvous place and then she walked by the river and did some thinking. She had a big problem which she was planning to tell you about but then she decided that she could not tell you. That is right, isn't it? She did not come and you never saw her again. You never learned why she had come to London.'

He waited but Harland didn't say anything.

'So here my story becomes less romantic, although you are not to blame because she believes that you really did love her. When she talked to you on the phone she did not explain that she was going to have an abortion? No, of course not. She would not do that.'

The word dropped to the pit of Harland's stomach.

'As you will appreciate,' continued Tomas, 'that kind of thing was then an impossibility in Rome. She made some excuse to leave Rome because she was desperate to tell you her news. I think some part of her believed that you could

71

make everything right. Yet she knew that she was caught in a trap. She had two choices – get rid of the child or have the child back home in Czechoslovakia. If she did the first she might be able to see you a few more times, but you were in London and she was in Rome and it wasn't easy. Some time during that day in London she made the decision to have the child and that was why she did not come to you. She could not bear to tell you that her decision meant she had to go back to Prague and that would mean she would never see you again. The choice she made is why I am here. I am that child, Mr Harland, and, incredible though it may seem to you, I am your son.' He picked up his beer and drained it in one, evidently relieved at having unburdened himself.

Even if he had wanted to, Harland could not react. He had no idea what he should feel or how he should deal with this boy. The only emotion he was aware of was annoyance. These were his secrets, his history that this boy was spilling out, telling him more than he had ever known about his own life. He was angry and appalled. The fact was that it had never occurred to him that Eva might have been pregnant. He'd thought of everything else, but not that. When she didn't appear he had been in despair, and so caught up in his own sense of loss that he didn't think it through at all. For weeks afterwards he called her number in Rome. He phoned people who might know where she had gone, but no one had any idea. Then he flew to Rome one weekend and searched for her in their old haunts. Eva Houresh had simply vanished and left Harland feeling jilted and exposed.

He was so distraught when he returned to London that he took a friend into his confidence, a good sort named Jimmy Kinloch who was in his SIS intake. Jimmy told him that he was well out of it – a relationship like that could ruin a man's career and get him into a lot more trouble besides. And so Harland had forgotten Eva, at least he had stopped torment-ing himself by thinking of her, which was an altogether different thing from forgetting her. What he did was to relinquish her, although some part of her was still in him.

'Tell me why your mother had to return to Czechoslovakia. Why couldn't she defect? If, as you say, she was pregnant, she could have defected and had the baby in the West. She would have been looked after.'

'It is obvious. If you'd listened to her, you would have known that she could not leave because of her mother – Hanna. Hanna was why she went back. She is still alive today. Do you know her story?'

Harland dimly recalled that Eva's mother had been in a concentration camp. He nodded to the boy to tell the story.

'In 1945 my grandmother, Hanna Rath, was found in Terezin. The place is called Theresienstadt in German. The Nazis made it the holding camp for the Jews of Bohemia and Moravia. She was nine years old and the last member of her family alive. All of them had been sent to Auschwitz on the transports but she managed to survive. Terezin was full of Jews helping each other. But without protection of any kind – no family, no friends – it was very hard for her. Somehow she escaped the transports. She has told me that she memorised the names of other children in the latest groups to arrive at Terezin and learned where they came from. That way she could pretend to be part of the new shipment. She also had a hiding place which she went to when the transports were being assembled for the death camps. Sometimes she stayed there for a day at a time, with just a little water. She told me that she imagined herself to be invisible and even today she says she has the power not to be noticed. She can walk down a street and not be seen. Can you believe that, Mr Harland?'

Harland nodded. He had met such people in his old trade. They were called ghosts.

'When Terezin was liberated by the Russians in May '45, she was found at the gates of the castle. She was the first to

73

receive treatment from the Soviet army doctors. Later in the summer of 1945 she was taken to an orphanage near Prague. She was one of just three thousand survivors of Terezin. Ninety thousand had disappeared into the camps, but this little girl had survived. She was alive yet she was never able to reclaim her family's property. The home and the business were gone. She could not say what her family owned and anyway she did not know where the proof of that ownership lay. She couldn't even prove who she was because there was no one left from her town who could identify her. No one – not a teacher, a doctor, a friend or one single member of her family – was alive to say who she was. They were all gone. She was left with a name – Hanna Rath – and that was all.

'And so she stayed in the orphanage. Then at sixteen she became pregnant – that was with my mother. There was some kind of scandal. She would not say who the father was. She had to leave. But Hanna was very smart. She got work and she raised my mother in a room in Prague with almost nothing – just the two of them together. That is the story of the woman you fell in love with in Rome. Maybe you did not know it all?'

'You didn't explain why your mother had to return to Prague,' observed Harland, apparently unimpressed. Inwardly his heart churned at the thought of Eva.

'That is simple. She could not leave my mother there. Remember what it was like at that time – the "Normalisation" after the Prague Spring. It would have been unthinkable for my mother to defect to the West and leave Hanna to face the authorities. Everything in her life depended on her keeping in favour with the authorities – her job, her home. As it was, she had very little. My mother could not do that to the woman who had made so many sacrifices for her.' He stopped and looked at Harland intently for a moment, then turned to signal to the waitress for another beer. 'I have told you my story. What more can I do to persuade you? I guess there is a DNA test which would prove it to you. But that would be humiliating and there is no point because – you must understand this, Mr Harland – I do not claim anything from you. I do not want anything from you.'

'So let me ask you again, Tomas, why have you come? You could probably have traced me before now.'

'I have known this story for only a little time. Before, I thought someone else was my father – the man she married. And I didn't know where you lived. There are many Harlands in the London telephone directory. Besides, I have had my own concerns.'

'What do you mean by that?'

'I don't want to talk about them now,' he replied, with an oddly grave expression. He looked away. 'Maybe I'll tell you some day, Mr Harland.'

'Look, forget the Mr Harland, will you? Use my first name if you must call me anything.'

'I think I prefer Mr Harland until things change between us.'

'As you wish.' Harland put down his glass. He acknowledged to himself that he was affected by the directness of Tomas's manner.

'Do you go to London?' asked Tomas, apparently composing himself.

'Yes, sometimes. I have a sister who lives in London, but I haven't spent much time there over the last ten years.'

'Will you be visiting your sister for Christmas?'

'Probably. I haven't decided yet.'

'If you go, we could see each other. My girlfriend is in London and I will leave her number with you, together with my own number. If you feel you want to see me again, you may call me.' He paused. 'I know you don't believe my story now. But maybe you could after a time.'

'Maybe, but I would like to speak to your mother.'

Tomas shook his head.

'You do see your mother?'

He shook his head again. 'No. I have not seen her for some time. Look, it's difficult to explain, Mr Harland. There are many things you don't know. And it is perhaps better that I do not tell you everything at once.'

'What do you mean?'

'I cannot say.'

'But you won't mind if I take her number?'

'No, but she will be angry that I've told you. She doesn't know I have come here.'

'Well, I'd like to speak to her about this. You can understand that.'

Tomas shrugged and for the next few minutes there was a silence between them. Harland studied him as he shifted his chair to make room for a couple of young women who had planted themselves with a great fuss at the next table and were unbundling in the warmth. There were a few sideways looks and some giggling, which Tomas returned with an offer of help to one of the girls who was coquettishly struggling to remove her jacket. He had something and it was working on these two girls, thought Harland.

Suddenly he felt incredibly tired. When he closed his eyes the golden light which he had noticed after the crash was flaring in front of him. He got up and indicated that he was going to the lavatory at the back of the restaurant.

Facing the urinal, he put his hand to the wall to steady himself, and thought about the young Eva. He tried to imagine how she would look now – dumpy and probably gone to seed, he thought. Still, he would have to call her as soon as possible because it was now imperative that he establish whether the boy was telling the truth. If this turned out to be an elaborate hoax inspired by Vigo, he would have to prepare his defence and work out what was behind it all. But it seemed unlikely because preparing Tomas's story and the fake identity cards, complete with the actual pictures of

Eva, would have taken longer than the few days since the crash.

Harland's thoughts were disturbed by a man coming in and entering one of the cubicles behind him. He zipped himself up and turned to rinse his face in the basin. He needed to pull himself together and concentrate because there was a lot more he wanted to ask this Tomas character – a lot more.

When he returned to the bar he instantly noticed that Tomas's chair was empty and the pile of cold-weather kit had gone. He glanced at the door and caught sight of him at the tail of a group of six or seven people who were leaving. Tomas gesticulated in a diving motion with both hands towards the two girls. Then he put his right hand to his forehead in a salute which flipped up into a wave. Harland went to the table. One of the girls looked up.

'Hey, your son had to go. He left this for you.'

'What do you mean, my son?' he said, seizing the scrap of paper she held out.

'Oh, I'm sorry,' said the woman. 'We just kind of assumed you were related.' Her companion worked the gum in her mouth and nodded.

There were two numbers on the paper. One was for a cellphone; the other had a central London prefix. 'Ask for Lars Edberg', said the note.

Lars Edberg, thought Harland. Why was Tomas using an alias? There was no number for Eva.

'Did he say why he had to go?' Harland said, looking down at the two puzzled faces.

'No,' said the gum-chewer. 'He was looking out onto the street and then he turned back and just kind of got up and left. He gave us the note and said you'd understand.'

Harland tossed down a twenty and worked his way through the tables towards the door. Out on the street there was no sign of Tomas. He hurried back to the intersection at the top of the hill and caught sight of a figure running down Clinton Street. Whoever it was, he was moving very fast, then he dodged to the right and disappeared from sight behind a truck. Tomas Rath had vanished.

7

THE PULSE

Next day, as Harland moved from a rotten night's sleep to a blank New York Sunday, he recognised that part of him wanted to accept the boy's story. But he consciously decided to suspend judgement and concentrate on the immediate mystery of what Griswald had been carrying with him.

Three hours later he stepped down from a train bound for Canada on to the platform of a small station some fifty miles north of New York. He waited there, looking across the sweep of the Hudson River towards the Catskills, and thought about Griswald. This part of the Hudson valley, Griswald once told him, had been settled by Germans, some of them Griswald's ancestors. It reminded them of the Rhine and their homeland which accounted for the names of the local towns – Rhinebeck, Rhinecliff, Staatsburg.

Sally Griswald's old station-wagon swept into the car park. She got out, looking much as he remembered her a dozen years before, and gave him a bereft, wordless hug. Then, taking his hands, she drew back and looked at him with a staunch smile. At length she said, 'If there was one man that Al would have wanted to survive while he was taken, it would have been you, Bob. Believe me, it is a consolation at this time to know that. There were very few people that Al admired and liked as much as you.'

Harland felt her loss with a sudden, useless clarity.

They drove to a large white clapboard house, set behind

some conifers in two or three acres of frost-scorched lawn. Griswald's boys, Eric and Sam, were waiting to greet them. They stood in the hallway, pretending to remember Harland from the past, sheepishly concealing their grief. They were unmistakably Griswald's progeny – big and friendly with Al's shrewdness lurking in their expressions.

She led him through to the kitchen where a pot of coffee was already laid out with some cups, and food was in the oven. They all sat down. The boys looked at him expectantly as if he was about to produce some news or insight.

'So it was you who answered the phone out there,' said Sally, shaking her head. 'How terrible for you to deal with that. I want you to know I totally understand why – you know – why you hung up. I'm glad you did . . . in a way. It gave me quite a chill to learn that you were out there with Al and that I was speaking to you at that awful moment.'

'Your call saved my life, Sally,' said Harland. 'They didn't know we were out there. I'm sure I wouldn't have lived if you hadn't rung at that moment.'

'It was lucky Dad kept the phone on,' said Eric, the elder boy. 'He should have had it switched off.'

'True,' said Harland.

'But if you hadn't been going to help him, you'd never have heard it,' chimed in Sam.

Over lunch they talked of old times in Europe, stories which fleetingly brought Alan Griswald to life in the minds around the table. Sally had to explain the circumstances of each of the stories to the boys – who the characters were and the politics of the embassy at the time. Harland filled in a few details, which briefly made her face light up. He let the conversation take its own course and only at the end of lunch did he begin to ask how Griswald had come to work at the War Crimes Tribunal.

She told him that he had left the CIA in 1994 and gone as an observer to the Balkans for the War Studies Forum in

Washington which put out reports on Western policy. He hadn't much liked the writing aspect of the job but he had become fascinated by the civil war in Bosnia and convinced that the West's policy hovered disastrously between inadequate help and criminal hindrance. They had been worried about money and she had found it a struggle for most of the nineties when Al had been travelling for the Forum. But she understood that he was obsessed with the failure of the West to capture the people responsible for the crimes that he knew about in Bosnia. For him there was a lot of unfinished business in the Balkans and she supported his determination to see some kind of justice done. Eventually he was suggested to the War Crimes Tribunal and created a job for himself, applying the skills he'd learned in the CIA to hunting war criminals – all the espionage stuff that she didn't have to explain to Harland.

In the early nineties she moved into the house that Griswald had been left, partly to save money, but more to give the boys a base in the States. Al continued to commute to Europe. He kept his work out of the home but sometimes she asked him things and he answered her straight. About a month before, on his last visit home, they had been out to dinner in Rhinebeck and he had talked about the cases he was working on. He had told her about five or six men who had been responsible for the massacres in Bosnia at the end of the war. She couldn't remember the details but he did say that there was another case which he had just begun which might prove to be very important. He hoped to be able to complete the investigation and then he would think about finding a job which would allow him to stay in the States.

'You don't know any more about this last case?' asked Harland.

'No, why do you ask?'

He would have to take this gently, he thought. Sally was as quick as her husband and he didn't want to alarm her.

'Well, there is an awful lot of interest in what Al may or may not have been carrying with him to New York.'

'From whom?'

'From the FBI, which is investigating the crash as a matter of routine, and, rather curiously, from my old lot.'

'British Intelligence? Why would they be interested?' Her eyes narrowed. 'Are you saying something else, Bob? Are you saying there was something sinister about the crash? I know the media was speculating, but that was just loose talk – wasn't it?'

'As far as I know, the crash was an accident. The Safety Board are going to announce their findings, and they apparently believe it was an accident.'

'Right, so what is it you're saying?'

Harland hesitated and looked at Eric and Sam, and the image of Tomas Rath flashed into his mind. He remembered Griswald's pride in his boys and he fleetingly wondered what it was like to have a son. Then he pulled from his pocket the wallet that he had kept with him since leaving hospital.

'I know this may seem odd, but I took this from Al's body when I answered the phone. I can't absolutely recall what was in my mind, but I suppose I wanted to make sure there was some identification. Yesterday, I remembered he said he was carrying some crucial evidence.' He placed the wallet on the other side of the table.

Confronted with something so close to her husband's extinction, Sally Griswald had put her hands up to her face and was looking at the wallet with horrified fascination. She picked it up and felt the hard, desiccated surface of the leather with her fingertips.

She said nothing as she went through the contents. Eventually he took the mini-disc out and handed it to Eric who shook his head.

'This isn't Dad's music,' he said. 'There are four hundred

82

records in the den and not one piece of music was composed before 1920. You know he was a jazz fanatic?'

Harland nodded. 'Famously so.'

'Have you played it?' asked Sam.

'No, I only remembered that I had the wallet yesterday. Anyway, I don't have a player for these things. Do you?'

Sam said he had one, picked up the disc and got up to fetch it. Eric went to join him, and Sally and Harland were left looking at each other.

Harland broke the silence. 'Is there someone at The Hague I can talk to discreetly about the investigations that Al was working on – a secretary, an assistant?'

'Yes, her name is Sara Hezemanns. She was Al's secretary but I'm not sure how much she will be able to tell you. You know how cagey Al was.' She wrote the name and Griswald's old office number on the kitchen pad.

'And what about this person he was travelling with?'

'On the plane? I don't believe he was with anyone, apart from you.'

Harland didn't press the point. 'And in Washington was there a hotel he stayed at regularly?'

'Yes, he went to the Fillmore Hotel on Tenth Street – he knows the manager there. He had some kind of deal.'

'He knew the manager?'

'Yes, but I forget his name.'

'Do you have any idea what he was doing in Washington?'

'Well, I guess he went to Langley. I know the Agency helped him with stuff like aerial pictures and radio intercepts. He visited there often because he was anxious to get these guys in Yugoslavia prosecuted.' She paused and glanced away, focusing on a pot of parsley on the window. 'We haven't got Al back yet. His body, I mean. That really hurts. It's ironic because Al said one of the things that obsessed those people in Bosnia was that they never found the bodies of their loved ones. They couldn't bear for them to be not buried properly. Did you know that?'

Harland shook his head.

'He told me it was a big thing for them,' she said, 'and I really begin to understand that now. It matters.'

The boys came back with the disc player and a portable speaker. 'I listened to some of this upstairs,' he said. 'Nothing strange about it, except Beethoven and Chopin was definitely not Dad's taste.'

They listened to the disc. Then Harland realised that the music playing was different to what was described on the disc cover, which listed highlights of orchestral works by Brahms, Chopin and Mendelssohn. What was playing now was the second movement of the Archduke trio by Beethoven. He picked up the cover and examined it.

'I noticed that too,' said Eric. 'This is the wrong cover for the disc.'

Before the next piece there was a sustained tapping – something between a Geiger counter and a door creaking open. The noise lasted five minutes more and was followed by the first bars of a Chopin nocturne. They listened to see if the noise returned, but heard nothing. Then Eric suggested that he could make a tape of the noise and slow it down. Both of them went off together, relieved to have something to do.

They returned ten minutes later, bearing Eric's recording equipment and arguing like young teenagers.

'It's code,' said Eric definitely.

'How would *you* know?'

'I just do. Listen.'

Eric played the tape he'd made, slowing it as much as he could on his equipment. There did seem to be a definite structure to the sound, almost like a pulse. As they listened, they realised that the individual taps consisted of many

84

different elements. 'If we could bring this down real slow, I think we'd find something there.'

'Maybe I could find someone to do that,' said Harland. 'Would you like me to?' Sally nodded. 'I'll take the original disc, then, and the slowed recording if that's okay.'

'I've got a copy,' said Eric, 'so if you lose it you'll know where to come.'

'Good. Look, I'm not going to mention this to anyone. Let's keep it between ourselves. If there is something here, I certainly don't want anyone thinking that you've got it.'

Soon afterwards, Sally drove him to the station. They waited in the car park until the train was about to arrive. 'Bob,' she said, staring ahead of her, 'find out if something's been going on – you know what I mean. Find out for my sake and Al's – he would want that.'

Harland promised he'd do everything he could.

He got to the UN late in the afternoon as the setting sun washed a pink light over the west side of the great monolith. There were still a few tourists about but the restricted areas were deserted. He was glad. He wanted to work in quiet and avoid the fuss which would certainly accompany his return to work on Monday.

He unlocked his office, noted the two-weeks' worth of mail and sat down at his desk to think. He got the number of the Fillmore Hotel in Washington, dialled and asked to speak to the manager, saying that he was a friend and colleague of Alan Griswald's. At length a wary English voice came on the line. Harland explained that he was making some inquiries for the UN about Griswald's expenditure prior to his death. Just tying up some loose ends, was the way he put it. If this worried the manager, he was welcome to call him back on the main UN switchboard. Harland heard the voice relax.

'You can never be too careful,' said the manager.

Harland smiled at the motto of British caution and

continued in a flat bureaucratic voice. 'We're dealing with the expenses incurred on his last trip. In the circumstances, we are concerned that they are fully reimbursed. I believe Mr Griswald was travelling with another gentleman who was also on United Nations business.'

'And you're doing this on a Sunday?' said the man.

'It's the Christmas rush. We need to make sure that his family is reimbursed before the holidays.' He grimaced at the lameness of his explanation and continued. 'The trouble is that we cannot immediately lay our hands on the name of the second party. Would that be something you have in your records?'

He heard the manager ask reception to look up the previous week's bookings. While he waited, the manager told him how he had met Alan Griswald some fifteen years before when he was deputy manager at the Jefferson Hotel. The death was indeed a tragedy, he said. Harland detected just the slightest strain of campness in his manner.

A voice sounded on the distant intercom. Two rooms were booked for two nights and paid for by Mr Griswald. Harland jerked his fist in front of him.

'The name of the other gentleman does not appear on the account,' said the manager, repeating what he had heard, 'but it does on the registration card. It is Luc Bézier, a French citizen apparently. No home address is given.'

'Anything else?'

'No. No passport number, no vehicle registration or contact number. Just the name Bézier.'

'Were there any additional charges to the bill – telephone calls? Meals?'

The manager replied that there were some other items. In a very short while Harland had persuaded him to fax copies of the bill and the registration cards. Five minutes later they slipped noiselessly from the machine by Marika's desk. He found what he was looking for halfway down on the second sheet of the bill – a telephone number recorded by the hotel's switchboard which began with the country code for France. There were two calls to the same number on successive afternoons, lasting seven and fourteen minutes respectively. Harland bet himself a cigarette that Luc Bézier was calling his wife or girlfriend.

He checked the number with International Information and found that it came from the Carcassonne area. It was nearing five – too late to ring. Besides, he wanted to know if the person who would answer the phone in France had been informed of Bézier's death. It seemed quite possible that they did not know, although they surely must have begun to suspect that something was amiss when the regular calls abruptly stopped after Monday. They would have started making inquiries, perhaps contacting Griswald's office in The Hague or the French embassy in Washington, and sooner or later someone would have suggested that Luc Bézier had been on the flight with Griswald.

Harland now felt sure that the FBI must have gone back over Griswald's journey and stumbled on Bézier's name. Ollins had been so interested in the fact that he had seen the compact-looking foreigner with Griswald at the airport that he must have traced the hotel booking and then, in all probability, located his name on a passenger list from France over the previous weekend. It would have taken one further call to acquire Bézier's passport details from the US Immigration Service. And that meant Ollins knew as much as he needed about Luc Bézier. So why hadn't he included Bézier in the final toll? Was that the reason for his shiftiness out at the airport? Had he been prevailed upon to keep Bézier's name secret, or was he doing it for reasons of his own?

Harland rang Sally Griswald and asked if she had heard of Bézier. The name meant nothing to her. Al had not mentioned that he was dealing with anyone from France.

Harland was about to ring off when she told him that she had been going through Griswald's recent mail and had found a sheaf of interview transcripts that had been expressed from his office in The Hague after he left. She had only skimmed them but thought they might be interesting. She would send the pages to his fax.

He made two further calls, the first to his sister, Harriet, to say that he would be in London for Christmas. Then he dialled the mobile number which Tomas Rath had left him. He assumed the phone was on a European service and so didn't expect an answer, nor was there one. He composed himself for the message service. 'This is Robert Harland,' he said evenly. 'I will be in London next week, so we can continue our conversation of last night. I hope that nothing is wrong. You departed in quite a hurry.' He finished by leaving his new mobile number and Harriet's home number and told him not to call before Tuesday.

He kicked his legs off the desk and went over to the fax to see if the documents had come. The engaged light was on. He waited while the cover sheet and the first of thirty-two numbered pages dropped into the tray. He read part of an interview with a Bosnian Muslim named Selma Simic. It didn't seem particularly important so he went off to the kitchen area to make himself some tea.

The floor was silent, except for the gentle background hum of the empty building. Most of the offices around him were dark. He made his tea, thinking about the order of phone calls he would place to Europe in the early hours of the morning, then returned towards his office.

As he stepped through the partition by Marika's desk he was aware of a rush of air to his left. He saw nothing, but felt a powerful blow to the ribs on his left side which hit the disc and glanced upwards to his Adam's apple. At the same time another force assailed him from behind. Two blows to the back of the neck, a jab to the kidneys, followed by a kick to the small of the back. Harland doubled up and threw himself backwards with all his might, flinging the tea, which astonishingly he still held, towards his left. A man cried out and lunged at him, but missed. Harland encountered the bulk of a second man whom he managed to propel with a crash into the partition on the other side of the corridor. He heard a gasp behind him but the fellow was strong and was soon up on his feet. Harland whistled round, aimed two punches to the stomach and brought his knee up to the man's chin. He fell. Then he felt a stunning blow to his head and knew nothing more.

8

WAKE-VORTEX

He came round with a flashlight in his eyes. Two men were standing over him. His office was very cold and he could hear the wind tearing at some papers on the window-sill. He lifted his head from the floor. A voice told him to stay still. Everything was going to be okay; an ambulance was on its way. Harland took no notice. He raised his head again and pushed the light away.

There was a chemical taste on his tongue and at the back of his throat. He moved a little more. His head hurt and his ribs and back were throbbing with new bruises. He rolled on to his side and pushed himself up to face two UN security guards who were crouching in front of him. He looked round, vaguely wondering why the window was open, and realised that he was some distance from where he had fallen. He had been out in the corridor and now he was beside his desk and there was a hell of a mess and the window was open.

'How are you feeling?' asked one of the guards, trying to get a clear look at his eyes.

'I'm okay.' In fact, he felt nauseous and irritable. 'Look, will someone bloody well close that window?'

'We can't,' said the other guard. 'It's jammed open – it's broken.'

Harland sat for a few minutes, consciously trying to still

his stomach. Then he wiped his nose with the back of his hand, cleared his throat and looked up at the guards.

'What happened?'

'Jim found you five minutes ago,' said one. 'He reckons he must have disturbed them when he came out of the elevator.'

Harland now recognised the taste in his mouth as cocaine. It was making him a lot sharper than he might normally feel after being hit over the head. He turned to the window and focused on the vibrating slats of the Venetian blind. Now he understood why the window was open. They were going to tip him out of it and make it look as though he had been on a cocaine binge and jumped. His single thought about this astonishingly crude plan was that Walter Vigo had nothing to do with it. Whatever the deficiencies and moral laxity of his former colleagues at Vauxhall Cross, they rarely behaved like gangsters.

'Did they take anything?' asked the guard called Jim.

Harland got up shakily and held on to the desk. Then he felt for the tape and disc in his breast pocket. They'd gone. 'I had some loose cash,' he said. 'Several hundred dollars – it's been taken.'

'They took your wallet?'

'The cash was in my pocket. My wallet was in my coat over there on the back of the door. Can you check for me?'

While one of the guards went over to check the coat, Harland scanned his desk. The copy of the hotel bill was still there and a glance at the fax machine told him that Sally Griswald's documents had arrived undisturbed. So, whoever had jumped him was simply interested in the disc and the tape. He thought of the copy that Eric Griswald had kept for himself and wondered if the Griswalds were in any danger. However, he was sure that he had not been followed out to the Hudson valley that day because he had taken the usual dry-cleaning precautions before leaving Penn Station, which had included loudly asking for a ticket to Trenton, New

Jersey. Besides, he was absolutely certain no one else had got off the train at his stop. So for the moment he guessed Sally and her boys were okay.

'Sir, the wallet's here in your coat,' said the guard.

He picked up the hotel bill and went to collect Sally's fax, ignoring the entreaties of the guards. Once he had checked that all thirty-two pages were there, he sat down in Marika's chair and asked for a glass of water.

The hospital had tried to keep him overnight for observation, but Harland had been at his most hostile with the young doctor and had eventually just walked out and gone home. The next day he felt as well as could be expected with a bruise across the back of his head, which a paramedic had ventured was the colour and size of a small aubergine. He had no doubt that somebody had been about to kill him, and that frightened him a great deal. But in another way it intrigued him and put him on his mettle. Old juices were beginning to flow.

He left his apartment at eight, having packed for a week, and took a cab to the UN building. When he arrived, he found his office had been tidied up and the window fitted with new locks. Marika was there and gave him a gushing welcome which involved a long hug. Harland had never quite got used to the American embrace and didn't know when to let go. Eventually he was released from her ample chest and allowed to make his phone calls. She said nothing about the strip of plaster at the back of his head, possibly because she assumed it was a result of the crash.

The first call was to Sara Hezemanns, Griswald's assistant in The Hague, who immediately insisted that she check his credentials with Sally Griswald.

Five minutes later she called him back and listened while he explained that he was interested in Alan Griswald's last investigation.

'It was the one involving a French contact.'

'I'm sorry I cannot help you with this,' she said warily. 'It is all confidential.'

'But you know the identity of the Frenchman and you knew he was on the plane with Griswald?'

She said nothing.

'Am I right in thinking that his name is Luc Bézier?'

Still no answer.

'Do you know whether he had any family in France – someone I could phone and ask what this is about?'

'I know nothing about him. He came to Mr Griswald out of the blue. Just rang up and asked to meet him. I was the first person he talked to which is how I know his name. Mr Griswald said very little about it afterwards and that is all I can tell you.'

'Have you been asked not to talk about this?'

'Look, Mr Harland, you must understand that much of the work we do here is very secret. I am not allowed to talk about current investigations with outsiders.' She was speaking very quietly now. Harland guessed that someone had come into her office.

'I'm going to ask you some questions and you can answer with yes or no, okay?'

'Yes.'

'Did this case involve the killings in north-eastern Bosnia in 1995? Is that what he was investigating?'

'Yes ... and ... also no.'

'Have you tried to contact Monsieur Bézier's relatives in France?'

'No.'

'So you don't know whether they have been told?'

'No.'

'Has anyone from the War Crimes Tribunal discussed the death of Mr Griswald and Monsieur Bézier?'

'Yes.'

'Who, the Chief Prosecutor? The Chief Investigating Officers?'

'Yes ... yes.'

'Did they suspect the plane was sabotaged?'

'No, I don't think so.'

'I have some documents which were sent to Alan Griswald's home by your office last week. Sally Griswald let me have them. They appear to be interview transcripts from 1995 and 1996. Are they relevant to the last case that Alan Griswald was investigating?'

'Maybe.'

Harland remembered Griswald's painstaking approach to any problem, the marshalling of every possible scrap of intelligence.

'Was he going to read them in the hope of finding something which may have been overlooked in the past?'

'Yes,' she said. He could hear she was pleased that he had guessed right and he knew she really wanted to talk to him.

'Perhaps it would be better for me to read these documents thoroughly, then ring you later?'

'Yes, that's a good idea.'

'Some time in the evening your time, say eight o'clock today, or tomorrow?'

'Yes,' she said, and abruptly hung up.

Harland looked at the number Bézier had rung from Washington and weighed up whether to dial it now or wait until he had talked to Sara Hezemanns again. A little reluctantly, he decided that it was better not to blunder in.

His next concern was the disc. Clearly the theft was significant, but he didn't want to alarm Sally Griswald, so when he rang he simply told her that the disc and tape had been stolen overnight from his office. He omitted all mention of the attack. Even so, it worried her that Eric had made a copy and she said that she felt threatened by its presence in her home. Harland suggested that it would be possible for them to send the recording by attachment to his e-mail address, or to express it to Harriet's home. He gave her both addresses, after fending off several more inquiries about the theft. For the next hour or so he sat, closeted in his office, thinking and making little diagrams. They resembled electrical circuit boards, with each component related to the other. Where Harland was unsure, which was often, he put a dotted line to indicate the tentative or unproven nature of the connection. He spent a good deal of time standing at the window looking at the gradations of blue in the distance of Long Island. Every so often he would dart back to his desk to add a few more lines or another box to the diagram. None of what he produced was very satisfactory because there could be no single interpretation to such random events – yet – but he was coming to grips with the problem, and when Marika brought him some coffee he was at least clearer in his mind about the nature of his task.

She set the cup down and looked over his shoulder with unconcealed interest. Harland asked her to book him on to the six o'clock flight to London and chase up the expenses from a trip in early November. At this, Marika clapped her hand to her forehead and said that she had quite forgotten to tell him about the press conference on the crash that was due to start on the third floor. Maybe he would like to go? Yes, thought Harland, he wanted very much to hear what the Safety Board was going to say about the crash.

He loitered a little distance from the conference room, mingling with a large group that had just emerged from the Security Council, and waited for the press briefing to get under way. Then he realised that he didn't have to go in. Behind him was a monitor showing the proceedings. He could see Frank Ollins from the FBI and Murray Clark from the Safety Board on either side of Martin Dowl, one of the UN press officers.

Clark, looking rather larger than normal against the

background of UN blue, had just risen and was taking the reporters through the procedure that followed the retrieval of the two black boxes. He said that the preliminary findings of the Safety Board meant that sabotage had been ruled out.

'This was an accident,' he said. Then he looked up and repeated the word 'accident'.

He reached behind him for some display boards which he held away from his audience of journalists. 'We now know that the Canadian Government Falcon 900, on loan to the United Nations, was subjected to exceptional turbulence caused by the preceding USAir flight that landed at La Guardia eighty seconds prior to the crash. This disturbance is called wake-vortex and it is associated with large airplanes, particularly the Boeing 757 which has a wing-flap design that generates a powerful vortex of air. This can force a following airplane into an unrecoverable loss of control. In this accident the preceding airplane was a Boeing 767 which is capable of creating the same type of hazard, although there are fewer recorded incidents involving 767s.'

Clark spun one of the boards round his fingertips to show a diagram of two planes on the same flight path, three nautical miles apart. The camera zoomed in and Harland could see that behind each wing was drawn a spiral.

'These are the vortices,' said Clark, pointing with his knuckle. 'At their core the airspeed may be as much as ninety knots. They can linger for a minute and a half after the plane has passed. Eventually they dissipate or move away. Some descend to the ground before dissipation and bounce right back up into the path of a following aircraft. And that is one of the big problems with this invisible phenomenon. The velocity at the core of the vortices is so powerful that it can affect a big plane like a McDonnell Douglas 88 – which is about three times the weight of a Falcon.' He turned to his audience. 'For your information that comes in at around twenty-two thousand pounds.'

He let this sink in then set off again. 'There used to be five or six serious incidents a year due to this phenomenon. There are fewer today because the Federal Aviation Authority and the National Safety Transportation Board have stipulated minimum distances between landing aircraft. These recommendations and the latest data on vortex incidents are printed in the *Airman's Information Manual*, which is readily available to all pilots.'

He turned another board which showed how the vortex had hit the ground and then risen to a height of 120 feet, where it encountered the Falcon.

'It's hard to estimate the speed and lifespan of a vortex because it varies according to wind gradient and strength. However we believe that a bouncing vortex intersected with the path of the Falcon at the threshold of the runway. The pilot experienced an uncommanded ninety-degree roll and pitch. He had no time to regain control and the aircraft continued in a right motion until the starboard wing appears to have collided with a light tower. There's evidence from the flight data recorder that the pilot applied a full left deflection of the rudder and aileron, but could not bring the aircraft under control in time. The pilot had only a fraction of a second to react. All the indications are that he did the best he could to respond to the situation.'

Clark paused to take a sip of water which allowed a journalist from the *New York Times* to throw in a question. 'The speed of reaction does not entirely release the pilot from blame,' he said. 'Your diagram shows that he was close enough to the Boeing to expose his airplane to these vortices. Was this his fault or Air Traffic Control's?'

Martin Dowl lumbered into action. He evidently knew the reporter.

'Mr Parsons, we will take questions at the end of this conference.'

Clark leaned forward and said he didn't mind answering

because it was important for the pilot's family. 'Our feeling is that he was well within the safety margin and he had little reason to believe the conditions were conducive to wake-vortex. No warning had been given by Air Traffic Control. This means that aircraft landing on the same runway during the hour prior to the crash had experienced nothing like the catastrophic vortex that he encountered.'

A woman's voice asked about the casualty list.

'We're coming to that now,' said Dowl testily. He picked up a prepared statement, which he began to read with the gravity of a judge. Harland listened intently, waiting for the official toll. But Dowl was taking his time, first describing the business of the UN officials on board, which turned out to be an informal briefing of Congress on the resources needed for peace-keeping operations, then touching on the reason for Canada's loan of the plane for the Secretary-General's forthcoming tour of South American capitals. He concluded with a passage about the Secretary-General's great sorrow at the death of twelve dedicated professionals in the service of the United Nations.

So, thought Harland, the corpse known as Male C was as good as dumped in the East River. Luc Bézier was never on the plane.

Dowl put the statement down. Then the camera focused on Parsons who had stood up and was asking another question. 'All through last week we were told that thirteen UN people had been killed on the plane. Now you're saying only twelve were killed. How could anyone make a mistake like that?'

Dowl took off his glasses and nodded to Clark, who began speaking with laboured patience. 'Sir, you have to under-stand the conditions at a crash scene where there has been a violent impact and wreckage is spread over an area of several hundred yards, where the body of the plane has been burned in a fire with temperatures reaching thousands of degrees.

These conditions do not aid the recovery of bodies. I am afraid mistakes do occur.'

'But surely,' Parsons shot back, 'there was some kind of passenger list you could check against?'

'Not in this case,' said Clark, making it plain with a look to Dowl that this was one for him.

'Nothing?' said the reporter, transferring his gaze from the right of the platform to Dowl at the centre.

'No,' said Dowl. 'The aircraft was returning to New York anyway. The UN personnel were making use of it as an economy measure. It will not escape your attention that many of the people on that plane had been at Congress arguing for the payment of late contributions to the UN budget.'

'So you didn't know who was on that plane. How can we be sure that you haven't made a mistake? There could still be people unaccounted for. Isn't that right?'

Dowl shook his head. 'No, that's not possible.'

'And you're saying that the next flight would have carried the Secretary-General. When was that trip scheduled for, Mr Dowl?'

'Last Friday. He was due to visit Colombia with members of the Economic and Social Council.'

'And the trip didn't go ahead?'

'That's correct.'

'Colombia, that's a dangerous spot. This must have occurred to the accident investigators and the FBI. I mean, if this crash wasn't caused by wake-vortex, you would have to look for another cause, wouldn't you? Have you ruled out any tampering with the plane's systems?'

'That's a hypothetical issue because the NTSB has established wake-vortex as the cause of this accident.'

'If I'm not mistaken,' returned the reporter, 'the only hypothesising going on around here is Mr Clark's. However convincing the theory appears to be, it is still only a theory – a hypothesis.'

Clark interrupted Dowl with a raised hand. 'Sir, we are certain that this accident was caused by wake-vortex. It's more than hypothesis – all the flight and cockpit data comply with the pattern of previous incidents. Since 1983 seventy serious incidents have been minutely studied, and that's just in the United States. During a ten-year period in Britain five hundred and fifteen incidents – not accidents – were reported at London's Heathrow alone. We know what we're talking about here. This is a well-documented and well-understood phenomenon.'

'Plainly not a well-avoided one,' said Parsons, and, before anyone had time to react, he added, 'If the Falcon was too close to the Boeing, someone must be to blame, Mr Clark.'

'The wake separation distance was satisfactory. We're looking at all the meteorological data of the time to see if the vortex was capable of an abnormal lifespan. These findings will be included in the final report. But I stress that we are not saying that the investigation is closed.'

'That's exactly right,' chimed in Dowl. 'This conference is an exercise to keep you, the media, abreast of the preliminary conclusions.'

Harland had heard all he needed.

9

THE QUANTUM FOE

He returned to his office to find Marika with arms imperiously folded across her chest, remonstrating with a man who was fiddling with the fax machine. She gestured Harland into his own office and said sternly, 'Why didn't you tell me what happened here last night?'

He shrugged. 'I didn't want to worry you. I just had some money taken, that's all. And I've got a bit of a bruise.'

'But you were mugged! Here, in the United Nations! It's terrible. Everyone is shocked that such a thing could happen to you after last week.'

'Well, there it is. I was a little shaken up, but I'm okay now. I'm looking forward to going away for a bit of peace. By the way, how did you hear about it?'

'One of the guards who found you came by. Asked if there was anything else missing. I said nothing except the fax roll. Somebody stole the damned fax roll. Can you believe that?'

'What do you mean?' He knew perfectly well what she meant and instantly realised the significance of the theft. The imaging film, which passed through the machine between two rolls, much like an old-fashioned camera, contained a complete record of the faxes he had received the previous night. All someone would need to do to retrieve the documents was to place the film, page by page, in a photocopier. It was as simple as holding an old piece of carbon paper up to the light – in fact simpler because each section of the imaging film was used just once.

Harland hid his reaction. 'Someone on this floor must've taken it when their machine ran out.'

This didn't satisfy Marika, but she had something else on her mind. The Secretary-General's office had called down. There was a brief gap in Benjamin Jaidi's schedule just after two, and he wanted to see Harland.

He arrived outside the Secretary-General's suite of offices a little ahead of time, and walked up and down the corridor looking at the framed pencil sketches of the UN buildings. Suddenly he was aware of the guard at the end of the corridor stiffening in his chair. He glanced to his left and found the Secretary-General standing almost next to him.

'It's a good trick,' he said, 'I learned it when I was a boy. The man who taught it to me said the secret of sneaking up on someone is to imagine that you are leaving half yourself behind. I am sure he was pulling my leg, but it seems to work, doesn't it?'

Harland looked down into the garnet-black eyes of Benjamin Jaidi. He had met him five or six times before and had always been struck by the man's eerily fluid presence. Diplomat, crusader, politician and seducer of despots, Jaidi inhabited many roles, but would only agree with the job description of a predecessor who said that a Secretary-General was like a secular Pope. There was something in that, but it didn't embrace the illusionist's craft that the neat, inscrutable little man practised in his every waking moment. Harland thought of him as a modern, dark-skinned Merlin. He was without obvious origins. He spoke with an unplace-able lilt, which someone once described as dockside sing-song, and his looks might have come from anywhere – the Middle East, Africa, India, even South America. In fact he was born in Zanzibar, was schooled in European universities and had spent most of his working life in the United States.

102

He took Harland by the elbow and walked him slowly back to his offices pouring out charm and concern for his ordeal. With Jaidi you felt immersed in sympathy.

They sat down in a sofa with their backs to the view.

'I must say, that looks a nasty injury on your head. Is that the result of the crash?' He paused. 'Or did you receive it last night?'

So Jaidi knew.

'Last night, but it looks much worse than it feels.'

'Yes, you certainly seem to have been in the wars, Mr Harland. You must look after yourself in future.'

'Yes.'

'So,' said Jaidi, clasping his hands over his crossed knees, 'Alan Griswald was a friend of yours?'

'Yes, a good friend.'

'Did you know he was coming to see me with information which he would only convey to me in person?'

'I had some idea. Would you mind if I asked what it was about?'

'It concerned his work in The Hague for the International War Crimes Tribunal, but I can't tell you more because I don't know.' He paused. 'Do you think this crash was an accident as they are saying?'

Harland weighed his reply. 'Well, I just watched the press briefing downstairs and the Safety Board's findings seem feasible enough. There's no evidence of sabotage.'

'Yes, wake-vortex is certainly a convincing explanation,' said Jaidi ruminatively. 'I haven't heard of such a thing before. But let me ask you what you really think, Mr Harland.'

'I think there are very good reasons to suspect that it was sabotage. Someone didn't want Alan Griswald to talk to you.'

'But you're right – there's no proof. It's disturbing that such a thing could happen – so many good people killed and

103

yet there's no evidence of a crime. It makes one feel powerless and angry.'

'Yes, it does.'

Jaidi sat in silence with a queer expression on his face. Through an open door beyond him, Harland could see the business of the Secretary-General's office in full flow, but Jaidi seemed in no hurry. 'I haven't had any lunch. Shall we see if we can get some tea? I think we need tea and cookies, don't you?'

He sprang to his feet and went through the open door.

Quite soon afterwards a very tall, Scandinavian-looking woman brought in a tray. Jaidi took a plate of biscuits and began to talk while steadily munching through them.

'I think we both know more than we are admitting, Mr Harland. Can I make that assumption without offending you?'

Harland nodded and wondered what the hell was coming next.

'You see, I've learned that you know about Monsieur Bézier and that you've made inquiries about the work being carried out by your friend Griswald.' He saw that Harland was about to interrupt and put up his hand. 'Please, let me finish. I understand that you may be upset by this, but I've had to acquaint myself with the facts as fully as I can. I am facing – or rather we are facing – a very difficult time. I think we have to embrace each other and share what we know.'

'What are you saying, sir?' asked Harland, tired of Jaidi's opaque formality.

'That we have a common purpose and we need to acknowledge it.'

'No, before that, about Bézier. How have you acquainted yourself with the facts?'

Jaidi sighed and bowed his head a little.

'Are you saying it was one of your people who took the fax roll from my office? And the break-in at my apartment, the attack last night? I can't believe it. Are you saying these were at your instigation?'

'I knew this would be difficult.' Jaidi sighed again. 'Yes, I plead guilty on two counts. Let me explain. It seemed to us, by which I mean Mr Ollins of the FBI and Sean Kennedy, the head of security here, that you might have taken something from Alan Griswald's body. We suspected that you knew what he was bringing me because you were friends. Old friends, I gather. There *was* something, wasn't there? But then last night it was stolen from you. Mr Kennedy wondered what else you knew and went to your office and found the fax roll. I'm afraid that he also arranged for a search of your apartment over the weekend, though he did tell me that he and his colleague were let in by a porter. So it was not strictly a break-in.'

'That doesn't make it any better, sir,' said Harland sharply. 'They read my private correspondence.'

'Yes, I agree, it's inexcusable, but up until this morning we weren't sure where you stood. Then it became clear that you were as interested as we were in finding out what had happened to the plane and what Griswald was doing. Those actions spoke well of your motives. But now you must tell me what you took from Griswald's body.'

Harland told him about Griswald's wallet and how he had found it on Saturday afternoon and then about listening to the disc and the pulse of sound which he suspected was some sort of code. He left out his visit to the Griswald family.

'And you no longer have that disc?'

'No, it was taken last night.'

'Yes, we thought something like that had occurred. It was a pity you didn't tell Ollins in the first place, wasn't it?'

'I didn't realise until Saturday afternoon that I had it. By that time I was beginning to think that Ollins was not being entirely straight. That impression was pretty much confirmed by the press conference this morning when there was no mention of the Frenchman.' He paused. 'Look, sir, can I ask you why you are so keen to conceal Bézier's presence on the plane? Sooner or later, someone is going to have to admit that he was killed with the others.'

'Yes, that's true. The answer is that Ollins and Kennedy, who I should mention used to be colleagues, wanted time to find out about Bézier. It's also important that the people who are trying to prevent me learning about Griswald's evidence do not know that Bézier was on the plane.'

'But if this was sabotage, surely Bézier was one of the targets.'

'Not necessarily. It's my conviction – no, my instinct – that Griswald was the lone target. I don't think they knew about Bézier. The important thing is that we learn how he fits in.'

'You keep on saying *they*. Who are *they*?'

'Are you familiar with quantum theory?'

'Yes,' said Harland doubtfully.

'Because that is what Alan Griswald mentioned in the one conversation that I had with him. He said he was dealing with a suspect who was like a quantum entity.'

'What on earth did he mean?'

'I'm not sure, but in the quantum world, as I understand it, very small entities can be a wave and a particle at the same time. They can also be in different places at the same time. This defies common sense.'

'Yes,' said Harland, dimly recalling a physics lecture at Cambridge, 'that's to do with the Uncertainty Principle. As one manifestation becomes definite, the other recedes and becomes hazy. The point is that you can never be sure of the hazy state.'

'Exactly! Griswald said he had managed to focus on one aspect of this individual which concerns a crime in the Balkans but he was hazily aware of this individual's other roles and his influence, which may even have penetrated the War Crimes Tribunal. He said it was almost inconceivable how this individual had multiplied his identities to operate on so many different levels. That's why he used the quantum analogy and why he was coming to me. The War Crimes Tribunal is, as you know, a UN-sponsored operation. He wanted to know that he had my support before he began to pursue this matter in earnest. Obviously he did not gain that support because next week Griswald will be buried along with all the others who died in the crash.'

'So you're sure that it was sabotage.'

'No, I'm not. I can only say that it's likely because this is not my forte. I rely on people like Sean Kennedy to keep an eye on things and he has his friends, but in the world of espionage we are babes in the wood.'

'Espionage? What has this got to do with espionage?'

'Didn't I mention that? Alan Griswald told me on the phone that the man he was investigating had important relationships with several intelligence services. I'm afraid I didn't ask which intelligence services because I thought we would be able to discuss it in person.'

'So what do you intend to do, sir?'

Jaidi paused and aimed a boyish smile at him.

'Well' – he took another biscuit – 'I was hoping that you would help. Your report on the water resources must be nearly complete. Is that right?'

Harland nodded.

'I was going to propose an extension of that contract, during which you'll find out who Alan Griswald was investigating. I believe things will follow on from there. Get that evidence and the people who caused the crash will not have won.'

'But,' protested Harland, 'even if I was to consider this, you're being wildly optimistic about my chances of success.'

'You underestimate yourself, Mr Harland. You're already doing what I am formally asking you to do.'

'Yes, but . . .'

'But what?'

'I have no authority.'

'You have my authority. You will be my personal representative, which still carries a little weight in some places. You will have a letter that states you are my representative and requests the cooperation of the government of any member state or agency thereof that you believe can help in your inquiries. This should be used only as a last resort because I would prefer that our arrangement remains *sub rosa*. You will learn far more that way. Shall we say an extension of current terms for six months? Afterwards you can deliver the water ownership report to me. Of course, in the long run that is the more important issue, but I'm afraid this is the more pressing one.'

Harland couldn't see a way out of it. Besides, he had already promised Sally Griswald that he would do much of what Jaidi was asking of him.

'Suppose I agree to this, how will it operate? Do you want regular reports?'

'You can call me any time, but you will liaise with Sean Kennedy. I suggest you go and see him now. He's aware of the proposal I'm making to you and has your letter of authority.'

'Okay, but I've got my doubts whether I'll find out anything for you.'

'Naturally you do.' Jaidi stood up. The interview was clearly over. Harland rose also and followed him into the corridor. 'I don't know how to say this,' Jaidi said, putting his hand out to shake Harland's, 'but it looks like this story is making its way to you. Call it what you will – destiny or just plain bad luck – but events seem to be reaching out to you, Harland. Much better that you go forward and meet them, don't you think? We'll be in touch after Christmas.' With a fleeting smile he turned and slipped back into his office.

Harland looked at his watch. It was three o'clock – nine in

Europe. He knew he had missed speaking to Sara Heze-manns; he would have to call the next day. Realising he now had little time before having to leave for JFK, he hurried off to find Sean Kennedy's office in one of the backwaters of the third floor.

Boris was right. Kennedy had a distinctly Clintonian hairstyle, a bouffant of wire wool, obviously kept in place by a daily application of lacquer. Harland noticed a slight sheen as he stepped forward to greet him with a handshake that was meant to be eloquent of Kennedy's no-nonsense masculinity.

'I knew you'd agree to the Secretary-General's proposal,' he said. 'Hell, this is the guy who persuaded a room full of Balkan mass murderers to demonstrate their national dances.'

Harland was already sure that he didn't like Kennedy. 'Has anyone spoken to Bézier's number in France?' he asked abruptly.

'No.'

'You mean his relatives haven't been informed?'

'No, not as yet.'

'Well, who's going to do that?'

'I thought we could discuss that now.'

'You mean you want me to do it?'

'Well, if you're going to be working on this thing, it would be for the best.'

Harland thought for a moment, then picked up the phone to Marika.

'Cancel my flight to London. I want the first available plane to Toulouse in France.'

'How do you know it's Toulouse?' asked Kennedy.

'I checked the number. It's from the Carcassonne area. Toulouse is the best airport at this time of year.'

'Right.'

'I'm going to call whoever is on that phone number this

109

afternoon. Then I want some back-up. Whatever is available in the way of insurance or hardship allowance must go to these people. And I want someone to call and explain these benefits as soon as I have been to see them. That must happen before Christmas.'

'Yes, I'm sure that's possible. I'll talk to the relevant department.'

'Next, I want a complete run-down of Griswald's cases from the War Crimes Tribunal – all his past investigations. I'll also need an idea of the set-up at the War Crimes Tribunal – the structure and personalities. You can send both these to my e-mail address. Naturally, you will not give them any idea why this material is needed. They are bound to suspect something, but nobody should know I'm working on this.'

Kennedy nodded. 'Pity about the disc,' he said, trying to regain the upper hand.

'Yes, it is,' said Harland tersely. He wasn't going to tell Kennedy there was a copy. 'Now, can you talk to Ollins and tell him that we are all in this together. He needs to share any information he gets. And I will do likewise. Tell him I will call him in the next few days. I have his numbers. Now all I want from you is the letter of authority from the Secretary-General and the fax roll that you took from my office this morning, plus any copies you have made.'

A few minutes later, Harland was back in his own office. He shut the door and thought for a long time about what he was going to say. Then he picked up the phone and dialled the number in France.

10

TWO OFFICERS

The phone rang for a full minute before a woman answered. Harland asked whether he was speaking to Madame Bézier.

'No,' replied the woman, suspiciously. 'There is no Madame Bézier. This is Colonel Bézier's residence.'

'Colonel Bézier?'

'Yes, Colonel Bertrand Bézier.'

'Not Luc Bézier?'

'No!' said the woman, a little crossly. 'He does not live here. He is a grown man. He lives in Paris.'

'I see,' said Harland, now understanding that Colonel Bézier must be his father. 'I am ringing from the United States. I think I should talk to the Colonel.'

'Impossible. He is a sick man. He cannot be disturbed.'

'It's very important. It concerns Luc Bézier. Madame, is Luc Bézier his son?'

'Yes, Capitaine Bézier is his son.'

'I see. This is going to be very difficult, Madame. I think I will have to explain this to you. Can I ask who you are?'

'Madame Clergues. I am the Colonel's nurse and house-keeper.'

'I see. I have some very bad news.' He paused for a fraction of a second. 'I believe that Luc Bézier was involved in a plane crash last week on Tuesday.'

There was a gasp at the other end. 'Is this a joke?'

He explained who he was and told her about the crash,

and after a little while she seemed to accept that he was telling the truth. 'It will kill him,' she kept on repeating. 'It will kill him. He is very frail.'

Harland told her that he was prepared to break the news himself, if she could wait until he arrived in France the following day. On the whole she said she thought that it would be better if the Colonel heard it from someone he knew. She had been with him for two years. She would tell him in the morning in the presence of his doctor, who was visiting anyway and would be on hand if the Colonel suffered a collapse. They agreed that Harland should arrive in the afternoon and speak with the Colonel, having first telephoned her from the airport.

Harland didn't ring off straight away but gently prompted the woman to tell him about Luc Bézier. It seemed that the Béziers were an old military family. During the Napoleonic wars, one of Luc's ancestors had served in the Imperial guard and fought at Waterloo. Luc had refused to use his father's contacts and had joined the French Foreign Legion, later transferring to the Parachute Regiment. He had left the military two years before and gone to work in Paris.

Harland rung off. He had been wrong about Bézier's calls to a wife or girlfriend. No cigarette.

He did not drink for fear of worsening the surges of pain from the back of his head. A whisky or two might have done something to dull his newly acquired knowledge of how quickly a plane is reduced to charred scrap, but he went on board sober, and as he dropped into the aisle seat he was aware of two things: the illusion of reliability about him and the slight tremor in his right hand. He knew he had to distract himself fast because he realised that the faith – or whatever he had left out on the East River – had indeed completely deserted him.

He took out the transcripts and began to read. There were

112

six interviews, all typed in single spacing. The first four were personal accounts of women whose menfolk had disappeared from a place in Eastern Bosnia called Kukuva, one of the 'safe havens' overrun during the Serb offensive in the summer of 1995. The last two were men who had apparently escaped execution and fled together through the hills to the Bosnian front line.

He picked up where he had left off in the account of Selma Simic. She was a dentist's assistant who lived with her husband and two boys in the town, which she described as a neighbourly place where everyone knew and helped each other. On a July evening her husband had taken her two boys, aged twelve and fourteen, into the hills overlooking the town. Knowing that she did not possess the stamina for what would be a gruelling march to Muslim territory, she had stayed behind with the older women and helped the mothers who were nursing babies.

The Serbs arrived early the next day, many of them reeking of plum brandy. The women were rounded up in the town square and questioned about their men, most of whom had taken flight in the previous twenty-four hours. By now the sun was beating down on the square and the women implored the soldiers to give them water and to allow the young children to rest in the shade. Selma Simic had been one of the women who had gone forward and talked to an officer. He told her and a friend that they could fetch water from a nearby bar. Inside she found a dozen Serb soldiers resting up. They let the women make four trips with a bucket and ladle, and then without a word they barred their way out.

The soldiers took turns with them, at first casually, as if they had nothing better to do. There was a TV on and some of them watched a news bulletin while the rape was in progress. Simic and her friend refused to cry out because they didn't want to alarm people outside, especially the children.

This enraged the men and drove them to more barbarous acts; they seemed to want to hear the women cry out. But still they refused. Selma remarked to the tribunal investigator that she endured by concentrating on some flies that were milling round a piece of food on the floor.

When eventually the soldiers had done with them they were thrown out into the square. The soldiers, she noted, were apparently sickened by their own behaviour, as though Selma and her friend had somehow encouraged them. At that moment, she felt they would be killed. But the men sloped away. They rejoined the group in the square and found that most of the younger women had been taken away and given similar treatment. One woman suffered a miscarriage and another died after an assault which Selma could not bring herself to describe to the interviewer.

The day wore on and eventually a bus drew up in the square. Fifty-eight people were pushed on board. Many of the older women were suffering from heat exhaustion and the children were hysterical. Before the bus set off, the women saw some of the older men who had remained in the town driven out of their hiding places at gunpoint. They stared at the ground and would not look up when the women called out to them. Selma Simic saw her neighbour, a widower of sixty-five who grew roses and carved wooden ornaments in his spare time. She could tell by the expression of terror in his eyes that he knew he was going to be killed, even though the Serbs insisted that they would be reunited after the men had been interrogated about terrorist activities. She said that among the group of men there were two boys a little younger than her sons. In all, there were forty-six men and boys. Not one of them was ever seen again.

As the bus departed, the women believed they were going to be killed and sent up a terrible cry. But instead they were taken on a meandering journey westwards, which included several stops while the Serbs debated which route to send them. At one crossroads they sat for nearly two hours watching columns of men and armour moving forward in the dusk for the assault on the Muslim stronghold to the north. During this time they caught sight of an infamous Serb general whose face they'd seen often on television. He was unmistakable, a huge, sweating man with a wide, red face and a beer drinker's stomach. She was shocked at seeing the author of the evil all around them standing so near. His voice carried across the road to the open windows of the bus and the women could hear his commands barked at a radio. These were interspersed with remarks about women and what he was going to eat that night.

At that time she did not know about the slaughter that would occur over the next few days. But thinking back on it, she could not get over the fact that he was talking about food and drink at the very moment that he must have been planning the operation to murder thousands of people. She told the interviewer that she could never rid herself of the image of him standing there in the sweltering summer evening. He perplexed and appalled her at the same time. He was not part of the universe she knew.

The other three women had equally harrowing stories of being separated from their men, terrorised and raped. The rawness of the experiences made Harland read them with more than an eye for possible leads in Griswald's investigation. He had seen plenty of similar things along the southern borders of Russia, but nowhere had he witnessed the pointless violence that they described. These women had been brutalised by their neighbours, men who lived a few kilometres away and who visited their towns; by mountain boys who had once brought their livestock to Kukuva market and who had given vent to their darkest desires and fears.

He read the testimonies of the two men, a tractor mechanic named Orovic and a school sports teacher who was identified by his initials DS. They had been captured a day later and sent to the killing fields on separate buses. There they were forced to watch from the windows as a dozen men at a time were taken from the bus, lined up in the doorway of a derelict barn and shot. The men had prayed, begged with the soldiers and even tried to bargain for their lives, offering their savings of Deutschmarks. Only a few went to their deaths cursing their killers.

Orovic's turn came early in the afternoon. When the shots rang out he fell backwards into the pile of bodies unhurt and lay there absolutely motionless, as more and more bodies were heaped on to him. During a lull in the slaughter, some time towards the end of the afternoon, Orovic had been aware of the general's presence at the mouth of the barn. He also knew his face well. Some kind of inspection was obviously taking place. The general had come to make sure the bodies were going to be properly disposed of and that his men had enough ammunition and would complete their quota of killing the next day. He heard him say that there were several hundred men being kept in a hall a few kilometres down the road. As the voices receded, Orovic squinted his eyes open and saw the general strutting away, talking to another man. They turned and threw a final contemptuous look towards the barn before getting into a vehicle and driving off.

Later, after darkness had fallen, Orovic heard a whispering in the dark. It was the teacher, DS, who had been winged on the shoulder but was otherwise unhurt. They waited until the early hours of the next day, then they extricated themselves from the mound of bloody corpses and from the terrible smell that already filled the barn, and escaped through some loose panels at the back of the building. Several shots rang out when the soldiers heard them running across the gravel road. The two men plunged into some dense undergrowth on the other side and began snaking their way up the hill.

Four days later they staggered over the Bosnian front line, suffering badly from blisters, hunger and dehydration.

As he read DS's evidence, which was nearly identical to the mechanic's, something began to fall into place for Harland. What linked all six people was the evidence of the general at the scene. But that could not be the point of interest for Griswald because the general was already the subject of an indictment for genocide from the War Crimes Tribunal. They had quite enough evidence of his involvement. Harland went back to the end of Simic's account, to the part where she described seeing the general on the roadside.

'There was a man with him,' she said, 'in a brand new uniform. I could not see his rank. All men in camouflage look the same. But this man was somebody of importance. You could see that by the way the general took care to consult him. I don't remember much of what they were saying now. We were too frightened to remember. But I am sure the man was a foreigner, not Serb. He had an accent and he could not speak the language well. A few times they had difficulty understanding each other and the general would slap the man on the back heartily. The general was anxious to please him, you could tell that.'

The investigator had prompted her to give a fuller description of the general's companion.

'He was shorter than the general,' she had replied. 'He was the same age – late forties, maybe early fifties. He was a dark man with a small face and a well-shaped nose and mouth. He might have been quite good-looking in his youth. The general was excited and pumped up with nervous energy, but this man did not move much. He was very composed.'

Harland realised that buried in each account was a mention of this man. All the women had noted his presence in passing and he had been seen by the two survivors of the massacre at the barn. The sports teacher had got a much clearer view than the mechanic because he had fallen to the side of the door and was able to watch undetected through a crack between the planks of wood. He said the man walked with quick short steps. He also heard a foreign accent.

Harland was sure that this character was the person Griswald was investigating. He supposed that hundreds, maybe thousands, of interviews had been combed for evidence of his presence in Eastern Bosnia during the final Serb push before the Dayton Peace Accord. The witnesses' statements which placed him at the scene of the massacre with the general were obviously of crucial importance in building a case against the man, whose identity Griswald must have known. But what did this all mean in the greater scheme of things? Why was Griswald being more secretive than perhaps he would have been about any of the other war criminals pursued by the tribunal?

Harland folded the transcripts and put them in his jacket pocket. For the rest of the trip he entered a shallow sleep. He awoke as the plane touched down at Toulouse in the dark, feeling dreadful. He bought himself breakfast and arranged for a hire car. Before leaving he called Madame Clergues to say that he was on his way.

Tomas Rath had slipped into Heathrow on a twin-engine turbo-prop from Reykjavik, having the day before flown from New York to Iceland in the hope that the route would make him a fraction less conspicuous. As he waited in the EU line for immigration control at Heathrow he turned on his cellphone and listened for his messages. To his surprise he heard Robert Harland's deliberate voice suggesting they see each other when he got to London that day. He noted down the numbers that Harland had left him and snapped the phone closed. That was really great news, he thought.

On the way into London he tried calling Flick a couple of times. He wanted to tell her about Harland, to say that his impulsive visit to New York had paid off. But he couldn't reach her. He supposed that she was at Covent Garden market because she often did the run to pick up the day's order herself. Tomas usually went with her. It was part of their life together and he loved setting off in the van, listening to Flick's collection of 'adrenalin rock', arriving at the huge flower hall just south of the Thames where he breakfasted on coffee and a bacon sandwich while Flick put together the order. His job – the lifting and loading – came later, so for the best part of an hour he watched her move between the stalls, haggling and flirting with the wholesalers. One morning a couple of weeks back he had caught sight of her in a shaft of light and his heart turned over. He knew then that he was falling in love.

He reached Belsize Park tube station and went through a complicated procedure which involved doubling back on the Northern Line to Camden Town, whereupon he left the station and walked to Flick's flat in Hazlitt Grove, South Hampstead. When he got there, it struck him as odd that her dark blue van was still parked outside her flat. By this time she was usually either at the shop in Hampstead or at the market. He unlocked the front door of the house and found a note on the doormat. It was signed 'Pete', who was the manager at the shop. The note, dated and timed the previous day, asked if anything was the matter.

With a sense of dread, Tomas climbed the stairs. On the first landing he waited and listened. No sound came from the floor above – another sign that things were not right. If Flick was there, she'd have music on. He continued up the last two flights, taking care to avoid the creaking floorboards, and arrived at the door. Standing under the skylight he pressed his ear to the door. He could wait no longer. He thrust the key into the lock and pushed the door open.

He found Flick lying naked in a foetal position on her bed. Her legs and arms were bound. She had been killed with a bullet in the head. There was blood on the wall and on a pillow which had been used to muffle the shot. Tomas dropped to his knees beside the bed and touched her hands, which had been yanked down to meet the twine around her ankles. He knew that she had suffered terribly. He saw marks on her arms, breasts and thighs – cigarette burns and welts that had risen into livid bruises before she died. In the corner of his mind he had already taken in that the place had been turned over and that they hadn't found anything. There was nothing to find.

He brushed her face with his hand. She was utterly cold. He let out a cry, not of self-pity, but of remorse. They had tortured her to find out where he was and they had tried to make her tell them what she knew about his activities. But Flick knew nothing. She'd never asked and he had never told her. This was it – the retribution he'd been expecting. At that moment he would have given his own life never to have met her. But she had smiled at him across that bar, walked over and sat down beside him. He should have done something to put her off, but he'd let her take him home to share her quirky, beautiful, decent life. And now she was dead. Dead because of him.

He sat there for some time, tortured by self-loathing. This was the end for him too. There was nowhere for him to go. He could not bring Flick's terrible fate on anyone else. Now he had to finish the job. He would let everything go – everything.

He rose and left the flat in a trance. On the first landing he stopped, unscrewed two locks, lifted the sash cord window and climbed out on to the narrow brick column which had been added to buttress the wall at the back of the house. Once he had got his balance he leaned over and pulled the window shut, then let himself drop three feet into a gully which was formed by the pitched roof of a Victorian extension. He edged along to a point where he knew the roof would take his weight and shinned up to a dormer window that faced the back garden. He reached the window and wrenched up a flap of roofing lead that concealed a small cavity. He groped inside with one hand, found the package wrapped in several plastic bags and slipped it into the big pocket inside his jacket.

When he had first moved in with Flick and was looking for somewhere to conceal the package, he had discovered that he could not take the route back to the landing window because the climb up to the buttress from the lower roof was too difficult. At the time he thought it was an advantage because it might deter others from venturing out there. Once he had got the package, he scrambled to the other side of the roof, let himself down to the top of a garden wall and into a paved area where refuse bins were kept. Within a few seconds he had left the premises and was walking down Hazlitt Grove – where to, he did not know.

Harland drove south towards the Pyrenees in bright sunlight. He made good progress and arrived at the small château on the bank of a river an hour ahead of time. He waited at the end of an avenue of lime trees until he saw a man leave in a Renault car, then drove up to the house and parked in front of the door. An attractive woman in her forties hurried out to meet him and introduced herself as Madame Clergues. Harland held out his UN identity card, but she didn't take it.

When told about his son two hours earlier, Colonel Bézier had said that he already knew. Something had told him that the silence from the United States boded bad news. Madame Clergues said he knew inside that Luc was gone and that this firm intuition accounted for his frail state in the last week. She asked Harland not to cause him undue torment.

He was shown into a conservatory where an old vine had run riot. Bunches of shrivelled grapes hung from the glass roof and dead leaves had gathered under the table. Colonel Bézier was seated in a green wickerwork chair with a tartan shawl thrown round his shoulders. He gazed through the open doors across some pasture to a line of poplar trees, beyond which lay the river. Beside him was a table with several bottles of pills, a book, *Le Monde*, mineral water, glasses and an old Lalique lamp. Harland saw that he spent nearly all his time there. A few seconds after he entered, the Colonel turned and threw a hand out in the direction of a chair where he intended Harland should sit.

He looked much younger than Harland expected – no more than mid-sixties. Except for his white pallor, there was not much of the invalid in his face. He had a strong jaw and cheekbones and close-cropped, dark grey hair. He examined Harland for a moment with watery, dark eyes, then wearily asked him to tell him as much as he knew about his son's death.

In rather mechanical French, Harland told him about the crash and his subsequent discoveries about Griswald and Luc Bézier's business in New York. He left little out because he understood that the Colonel needed to hear everything. He even told him about the disc and the transcripts. Throughout, the sick man nodded, as though Harland was confirming things that he had suspected for himself all along. Eventually he said he had heard enough and methodically took out a pack of Gauloises, lit a cigarette and held out the pack. Harland declined although his hand had involuntarily jerked forward.

'Good,' said the Colonel flatly. 'These things have put me in this chair.' He let out a thin stream of smoke from his closed lips. 'You know that my boy was a hero? Not the sort of hero you read about in the papers because he was on specialist operations. Four medals and too many commendations to count. That was Luc. That was my son.' He paused. 'I knew from the start that the business in the Balkans was a catastrophe. Those people massacre each other every fifty years. They're barbarians. The rest of Europe should have nothing to do with them. We French understood this, but the Americans and NATO, they had to get involved. Let them stew in their own hatred, is what I said. But Luc went because he could not pass up a challenge. He excelled at his job, you see. You know that he learned Serbo-Croat in a matter of months so he could speak like one of those damned peasants?'

Harland shook his head and smiled. 'What exactly was he doing there, sir?'

'He was running an undercover squad. They were trying to seize the war criminals. His work was like my own early service in Algeria. Most of it was surveillance, but they captured one or two of the bastards – just cow hands, nobody important. They shot a couple more, although my son said several of these men developed the habit of travelling with children in their cars, so it wasn't easy for the army. His longest job involved the man named Lipnik. Big Cat, they called him. For this operation, Luc's team had to go beyond the area where the French UN troops patrolled in Bosnia, right into Serbia. They watched him for about two weeks. They got to know his habits and routines although he was very discreet. The plan, I believe, was to snatch this Lipnik at a restaurant where they knew he was going to dine early one evening. Luc told me about it in detail. You'll see why in a moment.

'They knew they'd got the right man because the Americans had traced his phone and intercepted a conversation with Lipnik making an arrangement to be at the restaurant. Luc was doubtful about spotting their target, let alone being able to seize him and spirit him away without a fight. Their plan was to pretend to be Serb security agents who had been sent to protect him against an assassination attempt. It gave them the perfect excuse for hustling the man out of the place and into a car.'

'Sounds as though it might have worked,' said Harland.

'Well, they never found out,' said the Colonel emphatically.

Harland was worried that he was becoming too agitated. He wondered whether his son's death had sunk in properly.

'What happened then, sir?' he asked quietly.

'They saw him arrive at the front of the hotel. There were no guards in evidence – just a driver. To their amazement, Lipnik chose a table at the front of the restaurant overlooking the street. He and his guest were visible to the whole team. Luc got the vehicles into position and waited for a wedding party to pass inside. Then he gave the order to move in, but at that moment two men appeared from the throng of wedding guests and began shooting. The men at the table were killed instantly – quite an irony, considering the cover story Luc's team had made for themselves. In the confusion that followed, one of Luc's men went into the restaurant to check that Lipnik was dead. It was a terrible scene – complete carnage, apparently. Those men were dead all right – they were unrecognisable.'

'When was this?'

'Late '96 or early '97, I'm not certain.'

Colonel Bézier's gaze left Harland and drifted over the meadow in front of them. The sun had come out again to light the few brilliant yellow leaves that clung to the poplars and dance on the barely rippled water beyond. He fumbled for another cigarette. Harland understood that the Colonel was going to smoke as much as he liked now. There was no point in minding his health. They sat in silence for a long time before the Colonel shook a small hand-bell. A maid arrived. He ordered a cognac and cocked his eyebrow interrogatively at Harland. Harland said that he was driving.

'But that was not the end of the story,' he said. 'A little time afterwards Luc left the army. He'd had enough and he was interested in making some money and settling down. Sensible boy. He went into the art business. It sounds odd for

124

an ex-soldier, particularly of Luc's calibre, but he had a very good eye and he was ready to learn. He made a success of it because he applied himself. He'd been with a gallery for about two years last summer when he was sent to Vienna on business. He was walking in the street right outside a hotel when he ran slap-bang into Lipnik who was getting out of a car. This was only two or three months ago – about three years after the shooting in Serbia. But Luc was certain that it was the same man. Remember, Monsieur, that he'd studied his target minutely – he knew his mannerisms, his walk, everything. It was Big Cat! He was walking around, breathing like you and me – like you, at any rate.'

'Who is Lipnik? Do you know his first name?'

'A moment, Monsieur,' he said irritably. 'Let me finish. Naturally, Luc did his best to make some inquiries about the man he'd seen and eventually he told a friend in the State Intelligence Service. They took no action. But it was obvious to him that the whole thing had been a set-up – the shooting had been planned for the benefit of his team who, of course, had been made the unwitting accomplices to yet another crime in the Balkans. Two men were killed that day, remember, shot to pieces so no one would take a close look and ask whether one of them was indeed Lipnik. There was enough circumstantial evidence for the identification to go unquestioned. The restaurant booking, the fact that several people had seen Lipnik enter the establishment and the things they found on his body must have convinced them that this was indeed Lipnik. But it wasn't. The man was a double, somebody who was persuaded to act like Big Cat for an afternoon and got killed for his trouble.'

'But the tracing of the phone?'

'All part of the plan,' said the Colonel decisively. 'Luc realised that the whole thing had been a set-up. The phone was the lure that drew in Luc's team.'

'But surely they didn't suspect that the Americans were in on this.'

'Who knows, Monsieur, who collaborated with whom? It could be that they were really hearing Lipnik's voice on that phone and they had been genuinely fooled like we were.' He stopped and put his hand down to a tortoiseshell cat that had wandered in from the garden and was twirling round an oxygen cylinder propped against his chair. 'Or it might equally be the case that the whole thing had been American-inspired right from the start. Luc said there was no way of telling. About four weeks ago he was down here for some hunting and he asked my advice. I said if you feel strongly that you are right about this man and he has got away with something, then you should go to the War Crimes Tribunal. Let them handle it. This is how he met your friend Mr Griswald. And this is why he's dead.'

Harland was silent for a moment. 'To be frank, sir, I can't see why Griswald took your son along with him. He had all the information he needed. There was no reason why he shouldn't pursue his lead alone.'

'That might be correct if the Tribunal was immune to pressure from the United States and Britain and France. Apparently Monsieur Griswald did believe that. He felt Luc could persuade them of the importance of pursuing this matter.'

'Can I ask you again who Lipnik is?'

'Having heard the beginning of the story, I asked Luc to keep me up to date with developments. I was interested and it gave me something to think about sitting in this damned chair. Monsieur Griswald believed that Lipnik was not his real name from the start. It was a *nom de guerre*, used during his time dealing with the Serbs at the time of the war. He smuggled arms and ammunition and traded secrets with them and he acquired an identity to do that.'

'Did your son know what nationality he was? Did Griswald have any idea?'

'They thought he was Russian. That was their belief, but I cannot tell you why. They knew they were dealing with someone *comme Protée*.' Harland asked what he meant. The Colonel said someone who could assume different forms like the sea god Proteus. 'They believed he had several different identities – and lives to go with them.'

'Even so, supplying arms and selling secrets is not an indictable offence,' said Harland, now certain that he had been right about Griswald's purpose in gathering together the witness statements from 1995.

'The point is that they knew from other sources that Lipnik was involved with the implementation of the massacre. They knew that way back and they knew what he looked like. Otherwise they would not have sent Luc's team in. The question is, was Luc being used? He suspected that he had been. That's all I can say.'

Harland could see the Colonel was getting tired, and he said that he ought to leave. But before he could get up, Madame Clergues brought the phone to the Colonel and asked if he was up to talking to a person from the United Nations in New York about arrangements for the shipping of Luc Bézier's remains. He looked at Harland with an expression of great sadness, then shook his head.

'Will you deal with this please, Béatrice,' he said.

His voice had grown weak and his eyes were closing for longer periods each time he blinked. Harland rose and touched his hand.

'Thank you, Colonel. I think I should leave now.' He had planned to say something encouraging about continuing the investigation, but words failed him. He wished the Colonel well and thanked him for his time.

At that moment the Colonel propelled himself forward and clutched Harland's hand.

'As you can see, Monsieur, I will not live long. I am the last of the Bézier family now. We have served France for two hundred years and we have lived on this land for generations. All that was extinguished when my son was killed. If you can do anything to avenge his death and set things right, please remember that, Monsieur Harland.'

11

THE CRÈCHE

By the time he reached Heathrow, Harland was exhausted. He had taken a short nap on the plane from Toulouse but it had only made him feel worse. As he waited in a line of jaded businessmen on their way home for Christmas, he switched on his phone and called Harriet to let her know that he would be with her by nine. She told him that Robin was hosting his office party and he wouldn't be there until late.

A few seconds after he had hung up, his phone rang. He put his bags down and answered. It was Tomas.

'Mr Harland? Where are you?' He was shouting against the noise of traffic.

'I'm in London. Where are you?'

'In London too. I need to speak with you. It's very important. Something has happened.'

'Look, I've just arrived at the airport. It's a bit difficult now. Let's talk later.'

Tomas wasn't listening. 'My friend has been killed. She has been killed – murdered.'

Harland stepped out of earshot of the queue. 'Murdered? What are you talking about, for Christ's sake? Who's been murdered? Which friend?'

'Felicity – Flick. She has been killed ... She was in the apartment when I got back. They shot her and tortured her.'

'Have you told the police?'

'No, I cannot. I left her there.'

Harland gave him Harriet's address in St John's Wood and told him to go there immediately. He made him repeat the address then phoned Harriet to explain that a young man was about to arrive and that he would be in some distress. He'd explain when he got there.

He had missed his place in the queue and other passengers from another flight were now in front of him. Furiously wondering what the hell Tomas's call meant, he rejoined the line and moved slowly forward to the immigration desk where an official in an ill-fitting blazer was taking rather longer than usual to inspect the passports. Two men were looking over his shoulder and glancing along the queue. One of them appeared to focus on Harland and said something to his companion. As he approached the desk, one of them came forward, a thickset man with wiry black hair and ruddy Celtic cheeks.

'Mr Harland,' he said, 'my name is Griffiths.'

'Yes,' Harland said crossly. 'What do you want?'

'Would you come with us, sir? Mr Vigo wants a word. There's a car waiting outside. We'll have your luggage brought on, if you'll give my colleague here the baggage receipts.' A third man had appeared from nowhere and put out his hand.

'But what does Vigo want?'

'I'd rather not discuss it here, if you wouldn't mind. Mr Vigo wanted to talk to you this evening. It's nothing to worry about. He says it won't take long.'

Harland wondered how they knew to meet the flight from Toulouse, then realised that SIS would have had no difficulty in finding out about his departure from the US and would have then contacted the airline to alert them when he was on the London-bound plane. There seemed nothing else for it because he knew perfectly well that they could force him to go with them. He put the baggage receipt into the man's hand.

He was driven to a four-storey office block in West London, somewhere between Hammersmith and Earls Court. The car turned into a side street and passed a sign which announced FM AGRO PRODUCTS: NO DELIVERIES and then into a garage area where several cars were parked. A door closed automatically behind them.

Harland realised he was in The Crèche, an almost mythical establishment among MI6 staff, which periodically changed location but always served the same purpose. It was where MI6 conducted its initial interrogations and where various suspects and defectors were placed on ice in conditions of quasi-arrest. He had taken it for granted that all the dreary outposts of the service had been subsumed into the spanking new headquarters at Vauxhall Cross. Plainly not. This one still possessed the atmosphere of the Secret Intelligence Service that he had joined – the down-at-heel drudgery and suspicion of the Cold War. There was a feeling of impermanence about the building, as if its occupants were prepared to leave at a moment's notice.

He was led into a room where there was a small conference table, several chairs and a functional sofa at each end of the room. They asked him to sit down and told him he wouldn't have long to wait. Then they left, closing and locking the door behind them. He could hear voices recede in the corridor. He reckoned he had a very short time. He took out his cellphone and pressed redial. Harriet answered.

'Bobby, where the hell are you?'

'Listen, I want you to call the UN in New York. Get on to the Secretary-General's office. Make it clear that you are phoning on my behalf. Tell them that the British government is attempting to hold me without charges. It's got something to do with the affair that the Secretary-General has asked me to look into.'

'Where are you?'

'I'm in a building belonging to SIS – in West London

somewhere. A former colleague – Walter Vigo – had me picked up at the airport just after we spoke. Get the Secretary-General's people to phone the duty desk at the Foreign Office and kick up a stink. Tell whoever you speak to that I'm working on the Secretary-General's personal instructions. Got that? Good.'

While he was speaking he used his free hand to transfer the interview transcripts, which had been uncomfortably rolled up in his breast pocket, to the front of his trousers. The moment he hung up, he slid the phone's battery off, extracted the SIM card and placed it into the fold of material on the underside of his shirt collar. Then he opened his wallet and removed the bits of paper, on which he had written various numbers, and tucked them into the slit of a little coin pocket just beneath his waistband. None of these measures would be remotely effective if he was searched, but he hoped they weren't going to take things that far.

There was a murmur outside the door. Griffiths entered with two other men. They did not introduce themselves, neither did they smile or give any other sign of greeting.

As they sat down opposite him, he leaned forward, placed his hands on the table and said, 'Where's Vigo?'

'Mr Vigo will be along at some stage, I expect,' one of them said. He was in his fifties, dapperly dressed in a Windsor check suit, a cream shirt and a red tie which was embroidered with tiny fishing flies. Old MI5, thought Harland, no doubt brought up from some Home Counties village for the occasion.

'He'd better be. As far as I'm concerned, I'm here to talk to Vigo. I make it plain now that when I wish to leave, I will. If you attempt to prevent me from doing so, you will be breaking the law and, furthermore, you will find yourselves explaining your actions to the Foreign Secretary and the head of the Joint Intelligence Committee.'

'Yes,' replied the man quietly. 'We'll see how things go, shall we?'

The other man was vaguely familiar to Harland. He was heavier than his companion and wore large square-framed spectacles, behind which lay rather dead eyes. His mouth closed in an unattractive pout and he was less fastidious in his appearance – a sagging charcoal grey suit, a coffee stain on the cuff of his white shirt and a tie which showed its lining. Harland took him for a bit of a thug, an observation which helped him to remember his name. It was Blanchard – Derek Blanchard – and he had seen him in the eighties at meetings about the Soviet efforts to infiltrate the Campaign for Nuclear Disarmament. Blanchard was also MI5. Not top flight by any means and within five or six years of retirement, Harland guessed.

'I know your name,' he said to Blanchard, then looked at the other man. 'But what's yours?'

'Rivers,' he said. 'Anthony Rivers. Shall we proceed? This is not what I would call a normal interview, Mr Harland. We find we have very little to ask you, except in order to satisfy our curiosity about your motives. So I will come straight to the point. We know categorically that you have betrayed your country and are in contravention of the Official Secrets Act. Between 1975 and 1990 you worked under the code name *Lamplighter* for the StB, which I don't have to tell you was the Czechoslovak Security and Intelligence Service.'

Harland said nothing. He had been prepared for this moment and knew exactly how he was going to handle it. But why had it come now? And why had these two time-servers been fielded for the interrogation? He had the impression that this operation did not have the full weight of SIS behind it. There was something cobbled together about the whole thing.

Rivers produced a file from the chair beside him and opened it.

'You are Robert Cope Harland. After standard interviews and enhanced positive vetting procedures you were accepted as a trainee for SIS. At your first interview you were required to read and sign the Official Secrets Act.' Without looking up he flashed some papers, each of which bore Harland's signature, and continued speaking. 'Having completed your initial training in London and Portsmouth you were sent in 1974 for your first operational experience. This was intended as a purely observational role, a period of learning at the front, if you like. In those days it was customary to throw people in at the deep end a little earlier than we do today. You performed your duties with moderate flare and became involved in the operation to determine the extent of Eastern Bloc influence in a number of international institutions. We were also at that time concerned with the communist action against dissident groups that were based in Rome, principally those involved in the dissemination of anti-Czechoslovak propaganda following the Prague Spring. Is this all correct?'

Harland nodded wearily.

'At some point in your tour of duty in Rome – we believe it to be September or October of 1974 – you were introduced to a woman whom you discovered was an agent working for the StB. She was living in Rome under the name of Eva Houresh and her code name was *Lapis*. You initiated an affair with *Lapis*, knowing that she was a member of a hostile foreign intelligence service. Is that correct?'

Harland did not react. Rivers waited a second or two longer and pursed his lips, as if to indicate that he had had the misfortune to face many liars across an official table and Harland was no different.

'You returned to London and took up a number of posts, working in East European Controllerate. You joined the Intelligence Branch and worked in Berlin, Vienna and – briefly – in the embassy in the Soviet Union. You also spent short periods in the Middle East – the Lebanon and Turkey. I do not need to rehearse the details of your career; we all know it well enough. Suffice to say that you were approached by a man named Josef Kapek, an agent for the StB who was attached to the trade mission in London. He showed you a photograph of yourself in bed with *Lapis* which was taken in 1975. This we believe was in 1980, by which time you were regarded by your colleagues as reliable, even promising material.' He unclipped a photograph of Kapek taken in the street and showed it to Harland. This time he searched Harland's face for reaction. When he got none he gave a bleak, knowing smile and returned it to the file.

'Kapek threatened to send this item to the head of your department, together with details of the woman's back-ground. In consequence you agreed to his request to supply biographical sketches of the people you worked with in Century House and various embassies. He also revealed that there was a tape recording in existence. He told you that Eva Houresh is heard admitting to you her role in the StB and that you in turn reveal your own status in SIS.'

He paused. Rivers held up a cellophane envelope and withdrew a photograph with some flourish. It showed Harland and Eva making love, well, at least lying in bed together. Both faces were clearly visible. Harland didn't look at the picture closely. He remembered the image well enough, although he'd never been sure exactly where it was taken. He did notice, however, that the print was new, which was interesting because it might indicate that Rivers's dossier had only recently been assembled. He wondered whether they would produce even newer pictures of him speaking to Tomas Rath in New York. Was the boy part of this too? Was he an attempt to ascertain for certain his relationship with Eva Houresh? If that was so, what could possibly explain his call an hour before? Harland found no answers, but deep down he was convinced that Rivers and Blanchard were,

135

despite their self-assuredness, somehow uncertain of what they were doing. He returned to focus on Rivers.

'Over the ten years between 1980 and 1990 you are known to have cooperated with Kapek and his associate Milos Hense, a diplomat working in the Czechoslovak embassy in Vienna. Contacts in this period between you and Kapek and his intermediary were frequent and helped to build incremental understanding in the StB of Western signals and human intelligence. There is every reason to conclude that in your role as *Lamplighter* you served the KGB in the same way.

'In May 1981, for example, you reported to Hense on your part in Operation Stormdrain, an exercise in feeding the KGB a number of false impressions about the defence capabilities of Britain and her allies. Two years later you confirmed the identities of foreign journalists in Poland who were members of Western intelligence agencies. There are numerous documented examples of your disclosure of Western efforts to penetrate political institutions among Warsaw Pact member states. One particular instance that catches the eye is your contact with Kapek in Ankara, Turkey in 1987 during which you alerted the Czechs to the presence of a woman named Ana Tollund in the Secretariat of the Praesidium. Ana Tollund was subsequently tried and executed as an American agent. I do not have to explain to you that her death was the direct result of the information you gave Kapek.'

For several minutes longer, Rivers continued to read out a litany of betrayal. Harland sat back in his chair taking care to cover the slight bulge in his trousers with his jacket. He remembered a word that Griswald used when confronted with weak material. 'Scuttlebuck,' he would say. 'It's all damn scuttlebuck, Bob.' The dossier was exactly what Harland would expect from an investigation that drew on secondary sources, not his original file in the StB archives. And they could never get hold of that because Alan Griswald had burned it in front of him in 1990 – a late Christmas present, he called it.

Even if by some fluke there was a copy of the StB file, Harland had always known that he would be able to defend himself against allegations of spying for the East. In every instance he could demonstrate that he fed them misleading information or intelligence, which he was certain had already reached them from other sources. As to Ana Tollund, he knew Kapek had simply cited her as a source because he was anxious to claim a part of what was deemed to be a famous StB coup against the West. Kapek was a lousy, gullible second-rater. When he didn't know something he made it up. Harland could account for everything – every sleight of hand, dodge and manoeuvre which enabled him to keep the Czechs at arm's length while at the same time maintaining loyalty to SIS.

He concluded that Rivers's dossier had been assembled from brief references to him in other files. He'd always known that he was bound to appear in Kapek's own file, in Eva's and in a few others. Destroying his own file hadn't eliminated the problem, but it made it a lot less acute. It was obvious now that SIS had gained access to the StB archive which he knew still existed in Prague with orders to get as much as they could on him and as quickly as possible. The photograph must have been located in Eva's file or some other part of the archive. Its existence was embarrassing and Harland had dreaded it being found. But now the moment had arrived he knew he could handle it.

'There you have it,' Rivers concluded after a few more sentences. 'The A to Z of your betrayal.'

Harland paused, then allowed a smile to spread across his face.

'I suppose you expect me to roll over now and throw myself on your mercy. But, of course, you know this is all crap. For a start, not one of those accusations is backed up by independent evidence gathered by SIS or the Security Service. I don't deny that I was enticed into an affair – a young man's mistake that I regretted for its lack of professionalism, rather than any threat it posed. But I can show that instead of leading me to betray the service, I used it to our advantage. I even told Jimmy Kinloch at the time, so you can see it wasn't any big secret.'

Blanchard let out an exasperated wheeze, but Harland continued, holding Rivers's eyes.

'What you have there is a lot of gossip from a couple of bottom-feeders who were desperate to impress their masters. They had to produce fortnightly reports and because they were mediocrities they filled them with bollocks. We all knew that and moreover we used that need for a constant supply of information against them. Walter Vigo even knew about Kapek. It was he who told me how and when to use him and I distinctly remember filing reports of my contact with both Kapek and Hense, which doubtless you have got tucked away somewhere. Men like Kapek were the interface of the time. It was how we engaged the enemy. We used them while they thought they were using us.'

'Yes, but few of our people were stupid enough to have their pictures taken with a known agent,' said Rivers, rallying to regain control over the proceedings. 'You compromised yourself and then your loyalty, Harland. I don't think you have grasped the seriousness of your situation. You are facing a very lengthy jail sentence.'

Harland regarded him with a combination of wonder and disdain. 'Oh, for goodness' sake! Any public prosecutor would laugh at this pile of shit. Where are the covert pictures of my meetings with Kapek and Hense, eh? Where are the copies of bank statements showing that I received payments? Where's evidence of my ideological conviction? The men and women that I have suborned in the course of working for the Czechs? The transcripts of telephone conversations? The grainy pictures of dead letter boxes?' Harland stopped and looked at Blanchard and Rivers in turn. 'You don't have a thing, except a lot of fantasy scraped from the bottom of a few files in Prague. I doubt whether you can even prove that Kapek and Hense exist.'

Blanchard blew air from one cheek into the other and revolved his wedding ring with a thumb and one chubby finger.

'Oh, I assure you we have all we need,' said Rivers. 'We can produce Josef Kapek and Milos Hense any time we choose. You are forgetting that when Vasily Mitrokhin's archive was smuggled out of the Soviet Union to the West, it was taken as evidence of de facto guilt. We wouldn't have any problem gaining a conviction, Harland.'

'The Mitrokhin material led to no prosecutions – a bit of cheap sensationalism in the newspapers, that's all.'

'But those people weren't serving SIS officers. It's an entirely different matter to unearth evidence of this behaviour in a member of SIS. We know everything, you see, and frankly we are unable to ignore such a serious crime. We even know that you attempted to destroy your own files during or after the Velvet Revolution.'

'For heaven's sake, I was in hospital. I'd been beaten up by the Czechs – the very people you say I was working for! Doesn't that strike you as utterly illogical? I mean, why would they beat me up if I had been serving them all those years? Did it not occur to you that I was held and tortured for the very reason that I had misled them? Tortured, you understand. How many SIS officers go through that?' He was shouting now. 'Almost immediately after being freed I received treatment for cancer – surgery and chemotherapy. So you see I was hardly in a condition to run around chasing bloody files. By the way, how do you think that's going to look in court?'

'We know about your problems, Harland,' said Blanchard.

'But the fact remains that you did try to destroy the evidence. Luckily, you didn't get everything.'

'Well, if you're so bloody confident, why don't you have me arrested and charged?'

'In due course, we will. You may take that as a certainty,' said Blanchard.

Harland rose. 'I'm going to leave, this is getting ridiculous.'

'I am afraid that won't be possible,' said Rivers, also getting up. 'We will speak in the morning when I'm sure you will view your situation more sensibly. What we want from you is a statement, an admission of your role with StB. Then we will decide what to do with you. But we do need this from you, Harland, and I would advise you to cooperate as fully as you can.'

Blanchard by now had pushed his chair back and was making for the door.

Harland's temper snapped.

'You keep me here one moment longer and tomorrow you will be answering for your actions to the Foreign Secretary and the head of the Joint Intelligence Committee. I'm not pissing around. I have an authority from the Secretary-General which effectively makes me his personal ambassador. That means you hold me here at your peril.'

'Oh, in what capacity do you represent the Secretary-General?' asked Blanchard with laboured sarcasm. 'The investigation of the world's sewage treatment plants? The distribution of electrical appliances in the developing nations? Do you have proof of your role, or must we take your word on it?'

'Just accept that it exists.' Harland wasn't going to give him the letter yet. Much better for them to get a call from Jaidi's office. He prayed Harriet had got through.

'We will see you in the morning, Mr Harland,' said Rivers, opening the door. 'In the meantime, I recommend that you think very carefully about your position.'

Harland sat down. A minute or two later, the two men who had picked him up at the airport came in and told him to follow them. They showed him into what looked like an army barracks bedroom a few doors along the corridor where Griffiths asked for his personal possessions. Harland handed him his wallet, passport and phone and said he had nothing else. Griffiths seemed to accept this.

He looked around the room. There was a small window, high above the bed, a table, a chair and a reading lamp. He supposed it had once been a storeroom. On the walls regular indentations indicated that shelves had risen from floor to ceiling. The room smelt as though it had been sluiced down with cleaning fluid.

He sat down in the cold, stale air and unscrewed the top of a bottle of mineral water, left on the table together with some sandwiches. He poured the contents into a paper cup, peeled the wrapper from the sandwiches, and consumed them automatically. When he'd finished he lowered himself on to the bed and shifted to his side. There was no pillow and his head was still sensitive to the touch. He wondered about Tomas's call. Was he all part of some ludicrously Byzantine plan of Vigo's? If he had been, they surely would have produced Tomas in some shape in the general slew of allegations. The fact that they hadn't mentioned him made his story a lot more believable. Then quite suddenly his mind switched off. He shut his eyes and fell asleep.

At about six in the morning he was aware of the door opening. It caught him in the very deepest sleep and a few moments passed before he realised that Vigo was standing in the doorway. He rubbed his eyes as Vigo moved into the room and switched on the table lamp, angling it in Harland's direction. Harland swore.

'For Christ's sake, turn that off. What the hell are you playing at?'

Vigo nudged the lamp so that the light bounced off the

wall and threw an aura around him. He sat down and stretched out a leg.

So, Vigo had come to hear his confession: Vigo, the cardinal confessor.

'I imagine that you've been contacted by the UN,' said Harland.

He didn't reply.

'You know bloody well that you can't keep me here. That stuff your stooges from Five threw at me was grotesque. Not a word of it will stand up in court.'

'A matter of opinion, Bobby, a matter of opinion.' Vigo sighed to underline the gravity of Harland's situation. 'You know, I always had my suspicions. There was something too good about you. You were too anxious to please, too controlled. I knew that wasn't your character. I knew that there had to be a reason for this façade. And that reason, of course, was guilt.'

Harland propped himself up.

'What's eating you, Walter? I don't want to trespass on your problems, but all this does seem rather panicky and amateurish for you. I mean, for Christ's sake, we all talked to those termites from the East, so why on earth are you hounding me now? What's got into you all of a sudden?'

'Because you're a traitor – a traitor who's squared his conscience with a lot of sanctimonious nonsense about working for the international community. That's why.' He stopped and looked despairingly at Harland. 'Do you know about the poetess Sappho? Perhaps I can tell you about her. You see, none of Sappho's poems has survived. There are just fragments of poems which were used in the teaching of grammar. So we have some sense of Sappho's genius and we know from contemporary accounts that she existed, but we do not have her work. That's more or less how I think of your case, Bobby. There's now only fragmentary evidence of your activities, but from those fragments we can deduce a great deal about your importance as an agent for the StB.'

Harland got up and straightened his jacket.

'Sit down. I haven't finished yet.' The tone was surprisingly harsh. For the first time it occurred to him that Vigo would have no compunction about killing someone. Wet jobs were what the Soviets used to call assassinations. Vigo wasn't above resorting to a wet job, he thought. But that wasn't the point now. Vigo wanted something, something that he believed Harland had inherited from, or shared with, Griswald.

And then Vigo confirmed everything Harland was thinking.

'Unless I see some sign of cooperation, Bobby, you are going to be put away. At the very least your career will be ruined. My own belief is that higher authorities will deem your crimes to be so serious and so persistent that there is no other course but to prosecute you.'

'I've told you, I am not in a position to give you anything.'

'Of course you are. Why would the Secretary-General ask you to investigate the crash if he wasn't certain there was something to investigate – i.e. that you possessed some special knowledge? What is that knowledge, Bobby? Why you? What qualifies you? The only possible knowledge that you could have must derive from Griswald. Griswald, the man who accompanied you to Prague in '89; the man you travelled with to New York; the man who was taking his big secret to the United Nations. It all goes back to Griswald, doesn't it?'

Harland listened, fascinated by the movements of Vigo's face in the shadows. 'You're losing your touch, Walter. From what you say, I gather the Secretary-General *has* called the Foreign Office. Judging by the hour of your appearance here, I guess he must have talked to the Foreign Secretary. That means you've been told to release me pretty damned sharp.'

He paused. 'So, Walter, if you don't mind, I'm going to get the hell out of here.'

He moved to the open door. Vigo put up a hand.

'You've got absolutely no idea what you're dealing with, Bobby – no idea at all.' He shifted in his chair, then turned his face up to Harland. 'As to this investigation into your activities, don't for one minute think that it's over. Your head's in the noose and we're not going to let go of the rope.'

Harland left him sitting in the room and walked towards some light spilling into the corridor from an office. A man he hadn't seen before handed him his things. 'Order me a cab,' Harland demanded, 'and put it on your account.'

Harriet had waited up all night for him. It was seven o'clock when he was dropped outside her house in St John's Wood, a large neo-Georgian affair which Harriet called nouveau-Georgian. He saw her through the window, as he crossed a gravel drive which had been silenced by frost. She was asleep over the kitchen table with her head resting on folded arms. He stretched over a well-barbered box hedge and knocked gently on the window with his knuckle. She awoke, dragged herself up from the table, and gave him a despairing smile.

Their closeness was surprising: there were eight years between them and they were different in practically every way. Where Harland was tall, dark and concise in his movements, she was short, fair and animated. Harriet positively leaked energy. While his face, as he had been told often enough by Louise, gave little away, hers flickered with change, sometimes settling into a look of intense, happy concentration. She smiled when she was thinking hardest, which was perhaps why so few saw her coming. She would listen with that smile, her eyes oscillating ever so fractionally as she processed information at a ridiculous speed. And then she would dispatch her opponent with a few lines of deft logic, her expression becoming, if anything, sweeter.

144

She unbolted the double door and reached up to Harland to kiss his cheek.

'Bobby,' she said. 'You have to stop this. I cannot take the endless anxiety surrounding your travel arrangements. You can't seem to get off a plane like a normal person. First this terrible crash and now bloody Walter Vigo is marching you off to secret locations. God, I remember him! He married Davina Cummings. What a pompous creep! I don't suppose he's improved with age. Still, I gather by your appearance that the call did the trick. They seemed pretty concerned when I explained the situation.'

'Yes, thanks, Hal. Did the boy turn up?'

'No, he didn't. Who the hell is he anyway? What's this all about?'

'It's a long story. Wouldn't you rather hear it all tomorrow – I mean later?'

'No, I can't stand the suspense any longer. I've waited up all night and now I want some explanation.'

'But it's Christmas Eve, haven't you got things to do?'

'Not now, I haven't. And anyway everything is done: presents bought and wrapped; meals prepared; husband overdosed on champagne and flirtation. Look, Bobby, I want to know what's been happening to you. I haven't seen you for five months, for goodness' sake. And if it hadn't been for some providence of which you're entirely deserving, my darling brother, I might never have seen you again. So you have to tell me everything now. Please, I can't wait.'

They went into the kitchen. Harriet made tea and slapped some ham and cheese between a couple of pieces of bread and put them into a children's sandwich toaster shaped like frog. Harland told her everything and the familiar tremor entered her eyes as she snatched at the story. When he told her about Tomas she gasped and put her hands to her mouth to suppress a giggle.

'I know this is all very serious, Bobby. But you've got to see it's funny. I mean, it's like *Twelfth Night*. Lost love, people being washed up on foreign shores, relations appearing out of the blue. "What country, friend, is this? This is Illyria, lady." That's where you are Bobby – Illyria.'

12

A CHRISTMAS PARTY

After calling Harland, Tomas decided not to wait for him at the address. Instead, he checked into a small tourist hotel in Bayswater where the Lebanese on the front desk seemed to be glad enough of the business and didn't ask him for an ID. A rowdy couple next door might have kept him awake, if he'd wanted to sleep, but he had a lot to do, preparing the two small computers and encoding them with information. As he worked, he wondered furiously how he had been traced to Flick's home. It was baffling. There was no question of him ever using the telephones at her apartment and he'd never so much as touched her laptop. That side of things was watertight. He'd always made sure that he was absolutely untraceable. Yet something must have led them there – a mistake in the past six months which had been seized upon very recently and resulted in Flick's death. His body convulsed with a shudder as he saw her again all trussed up and broken. He had thought of calling the police after he'd left, but realised that the manager of the shop was already concerned and that she would be found soon enough. He stopped working and slumped in the chair, thinking back over the past few months. Then it came to him. It must have been the parcel from Mortz.

Mortz was his contact in Stockholm – a friend, though they had never actually spoken or met. Well, perhaps they had once in a bar in Stockholm two years before, but neither of them was sure and he couldn't put a face to Mortz, neither had he the slightest idea of his identity, his job or his age. Mortz could have been a college professor or a computer freak. Tomas inclined to the former because there was something thoughtful and restrained about his communications – a seriousness of purpose, for want of a better expression. They were very different, he could tell that, and yet they'd become friends, companions in arms, partners in the big project. He often wondered why Mortz showed such zeal for their work, and once he asked him about his motives in a rather cautious e-mail. Mortz did not reply. For a week there was silence and then he came back with new information from one of the half-dozen or so disenchanted intelligence people he'd cultivated over the Net. Things were back to normal.

Tomas composed new short bursts of information. That was his side of things. All the infiltration channels had been dreamed up by him. He started by using the phone-in programmes that are the standard fillers of airtime in radio stations the world over and during the calls played a tape of the condensed, coded message. He finessed his procedure by attacking the broadcasting computer systems with a benign virus – a vehicle which carried the messages. It was surprisingly easy – like a mosquito biting a sedated elephant. The stations, about thirty in all, were never aware of what was going on, but Mortz and he were certain that the messages were reaching their targets, causing acute discomfort and alarm in various intelligence services.

Mortz's idea was to reveal how the agencies of five or six Western powers, which were notionally on good terms, were using their resources to spy on each other. It was, he said in one of his oblique missives, a very wasteful hypocrisy. That was the nearest he came to articulating any motive.

Tomas had to admit that he had been caught up by his own ingenuity almost as much as he relished the revenge.

The information which arrived in the package – the very last means of communication that anyone would suspect – gave him a great deal more to play with. It was like an archive of their operation but there was also much that was new in the package, much that concerned him personally.

It arrived one day back in September. Mortz had told him to expect something addressed to Mr J. Fengel. There was no flat number on the parcel so it had been delivered to the house and just left on the table in the hallway. Tomas reckoned that the only way anyone would know to go to that house was if Mortz had kept a record of the address. And that meant one thing: Mortz had been tumbled and somebody had gone through his things and found it. He reckoned this must have happened within the last ten days because he'd received a couple of messages from Mortz on the Sunday before he left London for New York. Yet since then two e-mails had gone unanswered. The question was, how had they found Mortz? How had they located a man whose whereabouts Tomas didn't even know?

Both of them had always understood there were risks, especially for Tomas because his role involved using the phone system. In fact, there had been a problem nine months before when an Internet café he'd used in Stockholm just once was inexplicably raided. That was when he decided to leave for Britain and lie low for a while. Then quite by chance he'd come across the perfect way of using the phones without being detected, and Mortz and he had started up again. He'd encoded the photograph he'd kept all these years with a new algorithm and let the virus vehicle loose on a small radio station in Germany.

Tomas imagined the picture being passed up an intelligence hierarchy and landing in someone's in-tray and their having to work out who were the people in the picture and why the photograph had been published in this unconventional manner. They would take it seriously because they appreciated what else had come to them in this way. There was a hint of this in the feedback Mortz got from his sources. Some of the agencies would be baffled by the photograph; others, like the British and Americans, would have no difficulty in identifying the man in the foreground. They wouldn't, of course, recognise Tomas who stood to the side of the main subject, but he hadn't censored the image as a matter of honour – as a matter of admission, he told himself. Not long after Mortz had said he had used the photograph again. He exchanged it for more valuable information with a former CIA agent – new material on the practices of the CIA and National Security Agency. Tomas had sent a second photograph to Mortz in coded form which they were planning to use at some stage, although Mortz had already exchanged this for information too.

He worked through most of the night, his mind dodging between incidents in his past, to Flick and to Robert Harland. He was almost feverish with thought and yet he was aware of a manic clarity of purpose. He had little time. He knew they must be very close to finding him. They'd tracked him down to Flick's place, forced her to give them the name he was using and almost certainly learned that he had left for the States. Perhaps that's why they weren't watching the house when he returned? Or was it because Flick's body lay inside? Maybe they assumed he'd fled for good and were now looking for him in the States.

He thought of the bar in Brooklyn where he'd talked to Harland. Jesus, what a terrible misjudgement that had been! How could he expect Harland to believe his story? Harland was a suspicious, unyielding person, not at all how his mother had described him. But it was seeing that other man in the reflection of the mirror which he thought of now. The same character who'd got out of the car at the end of Harland's street and shown such interest in the building had walked straight into the bar. It couldn't have been a coincidence. That's why he'd left immediately, even though he knew it would only confirm Harland's suspicions about him. He had caught something in Harland's voice when he spoke to him on the phone that night. He barely reacted to what he was saying. He had just given his sister's address and told him that he would be there. That was not what he needed now. He would go tomorrow and tell Harland how he had found Flick and force him to understand that he wasn't making any of this up.

At about five in the morning Tomas completed his work and ran through a few procedures to make sure the two small computers were working properly. Then he left the hotel, telling the night porter that he couldn't sleep and needed a walk. He knew very little about this part of London but he was certain of finding what he wanted and within a few minutes he noticed the familiar oblong shape by a wall at the end of the street. He decided it was in too prominent a position so moved on and came to a quiet road of large, private houses where he found another slightly bigger cabinet.

People pass these waist-high boxes every day in London without knowing what they contain. Indeed Tomas hadn't noticed them until he saw a telephone engineer open one up near Flick's flat. The man explained they were officially known as Primary Connection Points – the first stop on the way to the exchange for an area's telephones. Tomas instantly realised that it would be possible to utilise the lines inside if he could open the cabinet. While talking to the engineer, he had discreetly jerked out the universal key that was lodged in the door and put it in his pocket. Thereafter he had used the boxes whenever he wanted, connecting his computer at random to one of the lines for a few minutes. It meant he could send the coded messages virtually undetected.

Now he worked fast. He opened the box, placed the computer on top of the panels of wiring, so that it was pretty much hidden, and connected it to several different telephone lines. That way the computer would use a different phone line each time it automatically dialled out. He knew that by the time anyone happened upon the irregular wiring, the messages would be sent, the battery spent and the information on the drive wiped.

He repeated the procedure a few streets away with the second computer and then returned to the hotel, feeling exhausted and cold.

Harland slept until eleven o'clock, then rose and checked the messages on his cellphone. There was still no word from Tomas, but when he got downstairs Harriet showed him a report in the *Daily Telegraph* on the murder of a thirty-five-year-old flower shop owner from Hampstead named Felicity MacKinlay. She had been discovered in her flat by the manager of her shop. She had been bound, gagged and tortured before being shot through the head at close range, said the police. The officer leading the investigation believed there might have been some sexual implication for the murder but he did not rule out other motives.

He was anxious to interview a man named Lars Edberg, a Swede in his mid-twenties who had returned to Britain at about the time of her death. A surprisingly sketchy description of Edberg was given and the manager was quoted as saying that he knew very little about Edberg and only saw him when he sometimes dropped flowers off in the morning. The Swedish authorities revealed that Edberg must have been travelling on forged documents. No passport had been issued to a Lars Edberg in the last five years, not to a man in this age bracket at any rate.

Harland put the paper down without saying anything.

'Do you think he did it?' asked Harriet.

'No,' said Harland. 'I told you he called me last night. I don't think he would've done that if he was guilty.'

'Unless he wanted help and somewhere to hide.'

'Could be, but I don't think this lad is capable of it. You can make your own mind up if he comes here.'

'Well, it will certainly make a change to have a fugitive from justice for Christmas lunch.'

The noise of Harriet's three children reminded Harland that he needed to buy Christmas presents and he ordered a cab to go to Regent Street. As he crossed the driveway, Harriet flung open the kitchen window.

'Call your friends in the States – you know, Griswald's widow – and tell her not to use your e-mail address. Vigo's people must have copied everything on your computer last night. You can set up another address from here.'

Harland phoned immediately he caught a cab. Sally recognised his voice and said that her son would send the material – she used that neutral word rather deliberately, he thought – when Harland got in touch with a new address. She told him that Griswald would be buried in a few days' time and that there would be a memorial service early in the spring. She hoped he would come.

After he'd hung up he ran through the conversation and realised that she had not used his name. There was also something constrained in her manner. He supposed that she might simply be depressed at the prospect of facing Christmas without Al. But it was possible that there was another reason. Perhaps someone had been in contact with her, someone who wanted to know the precise nature of Alan Griswald's last investigation, and, being no slouch in these matters, Sally had suspected that her phone was no longer entirely secure.

In Regent Street Christmas crowds had already thinned, leaving a rump of male shoppers desperate to buy presents in the few hours that remained. He quickly acquired a cashmere sweater for Harriet in the Burlington Arcade, then bought a couple of biographies of entrepreneurs for his brother-in-law at Hatchards. It was outside the bookshop that he noticed two men hanging back in the street – a fellow in his thirties hovering near a phone box and a man in a parka who was looking in the window of an airline outlet on the other side of Piccadilly. What was interesting about both, apart from a marked lack of urgency, was that neither of them carried shopping bags. By the time Harland had reached Regent Street, he was certain he was being followed by a surveillance team.

Quite suddenly, as if he had just remembered something, he plunged into a clothes store named Cavet and Bristol, which was still quite crowded, and took the stairs to the outfitting department on the first floor. Then he immediately turned right into the lift and descended to ground level where, as he expected, he found the parka hood hesitating at the bottom of the stairs. Showing no concern, Harland strolled to a table where some ties were displayed and selected a couple. He took them over to the counter and proffered them to an Indian woman who was bent over a stocktaking form.

Without changing his expression, he informed her that he'd just seen the man with the parka place two lightweight pullovers under his jacket. For good measure, he added that he suspected the woman thumbing her way along a rail of men's casual wear was working with him. Harland had spotted her when he entered the shop and just now, as he'd turned from the tie counter, he had asked himself what woman shops for her man with only a few hours to go to Christmas?

The assistant picked up the phone and in a very short time the man and woman were being accompanied by security guards to a back office. The man protested, wrenching his arms free of the security guards. But they caught hold of them more firmly and led him away. Harland nodded a smile of seasonal goodwill to the assistant and slipped away, somehow failing to hear her plea that he should stay and make a statement about what he had seen.

He soon completed the rest of his purchases and caught a cab back to St John's Wood. A palpable stillness was settling over the city as the first carols from the service at King's College, Cambridge came from the cab driver's radio. Harland thought of his father and a Christmas Eve twenty years ago when they went together to midnight mass in a big echoing church that rose above the Fens, half a mile from the family home. He could just hear the carol he particularly remembered from that service above the noise of the cab's diesel engine. He looked out on the emptying streets and wondered where Tomas was.

He arrived back to find his brother-in-law supervising the placing of presents beneath a perfectly decorated Christmas tree. He was dressed in a long collarless black tunic and slippers embroidered with his initials. He greeted Harland with a handshake that involved a brief semi-hug. Harland remembered that Robin had taken to bestowing this on practically anyone who came within range, as a declaration of his openness and modernity. Robin made the children sit down and listen to what was a condensed version of the crash. When Harland finished, he jumped up and gave him another brief hug.

'It's good to have you with us,' he said, silencing Harland's youngest nephew, Conrad, who wanted to know how many dead bodies he'd seen.

The news that Harriet had forgotten to tell him was that fifty people – locals, as Robin put it – would descend on the house at six-thirty for Robin's traditional Christmas Eve drinks party. Harland went off and set up a new e-mail address in Harriet's little office, sent it to Sally Griswald's address, then made himself useful, setting out glasses and lugging cases of drink into the kitchen.

At the appointed hour several couples arrived at once, one

155

or two of them having been dropped off by chauffeurs. The party very soon reached critical mass and for a time Harland avoided making conversation by handing drinks round, although this was unnecessary since a couple of waiters had appeared from nowhere and the children were already scurrying between guests with opened bottles of champagne. Eventually he was snared by Robin who introduced him to a couple named Lambton.

'He's the celebrity of the evening – the only survivor of the La Guardia crash. You'll have seen his photograph in the papers last week. We're very lucky and pleased to have him with us.'

The woman, a psychologist of some sort, goggled at him and, after listening to an even shorter account of the crash, urged Harland to find some counselling. The man looked on indulgently while his wife got closer and closer to Harland. When she drew breath, Lambton told him that he was in property and often visited New York. Could Harland advise him where to stay? He was tired of The Pierre and wanted somewhere younger and fresher.

'To take his girlfriends to,' chipped in his wife, with a high nervous laugh.

Harland's eyes drifted across the room to a pretty woman in her early forties who was talking to Harriet. At that moment Harriet revolved and beckoned furiously, which allowed Harland to excuse himself from the Lambtons.

'This is Anne White,' she said when he reached them, 'now divorced from one of Robin's partners. Anne has been telling me that she's going to dinner with Luke Hammick and his wife, around the corner, but that they are coming here first. Guess who else they're having to dinner this evening?'

Harland shrugged good-naturedly.

'Davina and Walter Vigo. And even better news is that the Hammicks are proposing to bring the Vigos here beforehand for a quick drink. You and Walter will be able to catch up on old times.'

Anne White looked on with interest, trying to fathom the underlined nature of Harriet's delivery.

Harland muttered, 'Don't worry, Hal, he can't come.'

'Oh, but you're quite wrong,' she said brightly. 'In fact, they're here now.' She left with a whispered, 'Bloody brass neck.'

Harland turned and saw a couple in the doorway being greeted by Robin who was bobbing furiously. Beyond them he could see Walter Vigo in the hall talking to one of the children. The sight struck him as bizarre. Children weren't part of Vigo's universe. Indeed, Walter Vigo at a Christmas party seemed an odd idea. Vigo looked up and caught sight of Harland and, without changing his expression, nodded imperceptibly. Harland turned back to Anne White.

'So you're a spy,' she said with a challenging smile.

Harland shook his head.

'You must be if you work with Walter Vigo. Everyone knows he's something important in the Foreign Office, which means spook in any language.'

'I don't work with Walter Vigo,' he said. 'I look at water pipes for a living.'

She continued with one or two more flirtatious sallies. Harland smiled down at her and parried a little.

Soon the children were lined up in front of the Christmas tree with two friends and required to sing a carol. Robin stood, hands clasped in front of him in frozen applause. When they had finished he turned to his guests with a wide grin, which Harland guessed had concluded many advertising presentations, and wished everyone a happy Christmas. He coughed once and added, 'We are also much relieved this year to have Bobby, Harriet's peripatetic brother, staying with us. As some of you may know, Bobby only last week escaped a terrible air crash in New York. He was the sole survivor and, as you can see, has managed to make the journey here to be with his family for Christmas. Bobby, we thank providence for your survival.'

Harland smiled and thanked Robin, although he heartily wished him dead.

Anne, who had been watching him, said, 'You're wondering why on earth your brilliant sister married him, aren't you?' She paused to take a drag on a thin cigarette. 'The answer is that he isn't threatened by her. Of course he's completely ludicrous in every way, but he's also very kind.'

'Yes,' said Harland.

'You know she's made an awful lot of money while looking after those kids, don't you?'

'No, I didn't.' He was genuinely interested.

'She's been trading on the stock market. Made her own little investment fund with various people's savings, although I don't think she actually took control of the money. That would be deeply on the wrong side of the law. Robin tells me she made two hundred thou' last year. Clever ole sis, huh?'

'Yes, clever ole sis,' said Harland. He watched Harriet weave towards Davina Vigo – who was plainly unaware of any difficulty – and thought glumly how little he knew of his sister.

Once or twice he could feel the weight of Vigo's gaze but turned to find him looking away into the middle distance. His presence didn't quite create a stir but everyone in the room was aware of him, even if most had not the slightest idea who or what he was.

The party swelled so that it became difficult to move in Harriet's sitting room and many guests spilled into a large conservatory area – the sort of sunroom that the English build without knowing what it should be used for. By now Harland and Anne had been joined by a lawyer with a blotchy skin named Deakin, who was clearly struck by Anne. Harland took a back seat in the conversation and wondered what precisely Vigo wanted. What was he afraid of? When he'd told Harriet the whole story she despaired of finding a unified theory of everything, as she put it. Sometimes, she said, you had to accept that things were simply unrelated.

Suddenly Harland became aware of Vigo moving in the side of his vision. He turned to find him making his way through the crowd, his mouth wearing a friendly smile, although his eyes told a different story. Anne made a tactful withdrawal, steering Deakin away into what he took for promising intimacy.

'Yes, Walter?' said Harland with quiet hostility. 'Have you come to apologise for that crap last night?'

'No. I just wanted to explain that this was sprung on us when we got to the Hammicks. I really had no option but to come.'

'But now you're here, you're quite happy to case the joint. I assume you already have this house watched.'

'Believe what you like Bobby, but I can assure you that's not true.'

Harland was aware of someone calling his name above the noise of the party. He looked round to see one of the waiters heading towards him after being given directions from Mr Lambton. At the same moment he saw Harriet with an alert expression making her way from another point in the room. The waiter got to him first.

'Mr Harland? There's a gentleman to see you. He's at the door. Says he won't come in.'

Vigo's eyes settled with interest on the waiter. Harriet arrived.

'Is there something wrong?'

'No, madam, there's a young gentleman to see Mr Harland. He's at the front door.'

'Oh,' said Harriet, without looking at Harland. 'That must be the Smithsons' boy, Jim. He's just left the LSE and I told them you might be able to get him something at the UN.

Why don't you go and ask him in for a drink, Bobby?' She placed a hand on Vigo's forearm. 'Davina's just been telling me how you took her for a surprise weekend in New York. I wish Robin would think of things like that.'

Yes, Harland thought as he left them, a surprise visit arranged instantly Vigo heard about the crash. That meant that Vigo wasn't on official business? He threw a glance in their direction as he reached the hall and saw that Harriet had shepherded three or four people into a group round Vigo, trapping him in the conservatory. She meanwhile had detached herself and by the look on her face was planning to follow him.

Tomas was waiting for him in a recess by the front door which acted as a cloakroom. He was plainly overawed by the size of the house.

'Jesus,' said Harland, 'you look terrible. Where have you been? Why didn't you come before now?'

'I stayed in a hotel. I had work to do.'

'Work! Look, this friend of yours – Felicity MacKinlay. You know the police are looking for you?'

'Mr Harland, I did not do this thing. You must believe me.'

'Yes I do. But you must talk to them.'

Tomas produced his crestfallen look.

'You don't understand. That's impossible. This is too complicated, too dangerous.'

'What's too complicated, for Christ's sake? You have to start talking, Tomas. Enough of this damned mystery. Why the hell did you leave that bar in New York?' Harland could hear himself. He sounded very much like a father.

Several people passed on their way out and threw rather puzzled looks in Tomas's direction. Harriet came into the hall, closed the door behind her guests and turned towards Harland.

'Look, you can't stay there. Walter Vigo is about to come out any moment.'

'Who is Walter Vigo?' Tomas asked both of them.

'He is a former colleague of Robert's and I don't want him to see you here, particularly with all that was in the papers this morning. You can go upstairs if you like and wait there until the party is over.'

Tomas picked up his bag. Then something seemed to occur to him.

'Mr Vigo is in the intelligence field, as you were?'

'Yes,' said Harland hastily. 'My sister is right. Why don't you go upstairs?'

'I don't think I should remain here with him in the house. I will come back. No, I will call your phone and tell you where to meet me.'

'Give it an hour,' said Harland. 'Do you need any money?'

'No,' said Tomas with a brief, shy smile to Harriet, who simply shook her head. 'I have money, Mr Harland.'

'Ah, there you are,' came a voice behind them. It was Davina Vigo and the Hammicks with Walter Vigo bringing up the rear. Harland saw him look over his wife's shoulder with interest at Tomas disappearing through the front door. But his view was blocked by Harriet reaching up to kiss his wife and then each of the Hammicks.

'What a lovely party,' said Davina. 'You must come to supper very soon in the New Year. I will get Walter to look at his diary.'

Harland and Vigo exchanged looks. The Hammicks and Vigos made for a Mercedes which had pulled into the gravel crescent at the sign of Davina Vigo waving a small purse through the open door. There was no sign of Tomas.

Harriet closed the door behind them, swivelled her eyes and blew out her cheeks.

'Why does he call you Mr Harland? Aren't you on better terms than that yet?'

161

Harland exhaled. 'He refuses to use any other name until I accept him totally. But I've only spent a couple of hours with him. How am I meant to react?'

'Well, I think you had better get used to him calling you something else. Bobby, he couldn't be anyone else's child. He's a dead ringer for you when you were that age – all gangly and intense. There's no question about it. He's yours.'

13

CLEOPATRA'S NEEDLE

Harland's phone rang at 9.45 p.m. but it wasn't Tomas. Instead, he heard some paper being shuffled and then the voice of Agent Frank Ollins.

'Ah, Mr Harland. I'm glad I've tracked you down. Is this a bad moment?'

'Could be better,' replied Harland.

'It won't take long, sir. There are just a few more questions I want to ask you about the period immediately before the crash.'

Harland slapped his forehead with annoyance. The last thing he wanted to do was block up his line. He was sure this could wait.

'Okay,' he said, 'but I may have to interrupt you. I'm expecting an important call.'

'At this hour? It's nearly Christmas Day with you, right?' said Ollins sceptically. 'Look, I want to take you through the last part of the flight. Can I remind you of the account you have given us so far?' He paused. 'Fifteen minutes out of La Guardia you get up out of your seat to go to the bathroom. Is that correct?'

'Yes.'

'At that moment the cabin lights are extinguished and you return to your seat?'

'Yes.'

'Then you notice that the heating in the cabin seems to be malfunctioning – it's gotten damned cold.'

'That's right,' said Harland wearily.

'The lights did not return before the crash?'

'No, they didn't. Look, is this relevant? I mean, does it have any bearing on the crash?'

'Hold on there, Mr Harland. This is important. We need to take this slowly. To answer your question – no, the lighting and heating systems are not directly relevant. We can see at what point they failed on the flight data recorder and there appears to be nothing to connect those two failures with the eventual destruction of the airplane. Does that answer your question?' He paused. 'Now, as I recall it, you said that as you were coming in to land, Mr Griswald held up his laptop computer and used the light from the screen to see what he was doing. You mentioned you could see his face in the light of the computer. It's here in the transcript of your first talk with me and Clark last week.'

'Yes, I remember that well.'

'In what way did he hold the computer up?'

Harland tried to remember.

'I think he held it up several times but I don't know what you mean by what way.'

'I mean, how did he hold it to maximise the light coming from the screen?'

'Well, at least once he held it up to see his seat belt and then I think he held it up several times to see how the table was folded away and to gather his possessions together. Are you suggesting that the computer being on might have interfered with the aircraft's systems?'

'I'd rather you let me ask the questions. But no, I'm not. Let me go over this again. First, did he hold the computer up as though he had simply raised it from the table, i.e. with the keyboard still horizontal?'

'I'm not sure, it was dark. It wasn't easy to see.'

'Is it possible that Mr Griswald turned the computer and held it like a book so that the hinge was vertical, that is to say that the screen and keyboard were also in the vertical plane? It would make more sense if you were using the light from the screen to see what you were doing, would it not, Mr Harland?'

'Yes, it's entirely possible that he held it that way. I guess he must have done so at some stage.'

Harland saw Griswald holding the computer, a cumbersome affair which he realised was protected by a special cladding.

'And he was holding it out in front of him, not to the side of his body or above his head?'

Harland sensed that he was on a speakerphone. There was the noise of someone moving beyond Ollins's voice. 'Yes, I'd say he held it out in front of him for a time although he must have moved it around a little to see what he was doing.'

'And you're sure about that?'

'As sure as I can be.'

'Thank you.'

'Can I ask what this is about?'

'We're just looking into every aspect of the crash – testing a few theories, that's all. Happy holidays, Mr Harland.'

'Wait a moment! I thought we had an agreement to share information through Kennedy at the UN. Can you tell me a little more?'

'I don't know what you're referring to. But if there was such an arrangement, that would surely take in your visit to the South of France yesterday. I don't remember you calling me about that, although what you learned may have a direct bearing on this crash.'

'Okay, what about a trade?'

'I'll think about that while I'm eating my Christmas cake.'

Harland tried another tack. 'Did you find the computer?'

There was silence while Ollins mulled this over. 'Well, I'll give you this one for free. Yes, we found the computer on the other side of the runway.'

'Was it burned?'

'No.'

'So you've learned what's on it.'

'No, the hard drive's all knocked to shit.'

This stumped Harland. What was the point of all these questions about the computer if it neither represented a threat to the plane's electronic systems nor provided any useful information about Griswald's activities?

'But you still think the computer is important?'

'Could be. We're just going over everything here, winding down for a day's R and R.' He paused. 'Oh, there was one other thing. Can you confirm that you removed the cellphone from Mr Griswald's breast pocket? You imply this in the transcript but do not actually state it.'

'Yes, it was in his inside pocket.'

'Would that be the right or the left breast pocket?'

'His right.'

'That makes sense. Mr Griswald was a left-hander. I guess he'd tend to favour the right-hand inside pocket.'

Just then Harland was alerted to an incoming call on his line by a series of beeps. 'Look, I've got to go.'

'That's okay. I still got plenty to do here. We'll talk after Christmas.' With that he hung up and Tomas's call came through automatically.

'Mr Harland?'

'Yes. Tomas,' he said, 'would you just accept that I accept that everything you've told me about your birth is true – okay? So call me something else. Right, where are you now? I'll come and meet you.'

'Be careful not to be followed. It was foolish of me to come to your sister's house. I was worried they were watching it.'

'Well, don't worry. The party was exceptionally good cover – a lot of people coming and going.' Then Harland thought about what the boy had just said. He couldn't possibly know about Vigo's people following him. 'Tomas, who do you think could be watching you?'

'The same people who tortured and killed Flick. The people who will kill me, if they find me.'

'Who are they? Why in heaven's name would anyone want to kill you?'

'It's a long story. I will tell you everything later. I will be at Cleopatra's Needle in half an hour. You haven't forgotten where it is?' he asked, and hung up after Harland said he knew precisely where it was.

He put the phone in his pocket and thought back twenty-five years and wondered whether he was on the point of understanding everything.

He went and found Harriet who was looking after a few stragglers at the party. He took her aside and whispered. Harriet smiled and briskly announced to the group that she was going to take her brother to midnight mass and would therefore be happy to drop off anyone who needed a ride home. Even the most determined couldn't fail to shift after her unambiguous hint.

It was Harland's particular request that Harriet should not bring her RV round to the front of the house, so they all had to file through the kitchen to the garage. He took the middle of one of the rear seats, having insisted that the love-struck Deakin sit in the front. As the garage door opened and the car moved out into the drive, he slid right down into his seat so there was no chance of him being spotted leaving the house.

After four stops they were left alone in the car. Harriet said she was sure she hadn't been followed, but to be on the safe side he told her to turn into the entrance of a large mansion block which was obscured from the road by a hedge. Harland opened the door and hopped out while the car was still moving. He waited a little time after Harriet had disappeared and then headed in the direction of Baker Street tube station.

He arrived at Victoria Embankment just before eleven o'clock and left the tube station by the north exit. Some way off he could hear the rumble of music from one of the clubs in the bowels of Charing Cross station. He walked quickly to a run of short railings on the right of the street and, placing his hand on the top, vaulted over into Embankment Gardens. Nothing much had changed in the twenty-five years since he'd last been there – the layout of the gardens was more or less the same and the gates which led onto the embankment had not been changed. He knew they were easily scaled. He moved quickly to the south side where he waited for a while. He could just make out Cleopatra's Needle from where he stood behind the gates, but he would have to get closer to see if Tomas had arrived.

He questioned why he was being so careful – after all, no one could possibly know where they intended to meet. Maybe, he thought, this tension was prompted by memories of when he'd come as a young man with a mixture of hope and dread to meet Eva. He'd taken ridiculous precautions not to be followed that day, applying the skills recently acquired during training at the Fort and, no doubt, looking rather foolish. All the business of doubling back on himself and popping in and out of pubs had caused him to be late. And when he got there Eva was nowhere to be seen. He'd waited and waited, then circled the area until nightfall. She never came. He obsessed about being late, although it had only been a matter of fifteen minutes – twenty at the most – and he imagined that she thought she'd been stood up. He expected her to call him later. But not a word came.

Grasping the spikes at the top of the gate, he climbed up the railing until he could place both feet on the top bar, and let himself down the other side. The gates stood back from the main boundary of Embankment Gardens so he could drop down without being seen. He glanced towards the obelisk and then back down the embankment to Hungerford Bridge, where two policemen stood drinking coffee by their car. The traffic was very light and there was almost no one about. He waited while his eyes ran over the scene. Then he made his move across the road and walked sharply along the river wall, noticing that the tide was low. The wind carried a faint smell of mud to his nostrils and his mind flipped back to the East River.

As he approached the first of the pair of huge bronze sphinxes that guard Cleopatra's Needle, he realised he'd forgotten nothing about the place. He found himself recalling its history – the hazardous journey across the Bay of Biscay when six men lost their lives; how the scars and pockmarks around one of the sphinxes had been left to commemorate the very first air raid by German aeroplanes on London in 1917; and the fact that the granite obelisk had been carved nearly one and a half thousand years before Cleopatra was born. Myth attributed the obelisk to Cleopatra although it was doubtful whether she had even laid eyes on it, unless she had happened to see it raised at Alexandria, a few years before Christ's birth and her own death. But Harland dwelled on that myth and as his search for Eva went on he had gradually merged Eva and Cleopatra into a single, mythic nemesis.

'Age cannot wither her,' he murmured to himself as he touched the flank of the sphinx, 'nor custom stale her infinite variety . . . She makes hungry where most she satisfies: for vilest things become themselves in her.'

He knew too much about the damned needle and it reminded him of the obsessed, cocksure young intelligence officer who thought he had all the answers.

He walked round the end of the sphinx to look over a short flight of steps, to the wide stone platform that projects from the line of the embankment into the Thames. There was no sign of Tomas so he moved past the obelisk to the second sphinx, whereupon he stopped and peered again. Nothing. He looked up and down the road as a shoal of seven or eight cars was released by the traffic lights a little further to the east, and then mounted the steps that led to the platform. He found him hidden, sitting on a ledge directly beneath the monument. He called out to him but Tomas didn't turn. He had his hands over a pair of earphones and he was staring down the river towards Waterloo Bridge and the illuminated cupola of St Paul's Cathedral.

Harland moved in front of him and placed a hand on his shoulder. He noticed that the stone was covered with a thin film of mud so he sat down beside Tomas and lifted his feet to the ledge. He was about to say something but was silenced by the view. He had never imagined London could be so still. Even the city's permanent background hum of traffic had faded with the approach of Christmas Day.

'So,' he said, 'what are we going to do about all this?'

Tomas looked at him. He was shaking a little and his face was pinched with cold, like the first time Harland saw him.

'What if my mother had come here that day? Would I have been born, I wonder? Would I have grown up with you as my father? Would I have lived in London? Would Flick be alive today? I was thinking about those things.'

Harland opened his hands in a gesture of helplessness.

'I don't know the answers to all that,' he said. 'But I'm certain that you should now tell me everything you've held back from me. Then we can decide what we're going to do about them. Maybe we should call your mother and get things straightened out.'

'I have not talked to my mother in two years.'

'Why not?'

'Because she deceived me about my father, because I could

not talk to her about the things I had seen and done – things that I cannot talk to you about, Mr Harland.'

'Call me Bobby, for heaven's sake. I'd find it a lot easier.'

'Bobby,' he said bleakly.

'Spit it out,' said Harland gently. 'Sooner or later you're going to have to talk to the police and tell them what you know about Flick's killers. Otherwise, they're going to think you had something to do with it.'

'Well, I did. I did cause her death, just like I caused the death of the man in Bosnia.'

'Bosnia? Why the hell are you talking about Bosnia?' His mind was flooded with all kinds of connections, but he wasn't going to push things. He told himself to allow Tomas to speak in his own time.

It had begun to spot with rain. Tomas got up, walked to the parapet and turned to Harland. He was about twenty feet away and reduced almost to a silhouette by the three floodlights that were ranged along the top of the parapet to light the obelisk. Harland watched the raindrops fizz on the floodlights and waited for his son to speak.

'It all begins here,' said Tomas, throwing out his hands. 'Everything in my life begins here. Tell me, is there somewhere like that in your life, Bobby, some very significant place?'

'Yes,' said Harland after a while. 'Here.'

'How strange that is.' There was a hint of a smile in his voice.

Suddenly his hand jerked upwards and he staggered forward. Then his body folded like a hinge at the abdomen and he was pushed back with a terrible force. Harland's mind took in two further shots. One hit the middle floodlight and caused it to explode; the second cracked into the parapet about a foot from where Tomas's head had come to rest. He flung himself forward to Tomas's body. Another shot came and ricocheted with a long whine between the parapet and the obelisk. He looked at Tomas and in an instant knew he was dead.

He scuttled back crab fashion to the steps which on his side were ten deep, as against the six on the other. He edged into the shadow of the obelisk and peeped over the top step. A flash in the shrubbery across the road told him the gunman's position. But he didn't register the sound of the shot, just the burst of mud and stone some fifteen feet behind him. He looked again. There was a slight disturbance in the bushes. The gunman was leaving. Maybe he was coming after him.

He crawled back to Tomas and looked down into his lifeless face. There was a mass of blood pooled by a wound in his throat and he appeared to have been hit in the stomach also. Harland felt the uninjured side of his neck where there wasn't a trace of a pulse. So he picked up a hand and fumbled beneath the cuff of Tomas's jacket. There was something, a very faint flicker of life, although he wasn't sure whether he was feeling his own racing pulse.

He looked up again and saw a movement. Someone was running across the road. Maybe there were two of them. He crouched down again and made for the gap in an iron railing which allowed access to a steep flight of steps running down to the river. He could see in the light from the street that their surface had been greased to a treacherous finish by the tide. He lunged to his left, found the handrail and plummeted down the steps, slipping and falling, but never quite losing his grip on the handrail.

He had some notion that he would be able to escape along the sandbank which was showing at the edge of the water into the shadow of the embankment wall. But that idea ended with the snapping fire of a different type of gun behind him and a sudden, livid pain in his shoulder. His hand instinctively released the handrail and he fell forward, somehow managing to propel his weight around the corner of the massive Victorian stone buttress and into utter dark.

He was convulsed with pain, but he was certain his wound wasn't serious. For one thing he could still clench and unclench the fist of his right hand. He hugged the wet stone, clinging to the crevices with his fingernails, and waited for his breath to subside. He strained to work out what was going on thirty feet above him, but the groans of an old pleasure boat buffeting against the wooden piles nearby made it impossible to hear. He waited. There was a brief sound of a siren and the squeal of tyres. More gunfire. Then right behind him there came a sloshing noise and a voice croaked in the dark, 'Hey, you! What's happening up there?'

He swung round to find a dim torch a couple of feet from his head and beneath it a very old face, much of it covered by a grey beard. The torch appeared to be part of some kind of headgear because every time the face moved the torch did. Harland was aware of a fretful pair of eyes looking at him.

'Get that light off,' he said under his breath, 'unless you want to get killed.'

A hand reached up and switched off the torch. 'What's going on up top?'

'Someone's been seriously injured – my son. Who the hell are you?'

'Saint George,' said the figure, apparently unconcerned by the news. 'Cyril St George – mudlark. This is my patch. Been here twenty-two years. Before that in Southampton – under the old pier there. Maybe you know it.'

Harland didn't reply. He realised that the old man must work the riverbank at low tide for coins.

'Can you get me out of here?' he said. 'I've been hit.'

'Not for a few minutes, I can't. Wait for the tide, because sure as eggs is eggs it won't wait for you.' He switched the lamp on and looked at a watch pinned to one of his many outer garments. 'Five minutes or so and we should be all right. Good conditions this evening. Couldn't miss a tide like tonight's.'

They waited without speaking, the old man's breath rasping in Harland's ear.

'Right, let's be having you,' he whispered, and took hold of Harland's left hand and placed it on the hem of some very coarse material. 'Don't lose your grip and follow me. If I take off into the current, don't be afeared. I know what I'm doing down here – I should do after all these years.' He coughed a laugh.

They set off and edged along the wall immediately below the obelisk in about a foot of water, then turned right so they were wading across the current.

Harland wondered why the old man didn't carry some sort of stick but he seemed to know his way. They moved out of the shadow of the wall into a part of the riverbank where there was more light. In the shallower areas he could see a number of weighted traffic cones which he guessed the old man had appropriated to serve as markers when the tide was not fully out.

'Nobody can see you down here,' he said. 'You think they can, but they can't. Don't you go straying now.'

They stopped while Cyril St George caught his breath.

'Guns!' he said with contempt. 'I find a lot of guns in here. They throw them in the river after they done their shooting and they 'spect them to stay put. But the tide brings them to me and I take 'em straight to the police. It's not just guns I find down here. Saint George knows where to look, see, and he finds rings and jewellery and very many ancient artefacts. And I see bodies. The suicides and murder victims all come past my bank.'

Harland could barely take this in. His shoulder was burning and it required all his concentration to stand still in the water without crying out. They set off again, tacking slowly towards a pontoon which was moored about a

174

hundred feet ahead of them. The water was getting deeper and Harland felt the combined strength of the outgoing tide and the flow of the river. The tugging and sucking at his legs took him back to the East River and he wondered whether this time the water would win. Twenty feet from the pontoon the old man stopped.

'You're on your own now, son. It'll go over my waders if I carry on. I'll wait down here until the coast is clear, then take the steps.'

Harland edged round the old man and went ahead, struggling to control himself. He was certain that at any moment he would put his foot down and find nothing and be swept away. Such was his fear that he had difficulty in committing himself to each step, but the old man urged him on until he was within a few yards of the pontoon. He made out a metal ladder fixed to the end but saw that the pontoon was rising and falling with the swell of the river. He realised he would have to time his launch so as to catch the bottom rung before it rose out of reach. He watched the pontoon and tried to accustom himself to its motion, all the while hearing the sounds of the water reverberating in its huge buoyancy tanks. As the ladder reached the zenith of its climb, he dived forward praying that he'd meet it on its way down. A few desperate strokes and he caught the rung with his good hand just as his legs were being dragged under the pontoon. The whole structure reared upwards with the next wave, pulling him out of the water like a bottle cork. A few seconds later and he had clambered up the ladder and was sprawling on the deck of the pontoon.

'Go on my son,' came the voice behind him.

Now the only thought in Harland's mind was for Tomas. He ran the length of the pontoon, climbed the gangway to the bank and scaled the padlocked gates at the end. He couldn't see any movement around the obelisk, but a police car was slewed across the carriageway on the far side of the road. Its blue light was flashing and both doors were open. Only when he reached Cleopatra's Needle did he see the bodies of the two policemen lying in the road. A car had just pulled up behind their vehicle and the driver was standing in the road speaking into his mobile. Harland shouted that there was another badly injured person on his side of the road, then leapt over the steps. Tomas was where he had left him. He knelt down and felt for the pulse again. He'd been right. There *was* something. A flicker of life.

He ripped off his own shirt, bunched some of the material together and held it against the neck wound with his right hand. At that point he realised that he himself had bled profusely. While he pressed the bandage home, he felt his own back with his free hand and located a shallow gouge aross his shoulder blade to the upper arm. He returned his fingers to Tomas's wrist, willing the pulse to continue.

They operated on Tomas for six hours, extracting a bullet from his stomach without much difficulty and patching the wound where a second had passed clean through his shoulder. But the greater proportion of that time was spent on a delicate procedure to remove a bullet lodged in his brain stem, the area at the base of the brain which leads to the spinal cord. The shot had been deflected off a metal clasp on Tomas's jacket and passed through his throat into his brain.

While Harland was being treated one of the surgeons came to see him to explain what they were doing. She said it was touch and go because Tomas had lost a lot of blood. At this Harland suddenly jerked up from the bed he was lying on. He'd remembered his own blood group which he had inherited from his father. Rhesus-null was one of the rarest in the world and the point about it – as he had discovered before his cancer operation – was that it clashed with O negative, which was used as a match-all in emergency operations. He told the woman that this might be a possibility. She looked at him strangely, then phoned through to the operating theatre.

As Christmas Day dawned, Tomas was placed in intensive care. The surgeon returned together with a distinguished-looking man in his fifties, who the nurses had informed Harland was Philip Smith-Canon, a leading neurosurgeon. The specialist introduced himself and asked Harland if he'd like some coffee in a nearby office.

'So I gather from the blood group of the patient that you're next of kin.'

Harland shook his head.

'I will be tracing his mother in the Czech Republic. It would be better if you regard her as his next of kin.'

Smith-Canon looked puzzled, but decided to ignore it.

'I ask because there are likely to be some difficult decisions to take over the next ten days or so. The patient is in an extremely serious condition and even if he survives the immediate threat to his life from this bullet and pulmonary infections, he is likely to face severe disability.'

'What do you mean exactly?'

'If you were to press me, I'd say it's probable that he will suffer total paralysis and lose the ability to communicate. I'm sorry to be so blunt but I cannot hide that the prognosis is very poor. This kind of injury is the equivalent of a brain-stem stroke or a serious tumour in that region of the brain. Whatever the etiology, that is to say the cause, we can predict the outcome with a relatively small margin of error. He's still at considerable risk, of course, but he's young and strong which may mean he'll live to regain consciousness.'

His voice softened. 'Mr Harland, he will wake to experience quadriplegia, mutism and facial paralysis, which may include the ability to blink. This is only half of it. There'll be numerous smaller symptoms, respiratory problems, altered breathing patterns, involuntary movements of the face, incontinence of bladder and bowel. You understand what

177

I'm saying? We're talking about a state of extreme privation, fear and discomfort. But inside he will be aware of what's going on and able to think normally.'

'There's never any chance of better recovery than that?'

'Not in my experience. The trauma suffered in his brain stem was very considerable and although he may not experience all the symptoms I describe, essentially my prognosis is right.'

'I see. But you knew this when you were operating to remove the bullet.'

'Not until we were well into the operation. But you have put your finger on something we must talk about and that's the question of resuscitation. There may be occasions over the next week or so when we will be faced with the decision of whether or not to continue to treat him. Often in these cases the patient is susceptible to pneumonia. That may be regarded – with the proper management – as a way out.' He paused and drank some coffee. Then he looked at Harland with genuine sympathy. 'I believe you to be his father, Mr Harland. I won't hazard at the reasons for your wish to hide this fact, but the blood group match is almost irrefutable evidence. There are questions which cannot be dodged. If your son lives there are enormous problems to be faced concerning specialised treatments and care. No person in this condition can live without round-the-clock attention.'

Harland thought for a moment.

'Look, as you have guessed, I am his father. I have known this for less than a week. The circumstances are extremely difficult to . . .' His voice faded. He felt almost drugged.

'How long is it since you've had a decent night's sleep, Mr Harland?'

'I can't think. Three days?'

'I suggest that you get some sleep soon.'

'Let me just finish. I was going to say that I cannot tell you why anyone would wish to kill Tomas, but I suspect that

178

there is a very evil man behind this shooting and the death of Tomas's girlfriend. It will help me greatly if you do not reveal that Tomas is my son.'

'You are asking me to lie?'

'No. If the police ask you, I would not want to prevent you from telling the truth. It's just that I don't believe that the police will ask you. After all, they have no reason to interview you.'

Smith-Canon nodded.

'Very well, I agree, and I will tell Susan Armitage, who came out with me just now, to do the same. But we will still need a next of kin to consult over the next few days. What of his mother?'

'I will try to trace her in the Czech Republic. But it's going to be difficult. She has changed her name several times.'

'I see,' said Smith-Canon.

'If I leave the country, I will put you in touch with my sister who will be able to get in touch with me wherever I am. Her name is Harriet Bosey.'

'Right, shall we agree on this, then – that your son remains here until he is out of immediate danger? I will then arrange for him to be transferred to my hospital and we will begin to assess the situation.'

Harland gave him his telephone numbers and dragged himself out of the chair. His arm still hurt like hell but the pain had faded as he learned of the true nature of Tomas's condition. He walked back down the hallway, away from the operating theatres, to where he knew the police would be waiting for him.

14

THE BITTER MADELEINE

Harland told two officers about the shooting and his escape along the riverbank. They said that one of the policemen had been killed, the other would recover but there was a likelihood of his not being able to walk again. After twenty minutes he began to feel faint. They called a doctor, who said he must have immediate rest, and he was driven to Harriet's house where two police guards were posted outside.

He slept until six-thirty that evening when Harriet woke him with a concise version of what had plainly been an elaborate Christmas lunch, which she brought to him on a tray. She didn't need to ask what had happened because she had learned all she wanted from the police guards to whom she had given lunch in the kitchen. There was also a detailed report on the evening news that made much of the tragedy of the young constable's death on Christmas Eve. Harland was sure there would be a lot more coverage. It would only be a matter of time before his name was released and someone linked him with the La Guardia crash. Then there was the connection to be made between the death of a young florist in a North London flat and the shooting of her boyfriend.

Robin joined them, stealing into the room with a stage tiptoe. He seemed genuinely horrified by the account of Harland's conversation with the surgeon and said that he would do anything to help with Tomas's care. All bills would be taken care of. Harriet touched him on the hand and smiled. In that instant Harland saw why their marriage worked.

'One thing bothers me,' she said, turning back to her brother. 'How did they trace you to the embankment? They must have followed you from here, I suppose.'

'No,' said Harland emphatically. 'They would have shot him outside the house, no matter how many people were around. They were obviously desperate to kill him.'

'Then they must have waited for you to join him before the shooting. After all, they'd tried to do away with you in New York.'

'That assumes a lot of things, the first of which was that they knew that it was me at Cleopatra's Needle. The second point is that they didn't make any real attempt to shoot me once I fled down those steps.'

'Not half, they didn't,' said Robin, looking at the bandage on his shoulder.

'No, I mean it. These were professional killers. If it had mattered to them, they would have gone after me.'

'But they saw or heard the police coming and made their getaway,' said Robin. 'So they couldn't chase after you.'

'No, that doesn't quite work either. The first shots were fired by a relatively quiet sniper's rifle. Only when they came across the road did they use a machine gun, which could be heard. That's what drew the attention of the police car. You see, I didn't hear its siren until I was on the riverbank.'

'What's all this add up to, then?' asked Robin.

'Bobby thinks that they haven't made the connection between him and Tomas,' said Harriet, 'or at any rate that they didn't identify him last night. That's right, isn't it, Bobby?'

'Yes.'

'But why didn't they shoot before you arrived?' said Harriet, then she clapped her hands and answered her own question. 'Because they had only just got there themselves!

And that's interesting, Bobby, because although they had only just arrived they knew enough about the meeting to position themselves across the road in that park. Right? And that can mean only one thing: they'd listened to the phone call that Tomas made to you. So, if we assume that they didn't know who he was calling – and we've already agreed that there are good reasons to suppose that – it means they must have been monitoring his cellphone. They knew his number – that's the only solution.'

'You could be right,' said Harland. 'And it would have been a simple matter to extract that number from his girlfriend, or even from some sort of record they found in the flat – a phone bill perhaps.'

Robin had sat down on the end of the bed. 'But doesn't it require considerable resources to do a thing like that? I mean, intercepting a particular mobile number needs a lot of sophisticated equipment. That's the sort of operation GCHQ goes in for – you know, collaring underworld barons in Marbella.'

'Yes, you're right, you do need pretty comprehensive equipment,' said Harland slowly, and he thought of Luc Bézier and the phone-tracking operation that had lured the French special forces team to a hotel in the Balkans.

'Well, perhaps you should point all this out to the police,' said Robin, pleased with his contribution. 'They're downstairs – two rather senior detectives. That's why I came up. I can tell them to go away if you want. After the last week and a bit, you've got every excuse to take a night's rest without being bothered.'

Harland said he would be down in a few minutes. When Robin had gone, Harriet helped him to put his shirt on.

'You're not going to tell them any of this,' she said.

'Of course not, Hal.'

'And you aren't going to let them know that Tomas is your son.'

'No, but they may work that out for themselves. And if the police don't, I'm sure Vigo will. He won't have forgotten seeing a young man disappearing out of the door. And since he's already claiming I spied for the Czechs and that I had an affair with Eva Houresh, it may not take him long to work out who Tomas is.'

'Which will make the allegations about your past much more difficult to deny.'

Harland nodded silently.

'What a terrible mess this is, Bobby.'

He went downstairs and found the two officers waiting in the sitting room. A short man with alert eyes and a brisk manner swivelled on his heels and gave his name as Commander Maurice Lighthorn. The other, a rather jaundiced fellow with watery eyes and a moustache, introduced himself as Chief Inspector Roger Navratt. Harland sat down but the officers remained standing.

'How are you feeling, sir?' asked Lighthorn.

'Better, now I've had some sleep.'

'And the injury. How's that doing? Much pain?

'No, but they expect it to heal quickly – it's a surface wound.'

'In that case, we were wondering if you felt up to accompanying us to the station.'

'Are you arresting me?'

'No, sir, but we do need your help and there's a lot to go through in a case like this. It will be easier at the station.'

Harland agreed to go, although both Robin and Harriet tried to persuade Lighthorn to wait until the next day.

Lighthorn listened, unmoved. 'I don't mean to be rude, madam, but this is a very serious incident and we have reason to believe that there is a link to another murder. Two people are dead, two very seriously injured. In my book, these circumstances require an urgent response.'

They drove to West End Central station where business

was slow. A few uniformed officers sat dejectedly waiting for the end of their shifts. Lighthorn explained that the investigation was being carried out at New Scotland Yard, but that they hadn't acquired all the space they needed yet. Lighthorn's appearance galvanised things and they were quickly shown into one of the station's interview rooms.

Coffee was produced. Navratt switched the interview tape recorder on and formally identified all those in the room.

'Mr Harland,' Lighthorn began after Navratt nodded, 'we have your account of the shooting which will form part of your statement in due course. What I want to do now is to ask you about your relationship with the man known as Lars Edberg. Can I start by asking how long you've known him?'

'I met him for the first time in New York last week.'

'In what circumstances?'

'Well, we had a few drinks in the bar around the corner from where I live in Brooklyn.'

'Did you meet there?'

'No, we got talking in the street outside my apartment and I offered him a drink.'

'Just like that?'

'More or less. He seemed a friendly young man – very bright and good company.'

'And you had no knowledge of him before that moment.'

'No, I had not set eyes on him or heard his name before that evening.'

'But you seem to have forged a strong relationship in that short time. Would you mind if I asked you the nature of that relationship? You will agree that it's unusual of a man of your age to strike up a conversation with somebody of Mr Edberg's age.'

'As I say, he was interesting.'

'And there was – how shall I put it – no sexual motive?'

Harland shook his head. 'No, nothing like that.'

'However, you were in contact this week after your return to this country.'

'Yes.'

'Were you aware at any stage that Lars Edberg was travelling on a false passport? No Swedish passport has been issued to a man named Lars Edberg.'

'Only when I read it in the papers yesterday.'

'Did Mr Edberg tell you about the murder of the woman he had been living with – Felicity MacKinlay?'

'Yes, in a phone call two nights ago.'

'Can you describe his state of mind at that time, Mr Harland?'

'It was a very short call and I didn't have a chance to ask much about it. But I would say that he was extremely upset. I gave him my sister's address and told him to go there.'

'And did he?'

'Not that evening.'

'When did you next hear from him?'

'Last night when he turned up at my sister's. It was difficult, though. There was a party on so we agreed to meet later.'

'Last night – Christmas Eve,' said Lighthorn significantly. 'That means that when you saw him you were fully aware that the police were looking for him. Because you yourself have just said that you read in the morning papers that Edberg was travelling under a false name. So the question is this: why didn't you phone the police then, Mr Harland? He was, after all, a major suspect.'

'I wanted to find out what was going on. In fact, I told him when I saw him by the river that sooner or later he would have to explain himself.'

'Still, it was a pity – some would put it a lot stronger – that you didn't phone the police at that stage. It would almost certainly have saved three people from being shot – four if we include your own injury, sir.'

'Look, I knew that he couldn't have had anything to do with the murder. I also knew he was frightened.'

Lighthorn's eyes darted to Harland's.

'Are you telling me that from one casual encounter you gained the certainty that this man could not have committed murder? You *do* know this woman was very brutally tortured before she was killed – tortured, sexually assaulted and executed.'

'I didn't know the exact details,' he said.

'But you read enough in the newspapers to know that her death was extremely ugly. Yet you still went to the Embankment to meet this Edberg – a man who you knew to be travelling on a fake passport, who was wanted by the police. That would suggest a very cavalier attitude to your own safety, unless you knew what Edberg was running from. Is that the truth of it? Did Mr Edberg tell you something in New York?'

'No, all I knew was that he believed someone was trying to kill him.'

'Why?' Again the eyes scanned Harland's face.

'He made veiled references to the danger he was in, but he did not specify what that danger was.'

Lighthorn seemed to digest this. In another context Harland would probably have admired his technique. He was clear-headed and possessed an unswerving instinct for the truth. But there was also something of the martinet in him.

'The reason I'm asking you these questions is not because we suspect Mr Edberg. We have ruled him out in the murder inquiry for the very good reason that we know he returned to this country about twenty-four hours after Miss MacKinlay was murdered. A baggage tag on the case that he left in her flat gave us the information on the flights he took. And we have since found the day and time of his departure to New York from another airline. What is significant is that the people who work at Felicity MacKinlay's flower shop told us that Edberg had said he would help with a large delivery of Christmas trees that day. Then without notice he left. What this suggests is that he left in a hurry and went to the States for a particular purpose. Do you know what that was?'

Harland shrugged.

'Come along, Mr Harland. You're an intelligent man – you must have asked him what all this was about?'

'I did, and he was about to tell me when he was shot.'

'Yes, by what appears to be a professional hit man. This was no casual drive-by shooting. This was the work of a top-notch pro who'd been hired to track down this young man. In the process he tortured and executed a young woman, murdered a police constable and crippled another.' There was genuine anger, genuine indignation in Lighthorn's manner.

The door opened and a young plainclothes policeman came in and whispered something to Lighthorn. Navratt looked at Harland, as if to deter him from listening in. Lighthorn left for five minutes then returned with an envelope which he placed on the table.

'In these circumstances,' said Lighthorn slowly, 'where a man has been shot at a secret meeting, it is often the case that one of the parties in that meeting has arranged the shooting.'

'What?' said Harland contemptuously. 'Are you suggesting that I arranged for the gunman to be there?'

'It's possible.'

'Then why on earth would they shoot me? And, second, why would I return to To—' He said the first syllable of Tomas's name, stumbled and said the name Lars. 'Why would I go back and wait for the police to come?'

Harland was sure Lighthorn had noticed the stumble, although he didn't pursue it.

'That's precisely the point I wanted you to make for me. Why in heaven's name did you go back to the scene of the shooting? I mean, you told the officers in the hospital how you fell down the steps at Cleopatra's Needle, and how you came across this character St George and then made good your escape. Remember, at this stage you were certain the young man was dead. You also told my officer that you felt for vital signs and there were none. So, I ask again, why would you return to the scene when it presented such obvious dangers? You were certain that Edberg was dead. Surely the most sensible course would have been to run in the opposite direction and find a phone box. Instead you returned to the monument.'

'Well, I wasn't sure he was dead. So I went back to check. By that time I'd heard the siren and —'

'And a lot more gunfire,' interrupted Lighthorn. 'That's what you told my officers.'

'Yes, and a lot more gunfire. So what are you suggesting?'

'I'm suggesting that your relationship with this young man was very important to you, important enough for you to race back along the embankment to be with him. Important enough for you to remain outside the operating theatre for an entire night, while you yourself must have been in some pain and suffering from your ordeal in the river.' He paused to pick up the envelope. 'I wonder if you would take a look at this, Mr Harland. It's a copy of the *Daily Telegraph* from last week.' He unfolded the paper and laid it on the table. 'It was found in Miss MacKinlay's flat in her recycling bin. As you can see, there's a large part of the front page missing. One of our officers decided to find out what had been cut out of this newspaper. He contacted the *Daily Telegraph* library a little while ago – fortunately they are publishing tomorrow – and found that it was the picture of your rescue in the La Guardia air crash last week.' He let this sink in. 'I remember the picture myself. You certainly have been through a lot this last week, Mr Harland. If you think about it, Mr Edberg must have cut this picture out of the paper before you say you met him. How do you explain this action?'

'I can't.'

'Is that all you've got to say? I mean, it's clear that this newspaper photograph acted as the prompt for Mr Edberg. Within hours of seeing it he was on a flight to New York, in all probability clutching this cutting – there is no sign of it in the flat.'

'Well, we did talk about the crash. He showed tremendous interest in it. Maybe that's why he stopped me in the street. He did mention that he had seen the picture.'

'Ah, but you're missing the point. This newspaper picture was the inspiration for Edberg's dash to New York. He plainly went to speak to you, showing, incidentally, the same devotion that you were later to show on the riverbank to him. This means he must have known where to find you.' He glanced at Navratt with just a hint of triumph for he knew that this must all be news to Harland. 'I've already had one of our officers check with International Inquiries and it appears that you are not listed in Brooklyn. Answer me this: how would he find you unless he knew where you lived? If he knew where you lived, it's a reasonable assumption that you had met before last week.'

'All I can say,' said Harland, 'is that I never saw him before that night, or spoke to him, or had any type of contact with him. I don't have the first idea how he traced me, although a determined person would not find it difficult to extract the number out of the United Nations.'

Lighthorn looked at him steadily.

'You're asking me to believe that this chap with a foreign accent appears out of the blue at your home and starts talking to you about a crash that you were in and you invite him for a drink, without having any idea who he is or where he comes from? It doesn't make sense. It's clear to me that Edberg went to New York for the purpose of seeing you.

189

During that visit I believe he gave you information crucial to the understanding of Miss MacKinlay's murder and to the shooting at the Embankment. I want to know what that was. I'm not pissing about here. We're looking for a man – or men – who callously gunned down two police officers and murdered a young woman. Those men may still be in the country. I believe that you may even be aware of their identity.'

'That's ridiculous. How could I possibly know them?' He leaned forward in his seat and couldn't help grimacing as the bandage on his shoulder shifted. 'I've told you what I know.'

'Then you give me no option but to hold you here. You may consider yourself under arrest, Mr Harland.'

'On what grounds?'

'On the grounds that we suspect you of an arrestable offence, namely involvement in the murder of PC Jeffrey Gibbon and shooting of PC Clive Low and the man known to us as Lars Edberg. I believe that you're withholding information which would help us make arrests, Mr Harland. I hope that over the course of the next few hours you will realise that your only option is to be completely frank with me.'

'But you don't believe any of this! You're making it up to keep me here and force me into giving you information I don't possess – that I couldn't possess. I have a statutory right to see a solicitor. I take it that you aren't going to ignore that too.' He noticed his hand was shaking and he knew his voice was somehow thinning.

'By all means make a telephone call,' said Lighthorn evenly. 'I will see you later.' With that he swept up the newspaper cutting and walked out of the room, leaving Navratt fumbling with the tape recorder.

He made the call to Harriet. She hurriedly told him that Robin had already been in touch with a solicitor named Leo Costigan who was standing by. She told him that she'd phoned the hospital and that the boy was still in a coma. They were doubtful whether he would ever wake.

Harland was taken to the cells. Several drunks and homeless men were there, who'd got themselves arrested in order to spend Christmas night in the warmth. There was a faint odour of urine in the corridor. Suddenly Harland experienced the stirring of blind panic. He reasoned to himself as he was led to the cell that he had already spent a night pretty much in custody and that he hadn't suffered unduly. But he found he couldn't control the fear and had to ask the policeman to wait for a few moments before locking him up. He said he felt faint.

'You ought to have thought of that before you dried up on Commander Lighthorn,' he said, and steered Harland into a cell. The door was shut and locked. He heard the policeman walk back down the corridor.

He tried to get a grip on his horror by sourcing it. What was it? Where did the panic come from? Of course! It was the smell of urine, the stench that had brought him round the first night in the villa in Prague. It was a smell he detested. He'd known it was his smell and that he must have pissed his pants while unconscious. And that was just at the beginning. There were many days more of him lying in his own filth, being woken up with a bucket of cold water and hauled into a room where a terrible intimacy was begun between him and his nameless torturer. For most of the time he was blindfolded and could not see who was in the room. But he learned by the echoes and the scuffling and the sniggering to count the number of men. Sometimes three or four; other times, just one. The man who spoke to him in the dark with that soft, cracked smoker's voice, and went over and over the past, insisting on more and more detail and, when Harland couldn't supply it, accusing him of lying and telling him he would be punished. Lying? About what? Things Harland didn't know. Things he couldn't know about because he simply hadn't been told, wasn't involved in this or that operation, or was somewhere else at the time.

He had worked Harland with a dedication that was senseless because all about them – although Harland didn't know to what extent – Eastern Europe was rising up against the communist regimes. Yet in the dilapidated villa and its fetid cellars remained a corner of Stalinist Russia. Seventy years of oppression and cruelty was channelled by the torturer into Harland's nerve endings.

It was the intimacy that Harland could not stand. Each day would start with the man hurting him. Then there would be talk, the offer of water or sometimes coffee, and the torturer would pass the time of day with him, discussing such bizarre topics as boar hunting in the Carpathians or the plum brandy to be had in Yugoslavia. He affected to be a man of the world, a man of taste with many high standards. Nothing was ever good enough for this connoisseur. As he talked, he tempted Harland into a man-to-man intimacy, in which Harland was required to give his opinion on the coldness of English women, the myth of French passion, the superiority of Russian hockey players and slovenliness of the Poles, the Turks and the gypsies, all of whom the man loathed heartily.

There was no question of Harland not responding because it would only advance the moment when the man hurt him again. His sole strategy was to delay being hurt. For the longer he put him off, the longer he would survive and the greater the chance of his being rescued. So he talked to the man, gave his all to the discussion. That involved relating to him, reacting genuinely to what he was saying, as though he was having a normal conversation and was not bound in a chair or stretched across a table, stinking of his own urine. It took all his energy to find ways of delaying that moment. But, of course, the torturer knew what he was up to. He let it be known – quite subtly – that he interpreted these ingenious diversions of Harland's as a peculiar confirmation of his own power: only he could drive this Englishman to argue that a salmon caught on a fly rather than a spinner tasted better, while that Englishman's body cried out from five hours of being bound on the stone floor.

As the day wore on the Russian would rib him about each red herring, like a parent indulging a child who is trying to avoid its bedtime. Then quite suddenly he would turn on Harland. It was back to business, he would say. He would start with his questions about an operation that Harland had never heard of or a piece of intelligence which had been fed up the line and had proved inaccurate. Why? Who? When? What motive? Harland was being called to account for everything he'd done, indeed for the entire Western intelligence effort over the past fifteen years. That was perhaps the only hint the man gave that he understood what had happened when the Berlin Wall fell. His world was over and now he was conducting a final inquiry. An inquisition. But it was also plain that he was exacting revenge. For what? The collapse of the communist system? The superiority of Harland's side? The end of his power and prospects?

Harland pathetically attempted to make a stab at the right solution and work it into a reassuring message during the conversation, but never to any avail. Sometimes the man would break into song or speak some impromptu doggerel, which wove Harland's observation into rhyme. Harland knew the man was watching his expression and he tried – oh, so very desperately – to hide his revulsion.

Before the man started hurting him again with the electrodes or the hot iron or the belts and clubs and needles, he would get very close to Harland, squatting or sometimes even lying on the floor beside him, and Harland would smell his breath and his aftershave and sense the slight aroma of a leather coat or a woollen jersey. Not once did he see the man's face for he always made sure that Harland was bound and blindfolded before he entered the room. He had seen the others though, the thugs who were called upon to beat him up, or do the lifting when the torturer wanted Harland stretched across a barrel or hung from a beam in the cellar. Even though he never laid eyes on him, he knew this man.

The truth was that he had succumbed. The terrifying, faceless presence had got to him. In his rare conscious moments in his cell he reasoned to himself that he was only trying to survive, but he understood that he had put himself in the position of the supplicant. Like a lover almost, he was dependent on the torturer's approval, alert to his whims and moods, desperate to please, but always knowing that in the end he would be hurt. It was intimacy of a truly demonic kind and it had left Harland with a peculiar terror. To him closeness was torture, except possibly in his relationship with Harriet. Somehow that had survived.

These memories ran unchecked through Harland's mind for the first time in the decade since he had taken a cab to a quiet North London street and talked to a very good woman about his torture. She had set up a discreet outfit for victims of torture like himself and he had gone on a doctor's recommendation, almost with the sense that he had something to confess. Torture, he was surprised to learn, had left him with a sense of guilt, just as severe bereavement can cause feelings of shame. The damage done is so great and particular that the mind can only express itself through one or other of the more common human emotions. He had returned many times to the woman who just listened and allowed him to voice the most dreadful thoughts. After six months or so he picked himself up and found himself a job. He never saw her again and never mentioned it to himself again, at least not in a way that would resurrect the images that played in his blindfolded mind all those years ago.

He thought of that woman now. She was the very antithesis of his torturer which was why it had been strangely difficult for him to talk to her on the terms and with the intimacy that he'd used in the villa. He had explained the irony and she had nodded and said she understood. He kept her face before him as he lay on the bed in the police cell and watched his hands shaking from what seemed like a very great distance indeed.

He noted that his detachment had come back again, the same part of him that had coolly advised that he was about to die in the East River. But now there was another message, an odd phrase that repeated itself in his head. 'Blank out. Blank out. Blank out.' He wanted blankness and the end of his terror.

Some time later that night he was aware of the cell door opening. In the doorway stood a man in a silvery blue suit who was rhythmically brushing the stubble on the top of his head. Harland scrutinised him with ultra clarity. A short man, a bustling man, carrying a briefcase, an overcoat and small black astrakhan hat.

'This won't do at all,' said the man several times. 'Look at him, for heaven's sake. When was he last checked?'

He knelt down by Harland's side. 'My name is Leo Costigan. I'm your solicitor. I'm going to get you out of here as soon as possible. These bastards will pay for this.'

Harland took in the ashen face of the constable who had locked him up.

'Mr Harland?' said the lawyer, shaking Harland's good shoulder. 'Mr Harland!' Then he turned to the policeman. 'This man is in shock. Don't just stand there. Get a doctor, you idiot!'

The policeman ran down the corridor.

'It's going to be okay. You're going to be okay, Mr Harland. Can you hear me? I'm your lawyer, Leo Costigan.'

He stopped speaking and put a hand to Harland's forehead and stroked it. For some reason Harland could not reply.

The officer returned with a uniformed sergeant and

Navratt, whose rheumy-eyed indifference had been replaced by a look of pure panic.

'It is plain that this man has suffered a nervous collapse while in your care,' said Costigan. 'I do not want him moved until the doctor has assessed his condition. You can all see that he has been allowed to wet himself and that his hands are shaking. He is unable to focus and cannot react. You lot are looking at the end of your careers. I don't suppose any of you were aware that this man is the personal representative of the Secretary-General of the United Nations?' He looked up at the three policemen. 'No, I didn't think so.'

Harland smiled inwardly. Costigan was doing a grand job. Harriet had been right about him – a good chap, a little terrier.

It was strange how he tried to talk but nothing happened. He was dimly reminded of the effect of a computer virus: the words seemed to move very slowly to the front of his mind and then disintegrate before his eyes. Still, inside he knew he was okay. He had come through and he was intact. He just needed sleep. That was all.

15

TWO HALVES OF A DOLLAR BILL

For the next few days no one was allowed to bother Harland. A visit from the family doctor confirmed the police doctor's view that he'd suffered a delayed reaction from the twin traumas of the air crash and the shooting. His problems had been compounded by lack of sleep. Harland went along with the diagnosis, but he knew very well that the shock to his system predated both these events by a long time. He was prescribed sleeping pills and a course of what the doctor described as mood improvers. He ignored the second bottle and instead buried himself in a biography of an aviation pioneer and watched old films on television with Harriet's children.

There was also a visit from Leo Costigan, who told him that the police had no intention of pursuing the case against him. He was pressing for an inquiry and had already made representation with the Police Complaints Authority. Harland asked him to inquire about Lars Edberg's possessions. Since Edberg was alive, he had every right to them. More important, a clue to his interests might be in that bag: the sort of music that might help wake him from the coma. Harland mentioned this because it had occurred to him that there was a lot in the bag that might eventually fall into Vigo's hands, in particular Eva's old ID cards. Costigan said he would do what he could but was doubtful since the bag

197

would almost certainly be regarded by the police as relevant to Tomas's identity.

By Monday evening he began to feel himself again. He lay on a couch in the conservatory thinking how he was going to find Eva. It wouldn't be easy, especially as Tomas had never given him any hint of her whereabouts or the name she was using. If he was to go to the Czech Republic, he would have to think very carefully about his departure and then his means of search. Suddenly he thought of Cuth Avocet – The Bird – and Macy Harp. He couldn't think of anyone who knew Prague better. He'd put money on the fact that The Bird still resided at a pleasant flint farmhouse between Lambourne and Newbury, where his wife ran a stud farm. And if The Bird was still there, Macy Harp would not be far away.

Late next morning Harland asked Robin if he could spend some time at his office. He said he felt like getting out of the house and he needed to make some phone calls. They drove together in Robin's Alvis to the White Bosey Cane building, just off Charlotte Street. Robin went into a large, sparse office where there was an exercise machine and a flat-screen TV, leaving Harland in the care of a whey-faced woman in her twenties named Cary who looked as though she suffered from multiple allergies. He explained that he wanted a private office, a phone and an Internet connection. She had no difficulty in finding somewhere since most of the agency had taken the week off. That was just what Harland needed – space to himself and the certainty that no one would be listening to his calls.

He took out some notes he'd made the night before. The first name on it was Sara Hezemanns', Griswald's assistant in The Hague. He dialled her direct line and got through straight away.

'Are you alone?' he asked her.

'Yes, there are many people on holidays,' she said. 'Why

did you not call before? I waited two evenings last week.' She sounded put out and slightly disappointed, which Harland took as a good sign because it meant she wanted to talk.

'I'm sorry, I was never near a phone at the right moment. But, believe me, I really do need to speak to you about Alan's last investigation.' He paused to read his notes. 'Tell me – did we discuss Luc Bézier?'

'We touched on him.'

'I have since read all the papers you sent to Mr Griswald. It's obvious that the man mentioned as being present in Bosnia in July 1995 was the subject of Alan's interest. He is not identified in any of the witness statements but I assume he is the individual that Bézier's group had been sent to Serbia to kidnap. That means he was under an indictment from the War Crimes Tribunal. Is that right?'

'Yes.'

'I understand from Colonel Bertrand Bézier, that's Luc Bézier's father, who I visited in France last week, that his name was Lipnik. I don't have a first name.'

'His name is Viktor Lipnik and, yes, it is true that he was the subject of a secret indictment. We believed it would be better if he did not know he was being investigated.'

'But he did know about the indictment.'

'Probably.'

'And that was all that was dropped when he was reported to have been killed. You see, Luc Bézier was the witness to the shooting at the hotel. I assume the report was filed to SFOR – that's the NATO commanders in Bosnia – that he'd seen Lipnik killed. I also assume there was no further investigation.' He stopped and briefly imagined Sara Hezemanns – an earnest, bespectacled blonde with an unswerving sense of mission. 'Look, Sara – can I call you that?'

'Of course.'

'Sara, I must tell you that I do have authority to pursue this matter on behalf of the UN. But I should also warn you that you may feel that my questions compromise your loyalties. If that is the case, just say you can't answer. Please don't hide things from me.'

'Go ahead,' she said.

'I suspect that Alan Griswald was working towards a second indictment of Viktor Lipnik, but that he was coming up against some resistance. People were either too sceptical about him still being alive or were motivated to obstruct Alan. If I read his actions right, he was gathering conclusive evidence that Lipnik was still alive, proof that no one could rebut?'

'Rebut?'

'Proof that no one could reject.'

'Oh, he had this proof,' she said. 'He was taking it to Washington and New York to show people. Luc Bézier was his proof. Monsieur Bézier saw Lipnik in Vienna.'

'Yes, I know, but what was the other proof?'

'This is difficult.'

'Why?'

'Because I'm not sure . . . At first everything was fine and Mr Griswald was given permission to find out what he could about Lipnik. Then he was told there were diplomatic interests involved.' She gave the phrase an ironic edge. 'He knew what that meant. This came from high up. Mr Griswald believed it originated in NATO headquarters or the UN – maybe his own country. He wasn't sure. He was very upset because he knew for sure that Viktor Lipnik had taken another identity and that he was a killer.'

'What was the proof?'

'I don't know. It came to him a few weeks ago. Maybe by e-mail. I am not sure. But not to his office here.'

'So it might have been sent to his laptop?'

'I think so.'

'You don't know what it contained?'

'No. Mr Griswald called them two halves of a dollar bill.'

'What did he mean by that?'

'At first I did not understand, but when I thought about it, I realised that the first piece of information was worthless without the second. Like two halves of a dollar. Only when you have the second half can you stick it together and spend it.'

'And these came at different times and Alan stuck them together?'

'I don't know.' She paused. 'I think Mr Griswald gave something to get the second. He talked about it vaguely with me. The morality of it. He hinted things. He said there was a higher purpose, though he had misgivings about what he was doing. There was a negotiation and he decided to give the source what he wanted. After that he got the second piece of information.'

Harland digested this. 'And they were in code, these e-mails?'

'How did you know?'

'It's difficult to explain. Not everything was destroyed in the crash.'

'But I think you are making a mistake, Mr Harland. I believe there was one e-mail only. He received the second piece of information personally. You see, he went on a trip to the East three weeks ago. No one knew where he was. He did not tell me. He did not claim for the expenses. He said nothing about it.'

All along Harland was thinking about the mini-disc. He was certain it contained the proof that Griswald was planning to show to Jaidi because he must have had everything he needed with him on the plane. Also he remembered Griswald tapping his pocket and saying how he would tell Harland one day because it would be particularly interesting to him.

Then something else occurred to him. Griswald and Bézier had spent two nights in Washington. That could mean that they were seeing someone else with the evidence. Washington was close to the CIA at Langley, Virginia, and also the National Security Agency's base at Fort Meade in Maryland. He might have been visiting either, perhaps gathering some confirmation for his material. He asked Sara Hezemanns what she thought.

'That's simple. He was seeing Professor Norman Reeve of the War and Peace Studies Forum. He used to work there, I believe.'

'But he wasn't just paying a courtesy visit?'

'No, he went to get some photographs that Professor Reeve had acquired.'

'Of what?'

'They were aerial photographs of a place in Bosnia. That's all I know. There were many taken during the civil war and also during the Kosovo war.'

'What did they show?'

'I cannot tell you. Mr Griswald was hoping to find something. But he did not explain this to me.' Harland made a note to find Reeve's number.

'You implied that there had been some discussion about Alan's death on the aeroplane. What were people saying?'

'There was nothing definite. When he died, some of his work was given to other people, although most of it only he could do.'

'Did they believe the plane had been sabotaged because it was carrying Griswald and Bézier?'

'Some people speculated. But no one knew about Bézier.'

'They knew about the other stuff, though – this proof he was carrying?'

'Yes, people did understand that he had something important.'

'Has the case been given to anyone else to follow up?'

'No, the case was never reopened. So as far as we are concerned it was simply a private theory of Mr Griswald's.'

He said goodbye to Sara Hezemanns, promising to let her know what he found out. Then he sat pondering Griswald's negotiation for the second piece of information. He knew that Griswald had given something of great value to his source, something, perhaps, that he had learned in the past with the CIA. Griswald wasn't in the habit of sharing his thoughts with those around him. For him to have talked to Sara must have meant that he was troubled by what he was doing. Was that why Vigo was so intensely interested in Griswald's activities? Did that explain Guy Cushing bumping into them in The Hague?

He looked at the desk clock and decided to call Sally Griswald even though it was only 7.30 a.m. on the East Coast.

She picked up immediately.

'Can you talk?' asked Harland, hoping she would recognise his voice.

'Yes,' she said straight away. 'I just wondered last week whether we had a problem. Perhaps it's best to be on the safe side.'

'Yes, concerning that material, it is.' He paused. 'Sally, do you remember a one-legged man on the circuit in Germany and Austria? He wasn't on our side of the business. The commercial end of things. Al made up a song about him. If you do remember his name, don't say it.'

Sally Griswald laughed. 'Yes, I believe I do recall the name.'

'Good, I've set up a hotmail address in his name. Could you have the material sent to that address in the next hour?'

'I'll get it done straight away.'

'There's one other thing. Is it possible that Al was seeing his old employer in DC? Not the CIA, but a later employer?'

'Yes, they were big buddies. Al respected him and often asked for his advice. Do you have his name?'

'Yes,' said Harland. 'Can I get his number from information?'

'Shouldn't be a problem, but let me know if you can't. He's worth talking to. I should have thought of that before.'

'I'll call him today,' he said, then hung up.

For the next hour or so he checked the in-box of the hotmail account he had set up in the name of Tony Widdershins. Eventually a message arrived with two very large attachments. The message from Eric Griswald explained that he and a friend had had a stab at decoding the pulse, but it hadn't yielded to the various algorithms that they had applied. The two attachments consisted of the original sound and a diagram, which Eric pointed out showed the patterns involved. Harland copied the two attachments.

Then he called Norman Reeve in Washington and, after listening to a detailed message about his movements, eventually located him in Florida.

As Reeve talked, Harland vaguely remembered reading something about him in one of the foreign affairs journals – an Austrian Jew with an anglicised name who'd survived the camps and had set up the War and Peace Studies Forum in the sixties. Reeve was cautious. There were no pictures, he said. He had not seen Griswald for over eighteen months.

'What did you think about the plane crash?' asked Harland. 'Weren't you in any way suspicious, knowing what Alan was investigating?'

'There is always conjecture with these things,' said Reeve. 'What I deal with is facts, Mr Harland.'

'If I was to provide you with some facts, would you help me?'

'That would assume that I was in a position to help. But I'm not in a position to help, whatever you tell me.'

'Can I put it this way, sir,' said Harland. 'If you knew of a Nazi war criminal who'd got himself another identity and escaped justice, wouldn't you feel that it was your duty to expose the man?'

Reeve snapped back at him. 'Don't you lecture me about the Holocaust, Mr Harland.'

'All I am saying is that Alan Griswald's final investigation was exactly that. He was trying to expose someone who faked his own death and escaped prosecution for terrible crimes.'

'You are obviously very inexperienced in these matters, Mr Harland. I accept that your motives may be honourable. But you just cannot telephone in the middle of my vacation and expect me to help when I have never heard of you and have no knowledge of your credentials.'

'What should I do to prove myself?'

'Again, this supposes that I have something to offer.'

'Yes, but the plane may have been sabotaged. I was on that plane, Professor Reeve, and I survived. Alan Griswald was a good friend of mine and I want to make sure his work does not go to waste. So I'm asking you again about those pictures. I gather they were aerial photographs taken in 1995, either by satellite or U2 spy plane. Alan believed they would establish some part of his argument.'

There was silence at the other end. 'You say you were on the plane with Mr Griswald?'

'Yes, and Luc Bézier and a number of other innocent people who were killed. This is to say nothing of the people on the other jet or the four people who were shot in London last week – two of them are dead. It's just possible that the man that Griswald was investigating is responsible for these deaths and shootings.' Harland knew he was on thin ice but it seemed to give Reeve some pause.

The professor sighed. Harland fancied he could hear him sit down and shift the telephone. He began speaking.

'Of course, there were many pictures taken by the US military during the Bosnian war and, no doubt, by other agencies too. A few have already been used to establish that major crimes did take place. They pinpointed the location of the crimes, of course, not the individuals involved, although this could be inferred by other knowledge.'

'Telephone intercepts, wireless traffic.'

'Yes, and eye-witness accounts that tally with the events picked up from the air.'

'So they can conclusively prove something happened on a particular date?'

'No, they prove that there was military activity in the area of a crime and that maybe some earth-moving took place contemporaneously. But they do not prove a crime.'

Harland thought for a moment and then had an inspiration.

'Is it possible that Griswald was investigating a crime which has so far gone undetected or ignored?'

'You would have to ask the War Crimes Tribunal about that,' said Reeve, returning to a defensive note.

'They won't tell me. Griswald's casebook has all but been abandoned. I understand that they viewed his latest investigation with scepticism, or that it may have been obstructed in some way. These are the things that Benjamin Jaidi has asked me to investigate and that's why I'm asking for your help. I'm sorry, perhaps I should have mentioned that before now.'

From the murmurs and exhalations at the other end of the line, Harland could tell that he had piqued his interest. Then the professor said abruptly, 'You say the Secretary-General has asked you to look into this. What precisely? The crash? Mr Griswald's investigation? The War Crimes Tribunal's behaviour? Which?'

'All those things and one or two other matters also. There's another aspect to this that I don't understand. Viktor Lipnik – if he exists – receives some special protection.'

'A veritable one-man crime commission, Mr Harland. I hope you're up to it.'

'So do I. Tell me what you need from me.'

'A date and a target area and I'll see if we can help.'

'But surely you know the date? Griswald would have told you.'

'He did tell me. But I never saw Mr Griswald before he went to New York. We had an appointment and I know he waited in Washington, but I was too ill. I'm down here recovering from pneumonia.' He paused and wheezed a cough as if to underline this. 'A date, Mr Harland. Give me a date and we'll do business.' With that the line went dead. The old buzzard was testing him. He wondered if Sally could bring any influence to bear. Maybe even Jaidi could phone him.

His eyes moved down the list and settled on Frank Ollins's name. But this set off an alarm at the back of his mind. He had increasingly begun to think that the protection that Viktor Lipnik received must have been provided by the Americans. Maybe the British were also involved. That would account for Vigo's manoeuvrings. Added to this was the probability that Tomas had been tracked by some exceptionally sophisticated equipment which only the major powers possessed. Britain and America were the big listeners and, of course, the Americans would have been the people tracking Lipnik's phone in Serbia before he was 'assassinated'. To talk to a member of the FBI in these circumstances required lunatic trust and cunning.

He dialled the mobile number and caught Frank Ollins in his car on the way to work. He sounded chipper and rested.

'I was just wondering how things were progressing,' said Harland.

'They're doing fine, thank you.' From the tone it was also clear that Ollins wasn't going to volunteer anything.

'I wondered,' said Harland nonchalantly, 'what you meant by those questions last week? This business of how Alan

Griswald held his computer just before we landed. What did you mean by that? What relevance does it have?'

'Look, I have a feeling that you haven't played straight with me, Harland.'

'Oh, why?'

'The more I thought about the people who attacked you in the UN building, the more I got to thinking that you had something that they wanted. I guess they probably took it from you too. Is that correct?'

'The answer to that depends on your position, Ollins. We don't know each other well. This affair gets more complicated by the minute and, frankly, I can't afford to talk to someone who is going to share what I have with too many people.'

'So you didn't lose everything that night in the UN?' Harland said nothing. 'Okay, so are you suggesting a trade?'

'That depends on what you have and what your position is.'

'My position is this: we're certain your plane was brought down, but as yet the Safety Board are out of the loop and it has not been disclosed to the public because it has terrifying implications. So, I want to find the people who did this. We are working on the same side.'

Harland decided to make the leap. 'Well, inadvertently I didn't tell you everything I knew.'

'Ah,' said Ollins. 'Would you mind waiting while I stop the car? I don't want to miss this.' There was a pause. 'Okay, what did you *inadvertently* forget to tell me?'

Harland explained about the wallet and how he had discovered after leaving the hospital that it contained a music disc encoded with some kind of message between the tracks of the music.

'That's certainly interesting, and since we are working on the same side, I'll tell you something that you'll keep under your hat. We found the phone that you took from Griswald's pocket and we got to reviving those little circuit boards in the phone, which incidentally is a WAP, and you know what we found? We found a stored e-mail message of precisely one hundred and eighty digits in length. That also is encrypted.'

'Then we may have two halves of a dollar bill,' said Harland. 'I've learned that Griswald's investigation received two separate messages which only work together. I happen to have the bigger half but it's worthless without yours.'

'So we're going to make a trade, aren't we? What do you say we send these two pieces of information by e-mail to each other at nine o'clock my time – two yours?'

Harland said that seemed fine. He gave the Widdershins address and wrote down Ollins's.

Then something occurred to Ollins. 'What happens if you decode this material before I do? You're going to send it to me, right?'

'If that's a reciprocal arrangement, yes.'

Ollins agreed, but Harland wasn't ready to hang up quite yet. 'What about those questions you were asking me? What did you mean? Obviously they had something to do with the phone because you asked whether it had been shielded by the computer.'

'Now, that one isn't for free.'

'But you think that this is part of the solution as to how the plane went haywire in the last seconds of the flight?'

'It's not the cause, it's a symptom. And that's all I am prepared to say. Be seeing you.'

Ten minutes later the strand of code arrived. Harland had not the first idea what to do with it and felt rather deflated. The three calls he'd made that morning had each brought him hard intelligence, but not understanding. Codes were all very well, but his interest and faith in that side of intelligence work had always been slight. They distracted from the human issues of motive and betrayal. But he did have Griswald's secret and he had to find a way of decrypting it.

His only idea was to see if The Bird knew anyone who could tackle it.

In the next hour Harland made a few more calls, the first to Philip Smith-Canon, Tomas's neurologist, whom he arranged to meet later in the afternoon. Then he put in a call to the Secretary-General's office and left a message requesting that someone, preferably Jaidi himself, prevail on Reeve to help him. Lastly he got hold of The Bird, who had been riding out on The Ridgeway.

Cuth listened with undimmed enthusiasm, but said the only hope of their being able to meet in the next twenty-four hours was if Harland was prepared to travel to Cheltenham for the New Year's Eve race meeting the next day. Cuth had a part share in a horse which stood a better than average chance in the 2.35. Macy was in the syndicate and would be there also. They would look in at the Arkel Bar in the members' enclosure periodically throughout the afternoon. Harland explained a few of the things he wanted to talk about in an oblique fashion and mentioned that he wanted something decrypted. Cuth told him to bring all the material. Then he inquired as to what sort of company he'd been keeping over the last few days. Harland understood that he was asking whether he was being watched. He replied that he had seen quite a few old friends since arriving in London.

'I see,' said The Bird. 'Well, let's keep this to ourselves. A private drink at the races, eh?' Harland smiled. It would be good to see both of them again.

The Neurological Unit to which Tomas had been transferred was contained in an unpromising red-brick hospital in Bloomsbury. Harland arrived there as it was getting dark. The lights shone out on a deserted pavement; there was very little sign of activity. A building in a coma, thought Harland.

He knew perfectly well that he should have summoned the energy over the weekend to visit Tomas, but the analogy with his own terror of imprisonment and pain was too close for him.

Dr Smith-Canon appeared soon after Harland announced himself at the reception and insisted they go straight away to Tomas's room. He said progress was good, considering the severity of his injuries, but Harland should prepare himself to see Tomas – it was an unsettling sight at first.

He was led into a soft-lit room. A nurse rose from a chair, clutching a magazine to her breast. She looked from Smith-Canon to Tomas and back again and said there had been no change in his condition. The doctor nodded and, sensing Harland's hesitation, guided him by the elbow to the side of the bed.

Tomas's upper body was raised at an angle of thirty degrees. His head was encased in a helm of bandages and elsewhere there were pads and dressings which marked the places where the bullets had entered. A tracheotomy collar had been fitted to his neck to allow him to breathe. Tubes ran to his nose and mouth and from under the covers to his stomach. The machines beside and behind the head of the bed hissed and sucked and occasionally gasped in a rhythm of their own.

Smith-Canon said Tomas needed constant attention at this stage. For instance, it was necessary to prevent the tracheotomy tube from becoming blocked by mucus. But Harland's attention was distracted by the air in the room which was warm and moist and overlaid by a brisk, medical odour.

Smith-Canon took hold of Tomas's right hand and felt the pulse. Then he bent over his face and shone a torch into an eye which he held open by pulling the eyelid upwards with his fingertips. Harland saw the light glance through a very small, expressionless pupil. The doctor let the eyelid drop and turned to Harland.

'I'm afraid there's no sign of consciousness but that can be deceptive: often a patient will creep towards consciousness and although he appears to be dead to the world he can be fully aware of his surroundings.'

He talked Harland through the equipment around Tomas's bed, explaining that he would have the tracheotomy for many months yet, probably for all his life. For the moment he was being fed by a tube which went straight into his stomach, but this might have to be changed over time because of the risk of the patient aspirating regurgitated food. Arrangements had been made to cope with the bowel and bladder, and these too would need to be reviewed.

Harland looked at his son's face. It wasn't quite vacant. There was definitely a look of his mother, and in the crease of his forehead he read an expression of frozen apprehension. He wondered whether this would be lifelong, but he didn't ask the doctor. He was too overwhelmed by the sense that Tomas, whatever his problems, had been effectively snatched from him just as he had come to accept him as his son.

The doctor looked at Harland sympathetically.

'I know, it's all rather unpleasant. But it's best that you're fully aware of the situation. He's going to need an awful lot of care, and there are many hurdles along the way which I can explain to you in a moment. But first I'd like you to do something for me. I want you to sit and talk to him. I think it would perhaps be best if you did this alone.'

He nodded to the nurse with a smile. When she had left, he said, 'I believe it's time we started using his real name. Of course I shall maintain his file and records in the name of Lars Edberg, but if we continue to address him as Lars, he may simply fail to recognise it. On the other hand, his real name is bound to mean something to him. The same may apply to use of the English language. I don't know how well he spoke English, but even if he was a fluent speaker, I believe his birth language would be better. His mother – have you had any luck tracing her?'

Harland shook his head.

'Well, it's imperative that she's found. When he comes round, his understanding will be not impaired, but he won't be able to communicate the slightest wish. It's an extremely frightening experience and can rapidly lead to depression. This is often expressed by the patients locking themselves in further by refusing to attempt to communicate – it's the only thing they can control. But there are several ways for him to communicate – for instance the use of an eyelid, or the vertical movement of a pupil. Locked-in patients can also be trained to alter the activity in their brain so that they can move a cursor on a computer screen.' He paused and glanced at Tomas. 'But this is all a little way down the road yet. The main aim now is to get him awake. So would you sit here for a few moments and talk about things that would mean something to him?'

Harland was aware that the very last thing he wanted was to be left alone with Tomas's lifeless form. In some way he was repelled by what he saw and that filled him with guilt.

'I know it will be awkward at first,' said Smith-Canon. 'But open your heart to him. Talk about things that mean a lot to you. The nurse will be just outside if you need assistance and when you've finished she'll know where to find you. Then we'll have a chat.' He smiled and departed.

Harland moved to the chair at the head of the bed and sat for a few moments, wondering how the hell to start. He cursed himself that he had asked Tomas so very little about his life.

'Tomas? I hope you can hear me. The doctor says that you may be able to even though you're in a very deep sleep.' He stopped, leaned forward to the boy's head and fought the fleeting fear of intimacy. His mind went back to the villa in Prague. How odd it was that now he spoke quietly into a person's ear, a person who could not interrupt, object or walk away. 'It's difficult for me to know what to say because I realise I was far too wary when we met for the first time. I asked you nothing about yourself . . . nothing about you . . . and so I don't know much about your life. If you can hear this, I'd like you to know how much I regret my attitude. I also want you to understand that I accept you as my son.' He faltered for a moment. His eyes came to rest on Tomas's hands. The fingers were long and delicate, almost like a woman's. He was shocked that he had not noticed them before.

He started again. 'Perhaps you'd like to hear how I met your mother. I know her as Eva, but she has a real name, which you know and I don't. I was a young man – younger than you are now – and on my first posting abroad. It was actually more of a training session with a little work thrown in. It wasn't difficult and I had a lot of time to get to know Rome and make friends. You know how we met because you told me about it. Your mother has remembered it more or less right. We were in a restaurant and I sat next to her and by the end of the evening I was lost to her. It's impossible to talk about these things without sounding like an idiot. But I was smitten. From then on we spent a lot of time together, but because we were both working in intelligence we had to keep our relationship secret. In the end we found it was easier to leave Rome at the weekends. We stayed in some pretty run-down places. One time we went to Ancona, a resort on the Adriatic, for a couple of days. That was a happy time. We could just see the Dalmatian coast from our bedroom window. The Romans used to call it Illyria. We promised each other that one day we'd go there together. Some promise. I suppose we both knew neither of us would be able to keep it.' He paused. 'God, I wish I was better at this. I feel I'm failing you again. Perhaps the doctor is right that you would respond better to Czech. That's why I'm going to try to trace your mother and bring her here. That's what I'm going to be doing over the next few days so I won't be able to come and see you. But when I get back I will come and we can work out a lot of things.'

At that moment Tomas's head jerked backwards, and his entire body seemed to be racked by an electric current. His arms flew into the air, his fingers splayed in fright. One leg kicked out, the other folded towards his stomach. Harland watched horrified as the muscles and veins just beneath the tracheotomy collar bulged and Tomas's face went puce. Then all four extremities began a slow rhythmic motion. Harland leapt up, tipping the chair over, and called out.

'He's waking. He's moving. He's coming to.' Before the words were out the nurse was through the door and pushing him aside. She snatched a syringe on a tray nearby, held it up to the light then injected Tomas in the buttock. The movement in the legs and arms began to subside and his head slipped back to the pillow.

'Why aren't his eyes open?' asked Harland. He turned and saw Smith-Canon.

'That was an involuntary spasm,' he said quietly. 'He'll be all right in a few moments. It's one of the problems with locked-in syndrome, though it usually occurs when the patient is conscious. I think we ought to leave Nurse Roberts here to deal with this. Everything will be fine in a few minutes.'

They went to Smith-Canon's room and sat on a small sofa. Harland felt exhausted.

'This kind of episode can be avoided once we get used to the patient,' said Smith-Canon. 'In each case we have to learn about the kind of things which set off a spasm. Sometimes it's associated with breathing difficulties or the use of a tracheotomy, other times with problems in the bowel.' He sensed Harland didn't want to hear. 'Okay, I can see you've had enough for one day.'

'Yes,' said Harland absently.

'Look, I'm not quite sure how to put this. But I had a visit

215

over the weekend from a man called Walter Vigo. I must say I didn't much take to him.'

'Yes, I know him. What did he want?'

'It wasn't easy to say. He was rather an oblique fellow, if you know what I mean. He wouldn't tell me what he did precisely, but he did stress that he was dealing with an urgent matter of national security. He was interested in Tomas's identity and wondered if I had any clue about it. He asked if I had been contacted by any relations. And he was particularly interested in his condition – whether he was likely to die and what the future held if he lived.'

'What did you say?'

'I told him that it was confidential information and that it was none of his business. However, I thought you ought to know. Clearly it has some bearing on the things you were telling me the other day. I think he thought that Tomas was going to be out of action and that he was no longer of much concern to him.'

'Thanks for that. Walter Vigo is a senior member of MI6. I'm not sure where they stand on all this. But you're right, his interest does have a bearing on what we were talking about.'

'Yes, I thought as much. Look, there's one other thing.' He opened the drawer of his desk. 'Bearing in mind your caution about revealing your son's identity, I decided not to hand this in to the police.' He placed a light Terylene wallet on the table. 'This was in your son's jacket. Actually, I believe it was in the lining. At any rate they missed it. I think it contains a lot that will help you.'

Harland opened it and found a smaller leather card-holder which held Eva's three identity cards and a couple of credit cards in the name of Edberg. There was some money – ten fifty-pound notes and a couple of hundred-dollar bills. 'Thank you. I can't hide the fact that I'm extremely relieved that you didn't give these to Vigo or the police. It might have proved very difficult for me to trace his mother without them.'

'Yes, I could see that. But you are, after all, his next of kin and I couldn't imagine that the police would have a better use for it.'

Harland rose to leave.

'I hope you find her, Mr Harland. It's very important for the boy.'

'I will. And thanks again.'

16

A DAY AT THE RACES

Harland caught the 10.30 Race Special from Paddington and arrived in time for the first race. But he did not see any sign of Macy Harp or The Bird until the middle of the afternoon. He hung about, watching the crowd – an untroubled mix of gentry, spivs and local farmers.

Before the 2.35 race he made his way through a wide tunnel which ran under the stands towards the paddock in the hope of spotting them. He felt a tug at his arm. It was Macy Harp who had darted from a doorway in the tunnel. 'This way,' he said with a conspiratorial smile. 'The Bird's got a private box. None of yer hoi polloi for Cuthbert Avocet these days.'

Macy hadn't changed a bit – a roguish red face, dancing eyes and quick, furtive manner.

They found The Bird positioned at the front of the box with his binoculars trained on the crowd below. Without removing them, he flapped a hand in Harland's direction and said, 'Bobby, grab yourself a drink. I recommend a whisky mac on a day like this.'

After a few moments he swivelled round and stood up. 'Good grief, Bobby, you look dreadful. Is that what aid work does for a man?'

'And a few other things too,' said Harland.

'So I gather. There's a good view from up here. We've been watching you plod hither and thither. We felt we ought to

218

make sure that you hadn't been followed here. There're one or two suspicious characters down there but I think your coat tails are clean.'

'They should be, after the palaver I went through leaving my sister's house in London.'

'Good,' said The Bird, with an encouraging smile. 'And I know you too well to ask whether you called from a safe phone yesterday.'

Macy planted a drink in one of Harland's hands and a large chunk of fruitcake in the other. 'Get that down you, laddie. It's Veronica Harp's renowned Christmas cake.'

They both picked up their binoculars and turned to the racecourse. 'Ours is the blue and maroon colours,' said Cuth. 'Maltese cross on a blue background. Can't miss her. She's a gorgeous animal but doesn't usually pull her finger out in the cold.'

Harland tried to show an interest in the fortunes of Manse Lady but was distracted by the realisation that both The Bird and Macy were extremely well turned out – tailored tweed suits, and, in Macy's case, a coat with chocolate brown velvet collar and expensive brogues polished to a military shine. Harland hadn't heard much of them in the last ten years but he knew that they'd extended their freelance interests in Eastern Europe into a number of enterprises that made use of their contacts behind the old Iron Curtain. They'd been into caviar, lumber, truck parts, aluminium, engineering tools – the lot.

The field laboured home with Manse Lady struggling up the hill to take third place. The Bird and Macy shouted a great deal, but to no effect.

'Damned jockey,' said The Bird. 'Thinks we're paying him to go on a nature ramble.'

Macy snapped his binocular case shut.

They had another drink and Harland began to feel the warmth of the whisky mac in his feet.

'You two seemed to have done well for yourselves,' he said. 'Business is good, I gather.'

'Can't complain,' said Macy, stroking a patch of blond stubble on his chin. 'Can we?'

'As you know, Bobby,' Cuth added, 'nature always smiled on us, now fate has joined her.'

They looked and spoke like a pair of amateurs, thought Harland, yet in their field they were unmatched. They were both in shape and The Bird in particular would still present a formidable challenge to anyone unwise enough to take him on.

'So, we hear you've been having quite a time of it,' said Macy. 'What's up?'

'Where do you want me to start?'

'Well, let's get something sorted out first,' said The Bird. 'You said you would bring something for us – some encrypted material. We have a friend on the course who might care to take a look at it now.'

'Really! How on earth did you fix that up?'

'We didn't. He's always here. Horse fanatic. Works at GCHQ and sometimes moonlights by operating the photo-finish camera. Good sort – listens to telephone conversations for a living and can decipher practically anything – except, of course, a racecard. But steady as a brass bedstead otherwise. Won't talk.'

'So where do I find him?'

'You don't. Macy will take it to him now. I told him that he was likely to need a computer. Is that right?'

Harland handed Macy the two discs, one containing the material from Ollins, the other from Sally Griswald's e-mail. He explained they were a pair and that they only worked in tandem.

'Now,' said The Bird, 'tell me what's been going on. I know that you've been shot at and that you've been in an air crash and I gather you were jumped by some heathens in the UN building. What else?'

'You're well informed. How did you know about the UN thing?'

'Word gets about. Look, why don't you tell me the whole bloody lot? The rest of the card's not up to much so we've got plenty of time.'

As Harland spoke, Cuth listened closely, his resourceful eyes darting from Harland's face to a hamper where he picked at the fruitcake. When Harland showed him Eva's identity cards he held each one up to the light, sniffed it and flexed it. Then he handed them back and returned to his chair to rock on the back two legs, his hands clasped round the back of his head. Harland talked for half an hour. He brought the story to a close with a description of Tomas's condition, and explained that he urgently needed to find Eva.

The Bird lifted a slender cigarette case from an inside pocket.

'Hell, Bobby, you're a dark horse. I knew you had some Czech connections, but I didn't realise you had a bloody family there.' He laughed, then his face grew serious. 'Vigo's interest puzzles me. I can't believe he's really concerned about you boffing some Czech teenager back in the Dark Ages. Did you give the Czechs anything?'

'Nothing of value. The odd bit that I knew they already had. I worked it to our advantage – you know how it was.'

'Yes, but you weren't always so canny. They turned the tables on you in 1990 and went at you hammer and tongs, didn't they, old boy? You looked a terrible mess, I can tell you. And that meant someone was pretty upset with you. What did you do to them?'

'I made the point to Vigo's friends from the Security Service, who are meant to be investigating me. They were hardly likely to beat up a major communist intelligence asset.'

'Yes,' Cuth persisted, 'but you didn't quite answer my question about what you might have done to them. I mean, the Czechs weren't into that kind of thing. They slung people into prison and roughed them up a little, sure – but torture wasn't their style.'

'I have no sense of having done anything to them. I imagined they were going to ransom me, then they started interrogating me about something I couldn't have known.' He paused, aware of The Bird's gaze. 'The Russians were capable of this thing. The man in the villa was Russian.'

'And, of course, you just mentioned that the fellow who was present at the massacres in Bosnia was also Russian. Are we talking about the same man?'

'Obviously I considered that because Griswald said I'd be particularly interested when he nailed this fellow Lipnik.'

'But still, it doesn't explain the motive, does it? I mean the savagery of it.' He rubbed his thighs vigorously and poured them each another glass of whisky mac. 'I wish Macy were here. He's good at this sort of thing. But anyway, let's just talk about Griswald for a moment. So, Griswald fixes up this business in Berlin which eventually results in the KGB selling the East Germans' archives to the Americans. Then you two go off to Prague with the idea of snaffling the Czech files too. You blow into town. You find the place is seething with revolutionary fervour and commence negotiations. Is that about right?'

Harland nodded.

'How much money did you take?'

'Fifty thousand dollars as a down payment. Half supplied by the Americans and half by us.'

'And who were your contacts in Prague?'

'They were Griswald's. I didn't want to use the man I had dealt with over the years. Too untrustworthy, too low down the pecking order.'

'And you didn't see this Eva woman?'

'No, not since '75.'

'So what happened?'

'Al went off to meet his contact and the next thing I know the place we were staying at was raided and I was under arrest. I spent the first night in StB headquarters, where they didn't seem to know what to do with me. Then I was handed over to this other lot. They took me to the villa.'

'Who knew where you were?'

'As far as we knew, not many, apart from our people that end and a few in Century House.'

'And Griswald – what happened to him?'

'He never got close to doing the deal. In fact, they took the money and left him high and dry. The Americans were pretty good about it, but Century House were not so understanding. Still, they did pay for you two to get me out.'

The Bird smiled. 'I think the terms of our agreement with Alan Griswald permit me to say categorically that Century House did not commission us. Now that he's dead, I can tell you that Griswald paid for the operation. There were a lot of expenses but we returned some of the money to him – having taken our standard fee, of course. I expect you can guess what he did with the rest of the money.'

Harland thought for a moment. 'I should have thought of it before. He used it to buy the StB file on me.'

'He certainly was a friend to you, Bobby, which makes his death all the more sad. Let's think about those files for a second. If Vigo's little helpers can ferret round those archives, there's no earthly reason why you shouldn't. That's surely your best bet, to trace Eva through her various changes of identity. At the same time you might also usefully learn who Vigo's people are.' He stopped and let the chair return to its four legs. 'You know, I think we may be able to swing this for you. But it'll take time.'

The door opened and Macy appeared, followed by a stout

223

woman in a blue housecoat who was holding the nozzle of a vacuum cleaner.

'We maybe ought to make a move in the next ten minutes or so,' he said. 'They want to clean the box.' The woman muttered something and left them.

'I have just been hearing about Bobby's troubles. They'll make what little hair you've got stand on end. By the way, what's our Nissen hut genius have to say about Bobby's codes?'

'He's rather agitated – to put it mildly.'

'Couldn't he do anything with them?'

'No, there was no difficulty. What's bothering him is the type of code used. He wouldn't say more than that. Apparently it's the same encryption used to leak damaging information about agency operations in Europe. Everyone – the British, Americans, Germans, French and even the saintly Dutch – is affected. He wants to know where it came from. Apparently it's a priority of GCHQ at the moment to find the source of this stuff.'

'What's the code say?'

'Nothing.'

'What do you mean, nothing?'

'It's a photograph – a video still. A man in a uniform on the side of a mountain.'

The Bird's gaze flicked to Harland. 'Friend Lipnik, I imagine. But I bet it's more than just a bloody holiday snap. Griswald wouldn't have taken the trouble to have kept the codes separate otherwise. Can we see it?'

'No. As I say, he's agitated. He suggested we meet at a pub about fifteen miles away just off the Oxford road – the Queen's Head. Says he'll see all three of us there in an hour.'

'He wants to see Bobby?'

'It seems so.'

As they left, The Bird muttered, 'Puts the bloody air crash into a new light, doesn't it?'

They set off in Cuth's Range Rover. He mentioned that a pub on New Year's Eve didn't seem ideal for a quiet meeting, but when they pulled up at the Queen's Head, an old coaching inn in a lonely spot, high on the Cotswolds, it was obvious from the empty car park that there would be little revelry to contend with.

Macy vanished into the pub to find their man. Harland and The Bird waited in the car, watching the rain turn to sleet until he appeared at the front door and waved them in.

'I've got some drinks coming. Our chap's in the back.'

They found him lodged in a tall wooden settle by the embers of a log fire. Harland had expected a desk man in his mid-fifties, a bureaucrat on the glide path to retirement. But a much younger man turned to greet them with a reluctant smile. He was in his early forties and had an alert, rather academic face. He sat with an anorak still zipped up, legs crossed, swinging one walking shoe towards the fire. On the table was a tin of tobacco and a cigarette rolling machine.

There were no introductions. Macy brought the drinks over.

'I've been telling them you're worried about this material,' said Macy quietly. 'You want to explain the problem?'

'Not really,' said the man disagreeably, beginning to feed tobacco into a cigarette paper. He looked up at Harland. 'Where did you get it from?'

'A friend.'

'And how did this friend come by it?'

'I'm not certain. I think he got it from a friend or two friends. What difference does it make?'

'Your disc contains a family of codes that are associated with one of the biggest intelligence disasters of the post-communist era. That's all.'

Harland remembered Vigo's conversation in New York when he had referred to an unusual source of intelligence that he insisted Griswald had access to. He had laboured the point and then refused to give Harland any detail.

'This is not really concerned with all that,' said Harland. 'I'm more interested in the picture Macy says you've found stored in the code. It may help with an investigation that this friend is no longer able to complete.'

'Believe me, the issue is not your damned photograph. Tell me, what form did the code come to you in?'

'One half came as sound, the other as a one-hundred-and-eighty-digit message.'

'Exactly,' said the man. 'Sound. And that's where your problem is.'

'Come on, loosen up,' said Macy. 'This is a friend of ours. Tell him what he needs to know.'

The man put down his pint glass.

'Look, this is not a question of favours, or what I owe you, or who the fuck your friend is. This is as serious as you can get.' He paused to light the roll-up. 'About ten months ago, maybe longer – no one is sure – our counterparts in Israel noticed that a number of radio and TV stations were subject to sustained bursts of interference. It sounded like the static caused by a prolonged electrical storm, and yet it was clear that this sound wasn't being caused by atmospheric conditions. They investigated and saw they were dealing with a set of elaborate, yet fairly unchallenging, codes. It seemed to be the work of a talented outsider who was getting his kicks from devising a series of puzzles, knowing that the only people who would possibly investigate his sounds would be professional listeners. Some of these codes were pretty ingenious. For instance, one was based on the Periodic Table and used the relationship between the symbols of the elements and the atomic numbers. Another was constructed on the position of the English Premier League on a particular Saturday last October.'

He took a draught of beer.

'The whole thing was seen as kind of game, this individual bunging his messages into the ether using the unsuspecting services of about thirty different radio stations. Everyone in Europe has probably heard this noise at some stage over the last year, but only a very few were in a position to understand it. No one had any idea where it came from but it was obvious that whoever was doing this had developed a virus to penetrate the phone systems of practically every broadcasting station. There's a lot of insecure equipment in a studio and somehow this joker had worked out a way of getting his hidden messages into the programmes.

'Then just as he'd got everyone's attention the messages became a lot more serious. He started talking about this and that operation – highly embarrassing for those agencies involved. He'd obviously tapped some good sources of information – people in the business who were feeding him. It was clear that a lot of his stuff was coming from renegade intelligence officers who may have used the Net to talk to him. Some of the information looked very much like the material being posted on the Net by known dissenters and troublemakers. He named agents, especially in the economic sector. For instance, a woman in the German finance ministry who was passing information to the French. There was no pattern to the messages in as much as they didn't favour one country over the other, but they did concentrate on corrupt deals, on high-level bribery and that kind of thing.

'Anyway, to cut a long story short, tracking down this individual or individuals became a priority in all the big Western agencies. They wanted to close him down big time. That wish increased when it was revealed in alarming detail how the Americans and British were supposed to be using their resources to gather intelligence on European business competitors. He was particularly accurate about the activities of the NSA at Bad Aibling.'

'Remind me what's there,' said Harland.

'At Bad Aibling the Americans can hear a man's teeth chattering in the Ukraine. It's a listening post, about fifty miles south of Munich, a very big one which employs a fair slice of the eleven thousand US intelligence personnel still in Germany.'

'I see. He's offended everyone – but why?'

'With respect, I don't think you see at all. The discs you brought to me use some of the same codes. They're pretty basic but I'm sure this stuff hasn't been seen before. It's new to me, anyway, which means there's a direct line back through the friend who gave you this material to the individual who's doing this. You may hold a key to the identity of the source and that makes it rather important.'

The Bird looked at Harland. 'That rather puts things in a new light. But perhaps they already know the identity.'

'That's not my area,' said the man. 'All I know is what I hear and what we filter from the air. But I do know there was a brief interruption of these messages about three weeks ago. We wondered if they had been closed down. There were a lot of people whose Christmas would be made if this fellow was deposited in a frozen river. But they started up again about a week later. Every bloody carol concert broadcast in Eastern Europe was interrupted by this interference.'

'Can I look at the picture you've got?'

'There are two. I found the second while waiting for you to arrive. But I'd rather do this somewhere else. I don't want some colleague of mine blundering in here on a New Year's Eve pub crawl.'

They went outside and got into the Range Rover. The man from GCHQ unfolded a slender laptop which had been concealed in his anorak and pressed a key.

'I'll show you the second photograph first.'

A picture of a middle-aged man appeared instantly. He was standing by a wicker table. His jacket was folded on the

228

arm of a chair and there was a swimming pool in the background. On the table was a tray of drinks, a newspaper and some documents. The man was holding some papers and appeared to be speaking. Clearly he wasn't aware of the camera.

Harland craned forward from the back seat to get a better look at the screen. The man was conventionally dressed – a businessman, still wearing a tie at the poolside. He was of average height and build, with a large head that was slightly out of proportion with his body. There was a dip at the front of his trousers to allow for the beginnings of a paunch, but otherwise he looked in reasonable shape. His eyes were in shade and it was difficult to read any expression in them.

Now Harland grasped the significance of the photograph. The folded newspaper might be German, but more important was that the front page would be dated. If this was Lipnik, it would prove he was alive after the supposed assassination. Enlarging the picture might also yield information from the documents – names, dates and the type of business he was engaged in.

'I'll give you the discs so you can take a closer look at this later.' The man clearly wanted to be on his way. 'But I'll show you the other one quickly.'

The machine hesitated before producing the second image from its memory. It unfolded from the top of the screen, first with a couple of inches of clear summer sky that lit up the interior of the Range Rover, then the top of some distant hills over which were traces of cloud. Then the whole picture materialised and Harland found himself looking at the same man, this time in khaki fatigues. He was standing in the foreground of a group of soldiers. They were gazing down into what appeared to be a ravine, for at the bottom of the picture was a very dark area, in shadow. The man was in sunlight, and despite the slightly liquid quality of the video, it was possible to make out a good deal about him. He wore a peaked cap and had his thumbs tucked into a canvas belt, from which hung a holstered pistol. He looked slimmer. Harland thought there were a few years between the two pictures.

He glanced over the rest of the scene and then his eyes settled on one of the soldiers. He didn't have time to know whether it was the angle of the head or the slightly diffident way the soldier stood back from the others that had attracted his attention. All he knew was that he was looking at Tomas. Tomas standing on a mountainside in the punishing summer heat of the Balkans. Tomas with a war criminal. Tomas in the uniform of a Serb soldier.

Harland began to breathe again and sat back a little. He could still see the screen through the gap between the front seats.

'Any way of bringing this up a touch?' asked The Bird.

The man muttered something and worked the keyboard for a few seconds. He turned the screen to face them.

'Yes, I thought so.' The Bird pointed with the nail of his little finger to the shaded part at the bottom of the picture. 'See here? I think you'll find those are bodies. You can just see the light on a leg here and over here there's someone lying on their side. I suppose they may've been chucked off the top into a pit. Who knows, but I think what we're looking at is the site of the massacre. Wouldn't you agree, Bobby?'

Harland nodded. 'Yes, I think you're right.'

17

NEW YEAR'S EVE

At eight-thirty that evening Harland was dropped off at Oxford Station by The Bird and Macy Harp. On the short ride from the pub, The Bird had filled Macy in with an expert summary of Harland's story. For them the story was a matter of professional curiosity – but only that. He imagined them happily chewing it over on the way back to Berkshire where their wives now prepared a New Year's Eve party. He wondered if their horsy neighbours had any idea what The Bird and Macy got up to when not running around the country in well-tailored tweed suits. As they pulled away, The Bird told him they would be in touch as soon as they'd found a reliable guide in the Czech Republic.

The trains were running infrequently, but at length a cross-country service pulled in. Harland boarded an empty first-class carriage and sank back in the seat, now alone with the knowledge of Tomas's presence at the scene of the massacre. Later he would look at the photograph again and enlarge it to see if the Bird had been mistaken about the shapes at the bottom of the picture. Broken branches or boulders in a stream might be the explanation. Whatever he found, he could not ignore the fact that Tomas was in the company of Viktor Lipnik, a suspected war criminal.

Dead tired, Harland tried to frame his thoughts unemotionally. The photograph did at least have the virtue of clarifying things. The process of reconciling two streams of events was over. There was a whole to consider now. And everything, as he had tired of telling people, sprang from Griswald. It was odd. As he learned more and more of Griswald's activities he seemed to lose the ability to bring to mind his face. Alan Griswald had become an abstract component in the mystery. That was all.

The important gain of the day was the information that the Americans and the British were exercised about the release of secrets about their spying activities against European powers. The probability was that Griswald had exchanged these secrets – easily gathered by someone in his position – for evidence that proved that Viktor Lipnik, far from being interred in a Balkan graveyard, was very much alive and prosperously in business. Whatever he hoped about Tomas's presence in the video still, he also knew that it was unlikely that Griswald had taken all that trouble to acquire the picture if it did not prove Viktor Lipnik's involvement in a war crime on a certain date. Christ, yes! There was a date on that video still. Harland had been so absorbed by the image that he had not taken it on board. At least it would prove useful in persuading Professor Reeve to provide the satellite images.

But how far was he prepared to pursue that line? After all, what was the point? Griswald was dead. Tomas lay in hospital unlikely ever to speak or move again. Others had been killed or crippled. Was it time to drop the whole business? For a full minute he thought of throwing the discs from the train window.

It wasn't that simple, though. The discs weren't the cause of the deaths and maimings, and getting rid of them wouldn't quiet Vigo, settle scores with Viktor Lipnik or bring Tomas out of his coma. The pictures existed as an ineluctable fact. He turned and caught sight of his reflection in the train window. A haggard, middle-aged man stared back at him. He thought of his younger self – the first-class degree, the fond

232

expressions of tutors who recognised promise, the absolute confidence, the ease of entry. The memory of himself for some reason brought back the image of Tomas on the mountainside in army fatigues, shrinking from the edge of the gorge – or was it perhaps a hurriedly excavated burial pit? If that image was a record of a massacre it meant that Tomas was a witness and that would certainly explain why he had been tracked down by a team of killers.

'Or would it?' Harland asked aloud to the empty carriage.

Tomas knew that he was alive. He had known that for some time. There were things that came to him from the world outside him – smells, noises and the lights and shadows which passed across his closed eyelids. But the pain inside his head and the clamour of discomfort from distant sites all over his body was too much for him and he had retreated back down the stairway. It was strange how he thought of it as a stairway. He could see it and feel it and as he got closer to the top there were certain things that he noticed about the stairway. The walls were cold to the touch and there was rope fixed to the side which he clung on to for dear life. He was never quite sure how he went back down again, whether he took it carefully, minding not to fall, or whether he just somehow arrived at the bottom where there was no light, no feeling – just dreams. He was content down there, though he only knew this once he had begun the journey up again and realised what he was leaving and what lay at the top. That was why he could never quite bring himself to leave the stairway for good. At the top he knew he would find himself, which was to say his body and his mind would be joined again and become aware of each other. Then Tomas Rath would live and act and do as other people did, but he didn't want that yet.

The clarity of these thoughts surprised him because he had been aware of a certain fogginess of late, quite separate from the pain that periodically surged in his centre and blotted everything out. He was thinking better and he'd quite consciously recognised that once he reached the top there were decisions to be taken. The nature of these evaded him for the moment, but he understood that they were there and that they would crowd in on him very soon.

He heard a woman's voice and he decided he would open his eyes and see who it was. He felt little pain at the moment – a hot, sticky feeling on his back and buttocks, tenderness in his neck and shoulders and a gentle throb in his head. But nothing he couldn't deal with.

He waited as the voice got louder. Someone was talking to him because they were using his name – Tomas. And they were speaking in English. That was inconvenient, but he'd handle it. He began to open his eyes and noticed only one was opening, and that it was pretty much blinded by the light. He blinked a few times so that gradually he became accustomed to the glare. Just then, it struck him that he was having terrible difficulty in breathing. There was a hissing noise in his ear and his heart was pounding as if he had just taken some exercise. The real pain now was in his throat. Not the agony of before, but a raw, scorched dryness like a very bad infection. He also had the sense that something was obstructing his airway. It was thirst. He had never known thirst which hurt. He tried to swallow to get some saliva down there but his throat wouldn't allow it.

He realised that a new note had entered the voice to his left and that the woman was probably speaking to someone else. But he couldn't listen because he was concentrating very hard on trying to move his head. He'd never had to think about how to do this before and now, quite inexplicably, he'd forgotten. But he *did* need to remember because he wanted water and he would have to get up and find that water or at least tell the woman, who was now talking to him in an odd, soothing manner, that he needed water above all else. Above all else, do you hear? He knew he was speaking. He was sure of it, but he could not hear the words. And then he understood that there were so many things in his mouth that he couldn't possibly speak. He would have to take them out in order to speak and to drink the water.

So he told his hand to grapple with the things they had shoved in his mouth and were causing him to experience that raspy, parched feeling at the back of his throat. Which hand he used didn't much matter – either would do. But nothing happened. He wanted to look to see if he still had hands. He thought he could feel them. But when you can't look down and they don't respond to your command, it's not easy to know whether you still have them.

Suddenly his other eye opened, and, although it took some time to get used to the light and he had to blink a bit, he was soon able to look ahead of him. There was a light on the ceiling and at the end of his bed he saw a man and two women. He was in a hospital. He looked down to see where his hands had got to but found that they weren't quite in his field of vision. He would move his head and check on them. That would be simple now he was fully awake. He moved, or rather gave the instruction to move his head but nothing happened. Again he wondered how he'd forgotten something so basic. Maybe they'd given him some drugs to keep him still.

He looked up ahead of him and a thought came to him that a preferable existence was to be had down the stairway, where at least he wouldn't experience this raging thirst and his limbs would move according to his wishes. But the man was saying something to him. He must be a doctor. He spoke very slowly and very insistently, as if he was stupid. Just because he was temporarily unable to move, it didn't mean he was a moron.

'Tomas,' he said, 'Tomas. That's your name, isn't it? We're

pleased to have you with us again. You've been unconscious for nearly a week. You've been in a coma.'

'Is he responding?' asked another woman's voice. 'His eyelids may just be fluttering as part of the aftershock.'

'For goodness' sake, Claire,' said the doctor, *sotto voce*. It was impossible to miss the impatience. 'If you haven't got anything better to say, do please shut up.'

Tomas could see the woman. She wore glasses. Straight black hair. Pretty but severe face. Quite sexy. He hoped he wasn't making a fool of himself in front of her. He must look absurd lying there.

'Your head probably hurts a bit,' continued the doctor, 'and that's because we took a bullet out of it on Christmas Day. You probably don't remember much of what happened, but you were shot and the bullet went up through your throat into the bottom of your head. Still, we managed to get it out pretty cleanly and you're healing very well. In fact, you're making excellent progress, Tomas.'

He drew breath heavily and came closer. 'The thing is, Tomas, you're going to feel a bit unwell for some time yet. Part of the effects of an operation like this is to render you paralysed.' He paused to let the words of this sentence sink in. All Tomas knew was that he was translating everything into Czech. The word *parolyzovany* repeated itself in his mind.

'You won't be able to move much for a while. That's a good thing in a way because it gives your injuries a chance to heal, but in other ways it's going to be very inconvenient and frustrating for you. But you can rest assured that we will be working very hard for you, pulling together to make things a bit more comfortable for you.' He paused again and put his face directly in front of Tomas's. It was difficult for Tomas to focus so close because his eyes now seemed to be bobbing up and down. He wanted to move his head back just to get a proper look at the man.

'I believe you're all there, Tomas. That's terribly good news. Really, I couldn't be more pleased. Well done, you.'

Well done, me? thought Tomas. How very English to say that. All I've done is walk up a stairway.

The woman came round to the doctor's side of the bed. Tomas saw a nametag on her breast and he could smell her scent.

'I'm not sure,' said the woman. 'He doesn't look as if he has taken in much of what you've been saying.' She appeared to be a doctor too.

'Oh yes he has,' said the man confidently. 'I know it.' He gave Tomas's hand a tiny squeeze. 'And I know he can feel that too. You're fully aware of what's going on around you, aren't you, old thing?' He paused again. 'So I thought I would tell you a little about what we're going to do. For quite a while we will be feeding you through these tubes here and helping you breathe with this machine which you can probably hear to your left. For that reason we've made a very small hole in the front of your throat to allow the air to pass into your body without something getting in the way. That may feel a bit uncomfortable and a bit strange until you get used to it.'

Now Tomas was registering what he had been saying, not the stuff about tubes, but about guesswork. Did they mean that he wasn't going to be able to communicate the smallest wish to them and that they would therefore have to guess his needs? How would they know that his throat was parched and his arse was sore and his side ached with a mysterious dull pain which reminded him of acute constipation? How could they possibly know these things? And how long would this state of total dependence last? When was he going to get better? He wanted to know the answer to that question most of all. There was an open-ended quality to the doctor's statements that made him uneasy. If he was going to be like this for months, he wished they would tell him.

He tuned again into what the doctor was saying.

'At the moment our first priority is to establish a way that you can use to communicate your needs. We want to be able to ask you questions such as – Would you like a different channel on your TV? And for you to be able to give us the answer yes or no. That can be done with your eyelids, which I'm optimistic that you'll be able to control.

'Now . . . I understand that you are a Czech speaker, but that you also speak English pretty well. Mr Harland, who you know, has told me that he will visit the Czech Republic at the earliest possible opportunity to contact your mother. He will bring her here and you'll be able to hear your native language. Of course, I have every hope that we will be able to work out this code in English. That'll make it much easier for us to get through the next three months or so.'

Three months, thought Tomas. He could just do three months – as long as there was going to be an end and he'd be able to move. Then he thought of his mother. Her lovely, dark, elliptical face came to him. The eyes that smiled and said nothing; the gaiety that defied confrontation; the conversation that left so many infuriating gaps – how would she cope with this? How would he?

His mind clouded with despair. He no longer had a choice in these things: if she came, he couldn't very well walk away.

God, he wished he could remember what had happened. He remembered he had been with Harland and that they were by a river. For some reason he was feeling optimistic. Harland had said something conciliatory to him. He had accepted him. Tomas was aware of his mind stalling in certain areas. Yes, he had been shot. The doctor said so, though he couldn't remember when it had actually happened. Was it after they'd been at the river? He remembered Flick. Flick was dead. He saw her bedroom and her body curled up on the bed. Had he imagined that? No, he hadn't because that's why he'd run and found himself in that little hotel room doing the final work. He noticed that his mind was vibrating so that it was difficult to hold on to a single thought: he would be thinking of Flick then his mother would come to mind; he would remember what Harland had said to him and then a big house full of people would appear.

He stopped scurrying between these images. Someone was laughing. He listened. Incredibly the noise seemed to be coming from his own mouth. The mouth which could not speak or drink or breathe by itself was now laughing. But there was nothing funny: he wasn't responding to a joke made by the doctor and he certainly hadn't been thinking of anything humorous. Yet his belly pulsated, his eyes were closing and the noise struggled past the tubes and hole in his throat to fill the room with a desperate, mirthless gurgle. Suddenly it stopped and Tomas realised – or rather suspected – that his face was frozen in a terrifying rictus because the doctor peered at him and he saw the horror and the pity in his eyes.

The female doctor asked her colleague something quietly. Tomas heard him pooh-pooh her suggestion, then he picked up the phrase 'involuntary motor activity', whose meaning he couldn't quite pin down because he was having trouble with words.

A terrible thought began to creep into his mind, a suggestion that this paralysis was not the side effect of drugs but was a permanent condition. Perhaps he would never again walk over to a basin and get himself a glass of water, never feel the weather on his face, touch a woman's breast, make himself heard, take a piss without someone holding his dick or plugging him with a tube. For some time now he'd been aware of the smell in the room and now he realised that it was his own smell. Would he have to live with that? With the leaking of catheters and bags? With the heat and accumulating sweat of his own body?

Panic flooded his head. He could hear his heart beating

239

very fast and something had happened to his breathing. First there was a total cessation so that he was fighting to get air into his lungs, then he could feel himself take tiny short gasps of air. He heard the doctors say something and the next thing he knew was that he was looking at his arms and legs, which had reared up in front of him and, in the case of his arms, were moving up and down as though he were conducting a very slow piece of music. The cramp at the back of his calves and in the top of his thighs was excruciating. But the one thought at the back of Tomas's mind was that he still possessed movement. This sudden reflex was evidence that he would eventually be able to tell his body what to do.

He felt the jab of the needle in his buttock and then saw his limbs fall back to the bed. The nurse who had administered the injection gave his legs some help by easing them down and placing the cover over them. But he didn't want that. He was too hot and he wanted to tell her to leave him alone and let him make his own decision about the cover.

The shot had an immediate effect. He was calmer and the doctor was talking again, but not to him. He was explaining something to the woman whose scent he longed for. He waited, wondering what would happen next. It occurred to him that he wasn't just a prisoner of his body but that it had declared a kind of independence and it was going to do anything it pleased, except serve its master. Was this the future? He had a superstitious sense that he had been occupied by a being that was going to force him to laugh and cry and gesticulate at inappropriate moments simply for the cruel pleasure of it.

He felt drowsy and began to slip towards sleep, knowing that he would never find himself at the bottom of the stairway again.

Harland arrived at Harriet's house, too weary to care much

about who might be watching his movements. Near the end of the train journey from Oxford it had occurred to him that Tomas's presence in one of the pictures had prevented him from seeing them for their true worth. Far from being a kind of curse, they endowed their keeper with a certain power.

He installed himself in Harriet's office at the top of the house and fed the disc into her computer. He looked at the picture of the mountainside first, isolating and enlarging the portion that contained Tomas. There was no doubt about it. Tomas was standing there with an oddly vacant expression, one foot lifting to the right, in the process of turning away. As far as Harland could tell, he was not armed.

He began to trawl the rest of the image for clues and information. He had been right about the date. It appeared over a patch of white rock that made it easy to miss. The events recorded had taken place at 2.15 p.m. on 15.7.95. That was probably all he needed to elicit the satellite pictures from Professor Reeve. He noted down the date and time, momentarily wondering whether the type of rock in the foreground was limestone. That might be a clue to the place. He moved over to the other side of the picture, framed the dark area at the bottom left-hand corner and instructed the computer to fill the screen with it. His first impression was of a detail in one of those mediaeval studies of the Day of Judgement – the souls of the damned cast into hell. There were five or six bodies lying there in the shadows. All of them appeared to be men. A glint of machinery caught his eye also, a crescent of metal, possibly the blade of a piece of earth-moving equipment.

Time and place were obviously important to Griswald's investigation and he realised that the mountains at the top of the screen might establish an approximate position. He flipped back to the whole image. There was a V-shaped nick in the furthest range which consisted of one fairly prominent peak. That might be identified if the direction of the camera was known. Yes, because a clue to this lay in the time that the image was made – a little over two hours past midday. That time seemed to tally with the amount of light in the picture and the shortness of the shadows. More crucial, however, was his observation that the shadows ran away from the lens, which meant that whoever had been filming the scene had his back directly to the sun.

Harland closed his eyes to assemble his little knowledge of using the sun as an aid to orientation. At midday a shadow cast by a vertical object would give a reading for north since the sun was in the south. As the afternoon wore on the shadows would swing to the right and, using the principle of the sundial, it would be possible to gauge the time and also to get a bearing between zero and ninety degrees. The further the sun went west, the more the shadows would veer to the east and a bearing of ninety degrees. He remembered that the season had to be taken into account in such a calculation but since the picture was dated to just over three weeks after the summer solstice of 21 June, he assumed that variation would not be great.

He was unsure of his geometry and decided to make a copy of the picture on Harriet's printer. Then he began to trace a series of lines fanning out from a point in the middle of the bottom of the frame. It was all very hit and miss, but after borrowing a protractor from his nephew's geometry case he estimated that the shadows were pointed at a bearing of between 20 and 25 degrees. That put the V-shaped incision in the range at a bearing of 15 degrees and the large peak at a few degrees east of due north – say 355 degrees. If he could get the profile of the mountain range identified, he'd be able to mark out a rough area where the massacre had taken place. And that process might be refined by estimating the distance between the camera and the mountain range – not, perhaps, a problem for a surveyor – and the safe assumption that this spot was probably close to a road or track because of the inconvenience involved in moving a bulldozer over a lot of rough terrain.

He called up the other picture and squared off sections that he wanted to examine more closely. The screen filled with the still life of the table – a German-language newspaper dated 29 May 1998, the tray of drinks which included a bottle of Pernod, Martini, whisky of an identifiable brand and various mixers. Harland focused on the papers in front of the drinks tray. They were in German and appeared to be some kind of report. The type was too small to read from the screen, but he picked up a couple of signatures at the bottom of one sheet and with greater magnification these could be deciphered.

He went back to the whole frame and tried to see what else might lie there. Way off in the background were two men in dark suits, standing with their hands clasped in front of them in the manner of silent heavies the world over. The landscape was rolling rather than mountainous, and it was possible to make out pastures and clumps of pine trees. It could be anywhere, thought Harland. There was countryside like this all over the Balkans and Central Europe but, given the newspaper, he'd bet on Austria or Germany.

Finally he addressed Viktor Lipnik, enlarging him to fill the whole screen. The three-quarter view gave him much more sense of Lipnik than the profile in the first picture. He had a rather long face with a nose that was slightly hooked at the end, a feature enhanced by the angle of his rather thin nostrils. His hair was straight and dark – perhaps dyed? – and he had a light beard which was only visible above his lip. All things considered it was not an unpleasant face.

Harland stared at the whole picture. He was aware of something speaking to him. It wasn't the sense of Eastern European style in the sheen of his suit, the angle of the shirt collar, the Windsor-knotted tie. Nor was it the suspicion that Viktor Lipnik had invested in cosmetic surgery, evidenced by a vertical scar in front of one of his ears. It was his Rolex watch – exactly the same chunky symbol of wealth that he'd been surprised to see on Tomas's arm in the first picture. He knew that Tomas had not worn it on the occasions that they met.

He printed two fresh copies of the pictures and two sets of the details he had examined, and placed them in envelopes. As he dialled Frank Ollins's mobile number, he let his eyes play over the photograph. As usual Ollins picked up immediately.

'Did you find anything in that material?' asked Harland.

'Not yet.' Ollins was unfazed by Harland's lack of greeting. 'The people who were looking at it haven't come back to me.'

'Which people were dealing with it? You see, some might regard this material as poison and its bearer as a national security risk.'

'Whoever you're talking about isn't going to get his hands on it. This is an FBI investigation into a very serious crime. We won't swerve from the completion of this inquiry, I can promise you that.' Harland was taken aback by this rather formal statement. Perhaps Ollins was speaking for the benefit of others.

'Good,' said Harland, thinking of that audience. 'Of course, anyone interested in suppressing this evidence would need to know that it's possible to place the information on the Web or to give it to newspapers. At this time of year they're always short of news.'

'So what did you find?'

'Two pictures of a man named Lipnik, who was indicted as a war criminal before he was killed off in an elaborately staged assassination. The pictures prove that Lipnik is alive and that he took part in a massacre of some scale. This man was the subject of Griswald's last inquiry and must be regarded as a suspect in the Falcon's crash.'

'What are you going to do with the pictures?'

'Send them to the Secretary-General's office.'

'Not before you give them to me as per our agreement, right?'

This was entirely within Harland's plan, but he wanted Ollins to know that he was doing him a favour.

'Why don't you tell me a bit more about the crash? What did you mean by the questions you asked me?'

'I'm sorry,' said Ollins resolutely. 'I can't say more.'

'Well, tell me whether you'll be keeping the Secretary-General informed on developments.'

There was a pause.

'Yes,' said Ollins. 'Look, to get back to our agreement. We said that whoever decoded the material first would send it to the other. That's what you agreed. Are you welching?'

'No, I'll send it in an attachment this evening using the same procedure as before.' Harland sounded reluctant but he knew that he was only too happy to pass the pictures to the FBI. The pictures represented power, but it was not the kind of power that needed to be hoarded.

They said goodbye, exchanging a sardonic New Year's greeting.

The next call was to Jaidi's office, which was still manned. He told the woman on the other end that he would be sending a two-page memorandum to the Secretary-General and that he would need a fax number or e-mail address that would ensure Jaidi read it the next morning. He stressed the need for utter secrecy and speed. She gave him a fax number in Davos, Switzerland where Jaidi had improbably holed up for a few days with his Swedish-born wife and child.

He slowly replaced the phone, already in the act of composition. But his thoughts were interrupted by Harriet telling him that there were just ten minutes to go before midnight. They were opening champagne.

Harland got downstairs to find Robin sprawled almost

245

horizontal, his long legs stretched in front of him. He smiled comfortably at Harland.

'So what've you been up to, Bobby? Haven't really had a chance to ask since you vanished from my office yesterday.'

Harriet looked on edge, as though she guessed he'd discovered something important.

'Oh, this and that,' he said, as pleasantly as he could. Whatever Robin's deficiencies of intellect, he was certainly a good host. He deserved politeness. The strokes of Big Ben came. They embraced, Harland enduring a longer than usual hug from his brother-in-law.

The phone went. It was Philip Smith-Canon breaking the news that Tomas had emerged from his coma. He had been awake for twenty-five minutes. He was very weak and there were problems with muscle spasm. They would be working on this in the next few days.

Harland hung up and told them.

'Well, that's some good news to start the year off with,' said Robin.

'I wouldn't be so sure,' said Harriet.

18

VIGO'S MAP

After a while Harriet and Robin went upstairs. Harland returned to the little office to begin a memorandum for Jaidi. It was a laconic affair which, if anything, underplayed the sabotage theory, although he did mention that the FBI had made unspecified discoveries concerning the electronics systems of the plane. The rest concerned the pictures of Lipnik whom he assumed was the man that Jaidi referred to as the 'quantum enemy'. He asked the Secretary-General to expand on his phrase for, as far as he knew, Lipnik had only one other identity – the one assumed after the staged assassination. He gave a hint or two about the evidence to be gleaned from a close examination of both pictures. He ended the note by saying that he was continuing his inquiries in Eastern Europe. He signed off in the hope that they would speak soon. He sent the e-mail with the photographs in an attachment, knowing that Jaidi would not concern himself with the identity of the young soldier in the background of the earlier picture.

As he was clearing up and preparing to go to bed, Harriet slipped into the office and perched, in an ancient woollen dressing-gown, on the desk beside him. Her face was scrubbed clean of make-up and glistened with moisturiser.

'Okay,' she said in a bad American accent, 'quit stalling on me. What've you got?'

'A lot,' he said glumly, and withdrew one of the prints

from the envelope and handed it to her. 'That was taken in Bosnia. It's the scene of a massacre. You can see Tomas in the background.'

Harriet let out a gasp. 'God! How on earth did you get this?'

'Griswald was carrying it on the plane. His interest was in the man in the foreground. That has to be Lipnik.'

'So everything does connect. What are you going to do now?'

'I'm going to go to Prague to try to trace Tomas's mother. It's essential that she's found to help communicate with him. But she must also be able to explain how he came to be in Bosnia when he was just twenty years old.'

'Who have you showed these pictures to?'

'So far the FBI and Jaidi. Both within the last hour or so.'

'I see.' She paused. 'Lipnik could reasonably assume that they were no longer in existence. After all, they took the mini-disc from you in the UN and wouldn't have expected you to have copied it. But that doesn't explain why Tomas was hunted down like that. It can't have been because he was witness to that thing in Bosnia because they would have found him before. So why now? What's the connection?

'Maybe Tomas knew Lipnik was alive.' Harland didn't sound very convincing to himself. He went on to tell her about his afternoon with the man from GCHQ.

'So the connection could be something to do with these codes.'

'Maybe.'

'So that means you're still much in danger?'

'I think not. But who knows? I haven't got to the bottom of this thing.'

'And you're going to Prague.'

This came out like an accusation. She knew about the last time, not the details of course, but she saw him in hospital only a few days after The Bird and Macy had delivered him

248

there. She sighed heavily and rubbed her hands together. There were tears of anger and frustration in her eyes. Harland started to say that he had to go.

'Oh, for Christ's sake, don't you think that you've run out of lives, Bobby? I mean, let's face it, you came back from the police station the other night in a terrible state. I know what caused it. So do you. You had a flashback. And now you're going back to Prague. What do you think will happen? Surely you can trace this woman and simply telephone her?'

'It's not that easy. I'll need to look at some old files there.'

She pressed her hands together and interlocked her fingers. 'You're a bastard to cause me so much worry. I hope you know that.'

He said nothing.

'I mean it, Bobby. You're a bastard.'

'I'm sorry.' He shifted in his chair. 'I really am sorry. But I'm stuck in the middle of this thing. I can't go back. I have to go forward.'

'Well . . . you'll need the things I've been holding for you. I always knew they'd be useful one day.'

She pushed him gently out of the way with her forearm, knelt down to the bottom drawer of a cupboard and pulled out a red petty-cash box.

'You remember you had me keep everything up to date when you were with SIS?' She looked at him despairingly. 'You know – your covers! You got me to maintain these bloody false identities and make sure there was activity in your accounts while you were away.'

Of course Harland remembered. From the moment he entered Century House on the Intelligence Officer's New Entry Course, he was taught how to build and maintain cover. In his time at SIS he had five or six. Each cover usually – but not always – included a false passport, a driving licence, a cheque guarantee card and one or two credit cards. It was drummed into them from the very first that these identities must have 'hinterland', by which it was meant a life that could be inferred from membership cards, receipts in the name of the cover, letters and so forth. It was advisable to have an ACA – an Alias Cover Address – where correspondence could be sent and someone would vouch for you if inquiries were made.

Harland was allocated a man in Wimbledon, a retired SIS officer who had settled down with a Dutch widow ten years his junior. His name was Jeavons. For a time the relationship worked well: Harland gained invaluable tips on trade-craft.

But it was a laborious business, keeping Jeavons sweet and making sure that there was enough convincing 'wallet litter' for the identities he used. Towards the end of Harland's time at SIS, Jeavons lost interest and his wife took over the running of Harland's affairs. But then Mrs Jeavons started to invent reasons for Harland to visit her, usually when her husband was out. It was plain that he had to go to bed with her, or move cover address. He opted for the latter and asked Harriet to manage things while he found someone new. It wasn't ideal but she had married and got a new name and as ever had inexhaustible energy.

By this time he had two main covers – Charles Suarez, a construction engineer from the British community in Buenos Aires, and Tristan O'Donnell, a salesman from County Cork. Both possessed false passports from the country of origin, arranged by SIS in the days when these things were less closely monitored. His colleagues who had been issued documentation by the passport office in Petty France were required to lodge them at Century House when they were not being used. But nobody seemed to mind the abuse of a foreign passport and Harland had been allowed to keep his.

Into Harriet's safekeeping also went the two bank accounts, one held at Coutts in the Strand and the other at the Royal Bank of Scotland in Victoria Street. Over the years, Harland had achieved a degree of realistic churn in the two accounts, using them occasionally to bank money of his own or pay off his and Louise's household bills. From these two accounts were also paid magazine subscriptions, video library fees, annual donations to Amnesty International, Shelter and The Salmon and Trout Association. In the days when he needed the services of O'Donnell and Charles Suarez he used in spare moments to write off job applications in either name so that he would have recent letters addressed to him to keep in a briefcase.

In the late autumn of 1989, when Harland travelled as an 'illegal' to Prague, he went without the protection of his own diplomatic passport and instead became Charles Suarez. This had been his own decision because he didn't want his name turning up on an immigration or customs list when he crossed from East Germany to Czechoslovakia. With his arrest, the usefulness of Charles Suarez and his carefully nurtured interests and ambitions ended. In fact, he never again saw the passport or the briefcase containing his reply from a construction firm in Reading. When he resigned from the service a few months later, nobody thought to ask him about any other identities he had cultivated alongside Suarez's.

Harriet unlocked the box with a key she took from the desk, and fished inside. There were bank statements, a driving licence, a video card and membership to a club in Mayfair called the Regency Rooms.

'Hal,' he said, 'the passport must be out of date. It's a decade or more since I looked at this stuff.'

'Nope,' she said, pulling a pristine EU passport from a brown envelope. 'In a bored moment I applied for a new one to see what would happen and they sent this back without batting an eyelid. Anyway, I somehow didn't want Tris to turn his toes up quite yet. Look, there's you.' She showed him the picture. 'Not bad. You gave me a whole strip of photos for visas. Don't you remember?'

Harland did vaguely remember. 'And I suppose the driving licence is current and clean?'

'What did you expect?'

He picked up some bank statements and looked at a recent sheet for 1999. His eyes settled on a column in the right. 'Hal! This was in credit twenty-five thousand pounds last year. Where did this come from?'

'That's why I didn't want Tris to die,' she said with a giggle. 'He's been quite a success on the stock market. In fact Tris is currently in the black to the tune of forty-one thousand pounds.' She handed him the latest bank statement.

'Jesus, is this your money?'

'Yes, it's all completely legitimate. I just wanted to keep certain transactions separate. Tris has two credit cards – banks kept on offering him gold, platinum and what have you, so he accepted. Last winter he paid for us all to go to Antigua, first class.' She handed him all the papers. 'It's all completely kosher. If you have to go to Prague again, you can go as Tristan O'Donnell.'

'You know Prague's a different place now.' He moved to touch the top of her hand but withdrew at the last moment. 'They're members of NATO. They're officially part of the West. The Czechs are a civilised people and all anybody wants to do is buy Gap and eat McDonald's.'

'Semi-West! I read the papers. Half the corruption scandals in East Europe are traced back to Prague and Budapest. Look, I just don't want you to be hurt – that's all.' She looked at him with an utterly vulnerable expression. He muttered some reassurance but knew he was pushing her away.

She rose from crouching over the petty-cash box. 'When this is over, you really ought to talk things through with a sensible shrink. You don't seem to be aware of what's going on outside you much. You seem to experience fear, but have no idea about danger, no concept of risk. You used not to be like that, you know. You were more balanced.'

'You're probably right.'

'I am.'

'I've been thinking about Vigo,' he said, shifting his position on the chair. 'How bloody odd it is that he's just gone off the radar. He went to see Tomas's doctor and asked about him. Then nothing. What's that suggest to you?'

'That he no longer needs to pressurise you, that he's found out what he wanted.'

'How would a visit to the hospital satisfy that, unless Vigo was somehow aware of the hunt for Tomas and was keen to learn whether he was effectively silenced as a witness? I think I'll pay Walter a visit. You know those people who brought him here for the party – the Hammicks? Do you think you could persuade them to give you Davina's home address?'

'We don't have to ask them. Davina Cummings is bound to be in the LMH Annual, even if only to let all her contemporaries know what a wonderful life she's enjoying.'

She reached up to a shelf at the far end of the room and withdrew a slender ring binder. 'Here she is: "Davina Cummings – brackets Vigo – twenty-three, Kensington Hill Square, London W11". Funny, I thought they lived in Chelsea. Still, the book is last year's so it ought to be right.'

Harland made a note of the address. 'There's one other thing,' he said. 'I'll be away for three or four days. Can you go and tell Tomas where I am and what I'm doing? He must be pretty terrified and I'm sure it would be good for him to see a friendly face. You'd better talk to the doctor beforehand. Tomas may not know how bad his condition is.'

'Of course. After all, he is my nephew.'

He rose early and took one of the Bosey cars to Kensington Hill Square in Holland Park. The day was cold and hazy and the sun had not yet dispersed the mist in the side streets. He parked outside number fifteen and counted the doorways to twenty-three, an averagely plush residence for the area with two conical bay trees at the entrance. Although the terrace was set back from the line of the road behind a run of nineteenth-century railings, it was possible to see the doorway to the house.

He decided to make his move at eight o'clock and spent the next fifteen minutes running through the questions he had for Vigo, and intermittently musing on the price of a house in the square. Two and a bit million pounds, he thought. Davina Vigo certainly had 'background'.

A little before eight a black London taxi passed his car and pulled up outside number twenty-three. Harland sunk a little lower in his seat and watched two men get out. As one turned to pay the driver Harland recognised his main interrogator at the Crèche, Anthony Rivers. The other was Derek Blanchard, the unlovely MI5 man. They appeared to be expected because they were let in immediately. A few minutes later a dark blue Mondeo saloon drew up and a further three men got out and went into the house. He was sure one of these was Griffiths, the thickset Celt who had approached him at the airport. And the parka? That must have been the same individual who'd followed him in Regent Street.

He waited for an hour, watching the windows for signs of activity. The more he thought about it, the more this breakfast meeting, held on a public holiday at the home of a senior member of SIS, seemed decidedly unofficial. He remembered that at the Crèche it had struck him he was being questioned by a couple of retreads. And there was a distinctly weekend feel to the others – the men who staffed the Crèche and had followed him so blatantly the next day. A proper surveillance operation would have used scores of men and women and however much he went through his dry-cleaning procedures it would have been virtually impossible for him to shake them off.

So Vigo was making do with limited resources, a group of individuals who came from intelligence backgrounds but who were no longer employed by MI5 or MI6 – people like Guy Cushing, who owed him. The purpose of this personal crusade baffled Harland. But plainly Vigo was at odds with his colleagues at Vauxhall Cross, and that knowledge gave Harland a lot more leverage than he had possessed when he set out that morning.

His thoughts were interrupted by a cab drawing up outside number twenty-three. Blanchard and Rivers reappeared and got in. The other three men followed them through the open door and, without looking back, climbed into the Mondeo and departed. Then a man and woman, who must have arrived some time before the others, left together. For a moment Harland wondered whether he should follow one of the vehicles, but realised that he stood to learn much more by catching Vigo off guard.

He waited ten minutes so that Vigo wouldn't suspect he had seen his visitors, then approached the laurel-green front door and rang the bell. A few moments elapsed before Vigo's voice sounded on the intercom.

'It's Bobby Harland, Walter. I thought we could have a talk.'

'It's not a terribly convenient moment, Bobby,' came the voice, unruffled.

'You'll change your mind when you hear what I have to say.'

The entry-phone went dead and the door opened a few seconds later.

Harland noticed his clothes first: suit trousers and a tie – a silk job with a plump knot. 'Off to work on New Year's Day, Walter? You must have a lot on.'

Vigo regarded him with wary interest.

'Can I come in?'

'If it can't wait, yes. But I do indeed have a lot on.'

He led Harland to the far end of the hall and into a small room lined with wire-mesh fronted bookcases and antique maps. All three windows were secured by impressive metal trelliswork. The floor consisted of old black and white tiles and above the carved eighteenth-century fireplace hung a bulbous convex mirror. On a Jefferson reading lectern lay a couple of closed volumes. The room had the air and silence of a scholar's retreat.

'So this is where you keep your incunabula?'

'Such that I possess,' Vigo replied tartly.

'It's a very soothing room. It makes me think that I should have paid more attention to where I live and what I surround myself with. I admire you for it, Walter. It's important in your job to maintain a balance. Do you still trot off to the London Library for an afternoon's reading?'

'Not as much as I'd like,' said Vigo. He was waiting for Harland to get to the point.

'I've come to talk to you about Alan Griswald,' said Harland. 'You know you were interested to find out what he was carrying. Well, I have the information with me.'

Vigo cocked an eyebrow.

Harland withdrew the envelope and selected the print of Lipnik by the swimming pool. 'This is Viktor Lipnik, an indicted war criminal who is believed to have been killed. Griswald knew he was alive. The picture was hidden in a code, which, I suspect, was your interest.'

Vigo looked at the photograph like someone who has been called upon to admire a child's painting.

'Well . . . thank you, Bobby. That's most helpful of you.'

He took out the second image and showed it to Vigo, having carefully placed his thumb over Tomas's head. 'And this one is of Lipnik at the site of a massacre in Bosnia. Enhancement of the bottom left-hand corner shows several

256

bodies. As you can see, it's dated to the period of the Srebrenica massacres in north-east Bosnia.'

Vigo put his hands in his pockets. 'It's good of you to show me these. No doubt you've forwarded your find to the relevant parties.'

'The UN and to the FBI as well. They're looking into the sabotage of the plane's electronics systems. Viktor Lipnik is therefore the chief suspect in the investigation.'

Vigo emitted a ruminative sound. 'Yes, I imagine that must be the case.'

'Walter, I don't seem to be getting a reaction here.'

'What did you expect?'

'For a start, an explanation for the investigation of my past by you.'

'That must be perfectly obvious, Bobby,' he said evenly. 'You are suspected of having committed serious offences against your country. In due course the authorities will decide what to do with you. It's out of my hands. I am not an officer of the law.'

Harland looked down and noted the impressions left in the seats of the two sofas by Vigo's recent visitors. He sat down and brushed his hand over the fabric.

'That's all bollocks, Walter. The only thing the authorities knew about the charade the other night at the Crèche was the call they got from the Secretary-General's office. I bet you had to do some fast talking to explain *that* to Robin Teckman and the Foreign Secretary. No doubt, they were rather bemused by the call, but I imagine you wriggled out of it. You knew you had to let me go and to pack the place up. You see, I know that wasn't the Crèche, Walter. You just borrowed some bloody building to give me a working over.'

Vigo removed his hands from his pockets and walked to one of the antique maps on the wall where he paused in rapt contemplation of a sketchy coastline of northern Europe.

'And if the Crèche was a fake,' continued Harland,

'Blanchard, Rivers, Griffiths and the others were operating outside the law, and – I'm certain – without the knowledge of the Director of SIS. What is interesting about this is why you have bothered with this elaborate charade. Clearly you aren't interested in the photographs of Lipnik because nothing as basic as evidence of an appalling crime motivates you. I remember you saying that Griswald had benefited from an unusual source to obtain his evidence. So it must have been the means of communication that interested you and the possibility that Griswald had exchanged something for those images. Am I right?'

Vigo remained immobile, then gestured to the map.

'You know, it's thought likely that this very map appears in the background of one of Vermeer's paintings, which is as good as saying that he owned it. There's no proof, of course, but it certainly is pleasing to have touched something that he handled. And that's the point. But if an expert were to come along and prove categorically that the story was myth, the map's charm would be drastically reduced.' He turned and studied Harland. 'It's the same with the snapshots of this man, Bobby. Your faith in them derives entirely from their recovery from the plane crash, about which, incidentally, you persistently lied to me. But leaving that aside, you have imbued them with a special significance, ignoring the counsel of your more rational self which must have suggested that these photographs could not be crucial evidence against a war criminal, whether alive or dead. For instance, the scene showing him in uniform could equally be interpreted as the excavation of a mass grave. An officer orders his troops to uncover the evidence of another army's crimes. How about that for an alternative caption?'

If only Vigo knew how that interpretation tempted him.

'There is the date on the image,' he replied, 'and the witness statements which put this man at the scene of the cleansing operation.'

'Very vague and circumstantial, rather like the provenance of my map. But look, Bobby, why are you concerning yourself with Bosnia? It all happened so long ago. There have always been massacres in the Balkans and there always will be; the people are intractable and murderous by nature. They won't change, no matter how much aid and intervention is advocated by the do-gooders at the UN.'

Harland had had enough of Vigo's diversion.

'This is not about Bosnia, Walter. It's about the release of intelligence secrets through the broadcast media in Eastern Europe. I know about the code and the way it's being used against the major intelligence agencies. The reason you were keen to get your hands on these pictures was that you thought they would lead you back to the original source. But that doesn't alter the fact that these pictures are valuable evidence and – much more important – they were probably the motive behind the crash.'

'Believe what you like, but I really must be getting on. Is that all you wanted to say?'

'Of course not. But I am surprised that you take the destruction of two aircraft and the loss of twenty lives so lightly. What I came here for is an assurance that your band of part-timers will not meddle in my affairs or obstruct my inquiry any longer.'

'Oh, that's another matter entirely, Bobby.'

'Well, it's one that you had better sort out, Walter, because you, Rivers and Blanchard were not acting in any official capacity and I'm quite certain that Robin Teckman would be interested to hear how you have been abusing your position. And what about Miles Morsehead and Tim Lapthorne, your two contenders for the top job at SIS? You deny your ambitions, but I know you too well. You want the power and the standard-issue knighthood. I'm sure they'd like to hear about all this.'

Vigo spun round from another excursion along the

coastline of seventeenth-century Holland. His face was distorted with temper.

'You seem to have been unhinged by your experience in the police station. A nervous breakdown, they said. Wet your pants, carried from the cell blubbering.' His tone softened, not with sympathy but menace. 'Let me make it utterly plain that I am in a position to destroy you, Bobby. Those files from Prague produced grade A material: the real thing. You were a bloody spy for the communists. You're bang to rights. In these circumstances you would be well advised to shut up and keep your head down. But if you persist in making wild allegations, these discoveries may well find their way into the press and then prosecution will be inevitable. You know how the press never lets go of a thing like this and you can imagine the fun they'll have with the pictures of the comely Czech seductress. And the recent dramas in your life – a plane crash, shootings, the torture and execution of a flower girl? It's meat and drink to those people.'

Harland cut him off. 'Still, your colleagues will be very interested to learn about your little group. Its mere existence will lead them to suppose that you are conspiring against them and the interests of SIS.' He stopped, placed his fingertips together and levelled his gaze at Vigo to tell the lie. 'You see, every one of them was filmed coming into this house this morning. Blanchard, Griffiths, Rivers – the lot. I can't name all of them, but I'm sure it won't take Sir Robin long. Naturally you will attempt to slide out of this one by giving them a lecture about provenance and the interpretation of images. You will perhaps explain that this is the early-morning meeting of the Incunabula Society, a seance of amateur cryptographers, a confessional meeting of the local AA chapter. The story will be ingenious, I'm sure. But they won't believe you and moreover they're unlikely to pursue the crazy allegations that you subsequently make about my past.'

Vigo sat down. He was at least going to deal, thought Harland.

'Why have you come here?' His voice showed no sign of anxiety. 'You're a clever man, Bobby, but it seems to me that everything you do betrays your guilt. Is that all it is – guilt? Or is there something you really want?'

'The links – I want the links, Walter. How does Viktor Lipnik tie in with this coded material? What does he have to do with the shooting of Lars Edberg? Why did you make inquiries at the hospital to find out about his condition?' Harland knew some of the answers but he wanted to see Vigo's reaction.

Vigo placed his hands on his knees and leaned forward.

'Lars Edberg,' he mused. 'I must say I'm touched by your devotion to him. It really is a fascinating aspect to this whole thing. I fancied I saw him at your sister's place on the evening of the shooting, but maybe I was mistaken. Possibly it was some friend of your sister's? Who knows? Who cares? You see, I no longer have the time to ponder your unlikely trysts beside the Thames. My interest has moved on from you, Bobby, which is why I would like you to leave now.' He stopped and looked away. 'I imagine you're still at your sister's place.' Another pause. 'Davina is right – Harriet has very special qualities. You can tell that instantly.'

His massive head turned back to face Harland. In the sunlight which now flooded through the lancet window, Harland noticed that the rims of his eyes were red and that the lower eyelids were drooping a little. It occurred to him for the first time that Vigo was under considerable strain. 'It would be regrettable if she became mixed up in this.'

'You're threatening me, Walter,' Harland said with surprise. 'You're saying that if I send that film to Teckman you cannot be responsible for my sister's safety. I won't tolerate that. If anything happens to her or her family, I will kill you.

261

It is as simple as that.' He felt angry and foolish in the same moment.

They rose together and looked at each other.

'I will say one thing to you, Bobby. Let this go. You have no idea what you're dealing with. If you persist, you will endanger other people's lives.'

Harland heard a woman's voice call out from the stairs.

'That's Davina,' said Vigo. 'I think you'd better leave now, don't you?' At that moment Davina glided into the room. 'Bobby was just going,' he said to his wife's surprised expression.

Harland nodded awkwardly and brushed past her to the front door. Even as he closed the door behind him he knew that he had made a bad mistake in coming.

19

BOHEMIA

The O'Donnell passport carried Harland into the arrivals hall of Prague airport without a hitch. The Bird had told him to look out for a driver with one of two names displayed on a board. If the name was Blucher, Harland was to walk past the man and catch a cab to the Intercontinental Hotel where he should await further instructions. If he saw the name Schmidt, he was to make himself known and the driver would take him to the meeting place.

Harland immediately spotted a young man by a coffee stand in a worn sheepskin jacket. He was holding a board, but the name was hidden by his hand. As Harland approached, the man raised the board up to display the name Schmidt, smiled imperceptibly and led him to the car park. Outside it was damp and snow lay on the ground. Harland noticed a metallic smell in the air that he associated with the uninhibited mining and smelting of the old Eastern Europe.

In a short time they were heading along the Vltava River. He tried to get his bearings. At the back of his mind he was orienting himself so that he knew the direction of an area named Dejvice where he was held the first night of his arrest in the StB building. The date was Friday, 17 November 1989, a propitious but bloody day which came to mark the beginning of the Velvet Revolution. Harland didn't learn the importance of the events he witnessed until long afterwards.

Harland looked out across the river to the Old Town Hall

and remembered Griswald going off to meet his contact. There had been little for Harland to do so he had spent much of the day sightseeing in the Old Town. As the day wore on it became obvious that something was brewing. Every so often he would come across furtive groups of students passing leaflets to each other, then melting away into side streets as the plainclothes security police arrived. A young woman in a white knitted hat had pressed a flyer into his hand, announcing a march in memory of Jan Opletal, a student who'd been killed by the Nazis a little over fifty years before. They talked for a short time. Harland said that it seemed downright perverse that while the world held its breath to see whether the East German uprising would spread to Czechoslovakia, the students were preparing to commemorate an obscure martyr of the Nazi era. She replied that it was a symbolic protest against the regime. In the two decades since the Russian invasion and the collapse of the Prague Spring, it had become second nature to the Czechs to make their protests metaphorically – at one remove.

Harland was much more alert to the movement of security forces than the students and, as dusk gathered that afternoon, he noticed the discreet arrival of troops dressed in khaki and red berets. It transpired that these were members of the Division for Special Purposes, an anti-terrorist group that had been infiltrated into the city to set a trap. A few hours later they would wade into the students, causing hundreds of casualties. When the fleeing students banged on the doors along Narodni Street to be let in, their fellow Czechs were too frightened to open up.

He had been tempted to stay and see what happened, but he decided to make himself scarce and returned to the ill-lit room where he and Griswald had camped out for a day and a night. Five StB men and three uniformed policemen were waiting for him. They were convinced that he had been sent by foreign powers to ferment revolution on the streets. The leaflet in his pocket about that evening's demonstration didn't help his denial. He was taken to StB headquarters and questioned. The next morning, as open dissent began to break out among all classes and professions in Prague, and Václav Havel hurried back from his retreat at Hradecek to lead the revolution, Harland was handed over to three men who took him to a villa. Time rushed forward for the Czechs but for Harland it went into reverse – back to the Stalinist purges.

All of that was very near the surface now. Harland made a conscious effort to think of something else.

The driver took a sharp right, away from the sweep of the Vltava, and rattled down a cobbled side street. As they waited at some lights, he turned round and handed Harland a monochrome tourist map of Prague Castle. Harland unfolded the map and examined it, remembering that before he was arrested he had planned to come up to the ancient citadel which overlooks Prague. In the second courtyard he found a red circle marking an object in the centre, which the key told him was a fountain.

They tore up the final few hundred yards to a deserted square in front of the castle. There the snow streamed across the headlights almost horizontally. Harland paid off the driver who responded by making a shooing motion with his hands to indicate that he should go through the gateway in front of the castle. It was bitterly cold. He passed between two sentries who did not seem to notice him and stole into the great, dark precincts of the castle. The fountain was ahead of him in the first courtyard, but not a soul was to be seen. Some way off he heard the stamp of more guards marching to their watch. He walked gingerly across new snow and passed under a second archway to find he had run slap-bang up against the west front of St Vitus's Cathedral. The façade rose up before him with the effect of a photographic negative, the snow picking out the details of the carvings. He looked up for a moment, then retraced his steps back to the fountain, followed by three guards in blue greatcoats and high fur collars who had appeared from the direction of the Old Royal Palace. From nowhere a tall figure had materialised by the fountain and was tracing a circle in the snow with his feet, as he talked animatedly on a phone. He raised a hand in acknowledgement of Harland and finished the conversation.

In an educated accent reminiscent of Tomas's, he said, 'You are Macy Harp's friend? Harland?'

'Yes.' Harland took in the gaunt, slightly hunched giant. He wore an ancient brown leather coat which rose up his back and sagged at the front. Under this was a suit and badly knotted tie. His dark hair was lank and long, parted at the side in a style that had been fixed in the seventies.

'I am Zikmund. Mr Harp is a friend of mine also. We have to wait a little so we should welcome the New Year with some beer – no?'

'Zikmund?'

'Zikmund Myslbek.'

They walked to a Skoda outside the castle and Zikmund folded himself into the driver's seat. Ten minutes later they were in a nameless bar full of smoke and the smell of beer. Zikmund gestured to a door at the back that turned out to be the entrance to a cavernous pool hall, at the end of which was a stage.

'No band this evening,' said Zikmund apologetically. 'The fun was last night.'

They sat down. Beers were brought, and two horseshoe frankfurters coated in mustard. Harland looked at his companion in the light. He guessed he was in his mid-fifties. His face had once been very striking, but now his cheeks were sunken and his skin was grey from work and cigarettes. He was evidently a prodigious smoker and forked the frankfurter into his mouth while a cigarette smouldered in his left hand.

They drank in silence for a while, Zikmund eyeing up a voluptuously built woman who was packed into jeans and a blouse and teetered on high heels. Without taking his eyes from her, he said suddenly, 'I am sorry for what happened to you here in Prague, Mr Harland.'

'Macy filled you in,' said Harland. 'Do you mind me asking how you know him?'

'Not at all. We met back in the seventies when he was working for your people.' Harland remembered that Macy and The Bird had briefly had legitimate jobs with SIS. 'I passed on the work of dissidents that could not be published here to Macy. He took them to the West.'

'And what do you do now?'

'I used to be deputy director of the new intelligence services for the Czech Republic.'

Harland couldn't conceal his surprise. Zikmund smiled again. 'We had an excellent chief after the revolution. I was his deputy when we set up the new service. Here we have one service that combines domestic and foreign work.'

'So what do you do now?'

'I do jobs here and there and get to sleep till noon when I want.'

Harland looked at Zikmund with new eyes.

'What did you train in?'

'Architecture. I was an architect but I could not have a job under the Communist regime. So I translated for a living and I cooked.'

'You cooked!'

'Yes, I cooked and I wrote a couple of cookery books – traditional Bohemian recipes and my own. Cooking became a passion for us after the Prague Spring. The Czechs hibernated. We each lit a fire inside and kept warm and waited for another spring to come. We made love, we talked to people we trusted and we cooked. Cookery was a good business to be in – more cookery books were sold than any other type of book in the seventies.' He paused. 'So, about this woman. Macy told me about her but none of the names mean anything to me. If she lived in Prague, I am sure I would know her. Still, a lot of those people who worked for the StB in the old regime keep their heads down now.'

Harland showed him the three cards – Eva Houresh's student ID of 1975 and the Communist party membership cards for Irina Rath from 1980 and Irina Kochalyin from 1988.

The last one appeared to mean something to Zikmund. He looked at all three again and seemed to be about to say something, then thought better of it.

'Are we to assume that her maiden name was Irina Rath?'

'Yes. Her son is named Rath and I know that Eva was not her real name.'

'But she is not in any phone book in the Czech Republic. I looked today.'

'But you have access to the old files?'

'Unofficial access,' said Zikmund, with a smile. 'I hear that this woman was once regarded as important. Her file is kept away from the others. We will have to wait until my contact calls me.'

'Tell me,' said Harland, 'do you know if anyone from the British SIS has recently had access to the archive?'

Zikmund looked longingly at the buttocks of the girl in stiletto heels who was stretching over the pool table for a difficult shot.

'This lady here, she is the girlfriend of one of the big Russian mafia bosses when he is in town. She is an athlete. She throws the discus for Czech Republic. A mighty woman, no?' He looked at Harland. 'Yes, they were here two weeks ago. I do not know what they were looking for. They spent a short time here and they didn't get to see any of the special files. Very few do.'

Harland explained that they must have seen something of

Eva's file because they'd obtained pictures of her from the early years.

'Maybe something, but not all. We will hear later. My friend will be able to tell you what they saw.'

They drank for a further hour. Harland found himself warming to the Czech's lack of ceremony. Secrecy for him was plainly a matter of occasional expedience, not a religious faith. He said something on these lines when he leaned over and grasped Harland's shoulder.

'Tell me why you English believe espionage is like gardening.'

Harland said he didn't know what he meant.

'Listen to the language used in intelligence work – you *cultivate* contacts, you *plant* listening devices or *bugs*, you have *moles* and you *weed* documents. Why is this so?'

'I don't know. But I think the mole was invented by a novelist.'

At half past midnight Zikmund received a call and they left, this time for a much longer drive to the southern outskirts of the city. Eventually they pulled up outside a building with an anonymous brick façade and got out. Zikmund pressed the bell at the only door and spoke into an entry-phone. There was a buzz and then a clunk as the action of a heavy electronic lock worked. They passed into a short corridor and repeated the procedure at a second door, which opened inwards into a long, cool space lit by fluorescent strips. Harland realised that the StB archive was housed in what had once been a refrigerated warehouse. A sprinkler system had been installed and rows of shelves stretched to the end of the building, but its original use was evident from the rails, chains and lifting gear that still hung from the ceiling. To one side was a long metal table with half a dozen reading lights, and beyond this four construction site offices joined together to provide desk space for the staff.

'Here the guilt of a nation is stored,' said Zikmund quietly.

'Every betrayal, small or large, of fifteen million people is in these shelves: every whisper of the neighbourhood informant, every dirty little compromise made by the ordinary man trying to keep his head above water. Every single squalid word is here, kept under lock and key. Very few of our people have seen inside this building.'

'Did you ever read your own file?' Harland now saw that the space was much greater than he had thought and that the archives ran off into the distance where the lights had not been turned on. He also spotted some sort of safe, way off in the distance.

Zikmund nodded slowly.

'It was the first thing I did when I got my job. One of the worst decisions I ever made. I discovered too much about the people I thought I trusted. I tried to put what I knew behind me, but it was difficult to forget that a friend I had known since architectural school had kept tabs on me for the authorities. Every conversation we had had was noted. It was for this reason that he found himself a very good job and that I was never permitted to work as an architect. I do not see him.'

A man issued from the office and approached them. He looked at Harland over a pair of glasses and started speaking rapidly in Czech. Zikmund translated.

'He says he has found the file you are looking for but that it only goes up to the early eighties. This he did not give to the two gentlemen who were here before Christmas. He says they were interested in seeing your file, but although there are cross-references to your name, it appears to have gone missing. He did not like the men who came. He says they were arrogant and he didn't oblige them too much. They took copies of some pictures from the Intelligence Operations Section. But they didn't get much information.'

'Would he mind also showing me the files that he gave them?' asked Harland.

The man appeared to understand. He handed Harland a green folder and pointed to the desk, then set off to the far end of the building.

'I must sit here with you,' said Zikmund. 'I'm responsible for you.'

Harland turned on a reading light and opened the file. 'I'm glad you're here because this is all in Czech.'

With little sense of expectation or dread, Harland began to sift through the pages of Eva's file, inspecting each entry then handing it to Zikmund for translation. Her full name turned out to include Eva. She was Irina Eva Rath, the only daughter of Hanna Rath. She was born in 1952 in Prague and attended school and university in the city, passing out top of her languages course in 1970. Zikmund remarked that it was unusual for someone to leave university so early and that she must have possessed a lot of natural talent. Copies of her grades in English and German were included, which confirmed this.

There was a long section devoted to her mother's circumstances and what her neighbours said about her and her daughter. They appeared to have kept to themselves, although mother and daughter were known to be active supporters of the regime and both possessed Communist party membership. The mother was on several local committees and was thought to be a willing, though unproductive, informant. When she left university, Irina Rath was recruited into the StB and trained. No details of this were given but it was mentioned that she operated under the code name *Lapis*. 'She was plainly very promising material,' said Zikmund, 'and attractive too. I understand what you saw in her, Mr Harland.' He picked up the black and white study of *Lapis* that had slipped from a cellophane envelope.

Harland had been looking at it too. It was odd: he felt none of the excitement that he'd experienced when Tomas first showed him the identity cards in New York.

Zikmund read on in silence, which made Harland impatient. He pressed him to say what he had found.

'Everything about Rome is here. It seems you were not her first conquest. There was an American named Morris who helped the StB at Nato – he was Drew Morris, a naval attaché, aged thirty.' That was news to Harland. Zikmund flipped a couple of pages. 'Her controller is this man who is referred to as K.'

'What else does it say?'

'This document has been *weeded*.' He looked up and winked. 'There are two pages missing. You see, you appear at the bottom of this page and then there is no mention of you again. Also a name has been erased here and here.' He held up the paper to show how words had been razored out of the typescript and replaced with tiny strips of paper which had been stuck over the back of the sheet. 'This must have happened before the revolution. Nobody would bother now. Nor would they get access to the files.' He stopped and looked again. 'From the sense of these pages I guess they have cut out mentions of the man known as K. But they have missed one or two, especially at the end. Do you know who K is, Mr Harland?'

'It could be Josef Kapek – but somehow I doubt it. Kapek was one of my contacts after 1980. He worked in the Czechoslovak Trade Mission in London and would be in no position to control *Lapis*. Besides, he was very low grade. He drank a lot and in the time I knew him, which was about ten years, he never gained a single piece of useful intelligence. A dunderhead.'

'Dunderhead,' repeated Zikmund, relishing the word. 'Then we look for another Mister K. But, still, Kapek tells us something, does he not? It means that you were being handled through the StB, not the KGB. That gives me an idea about K.'

'What idea?'

'All in good time. Tell me, did you help these dunder-heads, or were you leading them up the *garden path*? Did you give them much genuine information?' Zikmund contemplated him over narrow spectacle frames.

'No. I gave them things that would mislead or stuff they already knew. You're familiar with the nonsense of intelligence work: you know what I'm talking about. Look, why don't you read the file from beginning to end? I feel I'd get a better idea of it then.'

Zikmund began in a reluctant monotone. There was a lot of operational detail – the record of their being followed in Rome and to Ancona, but not Orvieto. The conversations they had about his exact role at the British embassy in Rome were also described. There wasn't much that surprised or shocked Harland. In Orvieto she had given him an account of everything that she could remember telling them. There were a few other notes. One stated that *Lapis* ceased all operational work in 1988 and that for five years before that she had served as a translator and code expert, occasionally on attachment to the service of a friendly power. 'That means KGB,' said Zikmund.

They looked through the file again. The librarian brought two much thicker folders from the dark interior of the archive before returning to the cabin where he put his feet up to doze.

'He makes no money and he came out as a favour to me tonight,' said Zikmund, looking at the librarian over his shoulder. 'Give him something when we leave. Foreign currency will do.'

Harland nodded.

They started with Hense's file, the smaller of the two, and found four mentions of Harland, including an overblown account of a cup of coffee they'd shared in Vienna. Harland could see how the details from Hense's reports of the time had been woven into the case presented by Rivers. Operation

Stormdrain, the disinformation campaign about Britain's military preparedness, had been worked up into a great scoop by Hense, although when they talked about it, they both knew the whole thing had long since ceased to have any significance. In all, five encounters with agent *Lamplighter* were recorded.

Kapek's was a much fuller account. The handling of *Lamplighter* appeared to be a major part of his career and he devoted much space to the analysis of Harland's character, which hinted at sexual promiscuity, a fondness for drink, his debts and a predisposition to melancholy. Zikmund read a passage which described a meeting in an art gallery when Harland was the worse for wear.

'I never met that little toe-rag in an art gallery,' said Harland, nettled by the slur.

'Toe-rag. I like that word too.'

Kapek had been careful not to overdo the character assassination. The conclusion his masters were meant to draw was that while *Lamplighter* suffered the symptoms of general cultural degeneracy, his information was still valuable. A couple of times he went out of his way to say that Harland had told him how he loathed Milos Hense.

'This guy wanted to keep you to himself and remain in London,' commented Zikmund.

Harland was aware that something was tugging at his mind. Suddenly it came to him. Kapek had shown him a copy of the picture of them in bed, but he had never actually produced the tape. He had mentioned it, of course, with a sly little smile, which was meant to keep Harland on side, even though he was being threatened. But he had never actually played it or even shown him a cassette. Harland had taken it for a bluff and ignored it. However, the important thing was that no tape was mentioned in any of the three files. That meant that Vigo had another source – but a source who was wrong.

They went through the papers for a second time. Then Zikmund produced a hip flask, popped a tiny cup from its top and filled it to the brim with liquid. Harland shook his head at the proffered cup.

'What's your theory about K?' he asked.

'Mister K, Mister K. You are aware there is another K in this story. It's Kochalyin. The name on your girlfriend's last identity card.'

'It was her married name. I know she's no longer married. Does it mean anything to you?'

'You see there was a man named Kochalyin – Oleg Kochalyin. He was KGB-active in Prague during the seventies. Not much is known about him, except that he was in the Soviet embassy here during the first years of the Normalisation. If this is the same man, it would explain the ambiguity that is suggested by *Lapis* working for the KGB while Hense and Kapek served the StB. Kochalyin was acting as a link between the two agencies.'

'But you say he was here in the seventies. Eva does not appear to have married until well into the eighties.'

'There are many things which would explain that. She might have been slow in changing her name. But the point is that when we came to set up the present service there was a lot of house-cleaning to do. We had to make sure that the people we employed had no connection with the StB and that they weren't tainted by corruption. It was in this time that we came across a former KGB agent. He was known as Peter and he was responsible for the Peter Organisation, which was notionally a new enterprise set up to trade with the West. It seemed to be based in Budapest, but we came to realise that it was based wherever this man Peter was. It possessed no office, no records, no accounts, no staff. Peter was the oil king. That means that he defrauded the state of millions in revenue.

'In Hungary the fraud relied on the difference between the

import duty on heating oil and diesel oil, which are virtually the same chemically. The Hungarians placed a dye in the heating oil so that it could not be resold as diesel. What the Peter Organisation did was to import tons of heating oil and remove the red dye with sulphuric acid. Another chemical cleansed the acid from the oil. A similar scam was used here in the Czech Republic. We soon understood that Peter was behind this and that the entire fraud was being run by ex-KGB people and their contacts in the intelligence services of Czechoslovakia, Poland, Hungary and Romania.'

'And Yugoslavia?' Harland cut in.

'Of course. Where there was an alliance between the KGB and the local intelligence service, Peter set up business. They were smart people and a lot quicker to realise the benefits of capitalism than the ordinary man. Within a year after the revolution they had a grip on the four main sources of illegal revenue – the sale of arms, illegal immigration into Western Europe, the drug routes and prostitution. The scams to avoid tax in different territories were the beginning of all this. The important thing was that these KGB people were used to dealing in strategic terms, thinking of the Warsaw Pact countries as one entity. Borders meant nothing to them. It took them little time to discover how to use the global banking system to hide and clean their money.'

'And you think Peter and Oleg Kochalyin are the same person.'

'He was one of our main suspects. But we never got any proof. Maybe they have now. I will ask.'

Harland showed him the picture of Lipnik by the pool.

'This is the man I'm interested in. Do you think this could also be Peter – Kochalyin?'

'He means nothing to me. I'll take a copy of the picture to show an old friend of mine. He may know him.'

There was one last file which had not been withdrawn by

Vigo's researchers because – of course – there was no reason for them to look into *Lapis*'s background. It was the slender dossier devoted to Hanna Rath. It gave a few personal details, but mainly dwelt on her exemplary service to the Communist party at district level, in particular her appearance at thinly attended meetings to hear the wishes and initiatives of the Praesidium. A note dated 1985 recorded that she had moved from Prague to a village in the area known as Jizerské Hory. Zikmund jotted down the address.

'She's old now, but she may be there still,' he said.

Her daughter was mentioned several times but there was no cross-reference which would lead to the *Lapis* file in the Intelligence Section. However, a recommendation, under-lined in red ball-point, directed the interested reader to a section where newspaper cuttings were stored. Zikmund was for leaving it, but Harland insisted they dig out the relevant file.

The envelope contained just one clipping – a yellow newspaper picture and caption in Russian from 25 August 1968. It showed a woman posing with Russian soldiers who were squatting in front of a tank. In one hand she held out a wicker basket, from which protruded a loaf of bread and a bottle; in the other was a plate of sausage and sliced meat. The headline over the picture read LOYAL CZECH WORKERS WELCOME SOVIET SAVIOURS. The extended caption described how Hanna Rath had given food and drink to the young Russian tank crew whose job it was to defend the Czechs from a Western-inspired coup. Harland read out the quotation from the tank captain at the end of the piece.

'We are honoured by the reaction of the ordinary Czech worker to our presence here. This was just one of many acts of gratitude that we have experienced,' said O.M. Kochalyin, tank captain.'

'Mr K!' exclaimed Zikmund.

'Yes,' said Harland, 'and maybe Mr Lipnik also.'

He unfolded the print of Lipnik again and placed it by the head of the young man who crouched in the middle of the tank crew with his helmet tucked under one arm.

Zikmund swore in Czech.

Harland said nothing: he didn't need to. The eyes were the same. The angle of the nostrils was right. The way O.M. Kochalyin held his chin had not changed in thirty years.

They put the files back into order in silence then tapped on the cabin door to wake the librarian. Harland held out one file slightly open for him so that he would notice the fifty-dollar bill lying inside.

'That was good of you,' said Zikmund as they left the building.

'Cheap at the price,' replied Harland.

20

THE BLINK OF AN EYE

It was the fly that made Tomas finally understand his situation. Somehow it had got into his room the day before and worked its way over every exposed surface of his body. He felt it on his face, on his ear, on his hands and arm. For a full day the trickling, cold sensation of the fly's legs drove him mad. And it was very smart, this fly. When a nurse was near, the fly would disappear for a while. He imagined it hid in the machinery until the coast was clear. Then it returned to complete its minute survey of his body. He wondered if it was going to lay eggs on him, eggs which would hatch into maggots in the warm atmosphere and begin to feed on him. He told himself that this would be impossible, but he became obsessed by the possibility that the nurses would miss the crucial part of his skin when they were washing him and allow the eggs to survive.

Eventually the fly disappeared of its own accord. But being at its mercy had in some way made him understand that he had lost all movement and that this was for ever. The doctor of course had been extremely vague, but in the three brief consultations – his word – that they'd had, Tomas had listened hard for any mentions of time. There were none.

He realised also that as well as movement he had been robbed of day and night. There was no natural light in his room, no darkness. Always the same gentle, pinky-orange glow greeted him when he awoke. There were no meals either; no clocks that he could see; or any pattern in the staff changes to give him a clue about the time of day. Whenever he opened his eyes a nurse was beside his bed or busying herself in the room, monitoring the various machines and pumps, emptying things, washing him and changing his position. He'd quickly become used to each nurse and familiar with their mannerisms and degrees of thoroughness.

His favourite was Nurse Roberts. She had a gentle manner and was unafraid of his condition. The others all in some slight way communicated their horror. One talked in a loud, distancing voice – like a teacher instructing a classroom of kids. Another fussed, endlessly redoing the chores that were part of her duty. A third, a large girl with a pink complexion, would occasionally stop and look at him – not as a nurse, but as a gawping bystander. This one had no imagination: she couldn't grasp that beyond all the tubes and the sighing machinery and the wildly gesticulating limbs, he was sitting quietly inside, as capable of being hurt as the next man. He disliked this woman. She had no more empathy than a suet dumpling. He called her the Dumpling.

Nurse Roberts disliked her too. He could tell that by the note in her voice when she talked to the Dumpling. It was formal and firm. Every time the Dumpling tried to prolong the conversation or make some remark about his condition or the abilities of the other staff, Nurse Roberts cut her off.

What was it about Nurse Roberts? Well, she smelled nice and she took care over her appearance. She was quick to read the expression in his eyes and would in this way consult him about the position he preferred or a change of television channel. They had a secret too.

Sometimes she would tell him about her evening out or something she'd read in the papers. What she had to say about these things was always clear and to the point. She would look at him as she spoke and she understood that he would rather listen to her than the damned TV.

At times there were more people in his room than he would have liked. He wanted to tell some of them to get out. After all, it was his room. But at least he could guess the time of day by the visit of the two doctors – the man who had introduced himself as Philip and the sexy woman in her thirties whom the doctor addressed as Claire. They came twice a day, in Philip's case sometimes more. Claire was cold and rather dogmatic, Philip a bit of an old buffer who didn't listen much to his colleagues.

These observations of the people in his new life absorbed him for only a little of the endless day-nights in the room. The pain in his head regularly built in a screaming crescendo then subsided but never completely disappeared. Sometimes he saw lights when his eyes were closed. They reminded him of the patterns he discovered he could make as a small boy when he rubbed his eyes very hard. They were brighter now and pulsed with the pain in his head. He was fascinated by them and imagined that they were somehow the manifestation of frustrated neurons firing in his brain.

He had made a list of his problems so he could decide which was the worst thing he had to put up with each day. Today it was his breathing and the pain in his right lung. It felt thick and congested and sometimes there was a stabbing pain in his ribs. If the machines were switched off, he was sure he would hear a rattle in his lung. Yesterday it was the heat of the bedclothes and the soreness on his back and buttocks. If only he could have moved to where there was a little fresh air. If only someone had thought to position a fan to cool his body.

Yesterday was the day of incredible thirst and dryness. He couldn't think of it now because it had caused him so much torment. Torment. That was the word he had been trying to find. Not a word he had given much thought to before. But it was exactly the right word. He was being tormented by his condition and the surprises it sprang on him. He would be lying there, trying to calm himself and suddenly he'd be crying, or a steady buzzing and tinkling would start up in his ear, or he'd be going into the upside-down-crab position with his heart pounding in his head and muscles burning. The point was that he couldn't let the pain out – he couldn't wince or cry out or clench his fists. He was locked in with the pain.

His condition kept him on his toes all right. And although his thoughts were on the whole quiet and controlled, there were periods of screaming red panic when his mind made no sense at all. It gave him very little time for the kind of thinking that he needed to do.

Yet he had arrived at a conclusion. He wanted to die. It was not a difficult decision in the circumstances and he was sure that he would be able to make himself understood with the blink of an eye. Already he had gained some control so that when Nurse Roberts asked him a question, he replied with a single blink for a yes, or double-blink for no. That was their secret. The Dumpling had tried this technique and breathed fumes of cooking fat and halitosis at him and he had not replied because he didn't want to encourage her. Besides, it gave him a feeling that he could at least control whom he communicated with. It was one of the very few things that was left to him, and even though it sometimes caused him to suffer when he didn't reply, he nurtured this tiny degree of independence.

The doctor was back again and the Dumpling was scurrying about trying to impress him with her efficiency, making nauseating purrs and coos as she went.

'Hello Tomas,' he said. 'Treating you well, are they? Good. I have someone here who wants to see you.' He stopped and told the Dumpling that she should take her break now. When she had gone he said, 'Her name is Harriet and she is your father's sister. I have mentioned before that your father has taken me into his confidence, but I wasn't sure whether

282

you had understood me. However, Nurse Roberts tells me that you are fully aware of everything that is being said to you and that you understand English.' Some secret, thought Tomas. 'That's very good news. Anyway, I believe your father is at this moment in Prague, getting in touch with your mother. His sister thought she would pop in and see you while he was away. I think you'll find her very refreshing company.'

Tomas was not at all happy at the idea of meeting someone who didn't know him. It was stupid to feel so self-conscious, but it *was* different seeing a person from the outside world. He prayed that his body would behave for the next few minutes and he cautioned himself not to let anything stressful float into his mind because those were the thoughts which seemed to set off his spasms.

The woman came in and showed her face at the end of the bed. It was a pleasant, animated face.

'Hi,' she said. 'I'm Bobby's sister. My name is Harriet. I saw you fleetingly a week or so ago, but I'm sure you don't remember me.'

He did remember her, but couldn't think where he'd seen her. His first thought was that she did not look at all like her brother.

He waited. He was the victim of conversation now. People came in and they talked at him and he had to listen. Sometimes he wished he couldn't understand. But his English had come back and, in fact, he was thinking in English most of the time. He believed his dreams were still in Czech, though.

She began to speak quietly and not in a rush, which most people did to fill the silence and cover their embarrassment. She looked at him directly in the eye also, which was a good sign. Only Nurse Roberts did that properly.

'I know Bobby will have told you nothing about himself so I thought you might like to hear a bit about him.' She paused. 'He's always been like that – not saying much about himself, but he's got a lot worse in middle age. He spends too much time by himself. He travels an awful lot and I suppose he's got out of the habit of talking to people properly. He's good at what he does and he's very persuasive and charming when he wants something. But it's such a pity that he doesn't let people see more of himself in other ways. You know, he can be really funny. Hardly anyone ever sees that side.'

This is exactly what he wanted – a story, the story of his father's life. Harriet moved to the chair that the Dumpling had just left and sat down. She leaned over to touch his hand and then decided to perch on the side of the bed.

'I hope you don't mind,' she said with a laugh. 'It's just a lot easier to see you.' Harriet was fearless, but she was not overpowering. She continued speaking, stopping to allow the ventilation that occurs naturally in a conversation. That was considerate because his brain didn't move as fast as it used to and sometimes he needed a moment or two to catch up. She was smart too: she anticipated what he wanted to ask her. Just as he was thinking that he would like to know something about Harland's background, she began to tell him.

'There's eight years' difference between us, so for a lot of my childhood Bobby was away. You see, our mother died quite early so having him home was just perfect. My father, whose name was Douglas, was a scholar – he lectured and wrote about theology. He used to go off to Cambridge University to do a spell of lecturing and he'd bring Bobby back with him for the weekend or, better still, the long vacation. Then things brightened up. My father started smiling again and we were a family. You see, we all missed my mother dreadfully.' She paused. 'She died in a road accident a few miles from our house. I don't remember much, except a terribly sombre atmosphere settling over our lives. And there wasn't any escape because we lived in a desolate and flat part of England, called the Fens. Things stay put in the Fens. Nothing shifts or moves on its own and that was the case with our grief. It stayed. My father never really got over my mother's death and died at quite an early age himself. I was twenty then and Bobby was twenty-eight. I suppose it brought us together. We've been pretty close for most of the time since then.'

She looked away. Tomas felt this was because of her own sadness and regrets and that it had nothing to do with him. She was behaving naturally and he felt complimented.

She continued in this vein for some while, telling him how her brother had given up the idea of doing physics and changed to an engineering course, a sign of his practicality as well as his basic modesty. He was much brighter than he ever believed, she said. Perhaps that's why he had gone into intelligence work. It had seemed to their father a waste of his talent and decency.

Harriet talked to him about meeting Eva.

'Was her name Eva? He thinks she has another name.' She looked into his eyes. 'I wish you could talk to me, Tomas. I really do. We shall have to work out a way of you communicating with me. The nurse says that you sometimes use your eyelid. Is that right?'

Tomas blinked once.

'That means yes?'

Tomas blinked again.

'And twice for no?'

Another blink.

'Now that I know, I promise I won't plague you with questions – not everything has a yes or a no answer. But can I ask if she's called Eva?'

Tomas blinked once and then blinked twice more rapidly.

'A yes and a no. Perhaps Eva is part of her name?'

Tomas blinked once.

'I see – she used her second name. Your mother was a big thing in his life. I don't imagine he has told you how important she was. I'm only just beginning to understand that when he stopped seeing her, a part of him closed down. I don't know the details. Maybe you do, but it obviously had something to do with your arrival.' She looked hard into his eyes. It was not a gaze you flinched from. 'How strange life is. Having a son is the one thing that might make Bobby connect with the world. Your coming to him has affected him deeply but I'm not sure he appreciates this yet. Was he very suspicious when you first met?' She smiled and waited.

A blink.

'I thought so.' She smiled again. 'That's typical. But you must forgive him. He's been through a lot. Do you want to hear more?'

A blink.

'Not tired?'

He lied with two blinks.

'Good. I'm going to tell you a little about him which will make you understand him a lot better.'

Tomas listened as she began to speak about his father's trip to Prague in 1989. She said he was badly treated – badly hurt. Tomas wondered what that meant exactly. Then he had become seriously ill. He had sorted this out, but she was sure that the effects of the beating had stayed with him.

Tomas was aware that he was suddenly having difficulty breathing. The machine pumped air into his body, but his body didn't seem to want it. And in some remote part of him – his legs? – there was a new tingling which was something between the sensation of a skin warming up after being exposed to extreme cold and a nettle rash. He made a conscious effort to divert his thoughts to the boy of fourteen that he had been during the Velvet Revolution.

He pulled the images from his memory and forced himself to concentrate on all their details. He saw the train ride to Prague. 'It was the first week. They had heard about the police attacking students in the city because way up in the mountains where they spent most of their time they could receive German TV. It was odd: his mother was usually so cautious and wary of the authorities. But a few days after that news she took him out of school and bought two train tickets to Prague. The day after they arrived – a Thursday – they went to Wenceslas Square to join the crowds. It was bitterly cold – the first day of winter. They waited from the middle of the morning to late evening. His mother was flushed and kept on plucking his arm and hugging him, which was a little embarrassing.

'Remember this, Tomas,' she had said, holding his face between her gloved hands, 'you're watching history being made. Promise me that you will never forget this.'

And he had remembered that day, mostly because of the aura that surrounded her. She had never been so alive, so passionate, so moved. It was as if she'd been pretending to be another person all those years.

In the following days the gatherings in Wenceslas Square had swelled. They went without fail each morning and stayed until the evening, buying food from the street vendors who materialised along the fringes of the crowds. At times he found it boring, listening to speeches over a poor public-address system. But eventually he understood that the crowds were holding vigil until the moment when freedom had been irrevocably seized. He was fascinated by his mother during those days. Strangers in the crowd would latch on to her, drawn by her infectious optimism. Everything she was thinking was expressed in her face and that gave it a new beauty. He would never forget those days in Wenceslas Square.

He was better now. The distraction had done the trick. He returned to Harriet.

'Can I ask you a question?' she asked.

He felt tired but he blinked once.

'Well – I think you have just given me your answer. So,

I'm going to go now. I'll be back tomorrow, if you like.' She paused and examined his face. Then she touched his cheek just above the stubble line. 'I have left some music which I know you like. I got the police to tell me what was in your bag. They wouldn't give me the original CDs, so my husband's secretary spent the morning getting duplicates.'

He said thank you, which he hoped she would realise was three blinks.

'There is one other thing,' she said, getting up from the bed. 'I have done some research about your condition on the Web. There are quite a few devices which will enable you to communicate more easily. Most will allow you to send e-mail. I'm going to talk to the doctor and see which he thinks will be the best for you. It's really important that you're able to say what you want.'

He blinked once and closed his eyes.

After dropping Harland off at a small hotel by the Old Customs Yard in the centre of the city, Zikmund did not return for a full twenty-four hours. He phoned mid-morning to say that it would take him all day to do some essential research. He would tell him about it that evening or the next day.

The city was choked with fog and few people were about. Harland spent a listless time walking around and reading in coffee shops. In the early afternoon he returned to his functional suite of rooms with a paperback of Dickens's *The Old Curiosity Shop*, which he'd bought at an English bookshop near the hotel. He read for a little while, opened some wine and looked out at the day congealing to dusk.

With a leaden certainty, he knew that nearly everything had fallen into place. Kochalyin was Lipnik. Kochalyin had also been Eva's husband. This explained how Tomas had come to be in Bosnia and why he'd been traced to London and shot. Kochalyin had ordered the death of his stepson and the torture and death of a young girl of whom he knew nothing. As for the plane crash, that too must have been Kochalyin's work, although the precise mechanism that caused the plane to swerve into the lighting towers as it came into land was only known to the FBI. He had pretty much everything he needed to make the full report to Jaidi.

At ten that evening he answered the phone to The Bird.

'Friend Zikmund gave me your number. Are you finding him helpful?'

'Yes, very,' said Harland. 'Why're you calling me?'

'Because there've been a lot of developments which are going to take the heat off you.'

'How?'

'It seems our country and western disc jockey got back to work yesterday to find a great fuss.' Harland remembered the old crack about GCHQ – it's in the country and west of London. 'Every spare man, woman and child with a gift for cryptography and other dark arts was deployed on tracing the source of these coded signals. Since Christmas there has been a burst of the stuff and the first few days of this week there was an awful lot of activity. The Americans and our lot at GCHQ were fairly hopping and decided they had to close this thing down once and for all. Macy heard from another source that they had wired up several of the radio stations used by these jokers in the past and started to trace all the incoming calls.'

'That's a big operation.'

'Yes. But it wasn't as though they hadn't thought of it before. Apparently these characters had some kind of routing system in Stockholm. Stockholm's full of Internet wizards, it seems. They bust a place last year and then just last month they pinned down the routing system and worked out who the sources were. A troublemaker named Mortz met a sticky end, I gather. God knows who killed him, but he was dead and things went quiet which is all anyone cared about. Then all hell blew up when the radio stations started pumping out more of this stuff during Christmas week. Again, they thought they had solved the problem – I don't know how they thought this, but they did. However, the coded signals kept coming. And guess what?'

'Just tell me, Cuth.'

'They traced this last batch of calls to London – to about a dozen numbers being used in rotation in the Bayswater area. With their usual towering incompetence, our former colleagues set about watching every house where one of these calls had come from. They assumed there was some kind of cell operating in the area – people running from house to house with a laptop. But this particular spot in London happens to be an area of high Arab ownership and Arabs do not spend the winter in damp old London. Most of the houses were empty and there was no sign of any activity. Then some bright spark realised that the telephone exchange must have been interfered with. They found two computers at different points in local junction boxes. Crisis over. Everybody goes home for tea and crumpets and hearty congratulations from the secret brotherhood flood in. Only problem is that they never find the bloke or blokes who were responsible. Still, the disc jockey tells me that there hasn't been a bleep out of any of the radio stations for thirty-six hours or more.'

'So whoever left these computers in the exchange boxes is free. He could be anywhere?'

'From St Bart's to St Petersburg.'

Or a neurological unit in central London, thought Harland. There was no other explanation. That was why they'd killed the young girl and pursued Tomas, using every possible tracking device. He wondered whether Vigo was part of the operation. Why else would he have gone to the hospital and cross-examined the doctor about Tomas's condition, unless he wanted to make sure that Tomas was effectively out of action? And once he knew this he had told Harland that his interest had moved on. Of course it had. He already knew that it was simply a matter of finding the devices that were sending out the coded messages. That's why he no longer needed Harland. But this supposed that Vigo knew of Harland's real connection with Tomas, and there was no reason to believe that because Vigo would have used it. Moreover he had approached Harland in New York before he knew of Tomas's existence. Something was still missing in the Grand Theory of Everything.

'Are you there?'

'Sorry, I was just thinking about Vigo's angle in all this. I can't work it out.'

'Well, you can be sure it has something to do with his own interest. He never stirs without a percentage of the action.' The Bird coughed. 'Look, I gather Macy and Ziggers have been on the blower all day. I'll let Zikmund give you the SP when he sees you. I'll only balls it up if I try to tell you.' Harland remembered that Cuth always deferred to Macy's intelligence-gathering skills and business sense.

'But surely you can tell me roughly what they've been discussing?'

'Friend Oleg – the man you discovered in the photo library.'

'Ah, I see.'

'Good hunting. I think things should be fairly quiet from now on. Come and see us when you get back.'

Harland hung up and sat for a while in the echoing, brightly lit sitting room of his suite. He noticed a couple of cigarettes that had been left by the cleaner in an ashtray, presumably dropped by a previous guest. He took one and went to the window where he lit up with a book of matches. He pulled the window open and looked down on the damp, cobbled street. A violin was being played in the apartment block opposite. The sound filled Harland with a deep melancholy. He was glad that he would not have to spend too much longer in this city.

21

EVA

The next day they set off early from the hotel in a hire car, which Zikmund conjured at a cheap rate from one of his contacts at the airport. He explained that he wasn't sure that his own car would go all the way to Jizerské Hory.

As they passed through the western outskirts of the city, Harland asked about the conversation with Macy Harp. Zikmund turned to him, his yellowish-grey complexion not improved by the morning light.

'Yes, I talked to Macy. I also talked to the FBI here. Did you know they have a bureau in Prague? How things change, eh?'

'What did they say?'

'The FBI clammed up when I started asking questions about Kochalyin. They said they weren't investigating anyone of that name. But that's not true. Macy told me he'd heard about the investigation of a particular bank account in London through which a very great sum of money has passed to New York. Macy would know about this because he does business here and all over Eastern Europe. There's this one bank account in the name of Driver. Driver is a Russian who took his wife's name when he married. She's an executive in the Illinois State Metal Bank which is why they didn't look so closely at the money going through his account. Eight billion dollars – maybe more – passed through and fanned out into a hundred different directions, mostly as payments to overseas companies. The operation was pretty hard to pin down because some money went the other way as camouflage. But the East–West flow was larger.'

'And this was Kochalyin's money?'

'Yes, certainly,' he said, flicking a cigarette out of the car window. 'But it's only one account and the FBI – though they do not confirm this – know there are a lot more involved.'

'Macy told you that?'

'Yes.'

'What's this add up to? Every Russian mafioso launders money through the Western banking system. There's nothing new in that.'

Zikmund looked mildly irritated. 'Listen, I'm giving you background, Mr Harland. You may need it. The point is that Mister K has become so powerful that Western governments rely on him for certain services. He negotiates contracts between East and West. He brokers information. He buys people off. He fixes elections. He makes sure there is just one bribe on a deal. That bribe goes to him, then he sees that the contract is completed on time. That's an important guarantee to have if you build a dam in Turkey or a power plant in Slovakia. Business will pay a lot of money for that.'

'You're saying he's so useful that Western governments ignore the money laundering?'

'Yes, but you're missing the point. Mister K is a very fluid, very adaptable man. He is nowhere and everywhere. He does not have a base, no single home, no single office, no single citizenship. He inhabits many different identities and owns many different businesses. He can control everything from a computer screen. Nobody has to see him for a deal to be completed. He is like a wisp of smoke and when a situation goes bad for him, like his interests in Yugoslavia, he becomes someone else. It's like that process – what is the word when a maggot changes into a cocoon and then a butterfly?'

'It's not a maggot, it's a caterpillar, and the process is called metamorphosis.'

'Metamorphosis – like the Kafka story. How could I forget? But there have been many more stages than with a butterfly. They are without limit but there is always some type of maggot at the end.'

'Do you get all this from Macy?'

'No, just the information about the Driver account. The rest came from my colleagues in the service here.'

'When you talk about the business in Yugoslavia, you mean his part in the war crime?'

'Yes – partly. There was a reason that it became necessary to have Lipnik assassinated. He had also been involved in taking money from the Serbs. At the beginning of the war the Serbs froze all private savings and took over the National Reserve – the part that was left in Belgrade. A lot of money was taken out of the country in the next three years. It went to Cyprus and then most of it disappeared. He was offering to launder money for the Serbs using the traditional import–export routes. But he took a very fat commission. He stole most of it. So in '97 the Serbs ordered him to be killed.'

Which led to the plan of the staged assassination, thought Harland. Settling Lipnik's account with the Serbs and the War Crimes Tribunal in one burst of gunfire.

'But he still has business in the Balkan states. My former colleagues are researching the illegal immigration that goes across the Czech Republic. The European Union requires us to do this. They know that the main routes being run from Ukraine and Romania go through Yugoslavia and Bosnia and Croatia. They suspect that Mister K is behind those too.' He paused to light up again. 'He's no idiot, this man. The Serb leaders imprisoned themselves in their own country. They cannot leave because of the indictments from the War Crimes Tribunal. K has done as much as them yet he can move anywhere at any time. He's outplayed them all. You know why I am telling you this?'

'Yes, you're warning me. You're saying that the proof that Lipnik and Kochalyin are the same person and the evidence that he is alive is a very dangerous possession.'

'Right, because you don't know of the alliances this man has made in the West. There are many who want to keep him alive and free to carry out their business for them. And you are about to contact the woman who was his wife. She may still be on friendly terms with him. Her home may be watched. They must know about you.'

'You're probably right. But this man tried to have her only child killed so they can't be on particularly good terms.'

'You are not listening to me. This is a very risky plan you have and I want you to think about how you are going to contact this woman. Remember, she worked for the StB. She was a spy for the Communists. She may not be reliable.'

Harland said nothing. He opened the window to get some fresh air. A few minutes later Zikmund motioned ahead of them.

'This place here is where the Warsaw Pact troops gathered before the Soviets ordered them to go into Prague in the summer of '68.'

Harland looked out at a featureless grey plain.

'And I want you to notice the road sign along here.'

'Why?'

'If I remember this road right, you will see, Mr Harland.' Harland noticed now that there was always an ironic edge when Zikmund addressed him formally.

A few miles on they passed a sign which directed drivers north, to a town twenty-five kilometres away. Its name was Lipnik.

'You see, this guy carries things from the past right through his life. He must have been here in August 1968 and he used the name in one of his false identities. Remember that, when you see this woman – he carries things through his life.'

They took another hour to reach the Giant Mountains and begin the climb to Jizerské Hory. Zikmund explained that the area had been cleansed of Germans at the end of the Second World War on the orders of the Allied powers. The property was given to the Czechs or seized by the government.

They pulled up in a village square and Zikmund went off to ask for directions. Harland got out and wandered into a nearby churchyard. Every headstone bore a German name. Along the street behind him the faded paint of German store signs was still visible.

It was odd then that Zikmund managed to find one of the few Germans whose forebears had not been tossed back into Saxony. He was a thin, bearded blond with a weather-beaten face, who had just tramped up the village street, prodding his way with a stave through the rutted snow. Two sheepdogs crouched and trembled in the snow as he stopped and answered Zikmund's questions. He spoke in broken Czech at first but then fell into German when he realised that Zikmund and Harland could understand him better. Yes, he knew old Mrs Rath. She was a good sort – she spoke German well. He used to deliver wood to her and she in turn allowed him to graze his sheep on her pastures in summer. She'd lived here fifteen years back, and her daughter and grandson had moved in with her for a period. They left about ten years ago. He had an idea that they were in Karlsbad in western Bohemia. He said the postman might be able to supply them with an address.

For the next hour they chased a post van from village to village. Eventually they caught up with him at a bridge and he gave them the address in Karlsbad.

'So we have learned something about the Rath women,' said Zikmund as they set off on the long drive. 'They are not poor. That German fellow said they had come into money. So perhaps Mister K has been generous to his womenfolk.'

An hour passed as they descended from the mountains and headed west across another flat expanse of landscape. They spoke little. At some stage Harland became aware that Zikmund was looking in his wing mirror more than seemed necessary, given that the road was free of traffic. He scrutinised the mirror on his side for a few minutes but saw nothing and sank back in his seat.

'Who knows you are here? asked Zikmund accusingly.

'No one but Macy, The Bird and my sister.'

'Someone else does. They follow, then they don't follow; then they follow. A car, maybe two. I'm not sure. But they are behind us, Mr Harland. I know it.'

Harland turned in his seat. The road behind them was still empty.

A few miles on, Zikmund pulled the car into a turning, then reversed at great speed on to a piece of ground that was hidden by a disused barn. He climbed out and peered round the barn. Harland did likewise.

'I was right, we do have a companion,' he said. 'This is the car.'

The blue Saab had to slow down before taking the bend in front of them and they were able to see that it contained two men. The car appeared to be in no hurry, but Zikmund was agitated. He took out a mobile phone, speed-dialled a number and began to speak slowly, enunciating the Saab's registration which he'd scrawled with his finger in the grime on the rear window.

'I called an old colleague,' he said, lowering the phone. 'He will arrange for the police to stop the car in the next town and inspect it for faults. That should delay them. We will take the road south so if there is anyone still following us they will think we are going back to Prague.'

They waited for ten minutes before driving on. The

landscape became a smoky blue and then for a brief period the setting sun appeared in the west. Zikmund said that even with the detour they would make Karlsbad by eight that evening.

'You know something?' he said, after another period of silence. 'I've been thinking of Ostend.'

'Ostend? In Belgium? Why?'

'It's a very interesting place. There are a lot of planes at Ostend and those planes often leave Ostend with no cargo. They fly to Burgas in Bulgaria where they pick up their cargo. Do you know what that cargo is? Military supplies. And then the planes leave for their destinations in Asia and Africa – sometimes South America. It has been the route for most clandestine arms traffic in the last seven years.'

'Ostend?'

'It's near Nato headquarters. Many of the illegal arms shipments are made with Nato's blessing because they are destined for the armies and militias that Nato supports. Kochalyin is very big in the arms trade and his contacts in Burgas are excellent. Is it possible that Nato owes him a favour or two?'

'You're forgetting something,' said Harland. 'During the Bosnian civil war, Nato was trying to stop arms shipments from the East into Yugoslavia. That's how Kochalyin got his foot in the door with the Serbs, by supplying them with arms and fuel. So he was never Nato's best friend.'

'Yes, but things change! Nobody cares about Bosnia anymore! Maybe NATO needed his help in making ship-ments to other parts of the world – you understand what I am saying? So they arranged to fake his death and then tried to prevent your friend investigating it.'

'What's Ostend got to do with this?'

'One of the enterprises that we know Mister K has an interest in is an air freight business in Ostend. Two modified

Boeings and a few smaller cargo planes that will go anywhere if the price is right.'

It was certainly a better theory than Harland had supposed at the beginning of Zikmund's little speech. He had always known that the phone-tracking operation which led Bézier's soldiers to the hotel must have involved some cooperation from Nato to pinpoint Lipnik's location and pass it to the French. The same influence that had staged his death could also be brought to bear on the War Crimes Tribunal, which was wholly reliant on Nato for the enforcement of the indictments. This wouldn't mean the corruption of the tribunal, merely a firm prod here and there to suggest that Alan Griswald's evidence didn't amount to much and that the tribunal could spend its time more profitably.

Harland straightened in his seat and groped for the cigarettes and lighter on the dashboard. Zikmund flashed him a saturnine grin in the glow of the instruments and told him to make sure his belt was fastened. The speedometer rose to 120 kph, then beyond.

'Is this necessary?'

Zikmund didn't reply. They took a turning on to a smaller road and moved at breakneck speed for about ten miles. Then Zikmund pulled over into a deserted depot, manoeuvred behind a rusting petrol tanker and switched off the engine and headlights. They waited. Three or four minutes later a car passed by travelling fast.

'Well, it wasn't the Saab,' said Harland.

'No, it wasn't. We'll go back to the main route and continue to make periodic diversions.'

Harland's mind returned to Kochalyin – anything rather than think about Eva and how he'd break the news to her. He thought about the code. Clearly the code's significance was twofold. In the wider context, it had become a matter of urgency for the intelligence organisations to stifle the random exposé of their operations. This was reason enough for the five or six big agencies to combine in tracing the source of the transmissions, which had been quickly achieved with the discovery of the two computers in London. So, in that respect, Cuth was right: the heat was off.

For Kochalyin, the interest in the code was acute because it revealed that Lipnik, the war criminal, was alive. Harland thought back to his conversation with Sara Hezemanns. She had said that Alan Griswald received the crucial part of his evidence after a visit to the East. That trip must have been to Stockholm. Because the images were hidden in the same code as the transmissions, it was reasonable to assume that they were either being prepared for broadcast or had already been used. Either way, it didn't much matter. The important point was that whoever killed Mortz must have learned that Griswald was in possession of the pictures. Plans were laid to destroy Griswald and the evidence. That left the only other member of the code-making syndicate to deal with. A week later Tomas was effectively silenced by the sniper's bullet.

Harland now dwelt on his son's motives. The more he thought about them, the more heroic they seemed to be. For in using the pictures, Tomas must have understood that he had signed his own death warrant. Kochalyin would know they could only have come from him. But why had Tomas released the video still which showed him with Kochalyin on the mountainside? Was it a kind of admission to the world of his guilt – a shriving of his sin? Or was he sending a discreet signature to Kochalyin? He must have appreciated that he would eventually be found and killed. It was at that point that the astonishing coincidence occurred. Tomas saw his picture in the newspapers and decided to risk going to New York. He knew he had very little time and he wanted to meet his real father.

Harland no longer needed to ask himself about Vigo. From the outset his only purpose had been to find out whether anything had survived the plane crash. All his actions were generated by the belief that Harland had retrieved the information or was somehow in league with Griswald and the code-makers. The cursory search of the files in Prague, the phoney Crèche and the clumsy deployment of the surveillance teams were eloquent of Vigo's agenda. Everything was designed to press Harland into giving him the evidence. That could only mean that he was working for Kochalyin.

Zikmund gestured to some lights in the hills above the road. 'Welcome to Karlsbad', they said. He pulled out the hip flask and raised it in the direction of the town. 'Let us drink to Karlovy Vary – as we call this city – and to the success of your meeting.' He passed the slivovitz to Harland who drank a silent toast. Then he remembered something Tomas had said in their last conversation. A man in Bosnia had been killed because of him. How could he have forgotten that?

The apartment building was not difficult to find. They drove past it quickly, then returned on the other side of the street to make a more leisurely inspection. The corner block had been built at the turn of the last century and was lavishly covered in art nouveau detail. Along the upper storeys ran metalwork balustrades which vaulted outwards in a series of balconies, each of which was supported by a pair of muscular hermaphrodite giants. At the corner of the building was a turret-like structure that rose high above the roof and was capped by a small cupola.

'Money,' said Zikmund, glancing upwards at the shuttered windows. 'These people are rich.'

They checked into a small hotel nearby, having left the car in a public car park some distance away. They asked for a room overlooking the street so that they could see the apartment building. A tree stood in the line of sight, but they could just see the entrance from the corner of the room. Harland suggested that one of them should remain in the room and watch the building, while the other took a closer look.

Zikmund left and did not reappear until the early hours. He came back slightly high and bubbling over with information gleaned from a cleaner, a neighbour and a bartender. The Raths had moved to the building about ten years before, the old lady having been advised by her doctors that the hot springs of Karlsbad would do her arthritis good. The younger woman – who *was* known as Irina – taught yoga. But this was not because she needed the money: the Raths were well off. As far as Zikmund could tell, the building wasn't being watched.

'Did anyone mention Tomas?'

'No one could remember a kid living there or visiting the Rath women, but this is an apartment building: people come and go without being noticed.'

From a supermarket bag he produced a royal blue jacket bearing a logo on the chest and back.

'This belongs to the company that services the elevator. The last inspector left this behind. The cleaner kept it in his storeroom and I bought it from him for fifty US. Wear it when you go tomorrow.'

They took turns to watch the building. Harland's shift ran to dawn. At eight he shook Zikmund awake and told him he was going. He put the jacket under one arm and a dark plastic folder used to hold the hotel stationery under the other. The folder would pass as an inspector's clipboard, he thought.

Ten minutes later Harland walked past the doorman in the apartment building and motioned to the elevator with a grunt. He got in and pressed the buttons for all five floors, in case the concierge was taking sufficient interest to notice where he got out. Flat seven was on the second floor, opposite the entrance to the lift. He moved to the double-door entrance and listened for any sign of life with his hand

303

hovering by the bell. There was no sound. He rang, and after a short pause a woman's voice came. She seemed to be asking a question. Harland said hello in English, which struck him as stupid, but it had the desired effect. He heard two bolts being drawn and the turn of a key. Suddenly he was looking at Eva.

She had changed little since the picture was taken for the last identity card. If anything, she had lost some weight. She was slightly flushed and her forehead was beaded with sweat. Her clothes – a black leotard top and baggy red pantaloons – also suggested that she had been exercising.

She was frowning slightly, trying to reconcile the English greeting and the jacket. She said something in Czech.

'Eva,' said Harland, looking at her steadily. 'It's Bobby Harland. It's me, Bobby.'

Her hands rose to her cheeks and her mouth opened slightly. But no words came out. Then three distinct emotions passed rapidly through her eyes – doubt, fear and pleasure. She took a step backwards. 'Bobby? Bobby Harland? My God, it *is* you.' She hesitated, then smiled.

The same perfect English, Harland thought, the same lilt in the voice, the same light brown eyes.

'I'm sorry to come like this,' he said. 'I should have phoned, but I felt it was better I came in person.'

'How did you find us? Why are you here?' She looked him up and down again. Her eyes came to rest on the logo of the jacket.

'Is it all right if I come in? I need to speak to you.'

An elderly woman's voice called out from the corridor to his right. She used the name Irina.

'I'm sorry, I forgot that you don't call yourself Eva. I can't get used to Irina.' He said it pleasantly but Eva looked at him as if he was accusing her of something. This was not going to be at all easy.

Eva's mother appeared in the light that was flooding into

the apartment. She was the type of small, well-dressed old lady you see in tearooms all over Middle Europe. She held a metal walking stick and moved with difficulty. Harland nodded at her and briefly looked past her into the apartment. It was large and comfortably furnished. The dark parquet floors were covered in expensive rugs.

The two women spoke to each other in Czech. Eva's eyes never left Harland's face.

'My mother asks the same question that I did. Why are you here?'

Harland waited for a moment. He had planned what he was to say.

'It would be better if I came in.'

Eva stepped aside and motioned him through a second pair of double doors to a sitting-room filled with scent from a large bunch of lilies. Eva moved to her mother's side, arms folded.

'Does your mother know who I am?'

'Yes, she knows who you are.'

'It's about Tomas,' he said.

'You've heard from Tomas?' There was a proprietorial edge in her voice which seemed to say, 'You have no right to talk about my son.'

'Yes, he came to see me in New York. He told me I was his father.'

'Where is he now?' she demanded.

'In London.' The old lady touched her daughter's arm. Eva's eyes betrayed relief.

'But . . .' Harland was appalled at what he was about to say, appalled also at the arc of fate that had brought him there to say it. 'But he is ill. He's in hospital. That's why I'm here, to tell you.'

'Ill?' she demanded. 'How? How ill is my son? What do you mean ill?'

'Please,' he implored, 'I think you will need to sit down. Your mother will need to sit down.'

Neither moved.

'Tell me why he is in hospital,' she said defiantly, as though he might be making up the story.

'He was shot.' The words were barely out before she had flown at him and slapped his face. She recoiled for a split second and then lunged again, beating his head and shoulders with her fists. Harland did not flinch. Eventually she fell back, head in hands, towards her mother's arms.

'Tell her what happened to Tomas,' said Hanna Rath in perfect English.

Harland exhaled. 'It is a very complicated story, but it ended with the shooting last week. I was with him when it happened. I'm afraid Tomas was hit several times.'

'But he is alive, yes?' said Eva, brushing back her hair. Her eyes blazed. There were no tears.

'Yes, he's alive, but he's not well. I have brought the doctor's phone number. You can talk to him and find out Tomas's latest condition. He was improving when I left England.' He waited. 'It's still only seven in the morning there, but we can call my sister, Harriet. She will know how he is.'

'Who shot him? Who shot Tomas?'

'They haven't caught anyone.' He had decided beforehand that he would leave out Kochalyin and Tomas's involvement with the transmissions. That was too much for her to deal with. He stood in silence for a moment. 'Look, do you want me to go? I can come back later.'

Eva moved to the window and looked out. Harland heard her saying something to herself in Czech – or perhaps it was to her mother because Hanna moved to the next room, to a kitchen and dining area. Eva now had her head down. Her shoulders were shaking with grief.

'Why didn't you come before?' she said through her tears.

306

'Because I didn't know where you lived.'

'But Tomas knows. Tomas has the phone numbers—' She searched Harland's face again. 'Why didn't Tomas tell you?' Harland shook his head helplessly.

'Because he couldn't tell you,' she said at length.

Harland moved two paces towards her, reaching out. But he stopped when he saw her recoil.

'He was in a coma,' he said. 'As I left England I heard news that he'd come out of it. Eva – they had to remove a bullet from the base of his brain. He may be permanently disabled.'

Harland saw Hanna looking through the door, horrified. It was as if both women had been scalded.

'I will go to London,' Eva said. 'I must go to London to see him. I will leave today.' She cast about the room, evidently trying to collect herself and think about the arrangements.

'I'll come with you,' said Harland. 'I'll take you to the hospital.'

Hanna came back into the room and motioned him to sit down.

'You will now tell us why Tomas was shot.'

'How much do you know about Tomas's activities in the last year?'

'Activities is a sinister-sounding word,' she said. 'It suggests something not legal. Tomas is a good boy. He needed to get away. He had his problems and we were content to let him work them out by himself. My daughter and Tomas have not spoken for some time. But we knew he was in Stockholm and that he had put his talents to good use there.'

'Do you mind me asking why you had not spoken to him?'

Hanna looked over to her daughter. Harland waited, but neither said anything.

'Well, it doesn't matter. I can tell you that he left Stockholm and moved to London. He had a girlfriend there.'

'We did not know that but, as you say, it doesn't matter now. All that matters is that my daughter sees him.'

'No,' said Eva from the window. 'I want to know everything. I have to hear the worse things now.'

Harland could not help noticing her beauty.

'How much do you really need to hear now?'

'Everything.'

Harland had no intention of telling her everything.

'Look, this is going to be very distressing. Why don't you take it one step at a time. We'll get the flights to Britain and we can talk on the way.'

'No!' she shouted. 'Tell me everything now.'

'Tell her,' said Hanna.

'Tell me, Bobby.' It was the first time she had addressed him by his first name.

'Well . . .' He paused and inhaled. 'I think there are very good reasons to believe that Oleg Kochalyin was responsible for the shooting.'

'That's impossible,' said Eva contemptuously.

Hanna studied Harland.

'Why do you say these things? Oleg would not hurt Tomas. They were close. For most of his life, Tomas knew Oleg as his father, and he was a good father to him. They saw each other after my daughter's divorce.'

'When was the divorce?'

'Nineteen eighty-eight,' said the old lady. 'It was amicable. Oleg took care of us. Irina and he still have an affection for each other, you see. This is why you are wrong.'

Harland wasn't going to pursue it.

'Look, I think you need time by yourselves. This is a terrible thing to happen. You will want to discuss what you're going to do without me being here. I'll go back to the hotel and wait to hear from you.' He pulled a sheet of notepaper from the folder that he'd been carrying and placed it on the coffee table. 'The telephone and room number is on this.'

He left the building. It occurred to him that he had eaten little in the last twenty-four hours, so he decided to find breakfast before returning to the hotel. He also wanted time to gather his thoughts before talking to Zikmund. Seeing Eva again had thrown him, though he barely dwelled on this because to do so would be to put his desire above her distress. He felt deeply for her, and it didn't matter that she had been cold and suspicious with him. That was natural. He knew he'd been the same with Tomas.

Half an hour later he went back to the hotel. As he climbed the narrow stairs to the third floor two men brushed past him. He thought nothing about it until he reached his room and found the door unlocked. He called out, then pushed the door open.

Zikmund was lying in bed in much the same position as he had left him a couple of hours before. He had been shot in the head.

22

ESCAPE

His first instinct was to leave the room immediately. The two men were bound to return once they realised that they'd passed an elevator inspector on the stairs of a hotel that possessed no elevator. But Harland was held to the spot. He looked down at the two small-calibre bullet wounds about two inches apart at Zikmund's temple and reflected bitterly on the waste. He had come to like the man, his decency and humour, and felt he owed it to him to stay and see that his body was treated with respect. But he couldn't.

He looked around the room. The contents of his bag had been tipped on to the floor. He swept everything back, knowing that there was nothing to reveal his false identity, and slung it over his shoulder. He felt in Zikmund's jacket pockets and removed the keys to the hire car. Then he left, without looking at Zikmund again, and hurried downstairs. He was still wearing the jacket that had saved his life when he sprinted across the road and burst through the entrance of Eva's building. The doorman, by now suspicious of his comings and goings, shouted something after him. Harland took no notice and bounded up the stairs to the second floor. Eva opened the door to his hammering and stared blankly at him. She had changed out of the exercise gear and now wore black trousers and a grey rollneck sweater. She looked composed – remote. He pushed past her, slamming the door behind him.

'The man who helped me find you has just been murdered. His body is in the hotel room over the street. He was asleep in bed when they shot him at close range with a silencer. The killing was ordered by the same man who shot Tomas.'

Eva looked at him and then at her mother who was still sitting in the same place on one of the sofas.

The lack of reaction annoyed him.

'Did you hear me? Kochalyin has killed again.'

The old lady was the first to speak.

'You have no proof, Mr Harland, that Oleg is responsible for the death of your friend.'

'No, I don't, but I do possess proof that he is a psychopathic murderer. It's the same proof that your son – our son – released to the War Crimes Tribunal in The Hague. This proof is so dangerous to Kochalyin that he has been prepared to cause the death of twenty-three people to suppress it. That figure includes a young woman named Felicity – Tomas's girlfriend. She was tortured to betray his whereabouts, then executed, like my friend. This toll includes many people who had never heard of Oleg Kochalyin – the passengers of two planes in New York, one of which he sabotaged. Then there was a young policeman in London who was mown down on the same evening as Tomas. His companion, by the way, is disabled for life.' He paused for breath. 'And Tomas? I'll be brutally frank about his prospects. Tomas will never move again. He will not speak again. He will never feed himself again. He is a prisoner of his own body.'

He reached into the inside pocket of his jacket. 'And the proof, that it was worth inflicting so much pain for? It's these pictures of Oleg Kochalyin, also known as the war criminal Viktor Lipnik.' He unfolded the print of the video still and placed it on the coffee table. 'This shows Kochalyin supervising the burial of victims of a mass execution in Bosnia. As

311

you can see, Tomas is in the background. It's clear that he was made to witness this disgusting event when he was not yet twenty years old – by a man who you apparently regarded as the perfect father figure.' He looked down at Hanna. 'Forgive me,' he said harshly, 'that wasn't quite how you put it, but it's clear that from the moment you welcomed Kochalyin into Prague in 1968 with that basket of food, you have never ceased to trust him. I don't know whether you knew his true nature, but you must have had some idea when Tomas came back from his little trip in 1995.'

'We did know something had happened,' said Hanna. 'But he would not tell us about it.' She was shaken.

'And you didn't press him?' Harland demanded. He turned to Eva. 'What did you think you were doing?' he said, jabbing at the photograph. 'How did you let Kochalyin take him to Bosnia?'

Eva shook her head. She looked as if she couldn't take any more.

Her mother spoke. 'You don't understand. Tomas had a drug problem. Heroin. Oleg paid for the clinic in Austria where he was taken off the drugs. Oleg was attached to the boy and Tomas listened to him. When he said he would take him on business to Belgrade, we thought it would be good for Tomas. We knew he was going into Yugoslavia, but we thought it was Belgrade.'

'And he told you nothing afterwards. No hint?'

She lowered her eyes.

'Did you know that your KGB friend was supplying weapons and fuel to the Yugoslavs? Did you know he was laundering their money and stealing a good bit on the way?' He threw his arms out wide, indicating the room. 'Eva, for Christ's sake, where do you think all this comes from?'

'My name is Irina.'

'Not to me, it isn't.'

The old lady looked at her daughter. 'Tomas *did* say he

had seen something terrible and we did think he had come back a very changed person. He would not talk.' She looked up at Harland. 'But you know he still went to see Oleg long after these events.'

'That's because he was gathering as much evidence as he could against Kochalyin,' said Harland. He placed the second picture on the table. 'This was taken on or after the twenty-ninth of May 1998 – probably by Tomas. It proves that Kochalyin – that is to say Lipnik – was alive after the staged assassination in Bosnia. Tomas certainly knew what he was doing. This photograph is in many ways more important than the first one.'

Both women looked at the picture.

Harland waited, then said, 'When did you tell him about me?'

'Two years ago,' Eva said, without raising her head.

'And he reacted by breaking off relations with you – is that right?'

She hesitated.

'We didn't see him, but he wrote to say that he had made a new life in Stockholm. He told me he'd done well and made some money for himself from an Internet company. He said he needed to get his life straightened out. He didn't send his address and I didn't try to find him.' She paused and moved to her mother's side. 'Of course we were anxious for him, Bobby, but what could we do? I knew he needed time to himself to sort out his problems. All I cared about was that he wasn't using drugs again.'

Harland watched her, partly absorbed by her face, and partly wondering at the compromises she'd made in marrying Kochalyin. Maybe they weren't compromises. Perhaps that was what she had wanted all along.

'I understand you've had your problems,' he said.

'Do you have children?' she asked abruptly. 'I mean other children. No? Well, how could you know about these things?'

'Well, maybe that's true, but I do know our son is lying in hospital and that I'm going back to Britain. You can come with me, or you can go separately. Either way, I'm leaving now.' He picked up the photographs. 'These have made me a marked man. And it's only a matter of time before Zikmund's body is discovered and descriptions of me are provided by the hotel staff.'

The phone rang. Eva moved to answer it but changed her mind.

'It's on the machine,' she said. The bell continued to sound. She cocked her head as it stopped and a recorded message played. A man spoke in Czech – a gravelly, controlled voice that did not hesitate. After a few short sentences he hung up without giving a name.

Eva looked at him to see if Harland had guessed.

He had. 'That was Kochalyin. What did he want?'

'He asks me to call him. There's something he wants to talk to me about. It's not important.'

'But he didn't leave a number, did he? That means you must be in regular contact.'

'I have a number where I can get him when I need to.'

'How often is that?'

She shrugged.

'A few times a year. A message is passed on and he calls me back.'

'And what do you talk about?'

'Nothing – financial arrangements. He has bills to pay for us.'

'And?'

'And he has sometimes made attempts to find Tomas. I didn't ask him to, but he has done this anyway. He says he does it to – how do you say? – to put my mind at rest.'

'And he calls to find out if you've heard from him?'

She nodded.

'Well, I'm sure he was very concerned,' said Harland. 'But

314

fortunately Tomas hid himself well. He got himself another identity. He has been living under the name Lars Edberg.'

Eva let out a weary, wry laugh.

'What?' It was at that precise moment when he became aware of something reaching deep inside him and snatching at his guts.

'The family trait,' she said. 'We've all pretended to be other people.'

Harland didn't respond. Now he knew what it was. That voice on the answering machine – he'd heard it before. It was in the villa. On the first day they'd tied him to a chair and left him blindfolded in the old air of the cellar. He was there for an hour or more in complete darkness and silence. And he'd thought he was alone, which is why he let out the sighs and self-recriminations that a person only voices when he knows he is by himself and facing death. Then the man spoke – the cracked smoker's voice he'd just heard. He was shockingly close and Harland had instantly understood that he'd been there, sitting beside him the entire time, watching his fear.

There was no conversation during that first session. But there was pain, a sudden, swift statement of the man's power. The first blow was to his groin. There were many more. He thought perhaps that it was a club or baseball bat, but it might just as easily have been the toe-cap of a heavy boot.

In some ways Harland was not surprised. All along he had wondered about the connection between the Russian in the villa and the elusive Kochalyin. He looked at Eva. Did she know about this? And what about the old lady who had made the first contact with the young tank officer, who had brought him into her home and practically offered her daughter up to him?

'How did you get here?' asked Eva.

'By car. We were followed. They know the car. They're probably watching it. But I have the keys and if there's no other way to leave I will try to use it.'

315

'Were you registered under your own name at the hotel?'

'No. Zikmund took the room in his name and showed his ID. They didn't see mine.'

'But the people who killed him must know who you are.'

'Of course. And they know I came to see you, which is why you just got that call. It is also probably true that they would very much prefer it if you didn't learn about the evidence against him. You must know a lot about Kochalyin's background which he would hate to see combined with the material I have. Everything you know will add to the case against him – for example, the dates of his business trip with Tomas in 1995. Soon, Eva, there'll be a point when Oleg Kochalyin will have to decide what to do about you. It may be that this man is still obsessed with you.' He paused, sat down on the arm of a sofa and removed the inspector's jacket. 'But how long is that likely to last now? It has only just occurred to me that while you didn't know what had happened to Tomas, you were no threat. But now he suspects that you've learned about the shooting and the reasons for it and about the other barbarities, he will come to see you as a danger to him.'

'He never will see her like that,' said Hanna.

'You seem very confident.'

'I am. She is the only person that man has ever loved. He could not harm her.'

Harland wondered how much the old lady had pushed Eva's relationship.

'Don't be too certain,' he said to her. 'He attempted to kill the boy and you yourself told me how fond he was of him.'

Eva squeezed her temples and rubbed her face.

'We'll leave now,' she said, looking at the floor. 'I already have my bag packed.'

She spoke a few words in Czech to her mother, then picked up the phone and dialled. This time she spoke in German, saying without preamble that she was returning the

316

call of fifteen minutes before. She informed the person that she was going out to give a class at the Thermal Sanatorium and to do some shopping. She would be back in the early afternoon, although she'd be on her cellphone in the meantime.

She went to get her bag and began to assemble a few more things for the journey – a book, her purse, passport, a cellphone and an envelope of money, which she took from a desk.

'You know that Tomas was probably traced by Kochalyin because he was using a cellphone,' he said. 'All he needs to do is to ring you to get a fix on your position.'

Eva thought for a second.

'We will need it,' she said firmly.

Having rung down and told the doorman to order a cab for her, Eva led Harland to the first-floor landing and through a metal door. They took a spiral staircase to the ground floor where there was a boiler room and service area. Another metal door opened on to a shabby little street at the back of the building, piled with dirty snow. She looked left and right, then bolted across the street. Harland followed, carrying both bags. At the first turning on the right she held her keys in the air. Harland saw the side lights of the dark green BMW blink ahead of him. She got in and started the engine before he had managed to sling the bags on the back seat.

'Now, get my phone out,' she said, scanning the street ahead of them, 'and also one of the credit cards in my purse.'

As they moved off, Eva wedged the phone between her ear and shoulder and asked for the British Airways number in Prague. Then she made another call. Realising she was booking flights on the afternoon service to Heathrow, he felt for his passport and held it open for her. She nodded to him as she spelled out Tristan O'Donnell's name. Harland had an idea what she was doing, but didn't say anything.

They left the side street and moved sedately towards the eastern fringes of the town. The traffic began to thin out. When they reached the open road Eva glanced in the mirror and put her foot down. For twenty minutes they drove at a remorseless speed, the needle of the speedometer never dipping below 140 kph. On the open stretches they moved at 180 kph. In a patch of forest they slowed down and took a turning left into a range of hills.

'Where did you learn to drive like this?' he shouted, as she accelerated round a corner to take the one-in-ten gradient.

'Russia. I was on a course there once.'

He'd ask her about that later.

'You think we're being followed? There's nothing behind us.'

'I hope they believe we're going to Prague – they will have got someone checking the flight bookings. But my instinct says they're not going to leave this to chance. They'll try to follow.' She paused. 'I guess they missed us on our last turning, but if they're smart they'll pick us up on the road to the north. It depends how quickly we can make it.'

She said there was a map in the pocket of his door and that he should start working out routes through northern Bohemia into Germany. She was planning to drive through Teplice and Usti. At each stage she wanted him to give an alternative route to cut through the mountains.

They passed through a forest of bare oak and beech, then dropped down to a plain, where they joined the road that would take them to the border. Harland was reminded of another trip in a BMW tearing through the Czech landscape to a border crossing. He had lain folded up in the back seat. Macy was at the wheel; The Bird was up front, but reached back and kept a hand on his shoulder for a lot of the journey. They thought they were being followed, but they were armed to the hilt and there was no question of them being stopped.

On the outskirts of a town called Chumotuv, Harland and

Eva entered a region known as the Black Triangle. All about them were tar-black scars of lignite mines and chimney-stacks pouring out thick, sulphurous smoke. Each town was a monochrome study of Communist functionalism – soulless prefab blocks drenched in pollution; factories of fantastical scale and filth. Everything was blackened – the piles of snow, the surface water, the road signs. Through it all the people moved as shadows. The towns looked as if they were still being run by Communist party bosses.

The country passed by in a toxic blur. At a place called Most, they halted for petrol. As Harland filled the tank, he gazed absent-mindedly across the road at an abandoned building. A prostitute dressed as a rodeo girl lifted a leg in the doorway in half-hearted enticement. Another joined her at the window and pouted. It was then that he noticed the blue Saab flash by. From the payment booth, Eva saw him duck and waited for a few seconds before returning to the car.

'Was it the silver Mercedes?' she asked.

'What Mercedes? This was a Saab.'

'I think there's a Mercedes also – German number plates.'

They didn't see either car again until Usti, where the Saab fell in a few cars behind them at some lights. They jumped the lights and lost it but Eva said she didn't think they'd shake it off for good. Five miles down the road they came to Decin, the last big town before the border. She turned into a desolate housing estate. A few hundred metres on she apparently found what she was looking for – four young toughs, three in skinhead uniform, loitering outside a bar. She got out and talked to them, gesturing and smiling. At first they looked wary, but she won them over within a few minutes. She returned with two, who sheepishly nodded to Harland, climbed in the back of the car and put the bags on their laps.

'What the hell are we doing?' asked Harland.

'I think it's better if we take the train. These boys are going to have a night out in Prague. I've promised them a hundred dollars. They weren't going to accept until I said it would be dangerous.'

As they prepared to get out at the station, Harland noticed Eva take her phone from the side pocket of her bag and slip it into the tray beneath the dashboard. That was smart of her: she was leaving it for the young men to use so they'd lay a false trail.

An hour and a half later the local train pulled into Dresden. They got out and separated. Harland went and bought two tickets to Amsterdam via Berlin and Cologne. At all three cities they would have the option to get off the train and take a plane to London. Having established that the train left in thirty-five minutes, he made for the spot where they had agreed to meet. Before he got there he was aware of her at his side in the crowd.

'I think they're here,' she said, looking in front of them. 'There's a train leaving for Warsaw in ten minutes. We'll meet on it.' She forged ahead of him and vanished towards the station's main exit.

Harland turned and walked quickly in the other direction and boarded the train waiting at the nearest platform – an express bound for Munich. He moved along two carriages and became stuck in the middle of a third. Behind and in front of him were passengers sorting out their seats and stowing luggage. He pushed back past a group of soldiers to the door. But this too was blocked. Then he realised that the door on the track side of the train would be just as easy. He opened it, dropped down to the rails and ran across to the other side where he scrambled up. He made the Warsaw express with thirty seconds to spare. There was no sign of Eva.

He gave up looking for her and sat at a table with two young German priests. About half an hour later she appeared and said she had a compartment to herself at the front of the train. She had bought two tickets to Warsaw where they could make a connection which would take them back to Berlin. He nodded to the priests and followed her to the compartment, on the way passing a ticket inspector with whom Eva was clearly already on good terms. They sat down opposite each other.

Now that they were alone, a rather odd formality settled over them. Eva tried reading her book but let her gaze drift to the unbearably bleak countryside. Their eyes fastened on the same village churches and impenetrable pine forests. Soon dusk snuffed out the landscape and they were looking at each other's reflections.

'I saw you on television,' she said suddenly. Her tone was matter-of-fact. 'I saw you on television in 1989.'

'I wasn't on television in 1989,' he said. 'I was still working for SIS. Serving officers don't go on television. It's one of the things they taught us.'

She didn't smile. 'But you were on television. That's how I knew you were in Prague. That's why I took Tomas to Prague and stayed in my mother's old flat. I thought I'd see you again in the streets. I must have been crazy.'

'How do you mean, you saw me on television?'

'It's true. I did. You remember how it started with the soldiers beating them up?'

He nodded.

'There was a German camera crew in Prague secretly filming in the streets all that day. They were waiting for something to happen like it did in the GDR. About four days afterwards, the film was smuggled out and shown on German TV, which we could receive where we lived. I knew it was you. I recognised your walk first. You were going away from the camera and then you stopped and someone gave you something. Your face looked directly at the camera for a few seconds, though you didn't know it was there. You were talking to a young woman, then you turned away. Bobby, I know it was you. You were near the end of Vaclavské Namesti – Wenceslas Square – by Narodni Street. That was where the police attacked the students. Why were you there?'

'Because of you,' he said simply.

'You were looking for me?' She was puzzled.

'No, I was there *because* of you. I was trying to eliminate my records of contact with the StB. Look, I don't have to explain this, surely. You knew about the photograph of us in bed. They threatened to send that other material to SIS. I had to get those files before the regime collapsed.'

'What are you talking about? There was no photograph.'

He contemplated her and wished he had a cigarette. 'The whole thing was rigged. I think it must have been at the hotel we went to near Campo dei Fiore. But I'm not sure, except I know it wasn't Orvieto.'

'You must believe me, Bobby. I never cooperated in such a plan.'

'Well, it doesn't matter now,' he said. 'But that was one of the things I was trying to get before everything collapsed in your country.'

'How could you hope to do such a thing?'

'The Stasi files were taken from East Germany at that time. The KGB ended up selling them in Moscow.'

'Yes, but these things were protected in Czech.'

'Less so, actually. My companion had a contact. We went to Prague to make a down-payment.'

She absorbed this and looked away. 'Do you know who your contact was?'

'It was my friend's. I was representing the British side of things. But he'd let me in on the deal because we were old associates. The Americans were going to bear most of the financial weight of the transaction, although we were going to get equal access to the files.'

'And did you get anything?'

'A little, but not enough to eliminate all trace of me.'

She was sailing very close to the subject of his detention and torture. That might be expected of someone who didn't know about it, but equally of a person pretending ignorance.

'Believe me, Bobby. I did not know of the photograph. I wouldn't have allowed it to happen.'

'Oh, for fuck's sake! What about the naval attaché? You compromised him before you met me in exactly the same way. You slept with him, right? Drew Morris was his name and he was forced to pass secrets to the StB – another victory for K.'

She looked appalled. 'How did you find out these things?'

'I finally saw the files. Zikmund got me in this week. I traced you through your mother's file.'

He could see her calculating what else he might know. The crease in her forehead had knotted and she wore the glazed, neutral expression that he remembered she used to hide her thoughts. A lot of him was still fascinated by her face; even in the unforgiving light of the compartment it was extraordinarily vital. For the first time he noticed half a dozen freckles on and beside her nose which were in fact tiny moles. Smile lines showed on either side of her mouth and she had one or two strands of iron grey in her hair. She was very beautiful, but for him now it was an entirely objective beauty.

'You know everything, then.'

'No, your file was remarkably slender. Kochalyin had long ago made sure that there was very little there.'

'But you have to believe me. I didn't know about the camera or the photograph.'

'It doesn't matter now.'

'No, this is the truth and it's important you accept it.'

Harland glanced at her reflection in the window.

'Why didn't you tell me that you were pregnant?'

'Because I knew you wouldn't be able to do anything. I

·had no choice: if I had defected, my mother would have been punished. That's why I didn't see you.'

'Yes, your mother – your mother has played a big part in all this,' he said acidly. 'Did you know there's a picture of her in the archive from '68, giving Oleg Kochalyin and his crew a basket of food? It was used in the Soviet papers. That act changed our entire lives. There is just one thing I don't understand. Was Kochalyin in the KGB then, or did he go back to the Soviet Union and train?'

'You want to know about all that?' she said, matching his vehemence. 'It is very simple. Oleg was undercover KGB in the army. They were worried that the troops would not do what was necessary. Oleg, who had been in the army before the KGB, was put in as tank captain to make sure there would be no sympathy for the Czech people, that there would be no weakening of resolve among the troops. When the tanks were ordered into Prague, they had no food. Did you know that? The great Soviet military machine forgot to give its army provisions. By the third or fourth day those soldiers were desperate. They hadn't eaten and they were out of water. It was very hot that August and they couldn't leave their tanks to find provisions. Anyway, the Czechs were not going to give them help.'

'But your mother did and then a Soviet army photographer happened by to capture the scene for the Russian newspapers.'

'It wasn't like that. This tank crew was outside our apartment for a day. They were suffering and so she gave them food. When the Russians heard about this they sent a photographer and they staged the scene again. Of course she was against the invasion – everyone was. But she gave them food because once a Russian soldier had saved her life. Did Tomas tell you she survived the camp at Terezin – Theresienstadt?'

Harland nodded impatiently.

'When the camp was liberated by the Russians a tank captain in General Rybalko's Third Guard Tank Corps found her. That night he looked after her – he gave her water and small amounts of food because she could only take a little. She was very, very weak and on the point of death. Maybe she reminded him of his own child – she never knew why he took so much care of her. But she says that kindness – the relief at finding kindness in the world again – was what saved her. It gave her hope. Do you understand? And then all those years later she saw a tank crew who needed exactly what that officer had given her – food, water, kindness. You see she saw them as people and she knew in her heart that she had a debt of honour and that was far more important to her than the issue of the invasion. It was a personal obligation. And for that act she paid greatly. We both did. We were hounded from the neighbourhood. People did not speak to us. They spat at us in the street. They called us Russian whores.' She paused and smoothed down the cover of her book. 'So, you see, not everything is as simple as it appears.'

'How did Kochalyin keep in touch?'

'Oleg stayed in Prague. He was working full time on the Normalisation programme and overseeing work with the StB. He was stationed in Prague permanently. I don't know how my mother found him, but she did and that was a good thing because the new regime was beginning to move against the Jews again. Those few Jews that remained in Czechoslovakia after the war were accused of anti-state and anti-socialist activities – a Zionist conspiracy. Oleg gave her protection. He found us another apartment and he got her a new job.'

Eva paused.

'People in the West don't understand now how difficult it was. She depended on him. When she came out of Terezin she didn't have one living relation in the world. So, you see, if I had defected in 1975, she would have lost everything for the second time in her life. I had to go back, Bobby, and I couldn't tell you why.'

Harland wondered if Hanna Rath had been Kochalyin's lover before he transferred his attentions to her daughter. Had he been waiting all that time for Eva? Had Hanna pushed the match to keep her protection?

'And you?' he asked quietly. 'When were you thrown into the bargain?'

She looked away. 'You're very cruel. I don't remember you being like that.'

He persisted. 'When did you become his lover? Before or after me?'

Her eyes darkened.

'After you. We needed to survive. I was pregnant, for God's sake!'

'So you had Tomas and resumed work for the StB, or was it the KGB? What did you do? You said you went on a driving course in Russia. That sounds like you were being prepared for some type of active service. What were you doing? Wet jobs? Courier work? I want the whole story.'

'You have no right to my story, Bobby. You were my lover twenty-eight years ago. That's all.'

'And the father of your child.'

'Biologically – yes. But that doesn't give you any kind of moral authority. Who are you to judge the decisions I was forced to take? They were very difficult and I made the best of my life after I took them. As for you, you didn't have any of these responsibilities, did you? You just continued your career in the British Secret Service.'

There was no longer even a pretence of politeness.

'Let me remind you of a couple of things,' said Harland coldly. 'You were living with a KGB butcher and a sadist. However much you averted your eyes, you must have known what he was. Second, you were serving a regime, the entire purpose of which was to suppress the Czechs and Slovaks –

your people. So when it comes to morality, even I may have the edge on you.'

'You spied for that regime,' she said. 'What does that make you?'

He looked at her with a new understanding. 'How did you know what I did?'

'You just told me.'

'I didn't say anything about that. I said that they just threatened to send the material to my superiors. I didn't tell you how I reacted.'

At that moment a door opened and an officer from the Polish border police asked for their passports.

'You are both travelling to Warsaw, sir?'

'Yes,' replied Harland. 'A business trip – one or two days.'

He examined the passport again.

'This passport was issued three years ago. The photograph is much older, no? You are more young in the photograph, Mr O'Donnell.'

Harland smiled ruefully and coughed.

'Vanity, I'm afraid. I liked that picture.'

The man seemed to accept this and turned to Eva.

'Have a pleasant journey,' he said.

23

A HALT IN POLAND

They remained in silence for half an hour. Harland wished he had something to read because his eyes kept returning to Eva's rigidly averted features. She knew more than she'd let on – he was sure of that. But he didn't want to have it out with her now.

Quite suddenly the train slammed on its brakes. Eva got up and angled her head to look forward out of the window. Harland went into the passage and opened a window on the right side of the train. They turned to each other. Eva left the compartment and hurried back to the doors at the end of the carriage. She wrenched open the windows on both sides of the train and peered up the line.

'There's a station about a kilometre in front of us,' she said.

Harland went to join her and leaned out of the window. The wind hummed in the electric cables overhead. He could just make out a row of white lights ahead of them and off to his right one or two clusters of orange lights that he supposed were villages. There was nothing obviously wrong, but he knew from the German travel schedule, issued with the tickets, that the *expresowych* wasn't due to stop until they reached Wroclaw in half an hour's time. What lay ahead was little more than a halt for local trains. He thrust his head out of the window and squinted. Now two or three pairs of lights were scything through the darkness towards the station. The

328

first pair stopped and were extinguished. Harland turned round to tell Eva to fetch the bags, but she'd already done so and was looking out of the opposite window. They waited.

The train began to ease forward, the wheels groaning with inertia. They travelled a further hundred yards but without picking up much speed. It was obvious they were going to coast into the station ahead of them for an unscheduled stop. He went through the possibilities. The engine might be malfunctioning; the line ahead of them could be blocked; or the railway was suffering from a routine delay. But it did seem odd that the cars had turned up at that exact moment.

'What do you think?' he shouted over to Eva.

Without saying anything, she tried the door handle and found the automatic locking system was on. 'Can you get out of this window?' she said.

She put the bag over her shoulder, gathered up a short blue duffel coat and swung one leg up in a balletic arc so that it rested in the top of the window. 'Like this,' she said.

'That's all very well,' said Harland, 'but don't you think it would be better to get out this side where there's no track?'

'It was for demonstration purposes,' she said with a sarcastic grimace. 'Perhaps we should stay on the train. You don't look in very good shape, Bobby.'

He poked his head out again. There were figures on the platform ahead of them. 'No, I think we should leave. We can catch another train at the station or thumb a ride.'

'In this weather? I don't think so,' she said.

She went first and with very little effort wriggled her legs through the window and then turned round so she could lower herself to a step below the door. She held the window with one hand and worked the handle of the door from the outside. It opened a fraction. She smiled up at him, then dropped from the train, squatted for a fraction of a second and rolled into the darkness, like an expert parachutist.

Harland opened the door, grasped the vertical hand-rail

and felt for the step below. Then he leaned back and slammed the door shut. The hand-rail allowed him to crouch down within two or three feet of the ground. He found he could hang there quite comfortably with his bag over his shoulder and so he decided to get nearer the station before launching himself into the dark. About two hundred and fifty yards from the end of the platform the train's brakes began to grind again. He shifted his bag from his shoulder and leapt, hugging it with both hands. His jump was not as neat as Eva's. He misjudged the distance and hit a mound of snow which sent him sprawling into a frozen ditch. He picked himself up, brushed the snow off and looked round to see Eva jogging towards him, taking care to keep out of the light thrown from the carriages.

She made her way to his side. The last coach passed and left them bathed in the glow from two red tail-lights. As the train juddered to a halt so that only the engine and the first coach reached the platform, four figures moved from the covered section of the station and boarded. Harland thought he saw uniforms.

'What's going on?' Eva said.

'I think they're police.' It was clear to him that the train had been ordered to slow down so that it wouldn't arrive at the station before the cars did. But it didn't make sense. Anyone who wanted to avoid them would simply jump down beside the track, as they had done.

They moved forward fifty yards to a piece of ground covered in rusting oil drums and concrete sleepers. Magnetic tape from a discarded cassette was caught in the branches of a stunted thorn bush and shimmered like Christmas streamers. They squatted behind the bush and waited. Harland was aware of two policemen moving towards them along the track. They were sweeping the snow with the beam of a torch, looking for footprints. They reached the last carriage and stopped. A man's voice called out to them from the other side of the train, where the same operation was apparently in progress. Then both men looked up as a head appeared at the door of the last carriage. They exchanged a few words during which Harland registered a note of dejection. Eva bent to Harland's ear and whispered that she'd heard that they had searched the train and found nothing.

The train eased forward with the police officers following and peering to see if anyone was hiding under the carriages. It drew level with the platform and stopped, whereupon the roof and the gaps between the carriages were searched. Eventually all the police officers assembled on the platform. There was a good deal of shrugging and gesturing and stamping of feet. Harland knew they'd given up on what was a hopelessly flawed plan. He rose a little, peered over the bush then edged round it and began to make his way towards the platform. Eva hissed at him to stay back, but he took no notice. She swore and scuttled after him, her blue duffel coat rasping over the surface of the frosted snow.

There was an officer in the middle of the group who turned from his men to someone hidden in the shadows. A lot of toing and froing ensued and now passengers were leaning out of the windows demanding to know why they were being delayed. A rail official came up and gesticulated, and then the man from the frontier police who had checked their passports joined in, insisting that the rail authorities hold the train at the station. He's been well paid, thought Harland.

'They're going to have to let it go,' said Eva.

'Well, let's go with it.'

'Get on again?'

'We can't stay here,' he hissed. 'No cars, no roads – nothing. There's bugger all here.'

Without consulting her further, he crouched down and slipped over the tracks into the shadows on the other side of the train. Eva followed so quietly that for a few seconds

Harland didn't know that she had joined him. She moved very close to him and stood, looking up at the door of the last carriage, her shoulders rising silently.

His plan was to step up and open the door as the train began to move off. But he saw the lights of another train approaching rapidly from the opposite direction and decided to make his move when it passed them. The murmur which preceded the express grew to a roar. It thundered through the station dragging a cloud of ice particles in its slipstream. Harland jumped up and wrenched the door handle downwards, but it wouldn't shift. He thought it might be frozen and reached up again to hammer it up with his fist. Nothing.

Just at that moment the wheels protested and moved a few inches on the track, paused then moved some more.

'Fuck! Fuck! Fuck!' Harland spat out the words.

Eva glanced at him and gestured with her head to the right. She dropped back behind the last carriage and jogged beneath the tail-lights. He followed because he didn't want to be left standing like an idiot in the middle of the tracks. There was about a carriage distance between them and the end of the platform. Just as the last few feet of the carriage passed the platform, he understood what she planned. She crouched and flipped herself over the rail and landed in the blackness under the concrete lip of the platform. The projection offered about two feet of shelter but much more shadow. A second later Harland dived too, but made a hash of it. The strap of his bag got snagged on a bolt that held the rail to a sleeper and he was forced to let go and roll over the bag. Eva's hand darted forward, released the strap and pulled the bag towards her. The train had travelled almost the length of the platform before they settled themselves under the concrete lip, knees clasped tightly to their chests.

Suddenly there was quiet. Most of the voices receded into the station buildings. But the sound remained of two or three pairs of footsteps moving randomly above. One pair came close to the edge about ten feet to the left of where they were huddled. The person seemed to be standing there in contemplation. Harland looked at Eva. She had put her finger to her nose and was lifting her head. He understood she'd picked up the scent of his heavy cologne.

Then came the voice, the voice of Oleg Kochalyin in the stillness of the deserted station. Eva flinched. Harland put his hand up to her mouth.

'We'll leave,' Kochalyin said in Russian. 'They're not here. Get the engine started.' There was no reply, just the scurrying of a pair of feet hastening to carry out an order.

He stood there for a few moments longer. Then he was gone and after a minute there was the cough of an ignition, followed by the whine of a helicopter engine. Harland realised that Kochalyin must have arrived at the station some time before the police. There was no mystery in this. It wouldn't have been difficult for him to work out which train they had taken from Dresden. The problem must have been to galvanise the Polish authorities to stop the train and have it searched. He wondered what story he'd used to persuade them to do this.

The noise of the engine reached a pitch behind the station buildings and then the helicopter lifted into the air with a sudden roar. It paused over the station and shot off westwards down the track.

'What do we do now?' asked Eva, shivering.

'It's still early. We'll get on the next train, whichever way it's going.'

Most of the lights on the platform were turned off and they were able to move away from beside the track. An hour later a slow service going east pulled in and they boarded for the next station down the line where they changed to a faster train to Warsaw. Late that night they boarded an overnight service for Poznań and Berlin. A bribe of fifty dollars bought them the last free couchette. Before they left, Harland found a phone and put a call through to The Bird to tell him that Zikmund Myslbek had been killed that morning. The Bird already knew but wanted to hear the details. He said that Macy was extremely upset: he'd known Zikmund for over twenty years. Then Harland phoned Harriet to say that he was on his way back with Eva. She was cautious on the phone and said that the patient had had one or two unexpected visitors, but he was doing well. Harland bombarded her with questions but she refused to answer.

He returned to the couchette to find Eva sitting on the lower of two bunks scrubbing her trousers with a nailbrush. She didn't look up.

'How is he?' she asked.

'She says he's doing well – improving.'

'Nothing more than that?'

'No, she couldn't talk.'

She turned her head up. The closeness that had come so naturally when they were relying on each other a few hours before had evaporated.

'I think you have to explain all this to me,' she said.

Harland waited.

'And you too – you have to tell me about Kochalyin and what you were doing in Prague in November '89.'

She looked puzzled.

'I don't know what you mean.'

'Well, let's have something to eat and and we can talk.'

They went to the restaurant car and ordered as the train left the station – soup, lamb and potatoes, and a bottle of rough red wine.

Harland drained a glass.

'You say I don't have a right to know your story. I disagree because the entire course of my life was affected by our . . . our meeting in Rome.'

'Mine too was changed,' she said sharply. 'I bore the child – remember!'

334

'Well, at any rate I'd very much like to know about your relationship with Kochalyin, especially after your divorce. I want some answers first, then I'll tell you why.'

'It's simple. I had to marry him because that was the only way we could survive. I told you that no one understands those days. Looking back now, we know that it all ended in '89, but in the early eighties communism looked as though it would last for centuries. The system seemed impregnable and we had to make arrangements accordingly. Oleg was my arrangement.'

'He was obsessed with you?'

'Yes, I suppose you could say that.'

'And he was your mother's lover before?'

She looked at him defiantly.

'I will tell you my story, not hers.'

'If you needed him, why did you divorce in '88?'

'These things are difficult.' A look of pain swept through her face.

'Was it the sex?'

'You're so crude, Bobby. Of course it was the sex. I could not love him. He knew about you and he blamed you for my failure to respond to him.'

'But you kept on good terms with him?'

'Oleg is not a normal man. He never knew his parents. They died soon after the war. He was an orphan and he plunged himself into our little family. He recognised certain things in my mother – her lack of parents for one – and in his weird, obsessive way he decided to become the man in our household. He spent much time away and so it was bearable. You ask about the sex. I will tell you. There was none – at least there was no conventional sex.'

'He was sadistic?'

'It's not so simple. Yes, he had those tendencies. He was abnormal – tormented.'

'Did he beat you?' Harland didn't want to know but something made him ask.

'Bobby, you aren't going to understand this. This man was distorted. He showed affection to me and my mother and Tomas, the only time perhaps in his life. But I could not return it. And when he understood that that exchange wasn't going to happen, he found gratification in other ways. There was a darkness in him. I don't know how I can express it any other way.'

'Humiliation?'

'Yes.' She was embarrassed.

'But I don't understand why he remained in touch with you after your divorce. It's been nearly fourteen years. And for all that time he kept you in some style.'

She looked at him coldly.

'Because I know him. I know his secrets; I know him like no one else can. I hold part of him. It was important for a man like Oleg, who is so much a mystery to himself, to feel that someone knew him.'

'And Tomas?'

'That was part of Oleg's idea of himself as a father. We did not have children – there was no chance of that. But Oleg wanted to give Tomas what he did not have himself. It mattered to him that Tomas did not have a father. It was one of the very few normal parts of him. That was another reason why he kept in touch with us after the divorce.'

'And did you tell him that I was in Prague that November?'

'No, why would I do that?' She paused. 'Bobby, I wanted to see you. Why would I tell Oleg? Besides, I did not know where he was. He was obsessed with keeping his movements secret. That was the way he lived. He phoned us, or made arrangements through an intermediary. Why do you ask about that time in 1989? What does it matter now?'

He smiled weakly. 'Were you working for the StB then?'

'No, I worked until 1988. This was not active service, as you said before. I never served as an illegal after Rome.'

'Why the training in Russia?'

'I had been suggested for a job with a high-security clearance and the Russians wanted to test me. So I was sent on this training course which at the same time was a type of examination of my trustworthiness.'

'In what field was this new job?'

'Signals Intelligence.'

'Ah!' exclaimed Harland. 'Code-breaking – that makes sense.'

She looked at him strangely.

'And you were based in Prague for this?'

'Yes – after training I got clearance and worked in Prague.'

'Tell me about the operation.'

Her brow knotted. The habit of secrecy dies hard, thought Harland. He poured her some more wine.

'We were concerned with acquiring cipher material from the Western embassies in Prague. We were breaking their codes and for this we needed cipher material.'

'But the Soviets ran the Sigint operation in the Eastern Bloc,' said Harland. 'All the friendly agencies, like the StB, fed into a central pool. As far as I remember, this was all part of the KGB's Sixteenth Directorate. Surely you didn't attend the training school of cryptanalysts as well?'

'No, I was trained at Moscow Centre. The training school was for Russians only. They thought it was secret, but we knew about it.'

'So you returned to Prague with this new skill of yours. Was Kochalyin a part of this set-up?'

She shook her head.

'But he would have had access to your material?'

'Yes,' she said.

'So you were working with him right up to your divorce?'

'Not directly.'

'Tell me, what success did you have?' This was interesting simply from a historical point of view to Harland. He recalled that the Americans and British were absolutely certain that the signals traffic wasn't being read by the KGB, particularly after the leaps in computer-generated cryptography in the eighties.

'We could read everything,' she said simply. 'Everything!'

'The British and American traffic?'

'Everything. We had been working on this for many years. Your people . . . your people were lax in many areas. There was a man in the US embassy. He fell for one of our agents. He never knew how much she stole.'

'So you were reading all the communications by '89?'

'Yes, we knew what your embassy was saying to the British Foreign Office.' She paused. 'We tapped the line from the telex centre to the encryption machine.'

So they had got all the telegrams. That must have been how Kochalyin had learned of his and Griswald's plan. Before they had set out from Berlin there had been furious exchanges between Prague and London, the embassy staff insisting that the plan to open negotiations for the StB files was fraught with danger. Three or four cables arrived saying that under no circumstances should it go ahead. What response these elicited from Century House, Harland never learned, but he knew they would almost certainly have told the embassy that the operation was off. But anyone with the slightest notion about these things or the way that SIS worked would have concluded that the operation was most definitely on. After that it would have been a simple matter to trace their entry into the country. And when Griswald started putting feelers out, well, there was no hope of them going undetected by Kochalyin.

They sat in silence for a long time. Harland was considering whether to tell her what had happened after that.

'I met your friend at that time,' he said. 'I encountered Kochalyin.'

She looked startled.

He exhaled heavily and drank some wine. 'I was . . . I was held by the StB then handed over to Kochalyin. But only this morning did I know for sure that it was him. I never once saw his face. I knew he was a Russian and one or two of the men with him were Russians. All I knew was his voice – the same voice that I heard leave a message on your machine this morning. I was absolutely certain at the station when we heard him again this evening.'

'I don't understand. Why did you never see his face?'

'I was blindfolded.' He paused, his eyes settling on a man at the far end of the restaurant car. 'It was a clever observation of yours when you said Kochalyin is a mystery to himself. I can understand that. But there again, we all live our lives like that. Our histories are hidden from us. For all these years I had no idea why I was taken by him. I only understood today what it was all about. I . . . he . . . he was taking revenge on me for you.'

'He hurt you?'

'Yes. I never understood the pointlessness of what he did – the attention to detail of inflicting pain. But now I do. He was taking revenge for you. He was taking revenge for that photograph of you and me in bed – the picture you say you knew nothing about.'

Her hands had risen to her mouth.

'And I imagine that the same motive was behind his taking Tomas to Bosnia. He wanted to contaminate him. He wanted to destroy him because he was my child, not his. There is no other explanation for what he did. You see Eva, he knew what was going to happen in eastern Bosnia that summer. He supplied the weapons and ammunition – the fuel. Kochalyin knew all along what he was doing.

'I've been thinking about those pictures I showed you and

339

I've come to recognise that Tomas didn't just witness the massacre – he took part in it. Just before he was shot he said he'd killed a man. I ignored it at the time Tomas was in hospital fighting for his life and forgot about what he'd said. But they wouldn't have let him see it without involving him – that was their way.'

He continued to look away from her although he felt the heat of her gaze.

'That's what they did in Bosnia. There are stories about the civilian bus drivers who were used to drive the Muslim men to the killing grounds. Each one was made to kill a man. That way they could never act as witnesses without admitting their own crime. I'm sure they wouldn't have let Tomas see the things that he did without involving him in it. They would've made sure he understood that it was either him or the man kneeling in front of him.'

'He could have told me,' she said helplessly.

His eyes returned to her. 'No, he saw where you lived. He knew how much money Kochalyin had put into your apartment. He knew he was paying your bills, paying for your life. And he knew you were indebted to Kochalyin for the drug treatment. He thought you wouldn't believe him, which meant he had to deal with this guilt by himself. That's why he left.'

'Yes, but he knew I and Oleg were no longer—'

'Were no longer what?' At that moment it dawned on Harland that Kochalyin had kept in touch long after the divorce for a very good reason. There must have been some residual sexual relationship – some service that only Eva could provide.

'When did it end, Eva? Or is it still a going concern? Is that what you mean by knowing his secrets, knowing him in a way that nobody else can know him? Jesus, Eva, what the hell do you two do together?'

He waited for her response. Nothing came.

'Well,' he continued, 'it certainly explains why Tomas had to get the hell out of your life, and I suppose that's why you never tried to contact me.'

She had lowered her head.

'You're right. There was something. But not now. Tomas knew that.'

'The thing I don't understand,' said Harland, 'is how your mother let this happen. She must have had a very shrewd idea what Kochalyin was about, even as a young man.'

'For God's sake, Bobby, you're so remorseless. Can't we stop talking about this?'

Harland pushed the plate of lamb to the side.

'The answer is, no, I can't leave this alone. You above all people know how this man has possessed our lives – yours, mine, Tomas's and countless others. He has infected us, Eva, he has used us, used you – he's a bloody aberration. He must be stopped. That's why I need to find out everything I can about him to nail him once and for all. It's not just Tomas I'm doing this for. It's for Griswald, for the people on the two planes. Those crimes in Bosnia extend right to the present.' He paused. 'You know, when I mentioned the plane crash this morning, you didn't bat an eyelid. You didn't ask about it. Perhaps you're no longer affected by these things. Just think of what he did, this man you've lived off for a quarter of a century. Two planes – twenty people wiped out like that. Good, innocent people, who were doing their unremarkable best in a bewildering world. People who worked for a living. They earned their keep, Eva. They didn't lie on their backs being fucked to get their money. They had families and friends and loved ones. Then nothing. And you know what? He still didn't destroy the evidence which Tomas gave to my friend. You see, I didn't tell you the final irony in all this. I was on that plane. I was with the investigator who was about to reveal that Viktor Lipnik was Kochalyin. I was

341

the sole survivor. In fact, that was how Tomas found me. He saw my picture in the papers.'

'A photograph again,' she said.

'Yes, a photograph again,' he said, without interest. Some part of him didn't care any longer.

'How did you get out?'

'Luck and a rear-facing seat.'

It was past midnight. He had said all he could. He paid the bill and they went back to their couchette. He waited in the corridor while Eva got ready for bed then entered to find that she had taken the top bunk and turned off her reading light. They said nothing. He lay down in his clothes and listened to the carriage wheels keeping time on the track. Twenty minutes later he gave up trying to sleep and went back to the restaurant car where an understanding waiter gave him a tumbler of whisky.

He sat nursing the drink for several hours as the black void of Middle Europe slid by.

Tomas was having difficulty with the name. Was it Lyhorn or Lithethorn? Or was there a hard sound in the middle of the name? He tried out variations in his head. He wanted to test the sound in his mouth, to bring his tongue down from behind the upper teeth to form the hard, explosive 't'. That was the thing about language, he realised. So much of it relied on the little womb of the mouth where the words were made and born. Now he no longer had the use of his mouth in this way he found difficulty in remembering the new words that came to him.

When the doctor addressed the man for the fourth time, Tomas decided it was Lighthorn with a hard 't' sound in the middle – Commander Lighthorn, evidently a policeman who had come to ask him questions. They had learned he was able to respond with his eyelid. But they didn't know about the equipment Harriet had obtained from another hospital. He'd been working with it all day, but Nurse Roberts had removed it a few minutes before their arrival. She said that the software was going to be checked and then leaned over him and gave him a conspiratorial wink.

Besides the doctor, three men were in the room now. There was the crisply dressed, unsmiling Lighthorn, a man called Navratt – no difficulty with that name – and a third character who was carrying a case that Tomas glimpsed as they came in. The atmosphere was tense. Smith-Canon wasn't bothering to hide his hostility and Lighthorn's companions plainly had their doubts about being there. He could see that Navratt was appalled by the sight of him and the man with the case was doing everything he could not to look down. However, Lighthorn's eyes fastened on him with a look of unfeeling appraisal. He moved to the side of the bed.

'So, the doctors tell me you are out of any immediate danger and that you have been feeling better. I've been wanting to speak to you since the shooting because I believe you can help us, Lars.' He paused. 'The first thing I have to tell you is that I know that you have another name. I'm quite sure that you are not Lars Edberg, and I've begun to doubt whether you are even Swedish.'

He peered at Tomas's face for a reaction.

'I have read that with your condition it is sometimes possible for the patient to use his or her eyelid to communicate. Dr Smith-Canon concedes you may be able to do this. You are lucky, he says, to be able to blink. So perhaps you could blink once to show me that you have understood what I've been saying?'

Was this man stupid? thought Tomas. He had few things left, but he'd still got the right to silence.

'Just blink once,' said Lighthorn. 'I know you can do it – a bright lad like you.'

'Look, this isn't on,' said Smith-Canon fiercely. 'I told you that it might be possible, not that he definitely possessed the ability. Please treat my patient with respect. There will be none of your bullying here.'

'I'm not bullying the patient, sir. I'm asking for cooperation in a very serious inquiry. Two of our police officers were shot and this man's girlfriend was brutally murdered because of him.' He returned to look at Tomas. 'That's true, isn't it? She was murdered because of you. I expect you have a fair idea who killed her, which means that you know who was responsible for the events on Christmas Eve. Look, Lars, I know you were up to your neck in something. We took fingerprints from the flat and the same set of prints have subsequently been found on a piece of equipment – two pieces of equipment, to be precise.'

Two, thought Tomas. They'd found both computers. He wondered how much had got out before they'd shut them down.

'I'm seeing something in your eye which says you know exactly what I'm talking about. Of course, you have much more idea about what was on those two machines than I do. Highly classified material, as I understand it. I believe those machines were set in operation by you on or before the evening you were shot. We're here to tie those machines to you, Lars, and to work out how they fit into this story, which brings me to the man you were with. The mysterious Mr Harland.' He stopped and put his face closer to Tomas's. 'Robert Harland has gone missing. He just vanished into thin air on New Year's Day and we haven't heard from him since. I believe he told you where he was going. It's a great pity that you can't tell me because I very much want to see Mr Harland again.'

Tomas stared at the wall that he had been looking at since he came round and wondered if Harland had traced his mother.

'I don't understand where Mr Harland fits into all this,'

continued Lighthorn. 'I know that you went specifically to see him in New York because you cut out his picture from the newspaper coverage of the crash at La Guardia airport. But why? What caused you to drop everything that day and fly to America? Perhaps it had something to do with the information on those computers.'

'This is ridiculous,' Smith-Canon interrupted. 'Have you any idea how taxing this is for a person in his condition?'

'Well, what am I supposed to do?' asked Lighthorn quietly. 'I believe he knows exactly what I'm saying and can answer my questions.'

'But you're not asking questions,' protested the doctor. 'You're telling him things which you know will distress him. I'm sorry, I can't allow it.'

'Doctor, I understand your concern for this patient, but has it occurred to you that he cannot decide whether he wants to help us until he has the full facts, which is what I'm trying to give him now?'

'There's no knowing what he understands.'

Tomas listened as from the room next door. It was odd how people talked in front of him nowadays.

'But, Doctor, in your office just now you said that it was likely that Mr Edberg had no cognitive impairment. That was the phrase you used. I didn't dream it up. So he can understand everything I say to him. You can't go back on that.'

'Yes, and a victim of a heart attack has no cognitive impairment,' said Smith-Canon, 'but you wouldn't treat him in this way. This man had a bullet removed from his brain less than two weeks ago. And I don't have to explain to you that there are few more distressing conditions than the one he is in now.'

This silenced Lighthorn for a few seconds. 'You won't object if we take his fingerprints?'

The doctor sighed. Tomas assumed that he had nodded his

consent. It was outrageous but there was absolutely nothing he could do, and before he knew what was happening the man with the case had grasped his right hand and was rolling each finger in turn along an ink-pad and then planting it on a strip of paper. The operation took some time. Tomas decided to remove himself and think about the things he had learned that day on Harriet's equipment.

It was quite a simple idea. A screen was placed in front of his head, while electrodes were attached to his forehead and behind his ears. Before Harriet and the technician even explained, he understood that the machine would measure the electrical activity in his brain. By simply thinking he could move a light point up the screen to hit a group of letters. At first it had been rather difficult to grasp the idea that he could actually move something in the outside world, but gradually he got used to charging his mind with thought and then emptying it when he wanted the light ball to drift to the bottom of the screen. He repeated the procedure, gradually eliminating all but the letter that he wanted. The program was designed to second-guess the operator with a version of a spell check. The letter T appearing at a certain stage in a word might mean that an H followed. There was some difficulty because the program was written for English speakers and his English spelling was not good. Also he had to get used to retaining in his mind the word that he wanted to spell out, at the same time as alternately filling and emptying his brain. Still, the first sessions had been successful and the technician Harriet had brought with her said he was the quickest beginner he had yet seen. Harriet clapped when he wrote his first message, 'hi thnk u email?'

There was a long way to go, but he was already thinking of short cuts. If only he could have a brief conversation with the technician, he'd be able to suggest ways of improving the software.

He returned to what was going on around him. The police

officer had taken his fingerprints and was now apologetically wiping the ink from his hands with cotton wool and cleaning spirit. Lighthorn appeared at the other side of his bed and scrutinised him.

'Of course!' he said. 'It's been staring me in the face all along. I couldn't think what it was. Now I see the resemblance plain as day. You're Harland's son, aren't you?'

The doctor coughed.

24

HISTORY LESSONS

They boarded the ferry from Calais to Dover late on Sunday night. A problem with the weather in the English Channel meant they did not set out until five the next morning by which time the gale had swept through leaving a nasty swell. Harland had called Macy Harp from France the night before to ask if he knew a safe place for them to stay in London. He said he would arrange for them to be picked up at Dover and taken to a place Harland knew well, but which no one else would think of.

Harland slept a little on the ferry then went out on the upper deck for some fresh air. Eva joined him on the soaking decks with two cups of coffee. They had said little to each other since the previous evening but now she seemed to want to talk.

'It's nearly twenty-eight years since I was in Britain,' she said. 'Do you like it here?'

'It's good to come home to. But I prefer to live abroad.'

'Was your wife English? You haven't mentioned her. You *were* married, weren't you?' He noticed her face and hair were beaded with droplets of spray.

'For nearly ten years. We divorced in 1991, although she had moved out before that. She was American – a banker. Louise Brinkley was her name. We met when I did a few months in one of the merchant banks after university and later hooked up and got married.'

She looked at him with curiosity. 'And no children. Why?'

'I was abroad a lot. Louise had a good job and she didn't want to be left at home with no money and looking after children. We said we would leave it until later.'

'Did you tell her what happened to you in Prague?'

He didn't answer. He remembered now that Walter Vigo had given her a bare outline. Louise liked Vigo and thought of him as the respectable side of espionage. She wanted the Vigos' kind of life and couldn't understand why Harland hadn't got it for her. By the time he returned to England, Louise had gone. She never came to see him in hospital in Vienna, but he suspected that this was because Vigo had been vague about the extent of his injuries.

'So you kept it to yourself.' She paused and shook her head. 'What was she like?'

'Restless, outspoken, mobile, ambitious, attractive.' Harland thought of her constant anxiety. She always looked as if she thought she was missing something. 'She lives on the West Coast somewhere now. We haven't seen each other for ten years.'

'And did she call you after the crash?'

'She wouldn't have known where to find me.'

'Tomas did.'

'Yes, he was very determined.' He thought for a moment. Somehow they were on neutral territory – they could talk. 'Tell me about him.'

'You saw him.'

'Only twice.'

She looked out to sea.

'He's a solitary person, like you. For a period his teachers at school were worried that he was withdrawn because he took no part in group activities. In a communist country this kind of individualism was considered a dangerous sign. But he did well at his lessons and he wasn't badly behaved. Later I

349

decided that it was better for him to go to a country school and let him find his level without being watched too much.'

'What did he study? What were his strengths?'

'Math and languages. But when he was a small boy he was fascinated with stories and history. He liked the Middle Ages – anything to do with knights and wars and the crusades.'

'You mean they dared to teach the proto-imperialist campaigns of the crusaders in a communist school?'

'He read about it,' she said impatiently. 'At thirteen he started showing incredible abilities, particularly in mathematics. He won all the school prizes and then a place at university. They said he possessed great intelligence – one of the best minds of his generation. The problem was that he could do everything so well. He left university early and went into music. He made friends for the first time and because he'd had so little practice he chose the wrong people. That is when the drug problem started. There was a girl – his first girlfriend. She introduced him to drugs. He was picked up by the police in a flat in Prague. Oleg got him released and paid for the rehabilitation.'

'Why did you tell him about me?'

'It was simple: he knew he wasn't Oleg's son. If what you say about Bosnia is true, then he had good reason to question that.'

'But he was in Bosnia a long time before you told him – what was he doing in that time?'

'He came back to Prague and became involved with computers. He understood what the Internet meant ahead of most people in Eastern Europe. He did programming and set up some sites concerned with music.' She paused. 'And he did some work for Oleg. I don't know exactly what kind of work – it was technical.'

'He was seeing Kochalyin regularly all that time?'

'Yes, before he went away.'

'And you don't know what he was doing for him?'

'No.'

'What was he like during this period? Your mother said that he was changed when he came back in 1995. How?'

She looked up at the cliffs to their right. 'He was hardened – more withdrawn than usual and he lost his temper. He never did that before. I found out he was seeing a therapist in Prague, but he didn't tell me this. I discovered a medical bill in his pocket. It was this doctor who suggested that he should ask me about his father.'

The sea was a good deal rougher on the British side of the Channel. There was an announcement that the ferry would have to lie off Dover until conditions improved. They passed an unpleasant few hours riding the waves with the boat's prow pointed into a north-westerly of renewed vigour. It wasn't until late into the afternoon that they finally disembarked and were picked up by Macy's driver.

Harland knew where he was immediately they passed the Imperial War Museum in south London. He looked out of the darkened windows of the Mercedes. The café was still there, the barber's shop and newsagent were unchanged along Kennington Road. The driver, a rather sullen ex-military type, said nothing. They had turned right into Westminster Bridge Road and passed Lambeth North tube station before Harland managed to stammer a question about their eventual destination.

'We're stopping just now, sir,' said the driver.

'But this is Century House, the old headquarters of . . .' His voice trailed off.

'Mr Harp told me to bring you here, sir.'

Century House, even when it was built in the early sixties, was an unremarkable complex consisting of a block of twenty storeys, a wing which rose just four storeys and a block which joined the two together. That had gone, together with the petrol station, once manned by SIS employees, in the

351

forecourt between the two buildings. But the main part of the building was still there, tarted up with chrome, wire and glass and a light-coloured brick cladding on the first few storeys. A sign invited interest in a unique conversion with apartments of one, two and three bedrooms with panoramic views.

They were dropped at a new entrance, away from the old security door which Harland had passed through for the first time in 1973. Eva hadn't any idea where they were and didn't ask. All she wanted was to get to the hospital.

'Before you go,' he said, 'we need to fix somewhere for you to stay tonight.'

They took the lift to the twentieth-floor penthouse and were greeted by The Bird, who had changed from his country tweeds to the camouflage of an executive.

'Always knew we'd rise to the top of this building somehow, but didn't think I'd have to buy it.'

'You bought the building?'

'No, just a couple of floors. I saw them up for sale last year and couldn't resist it. We do most of our business from here now. Frightfully central.'

He introduced himself to Eva who seemed unimpressed. Harland lifted his shoulders in apology to The Bird as they walked into what once had been the Director of SIS's office. He couldn't help but smile at the arrangement at the end of the room – a small partner desk with an old anglepoise lamp, flanked by a shabby sofa and an armchair. It was as if Ally Simmonds, the director of SIS when The Bird and Harland joined, had just got up and left the room.

'That's our Simmonds shrine. It's Macy's idea of a joke, though, of course, none of our foreign clients get it and it really has become too laborious to explain. I think he should have dressed it better with an old copy of *Horse & Hound*, a pair of ornithologist's binoculars – brackets unused close brackets – a white shirt, ready for formal evenings, a raincoat and a copy of the Moscow telephone book.'

Harland ignored Eva's rather contemptuous expression and peered through the door where there were five people working at computers.

'That's our staff,' said The Bird proudly. 'They're the core of the trading operation. God knows where we'd be without them. Recognise any of them? They all did a spell in the old firm.'

Harland shook his head. For a few moments he saw something else. Century House twenty years before, a secretary walking down a corridor with a cup of coffee passing a board on which were pinned notices concerning fire drill, the procedures to be followed at the end of the day, particularly in regard to the return of files to the safe, flat-sharing opportunities and the odd newspaper cutting – selected for some elusive irony. And off this corridor, which was much the same on any floor in Century House, were offices that owed their allegiance to one of the five controllerates – Western Hemisphere, Central and Eastern Europe, Middle East, Far East and Africa.

It was all remarkably normal, like the premises of a shipping company, perhaps, or an insurance office. To the initiated there were subtle variations of dress, character type and idiosyncrasy between the controllerates, but an outsider – of which, of course, there were none – walking through Century House would not have detected these differences. All he would have noticed would have been a series of nondescript rooms in which people worked over one or two files with remarkably little else on their desks. True, there were pot plants, mascots, pictures of loved ones, telephones and typewriters, but accumulations of paper were a rare sight. And, of course, there were no computers, it having been established by a team from GCHQ that the early models leaked enough radiation for someone to read a file from across the street.

Harland saw everything in the old secret capsule – the dirty magnolia wall paint, the tiled carpeting, the metal windows that didn't close properly and were plugged with tissue paper to stop the draughts, the secret servants – the inscrutable, the flirtatious, the drab, the reliable, the nervous and the new young Turks, straining for an effortlessness that fooled nobody.

The Bird touched him on the shoulder.

'Perhaps you should explain to your friend where you are.'

'Later. It's not important. We need to get over to the hospital. Got any ideas about accommodation tonight?'

'Well, there are bedrooms here. Should be as safe as anywhere else. I can give you keys. There's a chap who looks after these two floors – he's on site the whole time – and you have a driver who is handy in any situation. It's up to you.'

Harland looked at Eva. She shrugged a yes.

The Bird showed them to some rooms at the far end of the apartment. Eva stayed behind to wash and change, saying she wanted to look her best. Harland knew she was composing herself. Earlier, as they pitched and rolled off Dover, he had gently described the room that Tomas was in and the overwhelming amount of medical equipment and care needed to keep him alive. He also told her about the spasms and the sudden fits of meaningless sobbing and laughing. He did this because, since seeing her for the first time in Karlsbad, he'd noticed she possessed a curious ability to cut out and not take on the implications of a problem. That was presumably how she dealt with Kochalyin. But he wanted her to understand how bad Tomas was so that she could conceal her shock when she saw him. He tried to explain this but she accused him of taking a sadistic pleasure in telling her. The truce of the Channel was very short-lived.

While waiting for her, he borrowed a phone from The Bird and set about making some calls.

He found Harriet in the hospital with Tomas, which was

354

convenient because it meant she could tell him that Eva was about to arrive. He asked how Tomas was.

'Good,' she said. 'You'll be impressed, but somehow I don't think he's going to stick around for long. I just have a feeling.'

Then he dialled Special Agent Frank Ollins. He would have liked more time to talk with him but he was in a hurry.

Ollins took longer than usual to answer.

'I wondered how things were going,' said Harland, without saying who he was. 'It's a few days since we spoke.'

Ollins cleared his throat.

'I've been hearing some bad things about you,' he said flatly. 'I don't know if they're true or not, but either way these allegations make it very hard for me to cooperate with you.'

'What did you hear?'

'That you are under investigation for spying for the Iron Curtain countries during the eighties and that the case against you is watertight.'

'Where did you get this from?'

'It came down the line – the British have warned the US authorities about you. There's a lot of disquiet over the way you hid that material from the plane. People aren't happy about either your relationship with Griswald or the fact that these pictures were encrypted with the same code that has been causing our folks a big pain in the arse over in Europe.'

'And what do you think, Frank? You met me. Do you think I was a communist spy?'

'It's not relevant what I think. All I have to go on is the fact that you lied about what you found on Mr Griswald's body and that everyone tells me to stay clear of you.'

'The UN too?'

'I haven't spoken to them.'

'But you can at least tell me about the crash investigation.'

'I can tell you nothing.'

355

'Are you still investigating the possibility of electronic sabotage?'

'That was always your assumption. I did not state that as a fact.'

'You near as dammit did,' protested Harland.

'If you want to know anything about the crash, please address your questions to Mr Clark at the Safety Board or their spokesperson.'

'Does that mean that you are no longer investigating for sabotage?'

'It means this conversation is over. I'm going on vacation tomorrow and I need to get my stuff ready. It's been nice speaking to you.' He hung up without letting Harland say any more.

It was obvious that Vigo had been spreading his poison. But why? He himself had said that his interest had moved on from the pictures. Yes, that could be true in one sense. The pictures didn't matter much because they had presumably been broadcast in the same way as the other secrets. Now the much greater danger to Vigo's interest was the possibility that Kochalyin would be fingered as the leading suspect in the sabotage of the UN plane. That being so, he had pointed out the danger to the Americans and had besmirched Harland to make sure that no one would take him seriously. Harland wondered if he had pulled off the same deft footwork at the UN.

Before ringing Jaidi's office he put in a call to Professor Norman Reeve, the head of the War and Peace Studies Forum in Washington.

Reeve answered with an impatient 'Yes?'

'Sir, this is Robert Harland from the UN. I want you to listen to two pieces of information. First, I have the date you requested. It is the fifteenth of July 1995. If you have any satellite or U2 material from that date I would be most grateful. The photograph I have was taken at quarter past two in the afternoon, but anything immediately before that could be useful.'

'And the second thing?' said Reeve rudely.

'This is harder to explain because I'm not certain exactly what's going on. But I believe that there is some kind of international effort to have the plane crash written down as an accident. I suspect an alliance of intelligence agencies is responsible for this – the same people who have used the services of a war criminal known as Viktor Lipnik. In fact he is a Russian named Oleg Kochalyin.'

'I see,' said Reeve. 'Let me ask you how certain you are of what you've told me.'

'I can only say that I will be making exactly these points in a report to the UN Secretary-General. This is a complex matter, Professor, and there's a considerable effort to obstruct my inquiries, but at the core there is a war criminal and war crimes and I know that this will concern you.'

'Mr Harland,' he said wearily, 'I have asked you not to lecture me before, so please do not try and influence my decision with these trite points.'

'I'll do anything I can to influence your decision, sir. I asked the Secretary-General's office to contact you and persuade you to help me. Did they get in touch?'

'Yes, but what they had to say was of no interest to me.'

'Well, what can I do then?'

'Nothing – tell me about the photograph you have in your possession.'

Harland explained that there were internal clues about the location in the photograph. Using aerial surveillance pictures as well, it might be possible to pinpoint the site and mount some kind of investigation. Despite the original indictment, there could be no prosecution of Kochalyin without evidence that the murders had taken place. Harland added that some of the witness statements Griswald had been working on at the time of his death concerned a village called Kukuva, where some sixty male Muslims had gone missing at the time. The picture might be of their grave.

'It seems to me,' said Reeve after a short period of rumination, 'that you have an awful big tree to climb, Mr Harland.'

'Yes, but I have a witness – someone who can testify that Lipnik and Kochalyin are the same person and saw the massacre.'

'Then why can't he tell you where the site is?'

'We're working on that.'

Reeve said he would see what he could do in the next twenty-four hours. He gave Harland his e-mail address and hung up.

Eva appeared as he was about to dial the UN. He decided to leave it until later. There was still plenty of time left in the American working day.

Tomas was getting better at separating his mental activity into two streams – the hot lava thought, which he needed to propel the light point on the screen, and the articulation of what he wanted to say. Today most of the time had been spent working the machine for the technician so that he could make the adjustments that would allow Tomas to hook up to the Internet, open, write and send an e-mail file, and shut down the computer by himself. The procedure was quite complicated but the programmer was quick to interpret Tomas's thoughts and had some good ideas himself. The only problem was that he couldn't live with the electrodes permanently attached to his head. He still had to rely on someone to put them in position and turn on the machine.

Harriet had been in the room for most of the time. She suggested that an eye-gaze machine – a video camera which tracked the movements of a pupil – could be used in

358

conjunction with what was called the brain-computer interface. That way he could look at a particular spot and activate the computer.

He was impatient for these adjustments to be made because he knew he was fading. He felt wiped out all the time, which surprised him because he had not expended any energy on movement. He had thought perhaps that it was the drugs but now suspected that this inert body was running on very low reserves.

He was just thinking that he would have a sleep when Harriet answered her phone to Harland. Then she told him what he had already guessed. Harland and his mother were on their way to the hospital. Jesus, that was the very last thing he wanted now. Although he knew the meeting would require nothing from him – no reaction, no remorse, no apology – he still felt he ought to consider his attitude as though he was going to have to talk and explain things. God, it was going to be strange to see his parents in the same room for the first time.

He needed time to prepare. But he needed a lot else besides – to fill his lungs with the fresh air of a winter's day, a glass of red wine or a beer, the sensation of a woman's hair – Flick's hair – in his fingers, sex, a cup of coffee and newspaper, live music and a landscape. He wanted the sense of distance in front of him, to let his eyes travel over the fields and forests, taking in the extraordinary beauty of the world before he left it. It was odd because all his adult life he had tended towards music and the patterns of mathematics. That was the bent of his brain, but now he thought only visually and spent his time summoning places in his imagination, remembering the smallest details of bars he used to go to in Prague, a friend's apartment or the walks they used to take in the mountains – he and his mother and his grandmother, tramping through woods, the village below them like that picture by Breughel. What was it called? Ah, yes, *The Hunters in the Snow*. He missed snow and wanted badly to scoop some up in his hands, compress it and touch his lips with it.

He decided he would doze before they came. As he drifted off, he heard Harriet and the technician moving the equipment to one side, then felt her detach the electrodes from his head. She squeezed his hand and left.

25

DISASTERS OF WAR

Harland knew that the hospital would be watched, probably by Vigo's people. But there was also a good chance that the same men who had put a bullet in Tomas's head would be deployed to end Eva's life.

She was agitating to leave, wringing a scarf in her hands and glancing about as she had done in her apartment in Karlsbad. But he insisted he make a call to Philip Smith-Canon before they left. He got through and asked the doctor whether there was another way into the hospital. He replied that there was a staff entrance but it was just as public, then he said he would send someone to meet them a couple of streets away at a pub called the Lamb and Falcon. It would be a young woman called Nurse Roberts. She would bring a white coat and the essentials of a nurse's uniform. That way they could pass unnoticed through the staff entrance.

It was then that Smith-Canon dropped the news that the police had been to the hospital to take Tomas's fingerprints. They had made a connection between Tomas, the flat where the murdered girl was discovered and two computers found in London. But the more important point was that the policeman had noted Tomas's resemblance to Harland and said out loud that he thought Tomas was probably Harland's son.

They took their leave of The Bird, who said that he would be away for the night on unavoidable business, and set off through the damp early evening to Bloomsbury. On the way Harland thought about Vigo. It would be only a matter of time before Vigo heard about this. But if he had been working for Kochalyin he would surely have known who Tomas was all along. From all his actions, it was clear that Vigo hadn't known. Harland was sure that there was something he didn't understand, another level of the affair of which he had only the slightest intimation.

They arrived at the pub and found a nurse whom Harland recognised from his first visit to the neurological unit. She handed them a Sainsbury's supermarket bag which contained the coat and uniform. They put them on and the nurse led them back to the hospital. On the way she told them that Tomas had mastered a new piece of equipment which allowed him to write messages.

They passed through some iron gates and up a short flight of stairs to the staff entrance. Harriet was waiting for them outside the room on the second floor.

'He's pretty tired,' she said, smiling at Eva and taking her hand briefly. 'The doctor is with him. He said you should go straight in.'

Harland ushered Eva in, saying that he would join them later. He knew she would want to be alone with him.

Harriet took him for a cup of coffee down the corridor.

'How is he?' he asked.

'Weak – his lungs aren't very good.'

'What about the police?'

'Well, there's nothing they can do, is there? He won't respond to their questions and they can't lock up someone who's already in a prison.'

'So they don't know he can communicate.'

'They suspect it, but they've no idea that he can use this new equipment. He's really impressive, you know.'

'Eva says he has a very good mind – starred student and all that.'

Harriet looked at him with a significant arch in one eyebrow. 'And? What's it like, seeing her again?'

'She's not at all as I expected. Not at all. There're parts I recognise. But she's changed a lot.' He told her the story about Kochalyin. He took it at a gallop, throwing out shorthand observations about Eva's life and what he regarded as her eerie detachment. When he told her that Kochalyin was the torturer she touched him on the shoulder. For some reason he winced. He explained how Kochalyin's focus had shifted from Tomas to Eva who now represented a far greater danger to him.

'But you also,' she said quickly. 'You're still his major threat.'

'Which is why I'm going to write the entire report tonight. Most of it's in the bag. Once it's delivered, there's nothing he can do.'

'And Vigo? Where's he in all this?'

He felt himself smiling although he wasn't sure why.

'I wonder how many times we've asked that in the last three weeks,' he said. 'I'm almost at the point where I shall go and see him, hand him a copy of the report and say fuck you.'

'Are you putting him in it?'

'Not by name, because I don't have the evidence. I know that the intelligence services were all desperate to close down Tomas's operation and that they used Kochalyin to do this. But the UN will probably view this as simply a question of these different countries protecting their interests. Anyway, I haven't been able to make the leap to tie Vigo in with the plot to release Kochalyin from his obligations at the War Crimes Tribunal. And I have no evidence whatsoever about the crash because my one contact in the FBI has gone cold on me. So, it's down to the war crime.'

'What about Eva? Can she help with any of this?'

'Yes, I imagine with the background. Tomas can. He saw

363

the massacre. He can make a statement about the murders. That'll be an important addition to the stuff that Griswald was marshalling. The next step will be to find the site of the massacre. I have high hopes of that.'

His sleep had not taken him to some pleasant scene from his childhood, but to a hot mountainside where the noise of insects was deafening and his mind was clouded with fear and incredulity. How odd it was that now his eyes had fastened on to a tree with curiously black bark and limp grey leaves which he hadn't registered at the time. Now he could see it as if it were in front of him.

He knew she was in the room – he had heard the door. He opened his eyes and saw her beside him. She looked down at him as if she was waiting for a reaction. She wore the same perplexed expression she greeted him with when he returned from his classes and wouldn't tell her what his day had been like. He wished he could give her that reaction now – the smile and peck on the cheek that he'd always eventually conceded.

He saw she was shocked. She hadn't grasped that he would be *completely* paralysed. Her eyes moved frantically around the room alighting on each piece of equipment. She was trying to work out what they all did. She touched his arm and his forehead, but her eyes were still darting about the tubes and monitors. He knew he looked like some kind of installation, and he was aware that he was making one of his uncontrolled grimaces because he could see the horror in her face. It wasn't like her to be afraid.

He blinked a hello at her. This seemed to encourage her and she began speaking, jumping from one subject to the next without finishing her sentences. He wished she would relax and tell him how Harland had traced her and what she thought of him after all these years. Was she angry with him for going to find his father?

He waited. He had already learned that people calmed down after a while. Sooner or later they became aware that they were sounding stupid or hysterical. Then something else happened, to do with the lack of emotional feedback. They began to speak almost as if they were alone. He became a kind of bathroom mirror, a confessional.

His mother stopped and sighed. She picked up his left hand and drew it to her.

'Forgive me, Tomas, I'm in shock. I find this very, very distressing. I can't ... don't know what I'm saying. Forgive me for everything. God, how did we get here? When you went away, Tomas, I was so hurt. But I understood why you had to go and find your own life, away from me and Nana. She has missed you too. With her past, it mattered a lot that a third of her entire family had vanished. But we read your e-mails and we knew you would come back to us one day.'

She looked at him. Her eyes had softened; the fear was beginning to go.

'Did Bobby tell you who did this to you?'

At last a direct question, he thought. He blinked once, meaning that he knew who had done it to him.

'What else did he tell you?'

Wrong sort of question. He refused to blink in the hope that she would realise he was only capable of giving a yes or a no answer.

'I'm sorry.' She had understood. 'Did he tell you anything else?'

He blinked once, though it seemed to him that he had more to tell Harland.

'What did you feel? Did you like him?'

He blinked once.

'He told me what happened in Bosnia. Is it true?'

One blink.

'Oh, God, how could I have failed you like this?'

This was not a question he could answer in any circumstance, but especially now. Anyway she hadn't failed him. The truth was that he knew what Oleg was like – but when he was a teenager he had found him glamorous, a challenge, a rule-breaker.

Minutes passed during which she started several sentences, then smothered them. 'He said that you were forced to kill someone,' she said eventually. 'Is that true?'

One blink.

She hid her face and murmured something into her hands.

'And he put you here,' she said, dropping her hands. Tears were running down her cheeks. He had seen her cry only a few times. 'Do you want me to tell you everything?'

One blink.

She sniffed and composed herself.

'You remember how we went to Prague in '89? You know I took you out of school. I wanted you to experience this great moment because I knew you'd remember it for the rest of your life. What I didn't tell you then is that I had caught sight of Bobby Harland on television. It was fifteen years since I had seen him, but he'd changed very little. I recognised him immediately. Bobby was in Prague. I cannot tell you how happy it made me. I thought we were bound to find him. How crazy can you get? I was right, though – he was in Prague. But by the time we got there he was already under arrest. Then Oleg got hold of him. I don't know how he found him. Oleg always knew who he was and that you were Bobby's child. He was insanely jealous – you remember how he could be? He hurt Bobby very badly during that time. That's why I should have suspected that something would happen when you went to Belgrade with him.'

How he wished he could stop her. She was rushing over things. He wanted to know what Oleg had done to Harland. That was important – couldn't she see it was a pattern? How had Harland escaped? What had happened to him after that?

Did she know at the time what Oleg had done? Why didn't she find him then if she had been so damned keen to see him again? Tomorrow he'd put some questions on the screen for her and beg her to take things more slowly and to think of the things he would want to know.

'Bobby says that all this time you have been using your knowledge of Oleg to get back at him. Is that right?'

He blinked.

'And that you published pictures of him to help the War Crimes Tribunal?'

One blink.

She gave him a quick, ironic smile. She seemed to be about to tell him something, but he suddenly felt drained again. He thought of himself as diminished by the equipment around him – a lump of flesh in the middle of the rhythmic iteration of the machines. He couldn't keep up with them. He closed his eyes and sank into sleep, much quicker than usual.

A nurse came and told Harland that Eva was sitting with Tomas while he slept. He went in once to give her a cup of coffee and a sandwich. She thanked him but did not look up. He left because he felt she wanted to be alone with Tomas. His one impression of Tomas was that he was paler than before and a little thinner.

He spent much of the evening alone in the waiting area. Harriet had gone to fetch him fresh clothes, a laptop, a telephone, the War Crimes Tribunal interviews and copies of the two coded images. He would need most of these things in order to start work on his report later that evening.

At just past 10 p.m. Smith-Canon appeared in the corridor with Eva. She looked drawn and smiled nervously at Harland, shy perhaps of showing her grief to him.

Sensing that he should take his chance while he could, Smith-Canon had come back from a dinner engagement to talk to them. He took them to his office, produced glasses

367

and made them each a weak whisky and soda. Harland thanked him for all he had done, particularly for keeping Tomas's identity secret. It had bought them valuable time, he said.

There was a pause. Harland knew Smith-Canon was wondering how to approach Eva.

'Your son is a very resourceful young man. I've never seen anyone learn this brain-computer technology so fast. He must have extraordinary powers of focus – also a tremendous mental agility, I would imagine. Is that right, Mrs Rath?' She nodded.

Harland was grateful to him for talking about Tomas's qualities in the present, not in the past.

'I'm glad you're here because we really have to discuss some difficult issues. Unfortunately we can't leave them because a patient like Tomas may be struck down by an infection very rapidly indeed.' He paused and drank some whisky. 'A couple of days ago I explained the exact position to him. It was hard for him to bear this information by himself, with only myself and Mrs Bosey in the room, but I knew he'd probably already arrived at a fairly accurate conclusion about his prospects. I told him about the risks of infection, chiefly of the respiratory and urinary systems. The former is far more dangerous and I felt I needed to establish his views on cardiopulmonary resuscitation in the case of a life-threatening infection developing. If resuscitation – what we call CPR – is not wished for by the patient it is important for us to know that beforehand. Your views count too and I can give as much advice as you need. But the point is that Tomas has made his wishes utterly clear. This morning he wrote that he did not want resuscitation. I have a copy of his message here.' He handed Eva a sheet of paper. She looked at it for a moment and passed it to Harland.

There was just one line. 'I want natural death – not unnatural life – tomas Rath.'

'Of course,' Smith-Canon continued, 'he can revise his view. He can change his mind every day if he wants – in fact every hour is fine by me. It's his life, after all. Still, I thought you should know his thinking because you probably want to discuss it between yourselves and talk it over with him.'

Eva was looking down at her hands. 'Is he in pain, Doctor?'

'A fair amount of discomfort – yes. He suffers from spasms and these are very painful. The business of catheters and tracheotomy tubes is also unpleasant and there are numerous minor complaints which make life wretched for him. His head appears to have mended very well but I believe he is suffering from some pretty nasty headaches. Of course, there are some things which may improve as the tissue in his brain heals. We have noticed that the response of his eyelids has got much better and he has more lateral movement in his eyes than he possessed when he first came out of the coma. But I must emphasise that I think the chances of him regaining substantial movement are very slim indeed.' He stopped and puckered his chin.

'I'm very sorry, Mrs Rath. I hate to have to tell you these things. I am also very, very sorry that this should have happened to a clever young man like your son.' Harland saw that Eva was touched by his solicitousness. 'So' – he gulped the rest of his whisky – 'we shall have another talk soon, no doubt. Meanwhile, you must come and go as you please.'

As they neared Century House, Eva turned round to him in the back seat and said quietly, 'Bobby, whatever you need me to do, I will do it – anything.' She held his eyes for several seconds after saying this. He understood. They were on the same side now.

They took the lift to the top floor and were greeted by a young man in jeans and a heavy pullover who introduced himself as Jim, the caretaker. He said he would be a floor below them. His job was to keep watch on the two floors through the night, so if they needed anything they only had to ring down. He'd be up whatever the hour.

Harland settled himself at a long glass table with a view over Waterloo station and the Houses of Parliament and opened up the laptop. Eva sat down in a rectangular leather chair and contemplated him, one arm supporting the other and two fingers pressed to her temple.

'You're going to write this report?'

'Yes,' he said, without looking up. 'I need to get it off tomorrow. The sooner they have it, the less exposed we are.'

'You have had no sleep for two days.'

He looked up. 'I've slept a little, but I work best like this. Besides, I've always been able to concentrate in this building.' He tapped the side of his head. 'I'm sorry, I didn't tell you. This is the old headquarters of MI6. I worked on the sixth floor in the eighties – not such a good view as from here.'

She looked perplexed. 'But why are we here?'

'Because Cuth Avocet also used to work here and he thought it would be amusing to base his business in the building when it was converted. He says it's the one place nobody would look for us.'

She was unimpressed. 'That's a very British thing to do. Why does everything have to be *amusing* to you?'

'It doesn't – it's just a whim of his. That's all. It doesn't mean anything.'

She seemed unconvinced. She rose to find herself a drink. By the time she'd opened a bottle of red wine and returned to him with a glass, he had started an outline of the report.

'You don't show anything, do you, Bobby? You're sealed up like an old building that's dangerous for people to enter.'

He didn't reply but turned from the screen and looked at her.

'You feel things,' she continued, 'but you don't express them. I know you feel badly for Tomas – that's why you came to find me. But you haven't said anything about what you feel and you don't choose to acknowledge what others feel.'

Of course she was right. Louise had been right too. Harriet was right. Everyone was bloody well right.

'Look, a lot of time is wasted with people's pity for themselves. By writing this report I can at least affect something. I can begin to settle things with Kochalyin – and it won't be just for me.'

'Did he do this to you – did he cripple your empathy?'

'You speak as if it was some kind of physical organ,' he said sharply. 'If you must know, he didn't damage my *empathy*, as you put it.'

'See, look at you pushing me away. You don't like to talk about these things. Perhaps it's not your lack of empathy. Perhaps it's your inability to trust other people.'

'And where did you learn this sensitivity of yours – in bed with a war criminal?'

She was stung and turned away.

He softened his tone.

'Look, you're probably right about my faults – but you're not telling me anything I haven't been told before. Just now I need to focus on this. That's all there is to it.'

She sat down, stared at the view, then levelled her gaze at him.

'I hope it will be all right if I stay here,' she said quietly. 'I don't want to be alone.'

He didn't hear this. He had already started the first sentence of the report, which reminded Jaidi of the terms of his brief. He was eager to put everything on record because, apart from his letter of authority, no paper had passed between them.

By 5 a.m. he'd finished a draft. Most of it had come easily but there was a problem with the section concerning the massacre. He needed to be more accurate about the site and

371

explain the origin of the two pictures. He also had to have Tomas's statement.

He got up and arranged the blue duffel over Eva's curled-up form on the sofa. He stood and watched her for a moment, feeling the pity he had failed to express earlier. Then he slumped down on the sofa opposite her.

Tomas started making his statement at eleven that morning. Harriet was in the room with him. He took a short nap, then continued with Harland by his side until about two in the afternoon. At Eva's suggestion they had taken turns to be with him because she knew he found it harder to concentrate with them all there. No one looked at what was on the screen until he had finished. Then Harriet printed it out.

Harland sat down and read the single sheet of paper. In a glance he knew that it was exactly what he needed.

> i am tomas rath – a czech citizen – on 15 7 95 i was in bosnia with oleg kochalyin – aka viktor lipnik – and witnessed a massacre – this was arranged by kochalyin and serb army – we followed four serb trucks into the hills – they contained 70 muslim men and boys – when we arrived we heard first shots – i did not know about this until i saw bodies – the hands of victims were tied behind them – i helped a man who fell from truck – because i did this they kept him to last and i was made to shoot him – i killed this man – they said they would shoot me if i did not kill him – i am guilty of murder – i wish to say sorry for what i did – oleg kochalyin is my step-father – i have given two photos to tribunal – one of him in austria which proves he was not killed – the other photo of massacre was filmed by serb soldier – i took the film later – I testify this is all true – t rath.

Tomas was exhausted from the effort of writing but he could not sleep. He watched Harland as he read the statement, then his mother and Harriet. He felt an enormous shame. Taking so long over each letter and each word had meant that he'd dwelled on the scene for the best part of four hours. Yet he hadn't possessed the stamina to hit the thousands of letters it would have taken to express how he'd been trapped into witnessing the massacre.

Oleg had told him there was some action on the hill. They got into the army vehicle with the smirking Serb soldiers and drove the two kilometres up a narrow, unmade road. It was a long climb. The soldiers passed a bottle of plum brandy around. When they came to a halt, Tomas saw the men in the trucks ahead of them and it had dawned on him what kind of action Oleg had been referring to. The prisoners were terrified. They knew there was no escape because even if they jumped from the trucks and made a run for it, the hill was bare and offered no cover but scrub. The Serbs enjoyed their fear and toyed with a few of the Muslims, pretending to let them go, then shooting them.

They were taken out in small groups, lined up along a flat wall of rock and shot. Some begged for their lives, but most were so shocked they couldn't speak and faced their death with a leaden, drained resignation. Literally, their blood ran from their faces and they began to stare, almost as if death had entered them before the bullets. Tomas couldn't believe what he was seeing, the way the soldiers casually executed them. Oleg helped with a special, silent glee, standing with a younger Serb officer shooting his pistol. Tomas had started to edge away. His arms were free and he could run and he thought Oleg would stop them shooting at him. But as he slid round a truck a middle-aged man was rifle-butted out of the back of it and fell sprawling on to the stones. He was cut on the side of his forehead and instinctively Tomas went to help him, picking him up from the road and examining the wound. The bewilderment in the man's eyes was something Tomas would never forget. The man couldn't reconcile this simple act of human concern with what he knew was happening fifty metres away.

The Serbs saw an opportunity for some fun. They pretended to the man that he had been saved by Tomas, and he was allowed to stand on the other side of the road so that he could be taken back to his village. He stood convulsed by grief as his friends and relations were killed. At the end of the slaughter the Serb officer, a man in his thirties with narrow eyes and a vicious temper, marched over, pulled out a pistol and gave it to Tomas. Then he held his own pistol against Tomas's temple and ordered him to kill the man. Tomas refused. Oleg came over and barked at him.

'Don't think I will save you. It is him or you. If you don't kill him you will both be shot.'

He laughed as if he had made a joke and Tomas pulled the trigger. There was nothing else for it. A simple calculation – one death against two.

It was some days before he could think straight again but when he emerged from his shock he decided on two actions: he would eventually admit his own crime to whichever authority would deal with it and he would act as a witness to the massacre and Oleg Kochalyin's part in it. That was why he had remained in touch with Oleg after the return from Bosnia and why he went along with the fantasy that Yugoslavia had been little more than a hunting trip – a chance for two men to bond. Kochalyin had tested him, slyly referring to the events to see his reaction. Tomas had smiled knowingly, as if the whole thing had been an escapade. Over the months and years of this revolting pretence he'd got everything he needed. He had the evidence of Oleg's rapidly expanding operation and the enormous numbers of people who were corrupted by him. He came to understand that the man he had known all his life was not an individual but a force of evil. That was melodramatic, but there was no other way to describe it.

There was a heavy silence in the room. They had all read the statement. Harland coughed, came over to him, put his hand on the unbandaged part of his shoulder and said, 'You had no other choice. This is not your crime, it's his. Any court in the world would agree on that. The main point is that the statement is very helpful and perfectly written – well done.' He squeezed him gently and smiled.

His mother and Harriet added their congratulations. He wasn't fooled; he still knew he was guilty.

'Tomas is on the Internet now,' said Harriet brightly. 'The man came to fix it all this morning. He's got an e-mail address which he can open up by himself.'

'In which case you will need my address,' said Harland. 'Shall I put it in your contact list?'

Tomas blinked.

While he tapped at the keyboard, he said, 'I have been writing the report to recommend the opening of the investigation into what happened. I need a location for the massacre. Does Kukuva mean anything to you? It's a village in the Serb part of Bosnia with a Muslim population.'

Two blinks.

'It was a long shot anyway. Do you have any clear idea where you were on that day?'

Two blinks.

'I thought not. Still, we may be able to do it another way. I got some maps this morning from Stanfords and I've drawn over them so that we can use them together.'

He left the computer and rummaged in a plastic bag.

'But first,' he said, 'I need to go over the photograph with you. Can you face it?'

A blink.

He produced the video still. It was the first time Tomas had seen it for a few months.

'At some stage we will need to include this in your statement and then have both notarised, which means a

375

lawyer comes in here to see you swear that the statement is true and that the photograph was taken at the time of the events you describe.' He paused, swivelled the computer screen so that it was a couple of feet in front of Tomas's face and rested the picture against the screen.

'It struck me that there are one or two clues in the photograph that can help us. For instance, we know that the man holding the camera was pointing more or less north because of the time the film was made and the shadows on the ground. That means the massacre took place about forty kilometres south of that mountain range – maybe a little more. I'm not sure. If we can identify these mountains on the map, we can start plotting a corridor in which the site must lie.' Harland ducked down then bobbed up again. 'Right, here's the map I've prepared.' He folded it and propped it against the screen. His mother came round to stand beside Harland. They looked natural together, he thought.

He saw that Harland had drawn a grid over eastern Bosnia. It extended from the Drina River in the east to Sarajevo in the west, and from Foca in the south to Tuzla in the north. The vertical scale was numbered from one to twenty, while the lateral one was labelled A to O.

Harland had got a pencil out and was running it up the map, stopping at each line and turning to Tomas for a reaction. This was no good. Harland's hand was getting in the way and Tomas needed longer to think about where they went. The trouble was that they had dodged hither and thither with the Serb troops.

'He can't see the map,' his mother said, with an impatience that he knew well. 'Why don't you let him look, then call out the numbers and letters?'

Harland nodded.

Tomas was beginning to remember. They'd crossed the Drina River and had gone north to Visegrad, where they camped out the first night. They muddled on in the same direction after that. Then for two days Oleg had gone off and left him with a Serb detachment in a deserted village. He returned on the morning of 15 July. That was the day of the massacre and they had travelled west which would mean they had been somewhere north-west of Visegrad. He found the town on the map and blinked, indicating that he was ready. Harland failed to notice.

'I think he's ready,' said Harriet from the other side of the bed.

Harland began moving the pencil up the map. At each line he turned to look at Tomas's eyes. Instead of blinking no at each turn, he waited until the pencil reached lines 7, 8 and 9 when he blinked once each time. They repeated the procedure moving west to east. This time Tomas blinked once for the letters H, I, J and K.

Harland snatched up the map and squinted at the area.

'That means that the mountains in the video film are probably the Javornik group. What's brilliant is that you've picked the area that includes Kukuva.' He pointed to a speck on the map. 'I believe that's where these people came from and that's important because the authorities will be able to trace their relatives and look for DNA matches. Well done, it's really good to have pulled that off.'

Tomas thought it was probably the first time he'd seen Harland smile properly.

26

A LETTER TO TOMAS

The next two days passed with little incident. There was no sign of Vigo, and no hint either that they'd been traced by Kochalyin's people.

Harland busied himself with the report, inserting the pictures and captions into the text, together with a map. He pressed Tomas to add a little more to his statement about Kochalyin's trip to Belgrade and eastern Bosnia and his recollections of the people Kochalyin had dealings with, particularly the infamous Serb general who'd featured in two of Griswald's witness statements. He also asked Eva to swear an affidavit about her relationship with Kochalyin which she did in front of the solicitor Leo Costigan. The resulting text gave a lot more weight to the section dealing with Kochalyin's background and his business dealings in Eastern Europe. She outlined his career in the First Chief Directorate of the KGB (Foreign Intelligence), his period with the Sixteenth Directorate (Communications, Interception and SIGINT) and his roaming brief in Czechoslovakia and Hungary during the eighties, which fell under the auspices of the First Chief Directorate, Department 11 (Liaison with Socialist countries). She showed how this last shadowy role had developed into a criminal career during the first months of the liberation.

To Harland's surprise, her recall was clear and exact, particularly about his business dealings. For instance she knew a lot about the tax fraud involving heating oil and commercial diesel as well as about the shipments made by Corniche-HDS Aviation, Kochalyin's company in Belgium. After she made her statement she glanced at Harland with an expression of defiant innocence, a look which alerted him to a secret.

He was anxious to send the report, but felt he needed more on the air crash. As he redrafted this section, he thought it might be worth tracking down Murray Clark in the US. Clark was the proponent of the wake-vortex theory, but he might at least be able to provide some explanation for Ollins's odd line of questioning. Besides, it seemed unlikely that Vigo had blackened Harland's name with Clark's outfit, the NTSB, as he had with the FBI.

It was also worth bringing Tomas into this. Everyone agreed he was benefiting from involvement. Tomas had applied himself to his own statement and also to Eva's which he corrected here and there, adding dates. There was another sign of improvement. The nurses said that he was spending a lot of time using the computer, apparently following Internet trails and reading for his own pleasure. No one knew what he was doing because Eva had insisted the computer should be his private domain, unless he specified that messages were to be read. That seemed right to Harland.

One thing had stuck in his mind. Eva had said that Tomas helped Kochalyin on some technical matters during the period after Bosnia. He had asked about this again and she'd looked blank. Rather than trying to explain it to Tomas in person, he decided to send him an e-mail. This would allow him to digest the problem at leisure.

'My dear Tomas,' he wrote, 'I may see you before you read this, but I wanted to say now that despite all the terrors and tragedy of the past weeks, nothing in my life has meant quite so much as the discovery that you are my son. Thank you for having the courage to find me. I regret my initial reaction when you did find me and I hope to make it up to you.' He added a reassurance, again pointing out that Tomas's guilt about the killing in Bosnia was misplaced.

He was aware of a certain stiffness in his style, but he went on to ask if Tomas would apply his mind to the air crash. One of the things he understood about his son was that he possessed exceptional reasoning skills as well as being technically adept. Harland described exactly what had happened before and after the crash then went on to describe the mystifying call from Ollins on Christmas Eve. Why was Ollins so interested in the phone and the angle at which Griswald had held the computer in the last moments before the plane dropped from the sky? These two details seemed to concern Ollins more than what might be contained in the phone's memory and the computer's hard drive. That was surely significant.

He re-read the message, feeling that he was maybe asking a little too much of his son, but then sent it anyway. It was important that he say the first part.

Since he was on-line, he decided to look up the NTSB site to see if anything had been added to Murray Clark's preliminary finding that the Falcon jet had fallen victim to a powerful wake-vortex. There was nothing more so, before trying to track down Clark, he read through some other incidents involving wake-vortex so that he could talk knowledgeably to Clark. He found an accident synopsis concerning a Cessna Citation jet that had crashed in December 1992 after following a Boeing 757 into Billings Logan International Airport, Montana.

In this case the smaller Citation had been flying below the path of the Boeing and the separation distance between the two aircraft had been less than three nautical miles. Forty seconds before the plane encountered the vortex and went into a roll the pilot was heard to say, 'Gee, we almost ran over a seven fifty-seven.'

Harland made a note to ask about the separation distance. He seemed to remember that the Falcon had been about eighty seconds behind the Boeing 767. It had stuck in his mind because it seemed such a short time. What did that mean in terms of distance? In the Montana crash the Cessna had been seventy-four seconds behind the Boeing and had begun to roll at a distance of 2.78 nautical miles. So it seemed to Harland that the Falcon might just have been in the danger zone, under three nautical miles from the Boeing.

A few minutes later, his eye was caught by some general notes on wake-vortices. He read that the wing designs of the Boeing 747, 757 and 767 all left unbroken trailing edges from the fuselage to the ailerons. This was what caused the vortex to form. But wind conditions had to be right. Firstly, the wind speed had to be very low. A vortex which lasted over eighty-five seconds could only be generated in a wind of less than five knots. A wind of between five and ten knots cut the life expectancy of the vortex to under thirty-five seconds. He thought back to his struggle in the East River and instantly realised that the wind had been much stronger than ten knots.

He remembered looking up at the Manhattan skyline in the distance and feeling the ice particles against his face. The sea was choppy. The waves lapped against the mound of soil where Griswald's seat had come to rest.

He read on and found that the wind direction was also crucially important. A vortex usually lingered longest in a cross-wind that tended to increase the rotational energy. If the wind was against the rotational direction of the vortex it would radically reduce its life.

He closed the site and took Clark's card from his wallet. He dialled and heard the helpful but slightly self-important voice of Murray Clark answer.

'What can I do for you?' he said. Harland smiled. Unlike Ollins, Clark had not been got at.

'I don't want to bother you. It's just that the Secretary-General has asked me to find out how things are going along – on a purely informal basis, you understand.'

'I don't have much more to add to what is already in the public domain.'

'Can I ask you some questions? They're pretty basic.'

'Shoot. I have some time,' said Clark.

'The Secretary-General has a theory that the plane might have been low on fuel and he wonders if that has been considered in the investigation.'

Clark sighed. Harland could almost hear the word *idiot*.

'No,' said Clark. 'We've ruled out that possibility. The plane refuelled in DC. The extent of the fire indicates that it was carrying plenty of fuel.'

'What about pilot fatigue? Apparently there's been some concern at the Federal Aviation Authority that pilots are flying when they're exhausted. There was a crash a couple of years back when the pilot was practically asleep at the controls.'

'No, no. The pilot of your plane was well rested. A medical exam two months back shows he enjoyed good health. And his safety record was impeccable.'

'So it's got to be the ... what do you call it?'

'Wake-vortex. Yes, that is our thinking.'

'The planes were too close, then?'

'Not necessarily,' said Clark. Harland could tell his mind was elsewhere.

'The separation distance for the two aircraft was, what? Eighty seconds? What does that mean in distance?'

'A little over three nautical miles.'

'So normally that would be in the safety margin?'

'Yes,' said Clark, more alert now having noticed the change of gear in Harland's questions.

'What was the wind speed at the time?'

'Why are you asking these questions, Mr Harland? It sounds to me as if you have an agenda.'

'It is not my agenda, it's the agenda of the Secretary-General and the Security Council.' He added the 'Security Council' without a murmur from his conscience.

'I thought this was an off-the-record conversation.'

'It is. And I will have an off-the-record conversation with the Secretary-General when we've finished speaking.' Damn, thought Harland. That was stupid. There was no point trying to intimidate the man.

'I'm sorry,' said Clark formally. 'I feel I should seek advice before commenting on these matters to you.'

'Oh, forgive me. I'm sorry. I was getting carried away. I don't want to compromise your professional standards.' He waited.

'As it's you asking, Mr Harland,' said Clark at last, 'perhaps I should help if I can. But this *is* background?'

'Surely.'

'What is it you want to know exactly?'

'Just the wind speed,' he said innocently, then added, 'And the wind direction.'

'Let me see, the wind speed was between fifteen and twenty knots, gusting twenty-five to thirty.'

'And the wind direction?'

'South-westerly, as I recall. Yes, that would be it, south-westerly.'

Harland had what he wanted. He burned to get off the phone but rather than alert Clark, he thought of something else to ask.

'When will you make your final report?'

'Any day now.'

'Thank you so much. I'd better not waste any more of your time.'

He knew that it hadn't been a particularly subtle interrogation, but that didn't matter now. The wind speed was far in excess of the necessary conditions for wake-vortex, and the wind direction was completely wrong. He would check with a map, but he was certain that the landing runway pointed southwest – that's why the Manhattan skyline was way off to the right when he first struggled out of his seat. The plane had landed near enough smack into the wind and there could have been no side wind to give the vortex extra life.

The theory, then, was a fraud, but maybe the NTSB was not consciously guilty. It was possible that the readings from the flight data recorder so perfectly mimicked the action of a plane in the grip of a vortex that the board had opted for the only reasonable explanation – wind speed and wind direction notwithstanding.

He added a couple of paragraphs on the crash and then phoned Jaidi's office. Eventually a superior-sounding assistant came on the line and warned Harland that the Secretary-General wouldn't be able to read it for at least five days. Harland protested, to no avail.

He hung up, reminding himself that Jaidi was probably working with at least three of the governments who'd helped protect Kochalyin. These days the international agenda shifted with each revolution of the planet – an air crash that had seemed so tragic and puzzling a few weeks before was now of only minor historical interest. No one was waiting for his report. Indeed they'd probably prefer that it hadn't been written. And even if the great master of mobility and inclusion did read it, Harland had to face the fact that there was little hope of anything being done about Kochalyin. He would adapt and avoid and survive because he knew the global attention span diminished by the day.

But there were still one or two things he could do to hurt Kochalyin. He copied the report into another e-mail file and sent it to Professor Norman Reeve's address. Then he thought of the journalist at the press conference in the UN. Parsons was his name: he worked for the *New York Times*. If he delivered the report to him with background on Tomas's operation to expose SIS and CIA operations in Europe, it would, he was sure, make a hell of a newspaper story.

So he wasn't beaten yet. Not by any means.

Tomas had had a couple of good days – just two nasty spasms. The big problem now was the dreams – the dreams about movement. Some mischievous part of his subconscious had decided that he should only dream about the things he used to do. Last night he was cross-country skiing as he'd done in the mountains as a boy. He could feel the sweat on his face in the cold air as he pushed himself, arms and legs working to maximum exertion. He could see the winter landscape in every detail and taste the hot, sweet red wine that he shared with his mother at the end of each trip. He dreamed about walking, running and touching things, and each time his subconscious articulated the exact pleasure that he would never again enjoy.

He looked out of the window at his new view. A faint print of the half-moon was just visible in the late afternoon sky. Across the square, lights were being switched on in the offices and a woman had opened a window and was now leaning out to smoke. In the premature twilight of the square a figure in a bulky overcoat was standing beneath a cherry tree on which were still hanging a few vivid orange leaves. Tomas had gazed at the cherry often since his bed had been moved.

His attention returned to the room. His mother had come in and was saying an overly polite goodbye to Harriet. She smiled at him and briskly attached the electrodes to his head, switched on the computer and manoeuvred the screen towards him, blocking out most of the square.

He urged his mind to fill with hot thought and with little difficulty pushed the floating white light to hit the new e-mail icon. There was one message on his new server. He read the first paragraph, and smiled inwardly, then moved on to Harland's description of the moments before the flight. It certainly was an intriguing problem. He would enjoy working on it later.

27

STRANGE MEETING

Harland left Century House by the underground car park and walked eastwards through the dismal quiet of a public housing estate. He'd told Cuth's driver to stay with Eva, who between spells with Tomas was looking for an apartment near the hospital to rent for a few weeks. They were beginning to feel they were getting in the way at Century House.

A few minutes later he left the housing estate to cross a main road stalled with traffic, and merged with the crowds of commuters at Waterloo station. It was then that he sensed he was being followed, but this time by a more expert team. He stopped on the main concourse of the station, bought an evening newspaper and took the escalator down to the Underground, returning to the concourse on the upward escalator. He didn't spot anyone, but he felt the familiar weight at the back of his neck. He wondered whether they had picked him up at Century House, or later.

He paid for an all-zones travel card and for the next hour or so hopped on and off a dozen trains. Then he began to notice that the watchers were no longer bothering to hide themselves. As he travelled round the loop of the Circle Line he realised that there were now five individuals stuck to him. Every move he made they followed. Eventually he confronted a tall man in his mid-thirties who was carrying a knapsack, and asked what the hell he thought he was doing. The passengers around them looked on with the disengaged interest of London commuters. The man didn't reply but simply smiled back at Harland as though he was some kind of lunatic. At Victoria he got off and made his way to the street exit. As he fed his ticket into the automatic gate another man, in suit and tie, approached him.

'What the fuck do you want?' Harland demanded.

'Mr Vigo would like a word.'

'What for? To play charades in some clapped-out building?'

'No, sir. He suggests you meet in a place you know.'

'Where?'

'Carlton House Terrace.'

'Then why all this fucking around?'

'We were looking for an appropriate moment, sir.'

'Bollocks you were.'

'There's a car outside. We can be there in a few minutes.'

'I've been through this before. I'll go by cab, if you don't mind. Number three Carlton House Terrace, right?'

The man nodded.

Twenty minutes later his cab pulled up outside the familiar porch in St James's. Nearly thirty years before Harland had been there, invited by a man who called himself Fletcher. There had been three interviews in all and at the final session Fletcher had asked him to sign the Official Secrets Act, at which point his induction into MI6 had begun.

It was obvious that Vigo wanted to give Harland an unambiguous signal, firstly to demonstrate that he couldn't move in London without being followed and, more important, that he, Vigo, was no longer running a crew of irregulars. He had access both to a full surveillance team and official SIS premises.

Harland was shown into the grand but sparsely furnished room where he had once sat across from Mr Fletcher and his two silent colleagues on a warm spring afternoon. Vigo came in almost immediately.

'Hello, Bobby. It's good of you to take the time. I wanted to have a talk in what are rather changed circumstances.'

'Which are?' Harland noticed that the look of bustling confidence had returned to Vigo's expression.

'We met under rather difficult circumstances last time. We didn't perhaps have the kind of discussion that we needed to have. I accept this was my fault and I'd like the chance to clear things up now. That's all.'

'What do you want to clear up, Walter?'

'Any false impression you might have received.'

Harland laughed.

'I want to persuade you we have been working on the same side all along, Bobby.'

'No Walter, that doesn't work. You work for Kochalyin. I work for the UN, which despite its faults is still a force for good. You work for a man who has killed countless numbers of people.'

'I do wish you would stop being so dramatic, Bobby. What you say is simply not true.'

'You expect me to believe that after you tried to threaten me with an Official Secrets charge; after your band of occasionals chased me round London; after my son – yes, I know you must know he's my son – was tracked down using special equipment at GCHQ to locate his telephone? Walter, you're in this up to your neck and just because Tomas is no longer a threat to your grubby arrangements, don't think that I or the UN have any intention of hushing things up.'

Vigo sat with his hands across his stomach and produced a look of elaborate sympathy, which also included elements of pity, indulgence and disdain.

'That is in part why Robin has asked me to see you.'

He had dropped the name of the sainted chief of SIS, the

389

untarnished Sir Robin Teckman. That meant something too. Harland sighed.

'Okay, Walter, spit it out. What's been going on? Some kind of battle at SIS in which, no doubt, you have triumphed?'

'You know I'm not at liberty to discuss these things.'

'But the answer is yes, isn't it? That's what you're trying to tell me in your sly little way with all this – the crack surveillance troops, tea and cakes at Carlton House Terrace and using Teckman's name. What happened to Miles Morsehead and Tim Lapthorne, eh? Taken early retirement; fixed up with undemanding posts in the oil industry?'

Vigo said nothing.

'So,' said Harland, 'all that crap over Christmas was part of some SIS mud fight. You had your own pantomime season, Walter, mustering your little army and playing spies. You do know we're dealing with a war criminal? It's no more complicated than that – a very sadistic man who has killed an awful lot of people. You know that Oleg Kochalyin was the man who did me over in '89?' Harland looked at him hard. 'Yes, you bloody well did know. And you knew the reason behind it, didn't you?'

'I guessed at both, Bobby. I had no definite knowledge, certainly not enough to inform you that these were certain facts.'

'Did you know that Tomas was my son?'

'No, and we had no idea he was responsible for the transmissions.'

'That's rubbish. You knew. You must have known. That's why GCHQ helped track the signal from his phone.'

'You're wrong, Bobby, and you'd be well advised to keep such idiocies to yourself.'

'Then how on earth did they find him on the Embankment?'

'They followed him from your sister's house. When he

arrived early, they realised he was waiting for someone – a contact. That turned out to be you, which is why they opened fire when you arrived. We would have tried to give you protection but you managed to give my team the slip, and of course we didn't know what he looked like so he was able to leave your sister's house without being spotted by us.'

'But why didn't they kill me at the river? Why haven't they tried to kill me since?'

'I think they have. We heard about Zikmund Myslbek's death. We know that your journey after that was pretty fraught. In fact in many ways it's surprising that you made it back here. As far as the shooting at the Embankment goes, I think it's fair to say they thought you had been hit and were floating down the river. Anyway, by that time I gather the two unfortunate constables had arrived on the scene and the gunmen had to make good their escape. Believe me, we really were trying to protect you.'

'Crap,' snapped Harland. 'You were using me. You thought I knew a lot more about those coded transmissions than I did and you were using me as a bait.' He thought for a few moments. Vigo watched him working it out. 'But you had limited resources because someone in SIS was telling Kochalyin what was going on. That's why you were working with your little band of trusties. In fact I'd guess that a considerable faction was embroiled with Kochalyin in one way or another. But then the baffling part of it for you and everyone else was why the messages kept on being transmitted. You couldn't work it out, could you? You knew I wasn't responsible and you knew Lars Edberg was in hospital on life support.

'It was at that point your *interest* moved on. The Lipnik pictures were old hat. You couldn't give a fuck about them because they only represented a tiny fraction of what Mortz and Tomas had put together. You were obsessed with a far greater threat and also a far greater prize. The threat was to

391

your beloved service which was hurting from the sheer amount of detail that Tomas published – the eavesdropping operations against your competitors in Europe, the undermining of contract negotiations, the men and women hired to leak economic plans. And let's not forget the planes that left Ostend, collected their cargo of arms in Burgas and flew on to supply the nasty little wars in Africa. You couldn't afford for any more to come out – nor could the Americans, or the Dutch or the French or the Germans or the bleeding Belgians. So you had to stop it, and on the morning I paid my visit to your house, you knew you were within an ace of doing so. That's what that meeting was about: you were briefing your band of trusties after the latest batch of transmissions.'

Vigo tried to demur, but saw the look in Harland's eye and backed off.

'What a race that must have been,' continued Harland. 'Your lot against the official SIS team. And you won the prize. While they were watching the houses in Bayswater, you or one of your friends had the bright idea of searching the telephone junction boxes. That meant you got the computers with all their information and you could use it to nail the competition for the role of successor to Robin Teckman.'

'That's quite enough,' said Vigo. 'There are things that you don't understand and never will.'

'Oh, I'm nowhere near finished, Walter. You may think that you have arranged this meeting to silence me. But let me just tell you that I have all the cards. At the press of a key everything I know about this affair will go to the press and that means the government will be asking questions, which is hardly going to be conducive to your candidature. So if I were you, I'd sit tight and shut up.'

'Bobby, there's no point in this – really,' said Vigo. 'You don't have the whole picture.' He cocked his head to the sound of opening car doors outside. 'Look, I think we're about to be joined. I hope you will be able to listen to what is said to you.'

'No, it's you that has to do the listening . . .' His voiced trailed off because Vigo had got up.

'Would you just hold on a second,' he said irritably as he left the room.

Harland paced around the mahogany table for a few minutes. Then the door opened and Vigo came in followed by the gaunt, polished figure of Sir Robin Teckman. He sat down and smiled pleasantly at Harland.

'Walter's filled me in on your position . . .'

'Yes, I'm sure he has,' said Harland curtly. He liked and respected Teckman from his time with him in the East European Controllerate, but he wasn't going to be sweet-talked into silence. 'I was saying that there are outstanding matters to discuss. Kochalyin's crimes can't all be swept away. There's a massacre to consider in Bosnia, the plane crash that I was involved in and the killings and shootings in London. Just because you've sorted out your internal difficulties, it doesn't mean that we can forget what Kochalyin is responsible for.'

'And what did you have in mind, Bobby? How do you believe we should pursue these matters?' The eager, helpful smile had not faded.

'Firstly Britain should instigate the reopening of proceedings in The Hague. It's clear that we were involved in helping him fake the assassination in the first place.'

'That's not true,' said Teckman evenly. 'We believe another foreign power was responsible, probably the French, who kept their lines open to the Serbs all through the Bosnian civil war and the Kosovo conflict, as you probably know.'

'Why would they do that?' asked Harland.

'We believe it was some kind of deal involving an aero-industry contract. I cannot be more specific, I'm afraid, because we don't know. However, I suspect he furnished the crucial contacts which resulted in an order. They obliged by fixing up the drama in the hotel and putting their own troops on the job to act as witnesses.'

'If we weren't involved in that business there'll be no embarrassment at all to the British government.'

'Bobby, in the hope that you understand the spirit in which I make these remarks, I'm going to be open with you. Kochalyin has caused us considerable problems, principally because different parts of the service were engaged with different manifestations of him. It wasn't until Walter started pulling it all together two years ago that we understood that we were dealing with one man. I think the same can be said of a number of different agencies which have been equally compromised and embarrassed by these illegal transmissions. Tell me, have you learned anything about the motives of your boy and this fellow Mortz? Clearly the boy held a deep grievance against his step-father, and Mortz was a clever trouble maker from radical seventies stock. Put together they were a devastating combination. The motive puzzles me however. You see, the lad must have got very close to Kochalyin to have been able to gain the information he used. Was this premeditated – what was the trigger? What caused this resentment?'

That was something they didn't know and Harland wasn't going to enlighten them. 'He hated Oleg Kochalyin because of his treatment of his mother. That's obvious. But I haven't exactly had the chance to question him. He's frail and cannot speak.'

'But I understood he was capable of some rudimentary communication.'

'Occasionally, but he's not up to being questioned about this. His doctor says that he is prone to infections and needs to be kept quiet.'

'I see,' said Teckman.

'The point,' said Harland, 'is that I have a duty to report on all these matters to the UN Secretary-General. It's not just the massacre in Bosnia, but the air crash in New York. There's every reason to believe it was the work of Kochalyin.'

'What evidence do you have?' asked Teckman, in the manner of a tutor drawing out a pupil.

'I believe the plane was brought down by an electronic device – a virus maybe. I might have been able to pursue this further if Walter hadn't warned the FBI against talking to me, but I know that the crash wasn't caused by wake-vortex. The evidence of wind speed, wind direction and distance between the two landing aircraft at the time make a vortex virtually impossible.'

'Maybe what you say about the vortex phenomenon is true, but I don't think it quite justifies the claim that the plane was sabotaged. There could be said to be rather a gap between the two.'

Again there was no hint of a challenge. Harland could see that he was being manipulated into a position where he would be forced to concede he had little definite proof and therefore had no reason to take further action.

'Well, I've raised this in my preliminary report,' he said, a little defiantly.

A glint of concentration entered the Director's eyes. 'You have already sent this to the Secretary-General?'

'Yes, although there's much to add.'

'And what do you envisage the Secretary-General doing with your report?'

'I imagine he'll use the evidence to reopen the case into Kochalyin's activities in 1995 and maybe there are some lessons to be learned about the way powerful states employed this man.'

'And there again, he may do nothing,' said Teckman.

'That's up to him. It's his report – he commissioned it. But I will urge an investigation into the war crimes. By the way, you know there's evidence that Kochalyin was present at more than one massacre.'

Teckman exhaled and looked at Vigo. 'Naturally, Bobby, we're concerned that this report of yours doesn't fall into the wrong hands. It would be quite awkward for it to appear in the media in its unformed state.'

'You want me to wait until I've got more?'

'No, of course not. This is very dangerous material and it contributes to the sense that our institutions are degenerate. We want to build public confidence, not destroy it. I think that Walter and I have demonstrated to you that we rooted out the difficulty we were having and that these things can be addressed, without worrying everyone. That takes courage, you know. Look, I understand why you see this as something of a personal crusade – who could blame you after what happened in Prague and after what has been done to your boy? But I also want you to remember you are still a citizen of this country and that you signed the Official Secrets Act. If there is any publicity about this I think it would be damaging to the national interest in ways that you have perhaps not foreseen.'

Harland rose from his chair and shook the tension from his shoulders. Also, he wanted to show that he did not feel constrained in their company.

'In what ways will it be damaging?' he asked.

'With your background, you must understand that relations between countries are not a simple affair. Two states may be friends on one level, but competitors, even enemies, on another. For example, on drug-trafficking we are at one and there is a high degree of co-operation between states, but when it comes to crucial defence contracts or tenders to build a dam in Turkey each state pursues its own interests. The public finds this very hard to understand – but it's a system that works, after a fashion. When something like this gets into the open it tends to colour the entire relationship for a very long period. Politicians get hold of it and inflate the issue for their own purposes, which needless to say is not the common interest.'

'But there *is* a principle here,' said Harland. 'We know the identity of a war criminal who has also committed countless other crimes. What possible harm comes from putting him in the dock to answer for what he's done?'

'That assumes you can lay hands on the man. But let's accept that you effect this miraculous arrest, what then? Kochalyin appears at The Hague and, seeing that he is bound to be sentenced to a long term in jail, decides he has nothing to lose by telling the story of the last dozen years. You don't imagine the Americans are going to allow that to happen, do you? Or the French or the Germans? They have all used him in one way or another.'

'To say nothing of the British.'

'To say nothing of the British,' repeated Teckman, with a brief patrician smile. 'It just isn't going to happen, Bobby. And that's all there is to it.'

'Then what will happen?'

'Well, nothing immediately, but let me assure you that Kochalyin will not be able to continue operating as he has been. There are too many people who know what he did in his various roles. That is in large part thanks to your son. So, sooner rather than later, he will arrive at a messy end, in which case you can hardly be less than satisfied.'

'There's some kind of contract on him?'

'Good heavens, no. His time will come – that's all I'm saying. He's been exposed. People have made the connections; they know what he has done. For instance, Walter was telling me that he's stolen an awful lot of money. That does enrage people, you know.'

'But you don't believe there is any case to answer in Bosnia?'

Teckman looked pained. 'Of course I do, Bobby. Of course

397

I do. Please remember how much effort the British have put into capturing these people. No country has a better record of apprehending indicted war criminals than we do. None!'

Harland sat down again and looked at each of them in turn.

'I'm sorry, I can't wear this. The world may work like this, but it used not to. There were once ideas of right and wrong, however crude. We presumed to claim that we were on the right side because all of us knew of the evil of the regimes in the East. That was our motivating faith, however ragged and abused in execution. But now . . .'

'Now we have to make much harder choices,' said Vigo quietly. 'Robin is right. We can't have your report floating about and giving people the wrong impression.'

'The odd thing about it all,' said Harland, still looking at Teckman, 'is that there is almost nothing in my report about the transmissions. Do you know why that is? It's because I don't know much about them. I suspect that you caught a good deal before it was released from those two computers, in which I case I will never know. Tomas is hardly in a position to tell me.' Neither Teckman nor Vigo showed any reaction. 'So,' he continued, 'my report chiefly concerns the air crash and the war crime. As I told you, it has already been delivered to the Secretary-General. There's nothing you can do.'

Vigo cleared his throat. 'I think what Sir Robin wants is an assurance that you will not add to this report and that you will not seek to have the current draft distributed.'

Harland said nothing. He imagined a plan was already in place to persuade Jaidi to bury the report in exchange for some diplomatic favour. All they needed now was to ensure his silence.

'We all want to leave this room with a clean sheet,' said Teckman. 'Without acrimony or misunderstanding.' He paused. 'You see, we're working on the same side, Bobby, even if in the past there has been some doubt about that. You know what I'm referring to.'

Harland understood very well that he was being threatened again. A release of his report might not be followed by a charge, but certainly a campaign in the press to destroy him. He'd seen what had happened to younger members of SIS who had broken ranks recently and he knew that his former employers would not hesitate to use the material they had on his 'Prague connection'.

'Are we working on the same side, Bobby?' asked Teckman, with an interrogative lift of his eyebrows.

Harland was about to shake his head.

'I believe we are, perhaps more so than you appreciate.' Teckman nodded to Vigo who rose and left the room, closing the door behind him.

No more than thirty seconds later Vigo came in and waited by the door. Someone was hesitating outside. Harland leaned over and saw Eva standing anxiously in the light of the corridor.

'You see, we really are on the same side,' said Teckman.

28

THE FINAL WORK

There was only one thought in Harland's mind.

'How long?' he demanded icily. 'How long have you worked for them?'

Her eyes moved from Vigo to Teckman, whom she clearly hadn't seen before. He put out his hand and motioned her to a chair.

'Three years.'

It all made sense to Harland. Now he understood why she had remained Kochalyin's lover and how she'd been able to supply so much detail for his report to Jaidi.

'And you knew this, Walter? You knew who she was?'

Vigo nodded. 'Needs must, I'm afraid,' he said sombrely. 'We had to get the information on Kochalyin. You know how it is, Bobby.'

'You bastard, Walter.'

'But,' said Vigo, raising a hand to deflect the insult, 'Irina here will confirm that we had no idea that she was *Lapis* until late last year. We simply knew her as Kochalyin's former wife. We needed to build a picture of this man – his character, his habits, his business dealings. We needed to piece his different existences together. Irina helped us a great deal and we are very grateful to her. You may not believe this, but not once was your name mentioned. You see, you weren't in the picture until you got on that plane in Washington.'

'It's true, Bobby,' implored Eva. 'They didn't know about us until last month. They didn't know about Tomas – why would I tell them? I was just helping them with Oleg – that was all. Why would I discuss who Tomas's father really was? Tomas had his own life. And you? You were in the past.'

Harland sat down. 'Did you help them with information from the files?'

'No,' she said. 'He didn't tell me anything about you. Why would he?'

Vigo nodded in agreement.

'But why didn't you mention this arrangement before? We were travelling for nearly three days together. When we got to Century House, what happened then? You knew that Walter and I must have worked in that very building together. Surely that jogged your memory.'

'You didn't tell me where we were. You didn't mention the history of the building until after I'd seen Tomas. I didn't even know that you knew Walter. How could I? He didn't say anything to me and nor did you.'

'The penalties of discretion,' chipped in Teckman, who had sat down in his original place at the table. 'It's all true, Bobby. I have to say I was nearly as dumbfounded as you are when Walter unravelled this whole conundrum for me the other day. It does, however, rather underline my point about us all being on the same side. Everyone has been working against Oleg Kochalyin.'

Harland was watching Eva. For a fraction of a second she stared at him, her pupils dilating with significance.

'There's one thing that doesn't ring true to me,' said Harland. 'When Tomas was shot, why didn't you tell her, Walter? You could have called her.'

'Because at that stage we hadn't made the connection between Irina and Tomas and you. The police were late in telling us about the newspaper they'd found in his flat – the one with your picture removed. And by that time, you have

401

to remember, we were desperate to find the source of the transmissions. So the real identity of Lars Edberg wasn't a priority. We knew he must have had something to do with the transmissions, yet they were continuing after he had been shot. As you can imagine, Bobby, at that moment our sole aim was to stop the transmissions. Later, when we had located the source, I had the police take his fingerprints and we were able to make a match between those in the flat, the computers and Lars Edberg.'

Teckman took over the narrative. 'By that stage we had begun to sift through the information that Irina here had given us. We were comparing it with some of the things we'd seen in the transmissions. Suffice it to say there was an overlap. The information came from the same route. That was when Walter put all the pieces in place.'

'At what stage exactly did you know that Tomas was our son?'

'Some time in the middle of last week.'

'By which time I'd left for Prague.'

'Yes. We knew you would break the news to Irina and bring her back here.'

'And you were following us?'

'We have limited resources in the Czech Republic,' said Teckman. 'We caught up with you in Karlsbad and followed you to Dresden. Then we lost you. There was some confusion at the station. We were worried because our two men knew Kochalyin's people were following you too.'

'And here?' asked Harland belligerently. 'Here in Britain?'

'We've had you covered the whole time,' replied Teckman. 'The fact that Cuth Avocet put you up in the old building greatly aided us.'

'And the phones? Have you been tapping our calls?'

'No,' said Teckman. 'Our chief concern has been to see if Kochalyin would follow you here, in which case we would certainly have had a word with him.' He gave a bleak, deadly smile. 'His people are here, but he hasn't graced us with his presence, which doesn't surprise me in the least. It's far too dangerous. The reason you are still alive, I suspect, is because Walter has had you watched since The Bird's driver picked you up on the Kent coast. As to the phones, no, we haven't been listening. Besides, with the Harp-Avocet operation in full flow every day it would be difficult to pinpoint the calls.'

A flat lie, thought Harland. They were bound to have tapped into the phone lines. It explained why they had approached him now. They must have read every word of his report to Jaidi – they'd been forced to make their move and had produced Eva in a desperate attempt to stop him adding anything. He must also assume that they knew about the calls he'd made to Clark, the websites he'd visited while reading up on wake-vortex and the contents of his e-mails to Tomas and to Professor Norman Reeve.

'And The Bird and Macy? Were they in on all this?'

'We informed them this afternoon that you were in danger and that we were shadowing your movements,' said Vigo. 'They had suspected something. Their driver spotted a couple of our fellows in the course of the week.'

Teckman was winding a strand of cotton round a loose button on his jacket. Harland knew the distraction meant the head of SIS was concentrating very hard on his responses.

He would react accordingly. 'So it seems you've got us pretty much trussed up,' he said with a hint of resignation in his voice.

'I wouldn't put it like that,' said Teckman amenably. He looked up from the button. 'We just don't want any more killings on our patch. We want this business with Kochalyin to take its natural course, and I do promise you that it *will* take its natural course. That's why I've been anxious to point out that we're advancing on a unified front.'

'So what do we do now?'

'You carry on as you have been, while we watch your back

for you. I don't know how long this business will go on, but at some stage we will know when to make alternative arrangements for your safety. It will be clear to Kochalyin that he can no longer rely on Irina. After Tomas was shot he must have known that this would eventually happen, although of course he well appreciated that she didn't know where Tomas was and moreover she was unlikely to hear of the shooting for some time. So clearly Irina is a priority target for him but he also knows she will be well protected. My guess is that he will make a move later on, once he has settled other accounts. He will seek to eliminate her and possibly her mother. Oh, by the way, Irina, I should mention that we've found Hanna the accommodation I was talking about in Switzerland.'

He paused and placed his hands together on the table.

'So, to conclude, for the moment I think you should remain in Century House, where we can keep a close eye on you. You should continue to visit your son in hospital, where we can also make sure you are undisturbed.' He looked at Harland. 'In the meantime, I would very much like your assurance that you will not add to the report. What you have already said on this affair surely discharges your obligations. I don't want any gestures, Bobby, no desperate resolve. Just keep a low profile. Is that understood?'

Harland gave a brief nod. There was no mistaking the instruction, and there was little point in letting the Director know that he had no intention of obeying it.

'So I think that wraps up our business,' said Teckman, clasping his knees and pushing up from the chair. 'We'll be in touch. If you need anything, you can phone Walter.' He moved to the door. 'I'm glad we've had this talk. I can't tell you how important it is to know we're working on the same side.'

Tomas hadn't seen his mother leave because he was dozing.

He had worked steadily for two hours and then fallen asleep while she was with him. When he awoke, he noticed a very sharp pain which sprang from beneath his ribs every five or six breaths. He would have liked to have held his breath to see if the pain still came, but the machine took the option away. It commanded his lungs to inflate at regular intervals. He was forced to breathe – whether he wanted to or not.

There was another feeling that he hadn't encountered before, a general enervation which, on thinking about it, he likened to his body being drained of blood. This thought came from his paranoia. He was haunted by the idea that he was being kept alive for medical experimentation, involuntary blood transfusions, even organ donation. How could he tell whether he still had both kidneys? Did they have plans for his eyes – his heart, his liver? And his hands? Would the doctors take his hands from him and sew them on to someone's arms, fusing the nerves to another man's impulses? Or why not a woman's? Flick always said his hands were delicately made. They were sensitive, she said – artistic. She didn't know they were a killer's hands.

Nothing like this had gone through his mind when he was being taken off heroin. The sweats and arthritic fever of cold turkey were a picnic compared to this. Now, once his mind had got hold of a thought it seemed to take pleasure in supplying innumerable permutations of a particular horror. He had become fixated on what he regarded as the certain distribution of his body parts. Perhaps the intended recipients had already been matched with him and were waiting in beds around the hospital, longing for him to die and give them new life.

He sank a little more into himself. The pain was getting worse. Was this it? Was his heart giving notice of expiration?

He opened his eyes again and saw that the white ball light was quivering in front of him. The computer was on and the electrodes were still conveying the blistering heat of his panic

405

to the screen, making the light bob like a fishing float. He decided to continue with his work. Practically everything had been completed because his mother had very quickly grasped how to help him. It had given him a thrill working with her and for a few moments that afternoon he had forgotten where he was – and how he was.

He logged off to still the ball of light and struggled to put some thought to the problem his father had set him in the morning. There wasn't much to go on – the lights and heating in the plane had failed, then a little time later the plane had crashed. This might indicate a virus at work, but it would be a pretty crude one to knock out the lights needlessly. Maybe he was barking up the wrong tree. Perhaps the lights going out was only relevant in as much as it had forced Griswald to open up his computer and use the glow from the screen to see what he was doing. They had asked about the angle of the computer and where Griswald had held it in relation to the phone in his right-hand pocket. What could be the point of that?

He let his mind drift, hoping that something would occur to him. Five minutes later a glimmer of a solution came to him, but just at that moment he was racked with a particularly violent pain in his chest. The nurse hadn't noticed and neither had she bothered to ask how he was. He wished she'd give him something.

He thought again. That was it! The reason they wanted to know how the laptop had been held was because they believed it had shielded the phone. They wanted to know how it still came to be functioning in Griswald's pocket after the crash. Shielded from what? Not the impact of the crash, surely? Then he realised what the investigators were being so cautious about. He had heard of such things and, more important, he knew that Kochalyin was familiar with the device.

As he tried to remember exactly what was involved, the

pain returned and filled his chest. He was sure that he was running a fever, his eyes were stinging. There was a clamminess – hot and cold in the same moment. He knew this was the beginning of the end. He'd be going down that stairway and not coming back.

But he wasn't going yet. He still had things to do. He rallied himself. Yes! He remembered. Back in '97 – or was it '98? – Oleg had seen a man from a weapons research establishment in the Ukraine. God knows how he knew about the place – probably something to do with his past. The man came to him to explain the technology and, later that week, Oleg had sounded Tomas out about the production of such a device because he knew he was interested in radio frequencies. Tomas had been genuinely intrigued by the simplicity of the device.

He summoned all his will and laboriously went through the process of an Internet search. He read for over an hour then copied the relevant parts into an e-mail and addressed it to Harland. A second copy he placed on his hard disk for use later. Harland was right, he thought. It had been a logical problem and he was glad he had been able to crack it for him.

The pain was still with him and the fever was taking hold, but he had to get this one other thing out of the way. He prepared to concentrate for the last time that evening and visited his personal archive – a virtual locker which he had set up after Mortz sent him the package – and began selecting the coded information. Most of it had been used before, but there were one or two items that hadn't. He placed them in five separate files, attached the virus that his mother and he had worked up over the last couple of days, and began making calls to the numbers his mother had pinned to the laptop for him. Half an hour later everything had been sent.

But that wasn't quite the end of his work. He went back to the archive and withdrew everything – coded and uncoded material – and placed it on the old Czech website he had set up five or six years before – www.rt.robota.cz. For good measure he added the material he'd found for Harland.

29

DNR

'So that's all of it?' he asked. 'No more surprises?'

She shook her head, took two rapid puffs from a cigarette and inexpertly tried to stub it out.

'No,' she said. 'There are no more surprises, Bobby.'

She was sitting on the sofa with her legs folded under her. Harland had taken himself to the north window and was looking out towards the Houses of Parliament. They'd been through it all: how Vigo made contact with her; how he met her once in Hanover and how she subsequently communicated what she learned of Kochalyin's affairs through e-mail. It all seemed an extremely unlikely story.

He left the window and went to the fridge. There were a couple of bottles of white wine in the door. He withdrew the Chablis, pulled the cork and poured two glasses. He raised his glass to The Bird for putting it there and handed her the other glass.

'Vigo put up quite a case for my arrest and prosecution,' he said conversationally.

'I had nothing to do with that. I knew nothing about them going into the archive in Prague.'

'You know, seeing that picture of us made me feel very old.'

'You haven't changed much, Bobby. A little heavier and not so much hair. But you're the same man.'

'I ache all the time,' he said, smiling. 'I feel my age and I look it. But you, you've kept in terrific shape. It must be the bloody yoga.'

She returned his smile.

'Did you ever see the picture?'

'No, of course not. You have to believe me. I had nothing to do with that. But I knew that it existed, of course, because Oleg told me about it.'

'I do believe you.'

'Nor the tape recording. I would never have done that to you, Bobby – set you up like that.'

He looked at her hard. She was very beautiful. He believed her. 'I know that too. You see, there was never a tape of us talking. Kapek threatened me with it, but that was just bluff – something he pulled out of the hat on the spur of the moment and then boasted about in his report to Kochalyin. Maybe he told him personally. I don't know.'

'There was no tape recording?'

'No, just the picture of us.'

'I must have misunderstood.'

'Yes, you probably did. But your mentioning the tape is interesting because it indicates that at some stage Vigo and his friends were told there was one.'

'I didn't tell them.'

'I wonder where they got the idea?'

'I don't know.' She seemed genuinely perplexed.

'Who told you there was a tape – Kochalyin?'

'I can't remember – I have believed this for years. Oleg wasn't concerned with the operation in Rome. But he had access to the information. So maybe it was him. Why are you interested?'

'Because it means one of two things.' He put his glass down on the table and sat down opposite her. 'One solution is that they had another source to help compile the dossier about me before Christmas. But who could have helped them in that short time? Not Kochalyin, for obvious reasons. Not

Kapek because he knew there was no tape, and anyway no one knows where he is, and not you because Vigo didn't want to alert you to the fact that he was putting something together on me. Of course, there is another solution. Perhaps they already knew about the supposed tape. Perhaps they already had it on file and dug it out for the interview with me. You see what I'm saying?'

'No, I don't.' She searched his face.

'Originally I thought it was you. I thought you had worked for Vigo in the eighties.'

She shook her head. 'No, Bobby. I wish I had in many ways. It was what my heart wanted. But I couldn't have risked Tomas and my mother so I stayed loyal.'

'Yes, that was my reasoning. Besides, like every other intelligence organisation, the StB had firewalls between different departments. There was no way a code breaker like you would have had knowledge of how Kapek was handling me. And vice versa of course. Only a few individuals had total access and saw the whole picture. So whoever told them about the tape was either directly responsible for Kapek or was very high up. Kapek was Czech and so one presumes he reported to a senior StB man. Perhaps this individual was SIS's informant, but my inclination is that it was someone else.'

'But why are you interested in this now? It has nothing to do with the present.'

'But it does. There is one person who had access to everything the StB was doing – Kochalyin. He also told you that there was a tape, repeating Kapek's little myth. Perhaps he didn't know that there wasn't a tape. After all you said he had nothing to do with the operation in Rome. So maybe he just took Kapek's word for it. The important thing was that this was never committed to Kapek's file which means that SIS could only have got this information from Kapek or Kochalyin.'

'You're saying that Oleg was working for SIS? That's too incredible.' She paused and groped for another cigarette. 'Aren't you placing too much significance on the tape and the fact that it wasn't mentioned in Kapek's file?'

'Yes, perhaps,' he said. 'But there's something else. Over the last few days I've been thinking about Ana Tollund. She worked in the Secretariat of the Praesidium. She was a quiet little mouse of a person by all accounts, but she fed the West vital intelligence for twenty years after the Prague Spring. She was very good – subtle, courageous and discriminating in what she passed on to her handlers. Then in '88 she was caught, tried and executed. I heard about her a little time before her arrest, but I knew nothing in detail about the case and I certainly didn't say anything to Kapek about her. However, when I was questioned before Christmas, they accused me of tipping off the Czechs about Tollund. That was Kapek making it up to boost his own importance after the event. But somehow this was passed back to SIS. It could only have been Kochalyin.'

'Why weren't you accused then, if she was so important?'

'Because they knew that I had no access to the information about Ana Tollund. They knew I couldn't know but they kept what Kochalyin had told them on file nevertheless. Everything, you see, is noted down and kept.'

'But you have no evidence that it was Oleg.'

'No, and I never will have. On the other hand, we know that subsequent to the Velvet Revolution Kochalyin had a relationship with SIS. And we know one of his prime motivations is money. Does it not seem likely that he was on the SIS payroll *before* the revolution? He'd have been an incredibly valuable asset to them and when the collapse of the régime came they would have been very willing to extend the association. More than a few favours went his way, I bet.'

She drank some wine and absorbed this.

'It's true,' she said, 'that he always had money. Nothing

412

would stop him selling information if he thought he could get away with it. Maybe you're right, but you will never know. Perhaps you have become a little obsessed with this. Maybe you should stop thinking about the past, Bobby.'

'Possibly,' he said. 'But it is my past. Ever since I talked to Tomas in New York I realised how damned little I knew about my own life. You said something on the train about a person's history being hidden from them. I want to know my history.'

'But there's something more to this for you, isn't there? You think that Kochalyin learned from your colleagues about your plan to buy the intelligence archives. You're thinking that they told him you were coming?'

'Right,' he said. 'That's exactly what I believe. I had a theory about his interception of the coded traffic between here and the embassy, but it seems much more likely that his handlers here sounded him out about the plan. And that was all he needed. He knew exactly where to find me and he could do what he liked without anyone hearing about it in London.'

'Do you think they guessed?'

'That's an interesting point. I think Vigo had his suspicions. He may even have been responsible for alerting Kochalyin in the first place, but I doubt that he intended what happened.' He stopped. 'I'll tell you one thing, though. Kochalyin saved my life.'

'How do you mean?'

'Oleg Kochalyin saved my life. When the swelling in my groin didn't go down, the doctors investigated and discovered I had cancer in one testicle. They got it just in time.'

Her mouth opened in surprise. 'Are you serious?'

'No doubt about it. I didn't suspect anything was wrong. If Kochalyin hadn't done me the favour of whacking me in the balls on the first occasion that we met, I'd probably be dead now.'

She winced. 'Are you all right now?'

'Not a sign since. They did a good job. Everything is okay in that department.'

A silence ensued, both of them lost in their own thoughts. Harland got up and walked to the window again. It was odd that he should end up in Century House with Eva and the ghosts of old suspicions.

'You gave me a look when we were with Teckman and Vigo,' he said from the window. 'You were saying something to me. What was that about?'

She smiled. 'You'll see. You have a very clever son, Bobby. He's like you. He thinks everything through until he finds the solution.' She looked up at the ceiling then quite suddenly her composure collapsed. Her head sank to her chest and her shoulders convulsed with a sob. She began to run her hands distractedly through her hair as her shoulders continued to heave. 'I cannot believe what has happened to my beautiful son. It's my fault.'

Harland moved to her side, put his hands on her shoulders and held her. 'It's not your fault,' he whispered. 'You must understand that.'

She tried to speak but couldn't get the words out. He drew her to him and stroked her head with his right hand.

'He's going to die,' she said. 'I know he's going to die. He told me he wanted to die. Bobby, I don't know how I'll live without him being alive. It mattered when I didn't see him for all that time, but at least I knew he was alive.'

'Have you thought that he might have left you because he knew he was going to do something dangerous and he didn't want to get you involved?' he asked quietly.

'That's kind of you. But, no, he left because he couldn't tolerate me seeing Oleg. If only I'd told him what I was doing.'

'But you have now,' said Harland, knowing she must have shed the whole story during the long hours by his bed.

414

'Yes. Oh, Bobby, I can't bear what has happened to him. I cannot live with the thought of him like that. I know it's better for him to die, but . . .' She sank into herself, falling forward on to her thighs. Harland stroked her back, feeling inadequate to the task of comforting her. The intimacy of shared grief, he now discovered, was as difficult as the intimacy of love. He sat looking ahead at the empty, darkened suite of offices which lay beyond the living quarters, wondering why he'd never recovered that part of himself.

At length Eva sat up a little and dried her eyes. She had the glazed look of someone whose mind is utterly elsewhere. For a time she looked out of the window, her head nodding gently as her thoughts raced. Then she stretched for the bottle of wine on the other side of the table. Harland leaned forward, retrieved it for her and filled her glass. She thanked him and stretched again, this time going for the packet of cigarettes. As she did so her hair fell from the back of her neck and he caught sight of the oval of dark skin just beneath the hairline, the birthmark he'd kissed a hundred times during the long night in Orvieto. It seemed then to be the essence of her – the mark of her uniqueness. He leaned forward and kissed her neck as she came back to the sitting position. It was an impulse. He didn't think before doing it and for a fraction of a second afterwards he expected her to whip round in horror. She said something which he didn't hear and turned to face him, smiling weakly.

'I remember you doing that before.'

'In Orvieto,' he said.

'Orvieto.'

He bent down to rest his face at the back of her head and kissed the birthmark many times again. And he murmured the thing that had been formed in complete sentences somewhere in his mind, waited to be voiced for over a quarter of a century.

'I love you, Eva. I've always loved you. I never stopped loving. I cannot stop.'

She turned her face again to him. 'It's strange of you to go on calling me Eva. I like it.'

'*Eva*,' he insisted. 'I love you, *Eva*.' He was surprised. He wasn't watching himself. He had dropped his guard.

She held his face between her fingers as if trying to steady it and looked at him. Her eyes were desperate.

'You have to . . .' she stammered. 'You must . . .'

'Help you?' he asked. 'Of course I'll help you. You know I will.'

'He's going to die very soon,' she said, quietly and matter-of-factly.

In his former life – five minutes before – Harland would have sought to reassure her by saying that there was a chance that Tomas might recover some of his movement – it was after all a gunshot wound, not a stroke. He would have talked about Tomas building his strength and finding ways of living with his condition. But now Harland had bridged the void that existed between them, or, more accurately, between himself and the rest of humanity, he didn't say any of this. Instead he said exactly what was in his mind.

'When he dies, I will help you in every way I can. I will never leave you. I am here. Nothing else matters to me.'

She kissed him, first with gratitude and relief, then with passion. Her hands fell from his cheeks to the base of his neck and she pulled herself to him, lifting her legs to the sofa and moving against him. He held her close, feeling the softness of her breasts against his chest and the firmness of her arms and shoulders in his hands. Her lightness surprised him, as it had done when they were young. He marvelled at her and fell to her neck, then kissed her on her mouth, on her eyes, on her cheeks.

The scent of her awoke memories in Harland which were not exclusively erotic. He could hear the tolling of the clock tower near the hotel in Orvieto and smell the wood smoke that filled the town on winter evenings. There were inexplicable noises in the hotel. The wooden ceilings shifted and groaned in disapproval. Corridors creaked outside their door and the shutters on the windows juddered in the wind. He remembered her lying on the coarse linen sheets, twisted to an incredible degree at the abdomen so that her legs turned away from him but her torso remained flat on the plane of the bed. He remembered the miraculous curve of her hips – good child-bearing hips, he had said in a silly way, running his hand up the rise of her pelvis and down the slope of her leg and then back again, feeling the resistance of minute hairs on his fingertips.

At some stage in the long night of their weekend together, he had broken free of her and thrown open the windows and shutters and gazed down on the huge deserted square in front of the cathedral. The sight of this silenced operatic set – the illuminated façade of the mediaeval church, a cat slipping into the shadows at a low furtive run, the eddies of a few leaves in the recesses of the buildings around the square – had stayed with him in a clear, dream-like still, as if this moment had been the only time that he had seen the physical world as it really was. There was a ghostliness in the square and it prompted in him an equal joy and fear that they were the only people left alive in the town.

He had returned shivering to her warmth and laid his head on her stomach. She turned her legs and pushed herself up from the bed to watch him as his mouth drifted towards the line of her hair and down between her legs where he parted her flesh with his tongue. From the corner of his eye he could see her gazing at him with an intensely serious expression. Her hand suddenly reached down to press his lips closer to her and she came with a shudder, her head falling silently backwards so that he could only see the alabaster shaft of her throat. Quite some time afterwards she produced a gasp and

417

her head dropped forwards on to him and she smothered him in kisses and brushed her hair across his body. In the early stages of their affair, during the collisions in the hotels of Rome, Harland, who was used to the milk-and-water sex of the English, had been taken aback by the ferocity of her attention. Eva gave, but also took with equal passion, and when at last she had exacted what she needed she lay back on the bed with utter lack of modesty. He was amazed at the whiteness of her body and its strength.

The sequence in Orvieto – moving from the window to taste her body and watching her strain backwards – he had played over and over in his head, partly because it brought her to life like no other memory, but also because it was the only order of events he could remember from the entire weekend. By that stage they must have told each other everything. He often thought of the taverna where they had sat and she had taken hold of one hand and sternly made him listen. But there was no real order in his mind to the three days because apart from that couple of hours in the restaurant they'd ruthlessly shut out the world and greedily merged into each other.

Then as now. They stayed in the half-light feeling as young and awed by their delight as they had twenty-eight years before. Their joy was limitless and engrossing. But there were few words between them. He mostly kept his eyes shut to sense her the better, and in the rare moments he opened them he saw hers were closed too.

Some time in the middle of the night they made their way into her bedroom and sprawled on the bed where he struggled with her remaining clothes. Her head flopped lazily from one side to the other as he removed her bra and drew the white shirt from her arms. He stopped for a moment and absorbed her beauty, feeling less self-conscious than he could ever remember being. She looked drugged with expectation. As he kicked off his shoes and removed his own clothes, she began to weave about him, nipping at him with her teeth, clawing him gently, holding him to her to find the tightest fit. She didn't need to tell him that she loved him or that she had often replayed the way they made love in her mind because everything was as it had been, only more urgent, more serious.

He watched her moving to a climax, lifting her head from the bed and opening her eyes with a look of surprise.

About an hour later the phone in the sitting-room began to ring. Harland awoke and wondered furiously what time it was. He groped for his watch but found he'd left it in the other room and decided not to answer. But the phone went on ringing and after a couple of minutes, by which time he was fully awake, he dragged himself out of bed and went to pick it up.

'Mr Harland. This is Professor Reeve. I have the information you wanted.'

'Yes,' said Harland, and cleared his throat.

'Well? Do you want it?' demanded Reeve. 'After you sent me the report, I went to considerable trouble to get this information for you.'

'No, no – of course I want it, sir. Let me just get a pen.' He reached for his coat pocket. 'Right, I'm with you now.'

'From the information that you gave me,' said Reeve briskly, 'my contact was able to identify the likely location of the massacre site. So write this down – the position is forty degrees and two minutes north, nineteen degrees and thirteen minutes east. Computer models of the local topography confirm that the picture you sent me was taken by someone facing the mountains of the Javor and Javornik ranges. The profile of the mountains that you can see is about twenty-five kilometres north-west of the site.'

'Thank you,' said Harland, groping for the maps he had used with Tomas in the hospital. 'It'll be useful to be able to pinpoint the place in the report.' He paused, opened the map and quickly ran his finger to a spot not far from the road that meandered through the mountains.

'Are you there?' said Reeve, who had been explaining that his contact was a CIA target-spotter who was familiar with the terrain in the Balkans.

'I'm with you,' he said hastily. 'I was just glancing at the map and wondering whether it would be possible to learn if the grave was known to the authorities in The Hague.'

'You don't have to bother,' snapped Reeve. 'I've already checked on the data base we have. This site is new to us and will be to the people at The Hague. It was what Mr Griswald was undoubtedly working to expose.'

'Well, I'm most grateful to you. My heartfelt thanks, Professor.'

'But I haven't finished. I rang now because this site has suffered some disturbance in the last twenty-four hours. My contact has been doing some research into this area with the usual resources at his disposal. And he noticed in yesterday's pictures, which are exceptionally clear, that there was earth-moving equipment in the area. There is a two-hour gap between the first set which shows the equipment moving up a road toward the site and the second set which reveals the vehicles gathered round the site.'

'The evidence is being destroyed,' said Harland. 'He's digging up the bodies.'

'Precisely. With the harsh weather in those mountains at this time of year, it's unlikely that anyone would countenance carrying out large-scale construction work. The cold wouldn't allow it. So that is the only conclusion to draw. Someone should get some photographs of what's happening on the ground. But they'll need to get there during daylight tomorrow. It won't take long for those people to dig up and distribute the remains around the hills and then it will be a very difficult task indeed to prove that anything happened at that place.'

'I take your point,' said Harland

'So, I leave it with you,' he said. 'Good hunting, Mr Harland. I'll send you yesterday's images. You'll need them to find the exact spot. Let me know what happens.' He hung up without saying goodbye.

Harland thought of going back to bed but then he began to look at the map. He could fly to Sarajevo, hire a car and be there by early afternoon. All he would need to buy was a camera – maybe a video recorder too.

It was just five o'clock so he made some tea and returned to Eva who was lying on her side, sound asleep. He sipped the tea while his eyes moved over her face.

Harland's ears pricked up. Someone was moving on their floor. He put the tea down, crept to the door and peered through. The figure stopped and looked at the open map. As he moved against the glow of London in the window, Harland recognised The Bird's profile. He called out softly so as not to wake Eva.

'Hello, old chap. Sorry to wake you so early.'

'You didn't. What's going on?'

'Only the entire security establishment frothing at the mouth, but don't let it worry you. I'm sure it's all in a day's work for you.'

'What *are* you talking about?'

'Radio stations across Europe are spewing out the code again – just one code this time, and the whole bloody lot is being blasted out at the rate of knots. Vigo is named – so too Brother Morsehead and Friend Lapthorne. Did you know they were tied up with Oleg Kochalyin from way back?'

Harland nodded. 'I guessed.'

'But you didn't know that innocent-looking little fucker Morsehead was on his payroll. Apparently Morsehead used to pay Kochalyin. Come the revolution, Kochalyin paid Morsehead. It's the end for him and his ambitions.'

'Who's been translating this stuff for you?'

'The man you met after the races. The first broadcast came on the dot of midnight. Cheltenham went haywire. He was called in to trace it. Bobby, they're sure it's coming from London. Though they haven't got the exact spot yet. I've told him to keep me posted.'

'And you came to check it wasn't us?'

'It did occur to me that you'd rigged up some system here while you were canoodling away with the Bohemian Temptress.'

'Well, it isn't me.'

'What about her?'

'I don't know. She's asleep. I can wake her if you're worried.'

'Leave her,' said The Bird, looking down at the map. 'What's this all about?'

Harland told him about Reeve's call and his decision to leave for Sarajevo that day.

'So you're still pursuing this thing?'

'Yes. In all the fuss everyone forgets that there's a fucking war criminal walking about doing exactly as he pleases.'

'Why don't you let it drop, Bobby? This man is pure poison. You know that better than anyone. You'll just get yourself killed if you go.'

'It's obvious, Cuth. Oleg Kochalyin has affected every part of my life. I want to see him nailed. I'm going to get pictures of that place if it's the last thing I do.'

'It will be,' said The Bird. He examined Harland again. 'Are you sure the transmissions aren't your work, Bobby?'

'Yes.'

'Then who the hell is responsible?'

There was a noise in the passage leading from the bedroom. Eva appeared, wrapped in a towel. She looked at them in turn.

'I know what you're talking about. The answer is Tomas. I gave him help, but he did most of it himself. I told you,

Bobby, he's very clever. It took incredible willpower to do what he has done in the last two days.'

'But how?' asked Harland. 'How could he possibly do it from his hospital bed?'

She sat down on the arm of the sofa. 'He had stored everything in an electronic archive. The only thing he needed was the virus – but the codes and everything were there, waiting to be used. He learned to use that machine and we worked from there.' She looked at her watch. 'There'll be another one soon. I believe he intends this to be his memorial.'

'I'll say,' said The Bird, missing the point. 'People aren't going to forget this in a long time. The only mercy is that Fleet Street's finest can't read it on the bloody Internet.'

Eva looked down at the map. 'Are you going there, Bobby?' she said.

'Yes, I've just had a call from Washington. The satellite pictures yesterday picked up some activity at the site.'

She was about to say something when the phone rang. The Bird answered and handed it to Harland. A duty sister from the hospital was on the line. Tomas had contracted a case of double pneumonia and was running a high temperature. She said they should get there as soon as possible.

The Bird drove them there in fifteen minutes flat and went inside with them because, as he pointed out, the danger from Kochalyin was now very great indeed. In Tomas's room they were made to wear surgical masks. There were two nurses, each watching different monitors, and a woman doctor standing by his head. As Harland passed the end of the bed he saw the initials 'DNR' – Do Not Resuscitate – written along the top of his medical notes.

Eva made room for herself and sat by his bed, one hand touching his head, the other holding his hand. The nurses kept throwing glances in Eva's direction, trying to gauge her reaction. The respirator groaned and clicked with its usual rhythm, but from Tomas there came a new noise, a rattle, almost a bubbling sound, from his chest, which the doctor said had been drained but was already refilling with liquid. Harland looked down at his son's wasted limbs and then at the little knot of concentration in his forehead.

'He's exhausted,' said the doctor. 'His reserves are very low indeed.' This was aimed at Eva – a warning that she should expect the worst. 'The infection took hold late last night. We gave him some powerful antibiotics. But he was obviously in great pain and we have relieved that with diamorphine. The problem is that his defences are down, plus his stomach is reacting badly to the antibiotics.'

Eva took no notice. Her eyes were fastened on the clear plastic mask over his mouth and nose. Harland touched her on the shoulder and said he was going out. He went to find The Bird, who had made himself comfortable by a coffee machine and was absorbed in a nursing journal. He looked up and smiled sympathetically.

'It's not good news, is it?'

'No,' said Harland leadenly, 'I'm afraid it isn't.'

'Terrible for you, old chap. I'm dreadfully sorry for you both.'

'Thank you,' said Harland, for no reason thinking back to the Embankment and the sudden shocking grief he'd experienced while waiting for the ambulances to arrive.

'Well, at least you won't be able to hare off to the bloody Balkans,' he said. 'No good can come of that.'

'Yes, but it means that the evidence that Griswald and Tomas wanted to make public will be destroyed. Their work – their sacrifice – will be wasted. That does matter, Cuth.'

The Bird considered this. 'Look at it this way. They both did a lot to expose the links between Kochalyin and our former colleagues. There's going to be a dreadful stink when this gets into the system.'

'Yes, I suppose so, but it doesn't do anything to get Kochalyin.'

'But what on earth can you do? Running off to some godforsaken mountainside in Bosnia with your Sureshot camera is not going to help.'

Harland didn't argue.

Half an hour later, Dr Smith-Canon appeared and said he wanted to speak to Harland and Eva. It wouldn't take long, but it was important.

They went into his office.

'I'm not going to beat around the bush with you both,' he said. 'The situation is very serious. We might just be able to save him but it's going to take everything we've got and even then we won't know how long he'll last.'

Eva nodded dully.

He waited. 'You do understand what I'm saying?'

She nodded again.

'We have your son's wishes on record. You believe those are still his wishes?'

Without speaking she turned to the door. Smith-Canon searched Harland's face for clarification. He nodded and followed Eva back to Tomas's room. She settled by Tomas's side again, and Harland stood behind her, holding her shoulder.

Tomas could feel very little. There was some small part of him that was making decisions and taking things in and communicating these things to the centre of his being. It was like a voice on a bad telephone line, becoming fainter. He knew that he was fading with it. What more was there to say? He was going and soon he would not be having these conversations with himself.

It wasn't like this the first time. He had no sense of the definite surroundings of the coma. There was no stairway, no damp walls, and no warm place at the bottom where he

425

could rest. But his mind was full of something – tiny firings of light and flickers of memory. They didn't added up to much and he was tired of them.

One more time. He would open his eyes one more time and see who was there. It was difficult but he managed it, and when he focused he saw that his mother was very close to him. She looked so distraught that he almost didn't recognise her. He saw Harland too, leaning forward into his field of vision. They were standing together – mother and father. That was good.

She spoke in Czech, which was a relief: he couldn't handle anything else. She was saying how much she loved him and she wanted him to fight and struggle and beat the illness so they could go home together. She said she knew he could do it. He smiled to himself. She used to say that when he was small – she knew he could do it. But this time he couldn't. He'd done his best and he was going to have a sleep.

He closed his eyes. Then there was noise in the room. Raised, angry voices. He felt the bed move. What was going on? He couldn't be bothered to find out. No, he was tired and he was going to have a sleep.

The commotion started in the corridor. Harland heard Smith-Canon and The Bird's voice rebuking someone. There were other voices. He didn't turn towards the door because he knew the moment was near. Tomas had opened his eyes and gazed at Eva with pinprick pupils, then shut them with a flutter. The monitor on the other side of the bed had been showing an increasingly irregular heart beat.

A few seconds later the noise spilled into the room. Harland whipped round to see Vigo still in his overcoat march towards the computer stand which had been pushed against the wall. Smith-Canon came in followed by two other men who he realised must be Special Branch officers.

'Do you hear me?' hissed Smith-Canon, snatching at

Vigo's sleeve. 'My patient is dying! You have no right to be here. You must leave now.'

Vigo's face was set with purpose.

'This won't take long. We just need the machine. That's all.'

Harland leapt up, pushing the bed away from him, and placed himself between Vigo and the computer.

'Get the hell out of my son's room, Walter.'

The other men forced their way past him and began unplugging the computer and detaching the electrodes which still dangled from the stand. Harland swung round to them.

'Have you no sense of what you're doing?' he demanded.

Harland glanced at the monitor beside Tomas, then at Smith-Canon who had moved forward and stood shaking his head by the bedside. Eva lifted Tomas's hand to her cheek, closed her eyes and silently fell forward on to his chest.

In that moment it occurred to Harland that Tomas had not left him, but had simply withdrawn to a distant level of existence. It seemed possible that a body which had been all but lifeless for the past few weeks might still harbour a trace of him and that he'd make himself known as miraculously as he had done before. As if he had read these thoughts, Smith-Canon leaned over and turned the respirator off. The noise of the machine subsided and the gentle rise of Tomas's rib cage stopped. Harland moved to Eva's side and touched her lightly on her back, then felt Tomas's arm. It was already cold. He had gone.

Vigo hesitated a few seconds longer, then nodded to the men who had picked up the computer and its leads.

'I take it you have some kind of authority to do that,' said The Bird with deceptive mildness from the door.

'The Official Secrets Act,' replied Vigo, and left.

30

FLIGHT

An hour passed during which a startlingly bright day broke outside and the sounds of the city going to work reached their ears.

The room itself was silent and heavy with Eva's grief. Harland stayed with her for about half an hour but guessed she'd want to be alone with Tomas. He slipped out to find Smith-Canon and thank him for all he had done. On the way back to the room, he was approached from behind by one of the two Special Branch officers who had been waiting a little way down the corridor. The officer, a young man with sunken cheeks and a blond moustache, informed him that he and Eva should consider themselves under arrest.

Harland looked at him with disbelief.

'If I were you,' he said, 'I'd make sure that I had that instruction from the very highest level, because one word from me, and the whole of this business goes to the press. Now fuck off.'

'We have our orders, sir.'

'Nevertheless,' said Harland fiercely, 'you tell them that any discussions we have will be on our own terms. And during that meeting Mrs Rath will be treated with the respect due someone who has just lost their only child.'

With that he turned and went back into the room. Eva looked up. Evidently she'd heard something of the exchange.

'Don't worry,' he said. 'They're not going to bother you.'

'What now?' she asked at length.

'We must make arrangements,' he said quietly, looking down at Tomas. 'I guess we take his body back to your country.'

'Yes,' she said, 'but what are you going to do?'

'I'm going to Bosnia to get pictures of the site. It's now or never. Everything will be gone by tomorrow.' He stopped. 'I feel I ought to stay with you but . . .'

She shook her head. 'No, Bobby, you should go.'

'I'll only be away a couple of days.' He looked into her face. Her eyes were bewildered and shocked.

Half an hour later they left the hospital with the Special Branch officers. Notions of arrest had apparently been suspended – at least temporarily. They were led through a maze of passages near Admiralty Arch at the top of The Mall and into a large room, surrounded with a dado of Victorian ceramic tiles and hung with paintings of naval battles. A band of sunlight fell from the window across the centre of the room and heated the floor polish, giving the air a faint odour of resin and leather and a sense that the room was left over from an era of gaslights and plumed helmets. An odd place for Vigo to choose, thought Harland.

He sat with three other men in a crescent beside a conference table covered with a blanket of green felt to protect its surface. Harland guessed that two of them were from MI5 and he assumed the third was either from the Foreign Office or was a colleague of Vigo's from MI6.

Vigo motioned them to two chairs and then pulled his own slightly nearer the table.

'We all know what we are here for,' he said, without looking up. 'We're here to establish exactly what other allegations are going to be made in these transmissions.'

Harland coughed. 'But surely you have everything you need in the computer that you seized in the hospital.'

'The computer had a number of concealed files that

destroyed themselves when they were opened.' His eyes had risen from a blank notepad and were levelled at Eva. 'Tomas had learned something since we last took his computer away from him. Or perhaps that was your work, Irina? He plainly could not have done all this without your help. We also fully understand that the additional information which has been released in the last nine hours must have come from you. So, it is our urgent purpose to learn what else is going to come out. The Government needs to respond to this mess.'

Eva shook her head. 'It was my son's work,' she said simply.

'You must have helped him in the hospital?'

'Why are you so hot under the collar, Walter?' said Harland, seeking to draw the fire. 'All the material has been used before.'

Vigo leaned forward so that his shoulders and chest merged into one uniformly grey bulk. 'I don't think either of you quite understands the gravity of your position.'

'Nor you yours,' Harland shot back.

One of the two men that Harland had pegged as MI5 sighed. He had been studying Harland closely, as if watching for adverse character traits in a psychometric test.

'I mean it,' Harland insisted. 'For once your systematic hypocrisy has been exposed – spying on allies, using a war criminal to transport arms while paying lip service to his arrest and prosecution. It's going to come out.'

'We understand you were threatening to give this to the press,' said the Foreign Office type.

'Yes, when one of your police officers said he was there to arrest us. But as you know, I have had no access to the transmissions. I still have only a vague idea of their exact nature. So I'm hardly in a position to publicise it, am I?'

'However, Irina, you are,' said Vigo. 'Did you make copies of what Tomas has been putting out?'

She shook her head.

Vigo looked sceptical and returned to Harland.

'But the fact that you were prepared to make the threat underlines our fears. Only yesterday we had your word that your report would be taken no further and that its circulation would be limited to those who already have it. You appear to have abandoned that undertaking.'

This was all said with moderation, but Harland had no illusions about Vigo's intention. He was making the case for his colleagues, pointing up Harland's unreliability, his hot-headedness.

'You forget,' he said in an equally measured tone, 'that I am a servant of the United Nations. I work for the Secretary-General. I cannot therefore be subject to the interest of one state above all others. Of course this affair is embarrassing for you, but the fact remains that a man who had been indicted by the War Crimes Tribunal for Former Yugoslavia was working for you and the Americans. As a permanent member of the Security Council, Britain signed the resolution to establish the tribunal and is legally obliged to support its work. The same goes for the US. But both countries have done the opposite. Whoever set up Kochalyin's assassination in Bosnia is no longer of any real interest. What is relevant, however, is that Kochalyin relied on you from the winter of '96, '97 onwards. I accept that you were not responsible for this, Walter, but that's too bad. You're carrying the can for the flexible morals of your friends.'

'You have no proof that he has been used by either us or the Americans,' Vigo stated.

'Perhaps no direct proof, but if the facts were laid out about the crash and the faked assassination, together with all the other material – the pictures and so forth – then I'm sure people would draw the right conclusions.'

Harland had realised a while back that what they were worried about was the potential alchemy between his report and Tomas's transmissions. If the coded material ever reached the public domain, it would be denied by all concerned as a work of fantasy. But a UN report, commissioned by Jaidi, which supported some of the allegations, would lend credibility to the rest.

Vigo's attention flicked back to Eva.

'Of course, this is not quite the issue of high principle that you claim it to be – is it?'

She didn't respond.

'Irina, we know your son was involved in the murder of those Muslims – he admits it in the coded material of last night and he has apparently given the same statement to Harland.'

'How do you know that?' asked Harland, alert to the possibility that his e-mails had been read.

'Because he included it at the end of the last transmission and said as much. Was this his last word?'

'Yes,' Eva said. 'He was taking responsibility for his actions before he died. But it was not his fault. They forced him to kill that man.'

'As indeed he makes plain in his little account of the incident,' said Vigo with indifference. 'Was it his way of signing off? I mean, was this how he planned to finish the entire transmission?'

She looked up and nodded slowly. 'Yes, there's nothing more.'

'Good,' said Vigo. 'Then we know what we're dealing with and can plan our response. As to the report, I take it that your assurance of yesterday still stands?'

Harland didn't answer because he was puzzled by the sudden fading of Vigo's concern.

'Let me remind you,' Vigo continued, 'that you agreed not to distribute it further and that you would not add to it. I hope you're clear that you will both feel the full force of the state if you go against your word. So do I have your assurance?'

Harland shrugged. 'If that means you will leave Eva and me alone, then yes.'

'Our business here this morning is therefore concluded,' said Vigo. 'You may now leave. We don't expect to be in touch again, unless we learn that you've broken your agreement.'

Harland knew perfectly well that their business was nowhere near concluded. For Vigo, closure would only be achieved when he and his report had been neutralised.

They left the room and after retracing their route back through the dismal corridors, they broke into the sunlight of The Mall. He put his arm round her shoulder.

'I think we should go and sort things out at the hospital.'

'Yes, then you will go to Bosnia. I'll come with you.'

'You want to?'

'Yes,' she said. She had understood what the meeting had been about all right.

Later, at Century House, they were met by The Bird who had piled some anoraks and boots by the entrance to the lift. He greeted them with a cavalier look dancing his eyes.

'You've missed the flight to Vienna which connects to Sarajevo this afternoon,' he said. 'There's no point going to Zagreb because there isn't a connection to Sarajevo until tomorrow. So I've made other arrangements. A charter firm we use is sending a plane to Athens tomorrow to pick up a party of shippers. They're happy to send the plane to Sarajevo *en route*. But there are three conditions: you pay for the landing charges and a tank of fuel, you give the driver a steaming great tip, and you take me along for the ride.' He searched their faces for a reaction. 'I know some people in Sarajevo.'

'When did you ever go to Sarajevo?'

'Never, but one meets people hither and thither. I gather it's crawling with chaps pretending to their wives they're reconstructing Bosnia when all they're doing is banging Balkan beauties.'

'I know the type.'

'You are the type,' said The Bird, looking down at the mound of clothes and boots. 'Okay? Right, let's shift this kit down to the car. We've got to be at Blackbush airport in under an hour. Oh, by the way, I've got a good digital camera so you don't have to bother with that.'

'How much is this all going to cost?' said Harland, when Eva went to get her things.

'No more than three thou' – we'll sort it out when the invoices come in.'

'Thanks for organising it – thanks for everything, Cuth.'

'Think nothing of it. I want to get this fucker as much as you do.' He paused. 'Terrible shame about your lad.'

'Yes.' Harland paused. 'Cuth, you understand that Vigo will have us followed to the airport and he will get the flight plan within a few minutes of us taking off. He'll know where we're going and it won't take him long to work out that you fixed this all up. Are you sure you want him on your back?'

'Fuck him. Too slippery by half is Brother Walter. I didn't like the way he descended on that hospital one bit.'

Harland collected a few clothes, a phone, his map and the computer he'd need in order to download the images from Norman Reeve. Ten minutes later, Cuth's Range Rover exited the underground car park and sped out of London towards Blackbush. A dark red Ford, a motorcycle and a blue Nissan tracked their progress but were left behind when they drove through the aerodrome gates. Well before anyone had time to prevent them from leaving, the Gulfstream had taken off.

Almost subconsciously Harland settled himself in the rearmost seat of the little jet opposite Eva.

If he hadn't been so concerned for her he would certainly have been thinking about the risks of travelling on another plane. Once they were airborne, he snapped off his seat belt and leaned forward to hold both of Eva's hands between his. She smiled weakly, but her eyes quickly turned away, down to the English countryside lit golden in the early-afternoon sun. He knew she didn't want to talk.

Harland closed his own eyes to think about the task ahead, but within a short time he had fallen asleep. He was awoken by a hand on his shoulder.

'We've got less than hour.' The Bird was looking down at him. 'We need a plan of attack.'

Harland glanced out of the window to see the Alps ahead of them. A feather of vapour was trembling on the Gulfstream's wingtip.

'What information about this place do you have?' asked The Bird. 'Should we try to get as near as we can tonight, or wait until tomorrow?'

Harland showed him the position on his map.

'That's got to be an hour or two hours' drive from Sarajevo. It'll be dark long before we get there. Have you got the latest pictures of the site?'

'Blast,' said Harland, rubbing his eyes. 'I meant to log on before I left and collect my e-mail. I forgot.'

'That's all right. There's a phone socket by your elbow. You can log on through the plane's communications system.'

Harland downloaded his mail.

There were three messages – two from Norman Reeve with attachments and a third from an address he didn't recognise. The first included the picture from the day before, which showed the vehicles as little more than specks on the hillside. Harland made out some rocks and a road that had been cleared to the position of the four vehicles. The second picture was greatly magnified and had obviously been taken later in the day. It showed two trucks, a digger and a long loader. In the middle of the photograph was a black scrape where the snow and rocks had been removed by the digger. Around it were the marks of caterpillar tracks.

The Bird peered down at the screen from over Harland's shoulder. 'Could be anything,' he said. 'They might be making a reservoir.'

'At this time of year? Besides it's near the top of the hill. You can see from the light and shade. Who makes a reservoir at the top of a hill where there's no catchment area?'

He closed the picture and pulled up the second e-mail. Reeve had written: 'This was taken at 11 GMT, noon local time. Hope you bring home the bacon, Mr Harland – NR.' He opened the attachment. The trucks had changed their position, but the digger and loader were in more or less the same spot. They had been joined by a fifth vehicle, a smaller green jeep or pick-up. Harland squinted at the screen so that he could see the dots which made up the picture. He was sure the shape of the scar on the mountainside had not grown. He wondered: are those tiny strokes of shadow people?

He turned the laptop round to Eva. 'We may be in time. Nothing seems to have happened today.'

She looked at it doubtfully. 'I wonder if he knows this can be seen,' she said quietly.

'Well, they're lucky to have got the shots,' said The Bird. 'They've been having a lot of snow. We'd better get ourselves a bloody good vehicle if we're going to get up there.'

Harland had been on the point of saying something, but the thought left him. 'Any ideas where we can get that?'

The Bird said he had, but it would take the evening. They talked on for a while until the pilot shouted through the open door that they were twenty-five minutes from landing at Sarajevo. The Bird sat down on the other side of the aisle and fiddled with his seat belt. Harland scrolled through his inbox and found the third e-mail which came from an AOL address that meant nothing to him. It took him a few moments to see that it was from Tomas because the message was only signed T after the heading, 'Crash solution'. He realised that it had been sent just a few hours before his death. It was probably the last act of his life.

He decided to say nothing to Eva and began to read. It was clear that the material had been copied from various websites because of the different formats and typefaces used. All the quotations concerned high-powered microwave weapons and a new, cheap variant called a Transient Electromagnetic Device, which produced a devastating spike of energy. Harland glanced over a diagram showing a tube wrapped in copper wire and packed with high explosive at one end. It seemed that the detonation of the explosive sent a shockwave down the tube, generating a pulse of electromagnetic energy in the coils of wire. This issued at great speed from the nozzle of the tube and tore through every electrical circuit in its path.

Harland immediately realised the implication. A portable version of this weapon must have been set up along the shoreline of the East River and fired at the Falcon jet as it rushed across the water to land. The electrical circuits in the plane would have been instantly fried, causing a catastrophic loss of control which in every way mimicked the effect of a wake-vortex.

Suddenly he understood the meaning of Ollins's questions. The failure of the lights on the Falcon was only significant in as much as Griswald had held up his computer to use the screen's light to see what he was doing. When the pulse of energy struck the plane, the protective cladding of the laptop shielded the computer's circuits and – crucially for Harland – the phone in Griswald's pocket.

His respect for Ollins had taken a quantum leap. It was damned smart of him to have worked it out. But it was even smarter, not to say heroic, of Tomas to spend his last hours, paralysed and choked with fluid, battling through the problem.

The pilot announced they were beginning their descent and would be landing in fifteen minutes.

'I can't believe it,' said Harland, overcome with emotion. 'This e-mail is from Tomas. He's found out why the plane crashed in New York. It's incredible. He did it from his bed and sent this last night. What's more, the FBI reached the same conclusion long before he did. They knew it was sabotage and they've kept it quiet.'

Eva and The Bird listened intently as he explained the theory in quick clear sentences.

'Why would the FBI have covered this up?' asked The Bird. 'What was in it for them?'

'Who knows? I suppose they might not want to publicise the potential of this weapon. It would scare the shit out of a hell of a lot of prospective passengers. But perhaps we're looking at a cover-up involving all the major intelligence agencies of the United States and Britain. God knows!'

'Are you saying the US helped bring down that plane?'

'Not necessarily. Maybe Frank Ollins got to the bottom of the investigation and someone told him to forget the whole thing and go along with another theory involving the wake from the jet that had just landed. I don't know who pulled the levers and I don't know their reasons for doing it. But it certainly seems like a cover-up.'

'It would need careful planning,' said Eva quickly. 'They would have to know the likely times of departure and arrival and the runway that was going to be used. A lot could change at the last moment.'

'Yes, that's true. But remember Kochalyin owns an aviation company. Hell, he's used it to transport arms all round the world. Taking one of these devices into the States wouldn't prove very difficult. More important is that the people who work for Corniche-HDS Aviation must know a

438

thing or two about listening into communications between a pilot and the control tower.

'Christ, I wish you'd saved this until later,' said The Bird. 'It's giving me the bloody jitters.'

This made Harland suddenly concentrate.

'What was that you said just now?' he demanded of Eva.

'What do you mean?'

'About the satellite pictures. You wondered whether Kochalyin knew he could be seen. What were you thinking?'

'It occurred to me that Oleg appreciates what can be photographed from a satellite. Everyone knows that the graves around Srebrenica were picked up by US satellites and spy planes. I remember seeing the pictures in the newspaper.'

'So what would be a better way of gaining our attention and luring us out here than digging up that grave?' asked Harland.

'It's a bit late to have that thought now,' said The Bird, shifting in his seat.

'And why hasn't there been any further digging today?' Harland persisted. 'Maybe he had done enough to gain our attention and ordered the work to stop.'

'But he would have to be sure that *you* knew about the excavation,' said Eva.

At that moment the pilot dimmed the cabin lights: the plane was on its final approach. They had banked sharp right and were coasting along the side of a mountain. Harland could see houses, each with one or two lights shining in the prolonged dusk of a snowy landscape. On the starboard side he glimpsed the city of Sarajevo sprawling in the bowl of the valley. He heard the whine from the landing gear being lowered.

He unbuckled and rushed forward to the cockpit. 'I can't explain this now,' he shouted at the back of the pilot's head, 'but it's just possible some kind of device will be fired at us

439

which will knock out all your electrical circuits. Can you land without them?'

The co-pilot turned round and shifted his headset. He plainly thought Harland mad.

'Can you land it without any electronics? Because that's what you may have to do.'

'Take a seat, sir,' said the pilot calmly. 'We're very close now.'

Harland looked ahead of them and saw the lights of the runway approaching.

'Two thousand feet,' said the co-pilot.

The radio sounded and the pilot moved the flaps down. Harland heard the engines throttling back.

'Fifteen hundred feet,' intoned the co-pilot. 'One thousand. We're fully configured for landing, sir. Please sit down while we pop her on the deck.'

Harland reeled back through the cabin, knowing that it was now too late for him to avert the disaster. He dropped into the seat beside Eva and fastened his belt.

And then the miracle happened. They touched down – so quietly that it took a few moments for Harland to realise they were on the ground. The jet skated past a checkered military control tower and began to slow down as it headed towards the end of the runway.

'Welcome to Sarajevo,' said the captain with pointed calm. 'The local time is ten minutes past five. It's a clear evening. The temperature is minus seven degrees centigrade, nineteen degrees Fahrenheit. Wind-chill factor is high. Wrap up warm and have an enjoyable stay. We're aiming for a fast turnaround to get on our way to Athens, so I'd be grateful if you could leave the aircraft quickly.'

From sheer nervous energy, Harland had already flipped off the seat belt, risen and put on his anorak.

'Bloody hell, Bobby,' said The Bird. 'I'll think twice before getting on a plane with you again.'

Harland felt slightly foolish.

'I'm sorry,' he said. 'I thought he'd planned the whole thing so he would take the plane out when we came in.'

The aircraft came to a halt at the end of the runway. Eva got up.

'There's a truck in our way,' said the captain. 'It's going to lead us into the terminal. We'll just be a few minutes so you may as well make yourselves comfortable.'

Eva bent down and peered out of the window between their seats on to the uninviting wasteland of the airfield. Suddenly she recoiled back into Harland who was also looking out.

'Down!' she cried.

Harland had seen the flare of orange a hundred yards away, out to their right. But he hadn't reacted as quickly as Eva and only when the rocket hit the tailplane on the starboard side did he understand what had happened.

The pilot was also quicker to grasp the situation. He increased the power in the engines and the plane lurched forwards, sending his three passengers hurtling backwards.

The plane surged over the edge of the concrete runway and began to head across the snow towards the terminal building. The engines were kicking up a storm of ice crystals that were being whipped forward by the wind in rhythmic billows.

Harland struggled to his feet and threw himself towards the cockpit.

'What the hell're you doing?' he shouted over the noise of the engines.

'Trying to get away from him. There's no one out here who's going to help us.'

Harland looked out of the side of the cockpit across the deserted airfield to the small terminal building. Nothing moved. Ahead of them was a truck, on the back of which stood two men. One jerked something to his shoulder. The

441

rocket fired and passed just to the left of the cockpit. The pilot whistled in relief. Harland instinctively ducked.

He felt a tug on his arm. He turned to see Eva, pulling at his jacket. The Bird had both hands on the lever of the port door and was preparing to jerk it upwards. Harland lunged to snatch his and Eva's bags and turned to see The Bird wrenching the door inwards and then pushing it against the cabin wall.

The deafening scream of the engines entered the cabin with a blast of cold air. The Bird gripped Eva, but she signalled for him to go first. He jumped and she followed. Harland dropped out of the door shortly afterwards and crashed to the ground in a kneeling position. In the blinking light coming from the plane's belly he saw The Bird helping Eva to her feet. The plane had gone about thirty feet from him. At that point a third rocket hit it on the starboard side of the fuselage. Before the explosion ripped through the fuel tank on the far wing, a lone figure dropped out of the door.

The plane continued for a fraction of a second longer, then seemed to pause before shuddering and collapsing away from them. At that the second fuel tank exploded with much greater force and blew the fuselage apart. Harland got up and ran to where the man had fallen and recognised the co-pilot. He was lying in the snow. He called out that he'd hurt his leg and wasn't sure if he could walk. Harland could already feel the intense heat of the flames through his clothing. He took hold of the man's shoulders and hefted him upwards so he could drag him across the snow. The Bird rushed over to help him. Together they carried the co-pilot to a concrete block where they laid him on the ground and propped his head against the concrete.

Harland bent down with his hands on his knees, heaving from the effort.

'Better you don't tell them we got out. Play dumb. Say you

don't know who else got out. It's very important. Can you do that?'

The man nodded groggily.

'It's just for twenty-four hours,' said Harland. 'Then you can get your memory back.' He straightened and turned to The Bird and Eva. 'Right, let's find a way out so we're not seen.'

They ran towards the perimeter fence, away from the jet and the truck. Two military fire tenders had emerged from the terminal area and were lumbering towards the plane. From the centre of the airfield came a pair of military vehicles, bumping over the ruts in the snow.

Harland reached the fence first and looked back. The truck had vanished into the dark of the airfield in the east. He indicated that they should make for the terminal which was about 300 yards away. They passed a padlocked fence, then a single-engine Cessna whose wings were tethered to the ground, and continued along the fence until they were fifty yards from the concrete apron in front of the terminal building. All hell had broken loose. Troops had disgorged from the building and were rushing to their vehicles, while what seemed to be the entire staff of the airport were milling about, watching the fire.

No one noticed Harland approach and look through one of the windows. The terminal was a rudimentary affair, in fact little more than a large warehouse with its guts on display. Heating and wiring ducts were in the process of being installed and the customs and immigration posts looked more like ticket booths. Neither was manned.

He turned and waved the others forward. They walked smartly through the door and past the immigration post and in no time at all found themselves in a deserted car park on the other side of the building. Because the last of the commercial flights had landed there were no cabs to be found. They stamped their feet in the cold and searched each other's faces.

'You're a member of the UN staff,' exclaimed The Bird, eyeing a row of white four-wheel drives, each emblazoned with a UN crest. 'And you are on an important mission for the Secretary-General.'

They moved quickly along the line of cars until they came to an Isuzu with its sidelights on and the keys still hanging from the steering column. The driver had obviously left in a hurry to see what was happening on the airfield. They got in without a second thought and drove sedately from the compound into a desolate, ill-lit boulevard flanked by burned-out buildings.

They found a hotel in a street named Kulovića in the old part of the city and parked the Isuzu in a covered area at the rear, tipping the attendant more than his month's salary to watch the car overnight. They checked into the hotel but avoided having to leave their passports at the desk when The Bird deftly palmed another large tip to the young manager.

Half an hour later they all went to a restaurant near to the hotel where they ate from a menu of home comforts aimed at Western aid workers. As they walked the few yards back to the hotel, The Bird abruptly announced he was going to see someone and strode off down the street, hands thrust into a dark green jacket, scenting the wind like a lurcher.

Strung out and exhausted, Harland and Eva went to their room, where Eva went straight to bed. Harland drew back the curtains and looked down on a confusion of dwellings and terraces and arrested construction. Ahead of him was a pockmarked minaret lit by a single arc light. He thought unsentimentally about the trajectory that had brought him to this strange, persecuted little city, and the two spies who had danced a distant quadrille down the years – Walter Vigo and Oleg Kochalyin.

He went through the steps in his mind. The first involved

his own ensnarement in Rome. But Kochalyin, the instigator if not quite the architect of this embarrassment – for that was all it was – had himself been lured by SIS to sell the secrets of the East. There followed the collapse of the Communist system. Kochalyin lured members of SIS into arrangements which began as convenient exchanges of information in a world which SIS was struggling to make sense of, and ended in the total corruption of at least one individual – Miles Morsehead. In response, Vigo had hired Eva to find out as much as she could about each new incarnation of Oleg Kochalyin.

At that point they were even, but then came Vigo's move against his colleagues, a superb piece of footwork which eliminated Kochalyin's allies in SIS and left Vigo the uncontested heir, the saviour of the service.

Harland knew, however, that any ideas of pattern in all this were simply false. Everything was temporary and fluid. The moment it suited Vigo and Kochalyin they would join hands in a fleeting partnership. They had done so before and there was nothing to stop them doing it again.

That brought him back to the question that had hovered over their little party at the restaurant. How had Kochalyin learned of their imminent arrival at Sarajevo airport? Had he lured them using the bait of satellite pictures, or was someone in London keeping him informed?

He turned from the window, gazed at Eva for a few chilly seconds, and slipped into bed beside her.

They slept in each other's arms. At some point during the night, a bell rang out in the city of victims. They stirred and made love, almost in their sleep.

31

A NAMELESS MOUNTAIN

Eva was in the shower and Harland already dressed when he heard a knock at the door. The Bird looked strained. The skin around his eyes was taut and his optimistic manner had vanished.

'We should leave soon,' he said quietly. 'Let's try and get out of the city by six-thirty.'

He was holding a tray with bread rolls and a jug of white coffee that he had spirited from the hotel kitchen with the night manager's aid.

'Come on in,' said Harland.

Outside there was a steady dripping from the gutters and the lights were haloed with moisture. A thaw was setting in.

Harland downed a cup of coffee in a few gulps and looked at The Bird.

'What's up?' he asked. 'Where'd you go last night?'

'To a bar the manager told me about. It's where the diplomatic people hang out in the Old Town. I found a chap there who does the security for the British residents. I had a feeling I'd bump into somebody. Macy and I have been trying to get this fellow to work for us.'

Again Harland wondered dimly about the exact nature of Harp-Avocet's business.

'What did you find out?' he asked.

'That the attack on our plane is the only thing anyone's talking about. All the men involved are dead and it goes

446

without saying that the pilot was killed. The good news is that we weren't seen at the airport.'

'That's something. What about the car?'

'No mention of it. I gather that vehicles are nicked here then sold back to the dear old UN bit by bit as spare parts. Premature recycling, they call it.'

'What's eating you, Cuth?' asked Harland, focusing on The Bird's manner again.

'The same thing as you, Bobby, the same thing as you. Who the fuck told them we were coming?'

'Maybe nobody did. Maybe it was a set-up from the start,' said Harland. 'Maybe the business out there in the mountains is all designed to draw us here so we can be finished off. Maybe it was fixed from the very moment Reeve sent me those satellite pictures. After all, he got them from the CIA – the Americans are just as compromised by this affair as our lot and just as hot under the collar. They don't want my report circulated any more than Vigo does because it will add weight to Tomas's allegations.' He paused and thought. 'The alternative theory is a phone tap at Century House. I'm pretty sure that Vigo has been kept up to speed with my calls and e-mails which means he knows exactly what Reeve has been sending me. He knows I've learned the exact location of the site, and it wouldn't take a genius to pass our intention, together with the time of departure, to a man that half SIS have been talking to for the last twenty years.'

The Bird's eyes narrowed. 'Vigo's a cunt, but is he that much of a cunt?'

'He's desperate. They all are.'

'Yes, but it would have been a lot cleaner if they'd let you get out to the mountains before bumping you off. I mean, what the hell was the point of that mess at the airport last night?'

Harland didn't answer and instead poured more coffee.

Eva emerged from the bathroom, still drying her hair.

'It's simple,' she said, without looking up. 'We know that Oleg wants us dead and we know that would suit the British SIS. They both have equal motive. Therefore it's possible they are both trying to kill us – separately or together.'

'So the rocket attack was organised by Vigo?' said Harland. 'Is that what you're saying?'

'And made it appear like some kind of terrorist incident,' said The Bird.

'It's possible,' she said.

Harland thought again.

'Look, we'll work on the assumption of maximum jeopardy, which means that we take it for granted that both parties want us out of the way. In those circumstances it's sensible that only one of us goes – me. I will take pictures and if necessary bring back bones and then we'll get the site officially excavated – or at least guarded until they can get a team there.'

The Bird shook his head.

'Very noble, Bobby, but it's not on. Leave Eva if you want, but I'm coming. Besides, I've already fixed up a sort of driver-cum-guide. He only goes if I go.' He produced the keys of the Isuzu from his pocket and waved them in front of Harland to underline the strength of his position.

'We will all go,' said Eva.

Ibro stood waiting for them in the lobby, chatting to the night manager. His proportions revised the known limits of the human body. He was short – no more than 5' 2" – with a torso of near unimaginable breadth and strength. Harland saw that he had no neck to speak of and that he was compelled to hold his arms out at forty-five degrees because of the size of his chest muscles and biceps. His head poked out from the upturned collar of an old US airman's jacket. He smiled as they arrived in the lobby and wiped crumbs of pastry from a black chin.

'This is Ibro,' said The Bird, as though they were old friends. 'He speaks a little English and a lot of German.' They all shook hands. 'You are meeting quite a legend – one of the heroes of the siege of Sarajevo. He tells me he used to re-aim cannons by lifting their tow bars. Then he became the prime minister's personal bodyguard and now he's the hotel driver.'

They set out at six-twenty and travelled eastwards along the Miljacka River. Ibro pointed out sites on the way – the shelled-out National Library and a cemetery on the hill where some comrades were buried.

'*Weil Ich war,*' he recited, '*wie ihr wart und ihr werdet sein, wie ich.*'

'Come again,' said The Bird, trying to disentangle the German words from a thick Balkan accent.

'For I have been what you are now, and you will be what I am now,' said Eva. 'It's an inscription from a gravestone – a message from the dead to the living.'

'*Memento mori,*' murmured Harland.

Climbing out of the city, they passed a line of civil-war trenches, then a truck halt called Café Dayton, at which point they plunged into a tunnel that led them to the Republika Srpska – the Serb part of Bosnia. Dawn was breaking in the east. They were now moving through a softer, more rural landscape with well-tended smallholdings. The houses and barns along the way were no longer burned out. Nothing stirred.

They skirted the unremarkable town of Pale, the Bosnian Serb capital where the mass executions of 1995 were planned, and headed for the barren regions in the east. The road surface was broken and streaming with rivulets of snow melt. At a place called Rogatica they swung north, into the mountains. Harland began to feel they were getting near and once or twice he thought he glimpsed the range from the video still. They stopped the car in a wild, lonely place overlooking a valley and examined the map and satellite images again. Harland estimated they were five kilometres from the place where a road branched left and would take them to the site.

'What do we know about this place?' said The Bird.

'Not much. There's a small gorge at the top, which was the actual place of the massacre. A track leads past it and down the other side of the mountain. It's large enough to take trucks and a sizeable loader.' For a moment there was silence while The Bird pored over the map with Ibro, who at length gave his opinion that the road had been built as a short cut and that it would descend near a settlement on the other side of the mountain.

They continued on their way in silence until they reached a wooded area where they began to see clods of soil on the tarmac. Here and there they noticed evidence of the mud stuck to the snow banks either side of the road. Eva asked Ibro what the weather had been like over the last two days. He replied that temperatures had not risen above freezing for the past thirty-six hours.

Harland knew what she was thinking. The heavy frost explained why there was no change in the satellite pictures. They hadn't been able to work the ground.

They rounded a bend and came to the track exactly at the moment Harland expected. It was obvious from the marks on the road that the trucks had descended from the mountain, bringing the mixture of snow and soil with them. Ibro stopped, peered upwards and shook his head. The track was churned up and there were wheel ruts which would be too deep for the light Isuzu. They agreed to split up. Harland and Eva would climb the track, while The Bird and Ibro would drive round the mountain and look for another way up. If they failed to meet at the top they would rendezvous at this place in two hours' time.

As Harland opened his door, The Bird jumped out of the front seat and came round to meet him. He handed him a camera and then from his jacket pocket produced a Glock pistol which he placed firmly in Harland's hand. He gave a black CZ75 to Eva, remarking that it was appropriately a Czech-made weapon. It seemed Ibro came with a small arsenal of handguns.

They set off up the track, all the while seeking signs that trucks had passed that morning. They guessed not, since it was only just past eight-fifteen. Gradually the surface became firmer and they were able to make good progress. The mountain range in the distance came into view and they could see the track snake up the incline then skirt left of a rounded summit. They walked on. The landscape was very still. The only noise came from a pair of large ravens cavorting lazily in the updraft from the valley.

At the top there was a longer hike than they'd expected. They paused for breath and looked out across the grey and white mountain scenery. Eva touched him on the face with the back of a gloved hand and they continued on their way. Fifteen minutes on, the track climbed sharply for about fifty yards then took a sudden turning to the left by a large protrusion of rock. They found themselves on a plateau bordered by two walls of rock that rose twenty feet above them. The place looked like an old quarry and it had the acoustics of a natural auditorium. Every sound they made reverberated around them.

Their eyes traversed the scene. In front was a turning place where a battered truck stood, leaking oil on to the snow. It was obvious its wheels had become locked in the freezing slush. Beyond this was a large digger with its arm resting on the ground. A lot of tracks were visible in the snow, but no other sign of the vehicles shown in the aerial photographs. To their left the land shelved gently to form a depression, at the head of which was an opening in the earth. From this fanned caterpillar tracks of the digger.

Harland scanned the treeless slope to their right and

wondered about the squat shepherd's hut that hugged an outcrop of rock about two hundred yards up. He saw that the track led across the plateau and plunged down on the north side of the mountain. Here the snow was untouched by vehicles.

Eva muttered something about the place having a bad air. Harland didn't reply. He was listening intently to the mountains and he wanted to make utterly sure they weren't being observed. His eyes swept the whole scene again, taking in possible hiding places and routes of escape.

Eva inhaled. Visibly steeling herself, she went forward to the excavated area.

She bent down, grasped hold of something and heaved backwards. He went to help her and saw that large conifer boughs had been laid across the opening in the ground. They worked together to pull them away without getting down into the pit or letting their eyes stray to the earth. Soon they could no longer avoid it. The sun had surfaced in the east and threw a cold light into the pit.

What they saw was unmistakable. Eva drew back a few feet and looked down. Many remains were down there but only in a few cases was the natural configuration of a skeleton intact. The digger had worked against the general orientation of the bodies. The teeth on the end of the bucket had clawed across them laterally, mixing up the bones and leaving sets of long striations across the ground. Harland counted the remains of about twenty people, but realised that the grave was much deeper than he had originally thought. Bodies had been piled on top of each other. When the massacre was over they had filled the hole with rubble and junk with the result that before reaching the bodies, the excavator had had to remove a layer that included chunks of road tarmac, a car door, old tyres, a fridge and a buckled bed frame.

He got out his camera and began taking pictures, half his mind knowing that the camera would act as a barrier between him and the horror. He aimed the camera at the digger and the truck, taking care to include the registration plates. He stopped. Eva had sunk to her knees at the grave's edge. Her face wore an expression of measureless pity. He moved to her side and saw what she was looking at. At the side of the pit was the skeleton of a child – a small boy, judging by the shorts and faded red T-shirt still visible. His hands were tied behind his back with wire. His skull was averted to the left, the mouth open. A little distance away was the complete skeleton of a man.

'Was that his father?' she asked simply.

Harland took two more pictures but he was no longer able to distance himself from the scene. His eyes welled with tears of outrage and horror. He thought of the heat of that day, the certainty in each man and child's mind that the soldiers were going to do this monstrous thing. He thought of Tomas and the stumbling, tearful old man who was tricked into believing he was going to be saved. The casualness and cruelty of the act struck him as though he were witnessing it at that very moment. He thought of the jeering soldiers and wondered how they might remember that day and whether it haunted them as it had Tomas.

He was determined that nothing should be lost. He walked around the grave, shooting from every angle, climbed into the bucket of the digger and focused on some bone residues. He took pictures of the far wall of rock where the men had been executed and the bullets had chipped at the surface, of the shell casings that had been exposed by the movement of the digger and glinted on the ground. He made studies of how the wrists of the victims were bound with fence wire, of the crumpled shoes, of a green and red checked shirt and a belt buckle, which might subsequently be used to identify the victims. Then he walked over to the truck and let down the tailgate, to be confronted by half a skull lying on a mass of earth and bone fragments. He photographed this from close up, from above and from a distance.

He dropped down to Eva, overpowered by a sense of shame – shame for Tomas, shame for himself, shame for all men. It was by far the worst thing he had ever seen. Eva looked at him and shook her head slowly. After a little while he said they ought to be going because it wouldn't be long before the men would arrive to finish the job. He needed to get back to Sarajevo with the pictures before all trace of the massacre had vanished.

She turned her face to him again. An act of commemoration was needed, she said. They must do something to recognise Tomas's part in what had happened there. She did not use the words massacre or slaughter or war crime. What they were looking at didn't have a word, but they both knew that it was the result of an incomprehensible hatred, just as evident in the treatment of the remains. Eva muttered that the people in the grave were no less loved now than they had been on the day they were killed. Harland hadn't thought about it like that, and he realised how much she was feeling the loss of Tomas. He shook his head, not knowing whether it should be an act of commemoration or atonement.

At that moment they heard a loud report from the northern side of the mountain, not a gunshot but an explosion which sent two ravens wheeling into the air below them. They ran over to look down and saw the Isuzu on its side in flames about four hundred yards from them. The Bird and Ibro were nowhere to be seen. Harland took a few strides in the snow and then stopped, realising the car must have hit a mine. The road had been mined to protect the site from the curious but there wasn't time to communicate this thought to Eva. He turned to see her gesturing up the hill to several figures who had issued from the stone hut and were now moving with difficulty through the snow down to the car.

Harland and Eva bent down and withdrew to the digger.

Harland guessed the men had been sent to watch the site until the weather changed and work could begin again. They must have overslept or got bored – at any rate they hadn't thought to look down to the plateau.

From where he stood he couldn't see the car, but a little later the men, some of them dressed in old combat fatigues, reappeared, hauling Ibro along a bank of snow above the road. Their voices carried up the slope and it became obvious that they were moving directly towards them. Half of him wanted to run back down the way they'd come. But he couldn't leave Ibro and The Bird. Without saying anything, they slipped back along the wall of rock, at the end of which they found a good hiding place in a crevice, behind some pine saplings. But it wouldn't take two. He pushed Eva down and told her not to move, then scuttled around the top of the pit and down the other line of rock. He groped his way down to a point where the outcrop fell away into a void. He grasped hold of a narrow tree trunk and used it to swing round into a gap between two slabs. Below him was a drop of thirty feet.

Harland heard the voices come closer. A young man in a ski hat and leggings appeared and immediately noticed that the branches had been removed from the pit. He jogged to the edge, peered down and then shouted to the others. Two more came and finally a fourth man, dragging Ibro by the collar of his jacket. Harland saw he was cut on his head and bleeding from his right leg. He was prodded to the top of the pit and forced to kneel with his hands behind his head, whereupon they began questioning him. Much of it was abuse, but after a bit Harland recognised one or two of the words because of their similarity in Russian. He understood they were asking him who else had been in the car. Ibro looked up at his interrogators with silent contempt, for which he received several kicks and blows. At length they

455

tipped him into the pit and told him to lie face down by a mangled skeleton. That gave them great amusement.

Harland waited with his face hugging the cold surface of the rock. If he moved a little he could just see where he'd left Eva. He prayed she wouldn't do anything rash or betray her presence.

Suddenly the young man in the ski hat aimed his automatic weapon into the air and fired off a burst. Harland turned to see one of the pair of ravens crumple in mid-flight and fall to the ground. This seemed to upset two of his companions and they shouted and jabbed at him with their guns. A row ensued, but died as quickly as it had flared. It occurred to him that these men must have been in the paramilitary squad that had taken part in the massacre. They were being used to oversee the work because they could be relied upon to keep quiet. It was their crime as much as Kochalyin's.

He became aware of the sound of a truck, grinding and labouring up the final stages of the track. A few seconds later it came into view, throwing up a jet of mud from its back wheels. It pulled up and another man in fatigues got out. The new arrival sauntered over to the pit to inspect Ibro and hurl a few insults his way. The others called him back. Cigarettes and a bottle of liquor were handed around and they fell to laughing and needling each other. It was the familiar, easy companionship of any group of men out on a job.

One of the five moved up to a flat piece of ground above the main plateau and pulled out a cellphone. He was obviously having difficulty getting a good signal and he paced around trying to find the best spot. Once or twice Harland thought he might be in danger of being spotted, but the man was too absorbed to notice him. After about ten minutes he shouted to the others and slid down the bank to rejoin them.

Harland was extremely cold. The muscles that had been torn in the top of his thigh after the air crash at La Guardia were playing up again. He rubbed his leg, clenched and unclenched his hands and worked his toes inside his boots. Then he looked at his gun, slipped the safety catch down towards the double action trigger and tried to estimate the number of rounds in the clip. He stared at the blotches of pale blue lichen on the rocks and padded the cleft in front of him with damp leaves so that he could look through without chafing his face. Occasionally he glanced over to where Eva was, but saw no movement.

He was now certain that The Bird must have been killed in the explosion, which meant their only option was to sit tight and wait until the men had finished their work that evening. Why the hell didn't they get on with it? What were they waiting for, these cowherds and mountain men?

Another fifteen minutes passed. Harland pricked up his ears. He thought he'd picked up a faint throbbing in the air. Yes, it was the beat of a helicopter coming in from the north. He searched the sky and saw a Sikorsky rise above the wall of rock where Eva was hidden and curl up to the plateau. For a moment it hovered directly above him and he feared he would be spotted. He glanced over at Eva and saw a hand grasp a sapling to prevent it from being blown over in the downdraft. A leg of tan corduroy, however, was exposed for a few seconds. He raised the Glock and darted a look towards the trucks. The Serbs were shielding their eyes from the whirlwind of snow and grit. Thank God. They hadn't noticed her.

The helicopter swung into the wind, and landed with its pointed snout slightly raised at the place where one of the men had used his phone. He remembered the rosette-shaped swirl in that exact same spot on the satellite picture. The helicopter had visited this place before.

In the corner of his eye he saw a movement. Ibro was using the distraction of the helicopter to haul himself down the pit on his belly. His shoulders were doing all the work;

his right leg made no movement at all. The young man who had first noticed the disturbance of the branches caught sight of him and whipped round to spray the ground ahead of him with a well-aimed burst of automatic fire. The ricochets zinged into the rocks around Harland. Ibro's head slumped down. His arms remained crooked in a push-up position. Harland was pretty sure he hadn't been hit.

The helicopter's rotor slowed with a whine and the blades began to droop towards the ground. Eventually the engine was shut down and the cabin doors opened. A smell of aviation fuel reached his nostrils. He didn't dare to look up because he thought any movement would be seen from the helicopter. So he just held on, his right cheek pressed to the rock, watching the clouds out of his left eye and trying to ignore the insistent nagging of a bladder that had not been emptied since Sarajevo.

Harland picked up the murmur of respectful greetings. He lifted his head a fraction and saw that three men had got out of the helicopter, while the pilot remained at the controls. They had moved down the bank to the plateau and been led to the far side where they stood, looking down the side of the mountain. He could not see their faces but it was plain that an explanation was being given by the man who had made the telephone calls. He seemed anxious to please and there was much gesturing in the direction of the Isuzu.

Harland worked his head between the crack and looked out. The group had moved in his direction and spread out to reveal a figure standing squarely by the grave's edge. He wore a dark grey overcoat and a black cap with ear flaps. His gloved hands were clasped in front of him as he contemplated the prone figure of Ibro.

Oleg Kochalyin was shorter than Harland had imagined, but he possessed a palpable presence. To Harland, now lying in excruciating discomfort, he completed the dismal fear of the old quarry, a fear that penetrated his being and made him weak and nauseous. He moved his eye from the crack and for a few seconds consciously stilled his panic. Then he glanced up and saw that the darkened sky, which he had somehow attributed to Kochalyin's arrival, was in fact caused by a bank of low cloud that had snuffed out the sun and shrouded in mist the summit of the mountain.

He looked back at the group. Kochalyin had not moved and, as far as he could tell, had said nothing. He just stood taking everything in, his eyes flicking about him. He pointed to the branches pulled from the grave by Harland and Eva and asked something in Russian. The men did their best to follow what he was saying, then struggled to explain their failure to find out who had moved the branches. They looked at each other and fell silent. Suddenly, from above them, there was a noise which seemed to roll down the hill. It was a loud phut rather than a bang, followed by a more impressive rumble. Something had blown up inside the hut. The men shouted. He speculated that one of them had left the cooking gas on when they rushed to investigate the landmine explosion. At any rate, a fire had taken hold quickly and smoke was streaming from the door and one tiny window. Three of the men set off to rescue their possessions, paying no heed to the voices that ordered them to stay. Ultimately, thought Harland, these mountain men did exactly what they pleased.

He watched for a few seconds longer, wondering if the explosion could possibly have been contrived by The Bird. But there was no sign of anyone up there and he returned to peer through the crack in the rocks. Now something was happening. He shifted his head in the crack and saw two men drop into the grave and seize Ibro by his arms. They dragged him to the top of the grave where he was questioned again, this time by Kochalyin. Each time he refused to answer he was struck in the kidneys or stomach with a rifle butt, blows which would have felled and crippled a weaker man. Harland

459

couldn't watch. The pain was too familiar to him. Several times he was on the point of leaping up and firing off as many rounds as he could, but that would do nothing to save Ibro and would almost certainly jeopardise Eva.

He lay there feeling wretched and powerless, as if the blows were raining on him. And then a strange thing happened with his bladder. Some deep physiological memory stirred in him and he was beginning to piss, just as he had when Kochalyin, having kept him in some agonising position for hours, began to really hurt him. He flattened his back to the rock, withdrew his penis and let himself go. When it was over he shuddered, zipped himself up and looked through the crack. It was okay: they hadn't seen.

He felt better now, more capable of thinking about what to do. Kochalyin made a swift movement with his hand and now Ibro was being dragged to the side of the pit. He cried out as one of them kicked his injured leg. Harland thought he was being taken to the digger. He had to see what was going on. He flashed his head up and took one mental snapshot of the scene. Ibro was being bound by a chain so that his arms were pinioned to his side. They were knotting the chain and looping it around his neck. Harland knew what would follow. The digger's engine coughed and a plume of exhaust showed in the sky. He darted another look and saw that the chain had been attached to the bucket. The arm was rising. There was a clank as the bucket righted itself in the air and took up the slack in the chain. They were going to hang Ibro if he didn't answer their questions.

This he would not stand for. He slipped the camera from the jacket pocket and aimed it over the rocks, silently shooting off three frames. He checked the images on the camera's screen. Kochalyin was clearly visible in all three – as were the date and time. Then he put the camera in his glove and wedged the package in the rocks. Some day soon someone would find it and think to look in the camera's memory. It was a slight chance perhaps, but his report was out there, complete with accurate coordinates. If he disappeared, someone would come looking here, he was sure.

He drew his gun, rose to a kneeling position and aimed. The only face turned in his direction was Ibro's. So he scrambled over the rocks and began walking, holding the gun out in front of him at Kochalyin's back. What was going through his mind were the words of the instructor at the Fort – aim low and let the evil bastard inside you do the rest. He was perfectly calm and utterly focused on killing Kochalyin. He knew he would be killed too, but that now meant little to him as long as Kochalyin went as well. He glanced up at the helicopter, expecting to see the pilot, but there was no one sitting in the cockpit. Still no one turned round. And that, he realised, was because the digger's engine was revving and the hydraulics along the shaft of the arm were squealing for lack of grease. Besides this, the men were engrossed in what was happening to Ibro. The bucket lifted with a jerk, the chain strained and then pulled Ibro into the air. Harland saw his face going puce. He reached the end of the pit and was forty feet from the digger when he stopped, placed the gun on his left arm, and aimed. Only then did he see Eva walking towards them from the rock. She was calling out in Russian.

'Enough, Oleg! Enough!'

Her appearance seemed to surprise the men. They shifted and looked embarrassed. They didn't raise their guns to her because she walked to them with her hands empty. Kochalyin turned to face her. He nodded to the man operating the digger. The arm dropped and Ibro crumpled to the ground, gasping for breath. Eva bent down and loosened the chain around his neck. No one moved to stop her.

'Enough of this,' she said, straightening up. 'This killing, this torture – this shame.'

Then one or two of the men caught sight of Harland and levelled their weapons at him. Kochalyin turned and took

461

him in with an unsurprised nod. But that was not what froze Harland's blood. It was the face of the man standing next to Kochalyin. The obliging features of Macy Harp had also turned to gaze at him.

Kochalyin saw his expression and smiled.

'Not everything is as it seems, Mr Harland,' he said.

Harland couldn't take it in. Macy! Macy Harp, who'd rescued him with The Bird from the villa in Prague – from Kochalyin's clutches. Macy, the busy little fixer with the plausible, county manner. What the hell was he doing with Kochalyin? He struggled to make sense of it. Christ, he thought, was The Bird in on this too? Had they been working for Kochalyin all along?

Kochalyin was speaking again, very quietly so that Harland had to move a few paces forward to hear. Now every weapon was levelled at his head. He kept his aim, but he couldn't fire without hitting Eva and Kochalyin knew that.

'This man is the true killer of Tomas,' Kochalyin was saying. 'Tomas was like my own son, Irina. You knew that. I paid for his treatment. Whatever our disagreements, I couldn't have him killed. Harland was the only one who knew where he was. Ask yourself, Irina, is it more likely that I was working with them to kill Tomas, or that Harland was? He is still their spy. He led them to Tomas because he was the only person who could.'

Harland could hardly believe what he was hearing. He spat out a denial. Kochalyin took no notice.

'I was trying to find him,' he continued, 'but Harland got there first. He set up the hit by the river. If you don't believe me, ask this gentleman here. His name is Mr Harp. He knows the truth because he worked with Harland. He knows what sort of man he is.'

Macy produced an accommodating smile.

'I'm afraid it is true,' he said in English. 'Mr Harland was employed to hunt down Tomas and then Mr Kochalyin here. He is here to kill your ex-husband.'

As this was being said, Kochalyin moved a few feet towards Harland.

'This man has some crazy ideas in his head. He says I tortured him back in Prague. It is a condition he has – a mental condition. But even if you ask him now, he will tell you that he has never seen me before. And if you ask Mr Harp, who rescued him with his associate, Mr Avocet, he will tell you also that he did not see me there.' Macy obliged with a nod. 'Why would I want to torture this man, anyway? You maybe did not know that I was working for British Intelligence?' He paused. 'Yes, I, Oleg Kochalyin, worked for the overthrow of that corrupt Communist system. I saw what was going on around us. Everyone did. These were dangerous times, Irina. Naturally, I could not speak of what I was doing, but ask yourself – why would I celebrate the end of those bad days by torturing him? Why would I do that? It doesn't make sense at all.'

Kochalyin had adopted the rhetorical style he'd used on Harland, the probing interlocutor before administering the electrodes. Harland noticed his appearance with detached interest – a waxy skin, dyed eyebrows, an exceptionally cruel nose, a yellowish sickly colour to the whites of his eyes and pupils that yielded nothing. He noted the expensive but poor taste of his clothes and the flash of gold between his glove and the sleeve of his overcoat, the watch that he had first seen in the video still. Kochalyin was the picture of small-time crookedness, nothing more impressive than that. But what raised him above average evil was his sense of command.

He glanced at Eva and saw a flicker of doubt in her eyes. And then, as if to match Kochalyin's surreal challenge to the truth, the mist rolled down the mountain and in a very short time smothered the old quarry, isolating them from the rest of the world. The helicopter, the trucks and even the pit were

463

blotted out. Harland noticed Macy looking around, and the man who was clearly Kochalyin's bodyguard shifted a little and glanced up at the mountain.

'You surely don't believe this, Eva?' Harland demanded. 'This is a pack of lies. You know it is.'

Kochalyin smiled.

'You call her Eva when her name is Irina? See how crazy this man has become. Look at him. He is shaking.'

It was true. He was trembling, but that was because he had lain in the cold for so long.

Eva turned to Kochalyin with a look of interest.

'Then, Oleg, why are you here? Why were you going to kill this man?'

'Oh, this man is nothing. We knew Harland was here and we wanted to find out who else was in the car. I have to protect myself, you know. Anyway, he would not have been killed.'

If she believes that, thought Harland, she's lost her mind.

'But why are you here, Oleg? If you are as innocent as you say, why have you come here?'

'To protect the reputation of the boy I loved. I admit I have paid these men to destroy the evidence. They were all here that day and they got carried away. They're crude folk, as you can see, and Tomas was caught up with the excitement. There was nothing I could do. I wasn't even here when they started killing these people. It was a bad business, for sure, but Tomas was not responsible for his actions and I did not want his memory to be tainted by this.' He gestured to the grave. Then he turned towards Ibro. 'I have no intention of killing him, although he came here to kill me. They found many weapons in the car.'

'And the attack on the aircraft last night – did you do that?'

He shook his head convincingly.

'Of course not. It must have been your friends in British

464

Intelligence, Irina. They are your friends. Yes, I knew about your work for them. It hurt me at first that you would do such a thing to me. But then I let it go because I realised that we were all born to treachery. All of us at some stage have been Mr Walter Vigo's friend.' He smiled magnanimously at her and then winked at Macy, who returned a rueful look.

'You aren't going to believe this crap?' said Harland. 'He's not here clearing up some youthful indiscretion of Tomas's. He's been forced to dig up these bodies because the world knows about the slaughter that took place here. He will do anything to hide his actions. He sabotaged the UN plane. He had Tomas's girlfriend tortured and killed. His men murdered Zikmund Myslbek. There's nothing he won't do to hide the proof.'

'See what I mean, Irina,' said Kochalyin with a dismissive sweep of his hand. 'He has lost his mind. He believes that everything that is wrong with the world is the fault of Oleg Kochalyin. Does that seem likely? I do not have to listen to this. I could have him killed this very second, but I let him continue because I want you to see the man for what he really is. He is the murderer of your son. Tell him to put that gun away before someone gets hurt.'

Eva walked to Harland and put her hand out. As she did so, Harland thought he saw her light brown eyes pulse with a secret intent. She stood in front of him for a few seconds, shaking her head. He wondered furiously what she was going to do. Then Macy Harp, who was nearest to them, stepped forward and with both hands pushed the Glock upwards and wrested it from Harland's grip. He moved away, casually inspecting the weapon.

'Good,' said Kochalyin, his eyes playing over the scene with a deadly satisfaction. 'So it must be for you to decide what should be done with this man, the killer of your son.'

Now Harland understood why Kochalyin had been making his grotesque argument. He wanted to watch Eva kill him. That would be the ultimate revenge against their love – the payback for Eva's betrayal. He felt the resignation and blankness settle in him, as it had in the East River when he thought he was going to die. Although he'd seen that look in her eye, he didn't trust it. The bond she had with Kochalyin could not be doubted – it was evident in her every gesture. As that was the case, he really didn't mind dying. Now his life seemed nothing more than a series of calamitous misjudgements. Hell, he hadn't even seen Macy for what he was.

Eva seemed to have reached a decision. Kochalyin looked at her expectantly. She glanced round the group of men, then moved over to the young man with the automatic weapon. Kochalyin nodded to him. Somewhat reluctantly, he slipped the strap from his shoulder and showed Eva the safety catch. Harland didn't understand. He knew very well that she had her own gun.

Then she made her way back to Harland, motioning to the two men who had moved either side of him, to take him to the pit. The mesmerising look was still in her eyes, but now Harland was convinced that all it held was hatred.

'Don't you see, Eva?' he pleaded in English. 'He wants you to kill me. Then he will tell you he made the whole lot up and have you killed too. It's his revenge for you loving me – the final rape of your life by this man.' His voice had grown dull.

One of the men cuffed his ear with the barrel, then each of them took hold of his arms and frogmarched him to the edge of the pit. At the edge Harland stumbled and fell into the unspeakable grime. He pushed himself up and wiped the filth from his face. Except for Macy, who had somehow indicated his distaste for the execution and had withdrawn, the group of men moved as one nearer to the pit, Kochalyin and his bodyguard at the centre. Kochalyin nodded.

Harland looked up at Eva as she aimed the weapon at him.

'You were wrong, Bobby,' she said. 'I never loved you. I only ever loved one man.'

'Don't do this,' he said. 'For yourself – do not do this.' His voice trailed off and he looked up into the mist, certain that he was about to die. He glimpsed something in the periphery of his vision, an indistinct shape darting in the mist between the trucks. He turned to look at Eva. He blinked once.

There was a shout, followed by a prolonged burst of automatic gunfire that raked the ground around the men. In that moment Harland's mind registered Macy Harp diving to the snow with his gun and Eva whipping round to open fire on the men above her.

Harland was so stupefied by the sudden turn of events that he simply stood gaping at The Bird, who had emerged from the shelter of the trucks and was now advancing steadily, sweeping the area in front of him with his machine gun. Some of the men had turned to face him, but they were now being fired on from three directions and not one managed to raise his weapon. In rapid succession each crumpled and fell.

Harland blinked again. It was over.

Kochalyin had dropped to his knees at the grave's edge, right in front of him. His face did not betray the puzzlement which is said to fill the expressions of those who have been shot, but Harland did see a final look of anger in his lifeless eyes.

And that was all he noticed for several minutes. His breath, emotion and thought simply seemed to have vacated his body. When eventually he found his voice, he stammered, 'What the . . . what the hell was Macy doing with Kochalyin? Why was he on the helicopter for Christ's sake?

The Bird glanced over to Macy and Eva, who had gone to help Ibro.

'Our Macy's a shifty little fucker,' he said, without a flicker of humour, offering his arm to Harland so that he could haul himself out of the pit. 'When Zikmund Myslbek was killed in

Karlsbad, Macy was damned annoyed. You see, they went back a long way and they were good pals and all that. Macy wasn't about to let the murder of his friend go unpunished. He decided to find out about this character Kochalyin and we agreed that the only way that could be achieved was if Macy went to Kochalyin with information about you two. It turns out we had business interests in some of the same areas and, to cut a long story short, Macy and Mister K found they had a lot in common. They talked the same language, you see. Macy then tapped the phones in Century House for him. After that there was no question of him not trusting Macy. That was his *big* mistake.'

'And you knew about this?' Harland asked incredulously. 'You knew that Macy was feeding him everything?'

'Yep, which is why I stuck to you two like a tart on Easter Sunday. When Kochalyin made his move, Macy was going to tip me off. I knew he was with him, but I had no idea he'd be on his bloody chopper. I could hardly believe it when I saw him get out.'

'And where the hell were you? You didn't go with Ibro in the car, did you?'

'No. I thought it was best to stay with you two, so I followed you up the track at a distance, then made myself scarce.'

'And the hut? Did you do that?'

'Yes, an old trick. I gather it was a local favourite in the war. You place a lighted candle in the highest part of the building – in this case a beam by the chimney – turn on the gas and walk away. Being heavier than air, the gas takes a while to rise to the flame, by which time the whole place is full of the stuff. I learned the trick from Ibro. I believe it was used in the ethnic cleansing operations. Anyway, it certainly distracted those chaps for a bit.' He nodded in the direction of the hut. 'Two of 'em are unconscious. The other one got trapped inside,' he said absently.

They considered waiting for the helicopter pilot to recover from the blow delivered earlier by The Bird to his head, but decided he wouldn't be fit to fly them to Sarajevo. So they carried Ibro to the second truck and loaded him into the passenger seat. The Bird took the wheel and, once Harland had retrieved the camera from its hiding place in the rocks, Eva, Macy and he climbed into the back.

Harland wiped his hands of dirt and looked into Eva's eyes. 'You had me fooled back there,' he said. 'I really thought you were going to shoot me.'

'For a moment I thought so too,' Macy commented with a glimmer of a smile. 'Then I realised she must have had her own gun but was angling to get the better weapon from one of the men. Bloody clever to pull that off and then get you down into the shelter of the grave.'

They both waited for her to say something. But the engine roared and The Bird started the laborious business of turning the truck, pitching them forward then back to the tailgate with a series of jolts.

Eventually she shouted, 'You must have known I wasn't going to kill you. Didn't you see it in my eyes?'

'Not this time,' said Harland grimly.

He glanced at the pit and the grotesque figure of Oleg Kochalyin. His arms were limp by his sides and his head lolled a little to the right, causing his black cap to sit at a rather jaunty angle. It was as if some unseen hand had forced him to kneel and was now holding his body in penitence for the scores, maybe hundreds, who lay in that unquiet grave. Around him sprawled the men who had carried out the massacre – the perpetrators of a long-neglected barbarity. Justice had been served, Harland reflected, albeit crudely.

They began the descent to the road and dropped out of the mist. As they swayed with the motion of the truck, they fixed their gazes on the hills to the west, away from the shame of this nameless mountain. Out of the corner of his eye, Harland caught sight of a lone raven circling the crags below them, searching for its mate.